# CRUEL WATER

## a Portland ME, novel

*To Barb*
*Life Won't Wait!*

by

# Freya Barker

xox Freya B

Copyright © 2016 Margreet Asselbergs as Freya Barker

## ISBN: 978-0-9949514-2-7

Cover Design:
**RE&D - Margreet Asselbergs**

Editing:
**Karen Hrdlicka**

Proofreading:
**Prima Editing & Proofreading – Daniela Prima**

# DEDICATION

To my parents, who never asked anything more
of me than to simply be the best me I could be.
I hope somewhere along the line I made you
proud.

# CHAPTER ONE

*Viv*

The muffled sound of a phone ringing penetrates the remnants of sleep. I try to get up but find myself pinned to the bed by a heavy body. Right. Slowly the memories of last night filter back: the tall quiet man at the end of the bar who'd spent my shift at The Skipper following my movements without a word. Startling gray eyes, in a rugged face, that I could feel on me by the tingle they spread over my skin. Dark brown, long hair skimming the collar of his worn leather jacket, and the strong, long legs cased in dark jeans, had drawn my attention the moment he walked in. When he lifted his eyes to mine, as he took a stool at the bar, the impact of his gaze jarred me. His order of beer was the only time I heard his dark raspy voice. The rest of the night he simply lifted his empty glass for a refill, and my normally chatty self seemed unable to try for empty conversation. Tongue-tied. My brothers would have had a blast torturing me with that fact.

The man left the bar about half an hour before closing, and I'd felt a brief sense of loss before I scolded myself for even giving him a thought. I should know better. I thought I did, before walking out to cross the parking lot to my apartment building after closing and finding him leaning against the single light post at the end of the alley. Why I wasn't scared? I don't know. I should've been. Instead I watched with butterflies in my stomach as he purposely stalked toward me, stopping no more than a breath away, forcing me to tilt my head back to look at him. That in itself was a turn on. I'm not exactly short and am used to meeting most people at eye level.

His eyes roamed over my face before coming to rest on my mouth. Part of me wanted to bolt, but another stronger part of me wanted badly to give into a craving I've spent years suppressing. While I was waging this internal battle, his arms folded around me and pulled me hard into his chest. Strong, solid arms banded around me, and one hand slipped into the short hair at my neck, fingers curling tight to the point of pain. Still, I didn't move. The first touch of his lips on mine was brief, quickly followed by a toe-curling exploration of the recesses of my mouth. A kiss that satisfied a hunger I hadn't been aware of.

I did have the presence of mind not to take him back to my place. I simply climbed on, when he pulled me by the hand, to the black and chrome bike at the edge of the lot. Tucked in tight behind his broad back, I let him take me to the La Quinta Inn on Park Avenue.

That's where I find myself now, carefully trying to untangle myself from his limbs as I grope around for my purse and the offensive familiar tune on my phone, indicating a call from my oldest brother, Owen. Ignoring the inarticulate grumbling from the bed behind me, I snatch up my clothes, which his nimble hands had divested me of last night and unearth my ringing purse. With my arms full, I beeline it for the bathroom and lock the door behind me.

"What's up?" I whisper breathlessly.

"Viv, I ..." The hesitation in his voice sends chills down my spine as if I can sense bad news looming. "Dad's in the hospital. Mom found him this morning in the upstairs hallway. She just called me."

Already tugging up my jeans, I snap, "Which hospital?"

"Maine Medical Center. I'll come pick you up."

"No. I'll meet you there."

"You sure? I can be there in a—"

"I'm sure. Go. I'll see you there."

It takes me two seconds to finish dressing, desperately trying to push down the dark thoughts that want to bubble up. I don't even look at the bed as I tear through the room and out the door, the gray-eyed man I leave there all but forgotten.

"What happened?" Are the first words from my mouth when I find Mom in the waiting room the nurse at the front desk directed me to. I wasn't able to avoid thinking about the man I left behind in the hotel room while riding in the back of the taxi I managed to snag, just dropping someone off outside La Quinta Inn. Snippets of the heated grappling of hands to get clothes off, as fast as humanly possible, played out behind my closed eyelids. Guilt over the thoughts flitting through my mind wasn't enough to stop the slight clench of my thighs. It had been a long time ... only one rather disastrous attempt to wash away the harsh touch of my ex with a long-time friend, after a night of companionable drinking, about a year after I managed to leave that unhealthy relationship. A one-time mistake that should never have happened, left me locked inside my bathroom, sobbing on the floor. The friendship recovered, but I had become gun-shy after that, never allowing myself more than an occasional quick relief with a battery operated toy for assistance. Gray Eyes was the first man I'd been able to lose myself with, so much so, I apparently fell asleep in his strong arms in the early morning hours.

Mom looks like a deer stuck in headlights when her slightly wild eyes turn to me.

"I don't know … I noticed him leaving the bed at some point and I dozed off. Next thing I know he's still not back and when I went to look, I found him lying in the hallway outside your old bedroom."

A slight shiver runs down my spine and I swallow down the emotion. Mom seems so fragile, despite her normally unwavering strength. At seventy-three, she's as energetic and outgoing as she ever was, and I'm having a hard time seeing her so lost. Sitting down next to her I slip my arm around her rounded shoulders.

"Has anyone come to see you?"

She shakes her head no. "We just got here twenty minutes ago. I know nothing."

Just as I'm about to get up to find some answers, Owen walks in with his wife, Lydia, following behind. She slips into the seat on the other side of Mom, while he bends down to give her a hug. His eyes find mine and I shake my head in response to the silent question.

"I'm gonna see what I can find out, okay?" he says, walking back out the door, leaving Mom framed by Lydia and me, like bookends keeping her spine straight. I meet Lydia's warm eyes over my mother's head and give a tight smile.

"Where are the kids?" I ask, knowing that it's too early for the school bus to have picked up my seven and ten-year-old nephews.

"Neighbor," Lydia answers. "She'll make sure they get on the bus."

I simply nod in response and a heavy silence falls in the room. I want badly to cut through it with idle chitchat, to ward off my troubled thoughts, but can't bring myself to speak.

Owen's return, with a doctor in tow, cuts through the onslaught of unwanted memories threatening to suck me down. He introduces himself to Mom and just smiles at Lydia and me.

"Your husband seems to have suffered a stroke," he directs to Mom gently, who nods as if she'd expected it. I can't help the pang of resentment at her usual quiet acceptance, but I bite it down as I focus on listening to the doctor speak. "His vitals are fine, although his heart rate is slightly elevated— we'll keep an eye on that. We have him on medication to try to minimize the impact, but will need some time to evaluate the full extent of any possible damage. He's currently responsive but slightly confused and has difficulty communicating—something that's not at all unusual and not often permanent. Give us some time to run a few tests."

By the time the doctor finishes explaining the tests ordered for my father and promises to come back to get Mom to see him, as soon as they are done, my brother Aaron has arrived. As per usual, Owen and Aaron gravitate toward each other and start talking with Mom, leaving me out of the conversation, so I turn away and slip into my head.

My other two brothers don't live in Portland. Nolan stayed in Boston after his divorce, in order to be close to his teenage daughter, Chloe, who lives with his ex-wife. According to Aaron, he is on his way. Dorian is supposed to get the first flight out, since he lives clear across the country in San Francisco. The youngest of my brothers, he is probably the only one who never once treated me like an annoying little sister and instead became my best friend growing up. That is, until he moved to the opposite coast and broke my heart. I get it, I'm the only one who does get it. He needed a place where he could be himself, without the scrutiny of the small-town attitude still existing in Portland, despite its size. I think part of me always recognized that Dorian had a healthy interest in boys—men—especially when both of us admitted to having a crush on the lead singer for Duran Duran, Simon Le Bon. I remember my mouth falling open when Dorian confessed and rolled off the bed giggling. I was fourteen. It was the last time I told my brother my secrets.

"Hey, girl," Gunnar answers my call. Best friend to my brother, Owen, and permanent fixture in my life growing up, Gunnar has become a good friend in the past few years. He's also my boss and the owner of The Skipper, a restaurant pub on Holyoke Wharf in Portland, where I should've been prepping for the lunch crowd, right about now.

"Hey, Boss. Some bad news: my father is in the hospital after Mom found him on the floor this morning. Looks like a stroke, but we're still waiting on more news."

"Shit, honey. I'm so sorry. Need me to come keep your brothers in line?"

The immediate show of support has my eyes fill with the tears I've managed to avoid thus far. Gunnar and his wife, Syd, who has grown into the best friend a girl could have, would drop everything to be here for me, I have no doubt. But they have two kids that need looking after and a pub that needs to open without me to do it. He has also gone to bat a time or two with Owen, when he tried bossing me around like the little girl I'd long since left behind. There are things Gunnar knows about me that he has not shared with anyone in my family—things he reminds me are mine to share if, and when,

I'm ready. Don't know if I ever will be, but I'm grateful for the trust he shows me.

"Nah. I've got it covered," I bluff, and Gunnar knows it. I don't speak up in my family, not against my parents, not against my brothers. It's futile, since they don't hear me anyway.

"All right, Viv. We'll take care of The Skipper. No worries. Wanna talk to Syd?"

The thought of talking to her causes a few tears to push past my eyelids, rolling quietly down my cheeks. "Will you tell her for me?" I manage. "I'll give her a call when I know more."

"Sure thing, honey. Hang tough and we'll be in touch."

I'm sure Gunnar heard the hitch in my voice, but knows better than to draw attention to it, and simply hangs up without waiting for a response. I take a minute to slip into the washroom when I step back inside the hospital, and splash some cold water on my face. Shoring up my proverbial bootstraps, I walk back into the waiting room where the same doctor is talking to my mother.

"Viv, there you are," Mom says. "Apparently Dad is calling for you."

My breath gets stuck on the way out, and I have to forcefully push the air from my lungs. Ignoring the goose bumps that pop up on my arms, I turn to the doctor. "I'm sorry?"

"Your father became a bit combative during the CAT scan and keeps asking for "Vivvy." We can't seem to calm him down."

The use of my father's childhood nickname for me leaves a foul taste in my mouth, but I bite through it. "What would you like me to do?" I ask with a straight face.

13

"If you wouldn't mind coming with me to the radiology department, perhaps we can calm him down enough to finish the scan."

With a simple nod, and without looking at my family in the room, I follow the doctor out.

"Vivvy!"

I can hear him yelling from the hallway and walk through the door that is being held open for me. My eyes find him on the narrow table, being held down by two people in scrubs.

"Dad?" My voice croaks as I take in his disheveled look: one side of his face drooping and his eyes wild and red, shaking his head from side to side. "Dad! I'm here. It's Viv— look at me."

The red-rimmed eyes search frantically at the sound of my voice, and when they finally settle on my face, fill with tears. His mouth opens and closes, making him look like a fish on dry land, as he seems to be searching for words. "Vivvy," he manages, slurring heavily, his body relaxing under the restraining hands. But his next words send a cold stab through my heart and I have to fight to hold in the measly cup of coffee Lydia brought me earlier.

"Vivvy, I ... c-couldn't f-f-f-find you."

# CHAPTER TWO

## *Ike*

Like a coward I keep my eyes closed as she sneaks out of the room, without a goodbye or backward glance. I roll to my back and lift my arm away from my face the moment I hear the door click shut behind her. *Holy Christ*—that woman spells danger. I spotted her the instant I walked in the door of that pub on the wharf.

I'd stopped in on my way from the office of Maine Maritime Designs, located down the road, looking for a bite to eat. The Skipper had been recommended to me several times over the past few years, but I'd never had a chance to check it out. Last night was my first night back from a three-month stint in Norfolk, Virginia, where I'd been assigned to the refitting of a cargo vessel for use by my old employer, the US Navy. Enlisted at twenty, I'd spent ten years in service, before opting out the first chance I got after a couple of lengthy overseas stints.

The plan had been to come back to a fully renovated house, but the contractor informed me they needed another week to finish the bathrooms. Not happy with the wait, but unable to do anything about it at this point, I'd checked into the La Quinta Inn, where at least I'd be able to have a hot shower.

The promise of the hot dinner I'd been hoping for, before returning to my hotel, disappeared like snow from the sun the moment my gaze hit the clearest, ice blue eyes I'd ever

15

seen. Big and bright, surrounded by a dark fringe of thick
lashes in a face that could stop wars. Light blonde, choppy
strands of hair with a single streak of blue, framing her oval,
sun-kissed face with slightly pouty lips, and an athletic body
that immediately had my brain exploring alternative types of
exercise I'd like to engage in with her. Her voice, when she
asked me what she could get me, was sexy as hell. Slightly
smoky, but strong and assured. I notice she isn't as young as
she appeared initially, but that only makes her more
attractive. Mid-thirties would be my guess, and that still
means substantially younger than I am, although age
difference has never been an issue either way. My last
attempt at a conventional relationship was with a woman
twelve years my senior, and she was a firecracker. I stopped
trying after her: not like me to stick to one place, let alone one
person; not to mention the trunk full of baggage I tend to lug
along.

No, I'm a wanderer, which is why I'm lying here after
letting Blue Eyes slip out the door. I'll keep the memory, of
arguably the best night of my life, but force down the urge to
go after her.

"Hey, buddy, when did you get into town?" Tim asks me
over breakfast at the Denny's around the corner from the
hotel. It's a mild day, so I walked the short distance, choosing
to leave my bike. I shot Tim a message after I finally rolled out
of bed, needing a distraction from the nagging feeling I'd
fucked up by letting her walk out the door. I never did get her
name, nor she mine. The night had been all the more
memorable for letting just our bodies communicate. A slightly

illicit flavor added by not exchanging names or resumés, but rather allowing the physical expression to be the only language exchanged.

"Yesterday morning. Only to find my contractor needs another week to get the house habitable, so I checked into a hotel."

"That sucks. Didn't the guy start when you left?"

"Yup. Guess my hope that my not being around would expedite things backfired. Oh, well. One week I can handle."

"Sorry about that." Tim looks at me over the rim of his coffee cup. "Had I known, I could've kept an eye on things for you."

I hear the careful implication. I know he would've, that's never the point. There is a reason I don't have many friends, and the ones I do have, I seem to keep at a safe distance. Tim is a good man, someone I could trust with my life, let alone the care of my house. Rationally I know this, but it's still something I instinctively reject.

"Hindsight and all that," I reply lamely.

"You're an idiot," he states, but with a grin to soften his words.

Yeah. I fucking am.

We finish our breakfast talking about mundane stuff, weather, sports, and work. Safe topics of conversation until Tim asks what I'm doing tonight.

"Nothing planned, really. Why?"

"Remember the over-thirty ball team I play for? The Anchors? I don't know how long it'll be before you have to head out of town again, but we're looking for some fresh blood. We've got a game tonight, if you're interested. Short a few guys, so you can get your cleats muddy if you want. See how you like it, even if you can't commit, it might be a fun thing whenever you're in town."

"I might pop by, where is it?"

"Dougherty Field, just the other side of the highway. And we always hit our sponsor for a beer after," he says with a wink.

"Yeah?" I smile back. "Bet that's the best part of the night, am I right?"

"You've got it," he confirms, slapping a few bills on the table. "So I'll see you at seven tonight? We usually end up at The Skipper by about nine-thirty."

I work hard to keep my face straight. The Skipper, where a certain blue-eyed blonde mans the bar. *Fuck.*

"See you then," I manage with a lift of my chin, before adding my own money to the table and walking out.

The entire day I spend convinced I'd blow Tim and his game off tonight. The prospect of seeing her, too much of a temptation. I don't know why the thought of her comes with giant *danger* signs, but the mere fact I can't stop thinking about the feel of her, or her taste, tells me to stay away.

It's almost a surprise when I park my bike beside Tim's truck at the baseball diamond at ten to seven. It's just a fucking game, I don't even have to go out with them after.

So why does it feel like I suddenly find myself at a crossroads in my life?

"Ike!"

I'm still straddling my bike, helmet in hand, deciding whether there is still time to turn around, when I hear Tim calling. Looks like my decision is made for me. Swinging my leg over the seat, I switch my helmet for my cleats and glove in one of the saddlebags and walk over to the diamond, where

Tim is standing with a group of guys all wearing the same jersey.

"Tim. Guys," I greet when I reach them.

Tim makes the introductions and when he gets to the captain of the team, Gunnar, who also happens to be the owner of The Skipper, I look up to find a pair of intense eyes scrutinizing me.

"Tim tells me you're a local?"

I answer with a confirming nod.

"Then how the fuck is it, this is only the second time I see you?" he barks, squeezing the shit out of my hand he is still holding onto.

Well fuck. He must've seen me last night.

"Didn't realize you two had met before," Tim pipes up.

"Met wouldn't exactly be the right term. Let's just say he stood out, spending the entirety of last night eye-fucking my bartender." With a last firm press of his hand, he finally releases mine, and I can't help flexing to restore the flow of blood. If I'm not mistaken, I've just been handed a warning.

"Matt?" Tim says with eyes about to roll out of his skull, earning him a slap to the back of his head by Gunnar.

"No, you moron ... Viv."

Tim's eyes shoot to me, squinting, as if trying to read my face. "You be careful with Viv, she's fucking special."

Two good-sized guys stare me down. It should piss me off, but it doesn't. All I can think is—*Good, she has good men looking out for her.* Followed immediately by a pang of jealousy, wondering what exactly she means to these guys. The last thought through my head, as I kick off my boots and pull on my cleats, is that the name Viv suits her. That's when I kick my own ass for being a pussy and with a smile on my face, I grab my glove and take the field.

Three hours later, I'm nursing a beer at the big round table in the corner by the window of The Skipper. Scowling.

When I asked Gunnar who the new bartender was when we walked in—a petite, pretty, little thing with reddish hair, longer than I've ever seen on any adult—he about took my head off. "That's my wife, you asshole. Hands and eyes fucking off!"

I'd only brought it up because asking to know where my blue-eyed beauty was, would've been too obvious.

"And just in case you were wondering, Viv is off for an undetermined amount of time. Family issues," he added.

My second beer almost gone, I'm ready to pack it in: my body sore from being out of shape and getting way the hell too gloomy.

"Gonna be back next Wednesday?" Paul, one of the other guys on the team calls after me, when I say my goodbyes. I turn to find Tim's eyes on me as well.

"Sure. If I'm in town I'll be there. I'll let Tim know."

## Viv

With my father calm enough to stay still for the scan, I quietly slip out of the room and stumble to the first washroom I find. The coffee that has been churning in my stomach for the past twenty minutes finally finds its way up, and I drop to my knees heaving into the toilet. A purely physical reaction to my emotional turmoil. *Vivvy.* That fucking name. Ever since my fifteenth birthday, it made me ill to hear it. To my relief it got shortened to Viv over time. As I got older, on the odd occasion he'd revert to the old nickname, I would stare him down. He never used it again after I left the house at eighteen.

My stomach blissfully empty, I rinse my mouth and take a sip of cold water. A quick scan in the mirror shows my eyes, red-rimmed and dull with worry and the pain of long suppressed memories.

"Everything okay?" Owen's voice startles me as I turn the corner to the waiting room. He pushes away from the wall he was leaning against and steps up to me, lifting a hand to pull a strand of hair behind my ear. I can barely contain an inadvertent flinch, but he catches it anyway, lifting his eyebrows in question.

Stepping back, I swipe my own hair from my face. "I'm fine. He's fine, just a bit confused. They should be done with him shortly." I step around him and with my hand on the door to the waiting room, start pushing it open.

"Wait."

The word is whispered, but still causes me to drop my hand and allow the door to fall shut again. When I turn around, I see uncertainty and confusion mar my brother's face.

"What did he want?"

I shrug my shoulders, not quite sure of the answer myself. I look over his shoulder down the hall, doing my best to avoid his eyes.

"I can't help but wonder what he was doing on the opposite side of the hallway outside your room, Viv."

Underneath Owen's question I can hear a hint of fear and with a strength I summon from thin air, I straighten my shoulders and spine. Looking him straight in the eyes, I force a smile. "I can't imagine," I answer, pushing the door open resolutely this time, not giving him a chance to react.

# CHAPTER THREE

*Viv*

"Are you on your way?"

My mom's worried voice on my answering machine slices me. I've been a coward these past two weeks, avoiding visiting my father in the hospital, that is, aside from the times my brother Dorian hauled me there physically. He's been staying at our parents' house and is making sure Mom is taken care of, having taken an extended leave of absence from work. My other brothers have all gone back to work. Nolan was up from Boston, for a few days, before returning home and the older two have been in and out of the hospital. Everyone has been giving me a hard time for not sitting in his hospital room, along with the rest of the family every day. Everyone except Owen, who has kept quiet, simply watching me closely when I did show up under duress.

I've done my best to organize home-care for my father, making sure he has someone coming in daily to help get him showered and see to it that he's set to continue his physical and speech therapy from home. It's the least I can do for Mom, who will at some point be faced with caring for him alone. Even though he is already showing progress in his physical recovery, his confusion has not gotten any better. His physician warned us that given his age, dementia as a result of stroke is not uncommon, but not reason enough to keep him hospitalized. He's being released today, hence my mother's message.

I quickly dial her number, prompted by guilt. "Hey, Mom."

"Vivian, your father is coming home today," she blurts out excitedly.

"I know, I heard. Owen's driving?" I ask carefully.

"Yes. We're driving in convoy. Dorian is going with Aaron in his car, but said you're welcome to come with them, unless you prefer to ride with us?"

"Actually, I was thinking I'd rather wait at the house. I can make sure there is coffee warm and something to eat." I know this is not what she wants to hear, and I feel guilt clogging my throat when I hear her deep sigh.

"If that's what you want, dear." Dejection sounds in her voice.

"I was thinking of picking up some pain au chocolat from Standard Baking?" A shameless ploy to distract her with their favorite bakery in town works, because Mom enthusiastically adds to the list.

"Fabulous idea! Can you pick up some madeleines, as well? Your father still has a bit of trouble swallowing and the madeleines are nice and soft. Oh, and some of their five-grain bread too, please."

"No problem. I'll buy out the store, since the boys will be there with their customary hollow legs."

A niggle of guilt remains as I listen to her snicker. "Good plan. We'll see you soon, then? I'm hoping to get home by three."

"See you then, Mom. Love you."

The distracted, "Love you too," is barely distinguishable as she hangs up the phone, already getting worked up about getting him home, I'm sure.

I'm suddenly struck with a deep sense of loneliness. Ridiculous when you think about it: I have a large family, fantastic friends I get to work with every day, and therefore no reason to feel that way. Still, I have found myself thinking about rough, calloused hands, a scruffy jaw and piercing, pale gray eyes more than just a few times in the past couple of weeks. My bar shifts at The Skipper were spent jumping each time the damn front door opened, never finding those eyes meeting mine. They remind me of the waters right off the wharf, just before they turn rough. Smooth, silvery, and very unpredictable. Silence before the storm.

I shake my head to clear those thoughts and turn back to slapping on my minimal make-up before I run over to the pub to help with morning prep. I was lucky to find this fabulous apartment a couple of years ago, right at the end of Holyoke Wharf, and therefore within easy walking distance of The Skipper. I have a car, but it generally stays in the underground garage during the day. I'll need it this afternoon to haul the bakery order over to my parents' house, though.

The sun is out and the silty smell of the water fills my nostrils and settles my spirit, as I make my way down the alley behind the pub. The back door is already unlocked, and I push my way inside to find Syd elbow deep in chopped vegetables.

"Hey. What are you doing in so early?"

She swings her head around at the sound of my voice and smiles big, in contrast to the tears streaming down her cheeks.

"Onions," she clarifies, grabbing a towel and wiping at her face. "I'll never get used to it."

I chuckle, slightly relieved. For a moment there I thought—well—I don't know what I was thinking. Syd had quite literally crawled out of a dark, dank gutter since I first met her. Despite her tragic past, she managed to find her happy place with Gunnar, his kids, and at The Skipper. I'm ashamed at the pang of jealousy that occasionally stabs me when I think about the full life she managed to build. Just because I've resigned myself to live in some kind of numb suspension, doesn't mean she shouldn't reach for the moon. She totally deserves it.

I hang up the hoodie I threw on to ward off the morning chill and don my apron. Hauling a bin of potatoes from the cold storage, I wash my hands, move in beside her at the large counter and start peeling. My emotions already all over the place lately, I'm not up to examining my reaction, just now, too closely. I work silently beside Syd for a while when she elbows me in the side.

"A penny?" she asks, causing me to snort.

"Not worth it," I shoot back.

"Well, something has you disappearing inside your head lately. Wanna talk about it?" Her tone is light, but the intent underneath is very sincere. I've been open with Syd about Frank, my ex, and how I struggled to get away from him. I share other stuff with her, but there are some things I'll never bring up, simply because I'm working hard at denying their existence.

"This wouldn't have anything to do with a certain tall, built, and handsome, silver-eyed stranger now, would it?"

The paring knife slips from my hand and clatters on the stainless steel counter. Syd's soft chuckle has me look at her wide-eyed.

"Bingo ..." she says, gently smiling.

"How—?"

"He was in again last night, with the ball team. Except he wasn't so much interested in the beer or the conversation, but had his eyes focused on the bar, apparently hoping for you to magically appear. Unfortunately, it was just little old me, and

Gunnar about took his head off for staring, for the second time."

"Again? Second time? I don't understand," I mutter, confused as hell. Oh, I know exactly who she's talking about. But what I don't get is that he's been here again? Is he looking for me?

"He came with the team two weeks ago and kept checking behind the bar then, too. Gunnar says he's a new guy on the team. Does something in ship building, not sure what, and seems to have a healthy interest in you, according to my husband. He was away on business and showed up again last night, obviously looking for someone other than me behind the bar."

Not sure whether to feign ignorance or answer the obvious question in Syd's eyes, I opt for a shoulder shrug and muttered, "Huh."

"Viv? How do you know Ike?"

Should've known she wouldn't let it go at that. Ike? That's his name? Sighing I turn to face her. Confession time, it's easier than trying to keep something from her.

"I don't really know him. Didn't even know his name. He was in here the Tuesday night before my father had his stroke. Sat at the bar and other than his first order of beer, never said a word, just stared." An involuntary shiver runs down my back at the memory of those clear, intense eyes focused on me. "He was waiting for me outside after my shift and took me on the back of his bike to his hotel. That's all I know."

Syd scrunches her eyebrows together. "What do you mean, that's all you know? You didn't give him your number? What's wrong with you? The man is delicious."

My turn to raise my eyebrows at her. "Better not let your husband hear that. He's a bit possessive, if you hadn't noticed. That would turn ugly fast."

Syd tilts her head and sets her hands on her hips, looking at me expectantly. Nope—not letting go.

"Fine." I throw my hands up, capitulating. "We never spoke. Never said a word. Hell, I didn't even know his name was Ike. At some point I fell asleep, something I never, ever do, and was woken up by Owen calling me about my father. I grabbed my clothes and hightailed it out of there, without looking back." I turn back to my potatoes resolutely, but my friend is not done.

"Not looking back, huh? So how is it that you knew immediately and exactly who I was referring to?"

My hands still mid-air, I drop my chin to my chest.

"Because I haven't been able to stop thinking about him," I whisper, admitting something I hadn't wanted to admit even to myself. One fucking night with a perfect stranger: no history, no names, and no future—that's all it was supposed to be.

"Yessss!" Syd blurts out, enhancing with a fist pump.

"No!" I counter, causing her to turn to me with an angry scowl.

"You listen here, as long as I've known you, you have never expressed an interest in any guy. Not really. Finally one piques your interest, and you've obviously piqued his, but you're going to ignore that? Dammit, Viv. Not every guy is like that asswipe you scraped off. I mean, look at Gunnar, or Matt, even Tim, and he is friends with this Ike guy."

Her last words cause an immediate physical response: instant nausea. There is no way I can even conceive of anything with him now. Shaking my head I look at her. "Not for me, Syd. I don't do relationships of any kind, you know that."

Her eyes soften but her chin lifts stubbornly. "But ..."

"Morning, ladies," a familiar booming voice comes from behind.

Both of us turn to find Dino leaning against the doorway; a man of few words, chef extraordinaire and good friend. The smirk on his face as he makes his way over to pull his apron off the hook, tells me he heard more than I'd like. Dino is our resident sage, with an uncanny ability to see deeper than most of us are comfortable with, and on top of that hides a hefty romantic streak behind that imposing, brooding exterior. There is no way he won't meddle. *Fuck me.*

"There she is!"

Mom's voice, pitched higher than normal with anxiety, comes from behind my father, who is sitting in his wheelchair rather forlorn in the hallway of my parents' house.

I arrived ten minutes ago, my arms overloaded with baked goods. Just having finished finding those a home in the kitchen, I was making a pot of coffee when I heard the front door open.

My father looks like a stranger: his face drooping on one side, his body slumped to one side in the chair, and a blank look on his face. It's obvious that nobody's home right now.

Mom fusses with his coat when behind her, Dorian and Owen walk in the door.

"Where's Aaron?" I want to know.

"Late for a meeting, he just took off," Owen says. "Do I smell coffee?"

Glad for the distraction, I turn back into the kitchen to prepare a tray, trying not to look at my mom wiping some drool off my father's chin, while Dorian hangs up his coat.

By the time I walk into the room, coffee pot and mugs precariously perched on a tray in my hands, the boys have moved my father from his wheelchair to his favorite chair, and Mom is fussing with a plaid blanket over his knees that he keeps knocking off.

"Fergus," Mom exclaims. "Would you leave it alone? There's a chill in the air today, can't have you catching a cold."

The age-old dispute apparently hasn't diminished despite my father's confusion. Mom is still perpetually cold, summer or winter, and my father still grumbles at the near tropic temperatures in the house. Dorian starts snickering and before you know it, Owen and I join in a burst of laughter. Mom makes sure to give each of us the stink eye, but it's my father's intense gaze on me that wipes the smile off my face.

"Vivvy?"

"I'm right here," I say, squirming under his scrutiny. So much so, Mom turns to put a soothing hand on his arm.

"Fergus, you know Viv doesn't go by that name anymore."

He lifts his eyes to her. "No?"

"No," she says firmly and turns to take charge of the coffee, giving me an excuse to disappear to the kitchen to grab the pastries.

After half an hour of random chitchat, mostly with Dorian on the hot seat, since he lives farthest away, Owen helps my father to the bedroom, so he can rest. When he returns, he pulls out a proposed schedule of care. Typed out, we each get a copy.

"I gave Aaron his, and he said he'd look it over tonight. Let me know if this works for you, but with a nurse visiting daily, as well as the physical therapist, I think most of our focus should be on relieving Mom at night as long as she needs it."

Mom of course makes the appropriate sounds of protest, but I suspect she is secretly relieved not to have to tackle this alone. I bite down on my reservations when I see the two over-night shifts Owen's pencilled me in for. Since I'm not on the *schedule* until Monday night, four days away, I have some time to get used to the idea.

"I'm good for the meals three times a week. I actually brought in a pasta bake for tonight. We were prepping it for today's special anyway, and it's easy to reheat."

"You didn't need to do that," Mom objects, but I quickly shut her down.

"Mom, it's not a big deal to make extra for two people when we're cooking for the masses."

It's the least of my problems, preparing some meals for them. That's not what has my stomach in knots.

"You okay for the other stuff on there?" Owen asks.

"Sure thing," I assure him with a painfully fake smile that makes him scowl. I quickly get up and lean over to kiss Mom, before grabbing my bag and heading for the door. "Gotta go back to work, guys, I'll be back tomorrow around three with food. If there's anything before that, you know where to find me." Without waiting for a response, I slip on my hoodie and hightail it out the door, back to the safety of The Skipper's kitchen.

# CHAPTER FOUR

## *Ike*

"Morning, Mr. Hawkes," the receptionist at Maine Maritime Designs chirps. Her name is Pamela, I think. I keep forgetting, despite her continued attempts to get my attention. "So good to have you back. How was your trip?"

"Fine, thanks," I mumble as I slip past her to my office, more interested in my morning dose of caffeine than some idle chat with the much too young blonde. I'm about to shut the door behind me when David's voice stops me.

"Ike—a minute?" he asks, standing in the doorway of his much bigger office across the hall, fitting his position as VP of operations and my boss.

Letting go of my door, I follow him into his office where he waves me into a chair. "Sit. I was hoping you'd be in early. I have a conference call in fifteen minutes, but I want to hear how you made out in Boston."

"Good. The engine rebuild is back on track and should be ready for the scheduled launch in New Jersey, three weeks from now."

"You going to be there?"

"Sure. If you want me to," I respond, shrugging my shoulders. The frequent traveling for my work has always been part of the attraction for me, but somehow the thought of it now bugs me. My house is finished and last night, after striking out at The Skipper, I was finally able to enjoy a shower in my custom designed bathroom. The fifty-year-old,

33

two-story home had way too many small rooms that were in dire need of upgrading. After pretty much gutting the interior, the main floor was made into an open concept large room, housing both sitting and dining areas, and the single remaining wall was partially halved, to open up the dining area to the kitchen. The upstairs that housed four small bedrooms and a bathroom was reconfigured into a sizable master with en suite bath, as well as a small study and one spare bedroom. What used to be a full height basement, now has a proper stairway and is completely finished, with laundry room and cold storage. My weight bench and treadmill are down there, but the rest is still empty. I spent last night sitting on the bottom step of the stairs, considering what to do with the space. Seems contradictory but even with drywall dust and paint fumes still lingering in the air, the house finally felt like home—familiar. Something I'd never really felt before; it'd just been a place to park myself between projects. Now, even after only one night, I find I like the idea of going home later.

"You seem decidedly non-enthused with the prospect." David pulls me from my thoughts, and when I look up his head is tilted and he wears a grin. "Something happen I should know about?"

"Nah. House is finally done, and I actually like spending time there now."

"Taken a long fucking time for you to grow some roots, man. About time," he chuckles. He may be four years younger, but ever since marrying his wife last year, after only three months of dating, David has been pushing this *settling down* business on me, like it's the answer to all of life's questions. Maybe it is, but I'll limit it to staying a bit closer to home when I can. No plans to rush into anything more, although it's difficult to ignore the face that immediately pops into my mind. *Dammit.*

"Again?"

I slip onto the stool at the end of the bar, opposite from where Gunnar was wiping its surface. Now his almost-scowl is directed at me.

"Draft, please," I say, just shrugging my shoulders. When he slides the glass in front of me, he stays leaning on the edge of the bar.

"Thought I told you she was dealing with shit, man. Why are you pushing this?" His voice is quiet but holds a clear threat, and if I hadn't seen the pretty strawberry blonde he identified as his wife the other night, I might've thought he had a claim on Viv. As it is, I'm at a bit of a loss why he's so insistent I leave her alone. "What do you want from her?"

"Honestly? Not sure myself." I hesitate, thinking hard on that question, but all I come up with is that she's not one I particularly want to walk away from, and that's pretty fucking unsettling. Repeat engagements are rare for me, under the best of circumstances, meaning in those cases I've actually exchanged names with a woman. I never even got that far with this woman. "I just can't seem to stay away."

For a few moments, Gunnar stares at me hard before lifting his eyes to the ceiling. "She'd kill me if she knew I told you, she's like a fucking sister to me, but you seem like a decent enough guy. If you're really interested, you'll go easy. She's had enough asswipes try to stake their claim forcefully, and let me tell you—that shit won't fly. Not with me. Not with her four older brothers, and most definitely not with Viv. She's been there and has the T-shirt."

The mention of four older brothers is interesting, as is the information that Gunnar seems to be throwing in as a fifth

35

one. What has the hair on my neck stand on end is the implication of his words. It sounds like maybe someone wasn't so gentle with Viv, at a certain point in time. Despite the fact that it is obviously a thing of the past, it still makes me feel oddly violent.

Still, I face Gunnar calmly. "That is not going to be an issue."

"If you're smart, it won't be." A rap of his knuckles on the wood of the bar, and he turns to leave through the door at the other end.

I barely have time to think before the object of our conversation walks through that same door, freezing on the spot when she sees me. Not sure what emotions are flitting over her face, but it's a mixed bag. Hesitantly she moves closer, her eyes never leaving mine until a patron calls her over for a refill. The front door swings open and along with a strong gust of wind, a group of men comes stumbling in.

"Hey! Close the door, you guys," Viv yells from behind me. "You're putting whitecaps on the beer."

Snickering, the men make their way over to the bar, while one of them shuts the wind out. It's cold enough to drop the temperature in the bar by a couple of degrees. A spring storm is making its way up the Eastern Seaboard according to the forecast.

When I turn to the bar, I notice Viv still staring at the door, the color slowly draining from her face. I whip my head back around just to see the silhouette of a man moving past the window and out of sight. I look back at Viv to see her blink a few times before the beer orders shouted out by the new customers appear to penetrate. She wipes her hands on her apron and starts filling them. She still hasn't been near me.

I finally catch her eye about half an hour later and lift my empty glass. With only a nod, she fills another, places it in front of me and grabs for the empty one, but I'm a bit faster. My fingers curl around her wrist where I can find the rapid pulse of her heartbeat. She looks almost panicked, her crystal blue eyes wide open.

"Viv ..." Her name sounds strangely hoarse from my lips. It's the first time I've used it. I clear my throat and try again. "Viv, my name is Isaac—Ike for short."

"I know," she says, gently pulling her arm from my hand.

Before she has a chance to move away, I quickly ask, "Can we talk?" I follow her gaze as she takes in the crowd at the bar before she faces me with a shrug. "Sometime?" I find myself almost pleading.

I'll take the small smile she gives me for a yes. What can I say, I'm an optimist. It could just as well have been a pity-filled no. I have no idea what I'm doing, or what I actually would talk about if I did get her alone, but I'm trying to go with the flow. Or flying by the seat of my pants. Either one works.

"Need anything else?" She's poised to head over to the other side of the bar where someone is waving her down.

"Food. Have a menu for me?"

She reaches under the bar and pulls out a binder. "Pasta bake is the special for today and it comes with a house salad and fresh-baked bread. The rest is per the menu."

I shove the menu back in her direction. "Pasta bake it is."

She smiles before walking over to the computer screen on the sideboard and types in my order. I don't see her for the next fifteen minutes, as she's kept busy filling orders. I'm lost in a dart game on the other side of the bar, when a mouth-watering smell hits my nose. By the time I turn around, Viv has already moved away, but throws a little smile in my direction. Without delay because I'm starving, I dig into the steaming dish of cheesy goodness. Fuck me, it's been a while since I've had something this wholesome. Better than the usual quick meals, mostly ordered in or picked up at a drive-through window.

Within minutes I find myself mopping up the remnants of the spicy tomato sauce with the chunk of bread, still warm from the oven.

"You were hungry."

I look up at Viv, who's made her way back over here and stands with her hands on her hips, a smirk on her pretty lips. "Starving," I admit, making her chuckle.

"I can tell. Gotta be some kind of record, the speed at which you finished that," she says, indicating the now empty dish in front of me.

"Well, it was damn good—and a long time since I've had a meal like that. Compliments to the chef."

A blush creeps up Viv's cheeks as she avoids my eyes.

"You?" I ask with an eyebrow raised. Her response is a slight shrug of her shoulders before she grabs the dishes, turns on her heels, and disappears through the door behind the bar. Leaving me with a satisfied smile on my face, lifting my beer to my lips.

"Looking way too fucking smug." A slap on my back accompanies Tim's voice behind me.

"Whatever," is my intelligent response, as I turn to face him, still sporting that dumb-ass grin on my face. I'm feeling fucking great and no amount of heckling is going to bring me down. Tim pulls up a stool beside me.

"Not gonna elaborate?" he asks.

"Fuck no. Leave it at the good food. I just had the special."

"Hey, Viv!" he yells out beside me, just as she walks through the door with another steaming plate. Her head turns toward the sound, and the bright familiar smile on her face for Tim, leaves a sudden bitter taste in my mouth.

"Right with ya!" she yells back, as she slides dinner in front of a patron sitting in one of the booths.

"Just get me one of those when you've got a minute," he says, indicating the dish she just dropped off.

I follow her across the bar with my eyes when I sense Tim staring at me. "What?"

"Interesting," he says, leaning in. "If I didn't know any better, I'd think you were interested in my good friend, Viv."

"How good of a friend?" I bite out, rising to the bait.

"Good enough to know you don't stand a chance. Viv isn't interested. At least not in anything remotely serious."

I stare him down. Don't like the feeling he knows a little too much about Viv's preferences. Part of me wants to tell him I've already had a taste—a smorgasbord would be more accurate—but something tells me to suck that back. Good thing too, because next thing I know Viv's sexy voice pipes up. "Another brew?"

"Sure," I tell her, holding up my empty glass.

"Tim? Regular?" She's looking at him, but I can tell she's keeping an eye on me. She seems uncomfortable.

"You bet, sugar," Tim answers way too enthusiastically. With a last nervous flick of her eyes in my direction, she turns her back.

## Viv

*Son-of-a-bitch.*

Don't know whether the churning in my stomach is butterflies, nerves, or dread.

Seeing Ike sitting at the bar earlier sent me into a tailspin of emotions. Part of me was thrilled, the intense way his eyes followed me around a turn on, and I admit I was playing coy. The moment that group of guys walked in, and my attention was drawn to the door, the blood froze in my veins. The eyes staring at me through the window instantly filled me with panic. The contact so brief, I was already questioning what I thought I'd seen the instant the person walked out of view.

Now Tim has joined Ike at the far end of the bar. The tension at that end is palpable, and I don't even know what they're talking about, but I'm afraid it might be about me.

"Watch it!"

My head down, deep in thought, I don't see Matt coming out of the kitchen, a large serving tray on his shoulder. He's serving tonight, while I tend bar. Something we regularly mix up to keep everyone on their toes.

"Sorry," I offer, raising my hands apologetically, before slipping around him and into the kitchen.

"Can I have one more special?"

"Stuff is flying out of here tonight." Dino turns to me with a broad smile on his face. "Thinking of adding this one permanently to the menu."

I shrug my shoulders, feigning indifference although I'm secretly tickled.

"You've been quiet these past few weeks, everything okay at home?" he asks with concern on his face. Dino has always been the quiet but intuitive one. Maybe long-term marriage and a house full of kids does that to you, but it's like he has some kind of radar.

"My father just got home today. Seems weird, to see him so helpless. He's always seemed larger than life, especially at home. To see him shuffling around, confused look in his eyes is a bit disconcerting. Very unlike him. I guess it's the new reality."

Dino nods while opening the oven door to pull out my order. "It's just been two weeks though, right? He probably still has a lengthy road ahead. Give him a chance to recover," he says. I manage to disguise the slight shiver his words cause by turning away and prepping my tray with cutlery and bread.

"Maybe," I say a little weakly.

Dino lets the oven dish slide from his gloved hand on the tray and pins me with his stare. Uncomfortable with the intense scrutiny, I mumble a quick, "Thanks," grab the tray, and hurry out of the kitchen before he has a chance to dig down.

I can hear the commotion from the other end of the hallway and rush into the bar, almost bumping into Gunnar, who comes rushing out of his office.

"What the fuck?" he bellows, as he passes through the doorway ahead of me into what looks to be a brawl. Slipping through behind him, the first thing that draws my attention is the sound of breaking glass to my left, where one of the young guys from earlier is now swinging around a broken bottle. I don't think, just set the tray down, grab the steel pipe we have hidden under the bar, and head over there to intervene. All around the bar fights seem to have broken out, and Gunnar is already elbow-deep, pulling bodies off each other.

"Hey!" I yell at the young punk waving the broken bottle in the face of one of my regulars, lifting the pipe over my head. "Drop that fucking bottle, asshole!"

He turns, bottle in hand and tries to swipe it across the bar at me. Without another thought, I swing the pipe down, hitting the offending arm as hard as I can. He fucking screams

41

like a baby, dropping the bottle and cradling the now awkwardly bent arm with his other.

"You fucking bitch!" Anger racked up, with adrenaline and alcohol flowing, he comes charging over the bar, only to be hauled back by the scruff of the neck.

"You be nice to the lady, or I'll break your other fucking arm. And word of warning, I might not leave it at that." Ike's voice is deceptively quiet amid the melee around us as he twists punk-boy's good arm behind him, while keeping him in a chokehold. Somewhere over the ruckus I hear Dino, who had also come storming in, yell the cops are on their way. Unfortunately, this bit of news doesn't seem to penetrate the mass of twisting bodies. So I turn, leaving Ike to handle the punk and climb over the bar, pipe in my hand.

It is likely only a few minutes, but it seems like hours, before a surge of police officers pushes through the crowd, slapping cuffs on whomever they encounter. I find myself lifted on the counter by Gunnar and have a chance to think. Where the fuck did all these people come from? When I went to pick up my order, the bar was about half full and now it's teeming with bodies. Many of whom I didn't see earlier.

Tim steps behind the bar, blood running from his nose. "Bunch of morons. Those punks who came in earlier seem to have drawn a crowd. Some kind of turf war. I don't know."

From the corner of my eye I see a cop approaching Ike, who is still holding onto punk-boy. Before I have a chance to call out, the cop is wrestling Ike to the ground and the kid is trying to take off.

"Hey!" I yell, jumping off the bar, taking after him. He's almost made his way to the front when I catch up with him, grabbing onto his shirt. He swings around and before I can react, I have a fist coming at my face.

I register a crunching sound just ahead of the pain, when darkness sucks me under.

# CHAPTER FIVE

*Ike*

"Fucking told you."

I give the cop, who tackled me a second time when I went after Viv, a dirty look.

It had taken two of them to cuff me and toss me into the back of a patrol car, after seeing Viv go down. If not for Tim's calm intervention, I would have been taken to the police station. I was trying to kick out the back window after I saw her being loaded into a waiting ambulance, when Tim spotted me abusing municipal property.

"I thought you were a pacifist," he says, grabbing me by the arm and pulling me away from the cop and toward his ride. Good thing too, since the cop looks like he might be changing his mind about not charging me.

"The guy was coming after her with a bottle," I say, by way of explanation, but Tim only chuckles.

"He'd already dropped it when she broke his arm."

"Yeah," I semi-groan, the memory of the blonde Amazon not blinking as she faced off with the guy still heating my blood. She's something else. That was fucking hot, watching her fearlessly jumping into the fray. Even for a pacifist.

"That was fucking awesome!"

Viv is sitting up in the hospital bed when we finally get there an hour or so later. Her face is bloodied, one eye is swollen shut and turning black, and the other looks wild.

45

Even though no charges had been filed against me, the cops still wanted a detailed run down of what I knew. It had taken me some time to convince Tim to wait for me when he announced going to "check on Viv."

Gunnar's pretty redhead is standing beside her, trying to push her back down, while he is in the corner scowling.

"Dammit, Viv. Lie the hell back down," he barks, when he spots Tim and me in the doorway. "Damn woman's probably got a concussion. She sure as fuck is out of her mind."

Giggling from the bed has me turn my head in that direction. Sure enough, it looks like Viv has become slightly unhinged. *The fuck?*

Gunnar's wife, Syd, must have spotted the confusion on my face, because she sits down on the edge of the bed, making sure Viv stays down before she explains. "She has an orbital fracture. When she woke up earlier she was in a lot of pain, so they gave her some narcotics. Seems to work, she's not feeling any pain now, but it does mean they'll keep her overnight for monitoring."

"Reckless," Gunnar is still grumbling in the corner.

"She gonna be okay?" I ask Syd, moving to the other side of the bed.

"Should be. Maybe blurred vision for a while, and headaches, but they say it looks like nothing's been displaced, so she should be all right."

"Heyyyy, lover," Viv slurs from the bed in my direction, causing all eyes in the room to turn to me. Great.

"Hey, slugger." I smile at her, avoiding the heated glares. She looks like shit. Partially obscured by the single strand of bright blue hair, a small cut above her eyebrow looks to be the likely reason for the blood on her face, and her eye is a mess. Still she's beautiful.

"You s-saved me," she stutters, reaching her hand out.

"More like you saved yourself, gorgeous." I take her offered hand and squeeze it, still ignoring everyone else in the room.

Before anyone can say anything else, a nurse walks in telling us visiting hours are long over and before anyone else has a chance, I lean over and kiss the back of Viv's hand.

"Night, Viv."

She just smiles a big goofy smile at me, when I'm physically shoved aside by Tim. Not trusting myself to watch his hands on her, I make my way out of the room. Waiting outside the lobby doors, I have my back against the wall, sucking in fresh air.

"The fuck was that all about?" Tim wants to know when he joins me outside, getting in my space.

"None of your goddamn ..." I start when Gunnar and Syd show up behind him, Gunnar clasping a hand on his shoulder.

"Ease up there, Tim. I'm thinking Viv's got enough big brothers to defend her virtue." I'm surprised at Gunnar's words. Would have thought for sure he'd be next in line to question me, but when I see Syd's smile for her husband, I have a feeling she may have had a quick word before they came outside.

Tim takes a step back. "She's a friend, Ike."

"I know. You mentioned that before. And for the record, so has he." I indicate Gunnar beside him.

With just a nod, Tim turns and walks to his car, getting and driving off without giving me a second glance. *Fuckin' A.* I'm stranded.

I'm surprised when Syd hooks her arm with Gunnar's and slips her other one in mine. "Looks like we're gonna share a cab," she chuckles.

We all end up back at The Skipper, where some guy named Dino is in charge of clean up. Surprisingly, the actual damage to the place is minimal. One broken barstool, a hole in the drywall, and some broken glass is all that's visible of the brawl. After Syd fills him in on Viv's condition, she pulls out an expensive bottle of scotch and a bunch of shot glasses, planting them on the bar.

Gunnar groans. "Bird, really? You have to grab the most expensive bottle again?"

"Whatever," she mutters with a grin, shoving a shot glass at each of us.

By the time I get home that night, after helping with clean up and tossing back a few shots, it's past three in the morning and I'm pretty buzzed. Going to feel it tomorrow morning. With my clothes still on, I roll into bed. My last thought, before I pass out, is of Viv wielding that damn pipe over her head, grinning like a fool.

## Viv

I wake up to Dorian, sitting by the side of my bed. "Hey, Sissy." He smiles gently. Good thing too, because my head and face are throbbing.

"Hey," I croak, my mouth tasting like the inside of a sceptic tank. *Yuck.*

Slowly, last night's events roll by, up to and including some vague recollection of my *Skipper* family and Ike. *Jesus.* Ike. I remember feeling almost euphoric and rambling, yet can't quite recall what came out of my mouth. I think I may have thanked him for coming to my rescue. Better do it properly, whenever I see him again.

Damn. Can't do narcotics, they make me loopy and give me a giant hangover. Like the one I have now.

"How did you get here?" I ask my brother, who looks almost angry.

"Gunnar called Owen, who called me. At fucking seven o'clock this morning." He leans back in his seat and folds his arms. Uh oh, a sure tell for Dorian that he is majorly pissed. "Wanna tell me why it is that we find out our sister is in the hospital as a result of a bar brawl, the morning after? Dammit, Viv, Gunnar said you had insisted not calling us last night. Why the fuck not?"

I wince at the combination of anger and hurt in his voice. My brothers, who are always ready to jump to my rescue, bristle whenever my independent side overrides. I stopped turning to them when I'd gotten myself in hot water with Frank, my ex, and was afraid of what the boys would do to him if they found out. They never knew my struggles at the time. The one good thing that came out of that was finding better ways to cope. I'd been a pain in everyone's ass for years before I even met Frank. Then he became a pain in *my* ass. Quite literally at times.

For the life of me, I can't figure out how my mind went there, with Dorian sitting next to me, glowering. "Sorry," I offer weakly. "I didn't want to worry you guys. We have enough going on with Dad. I promise, I would've let Gunnar call you, had it been any more serious. But as it is, it's only a black eye." I reach out to place a soothing hand on his arm, but the IV line I'm still attached to restricts me.

The scowl on his face gentles fractionally before he reaches over, grabbing my hand in his. "Think we all know you can take care of yourself by now, Sis, but we're family. You were there for me for years. How fair is it not to give me the same opportunity?"

I could argue with that, but I don't. Not the right time or place, if ever. Instead I give him what I hope is an apologetic, slightly watery smile.

By noon we're finally on our way home. Dorian had waited with me until the doctor finally appeared with my release papers and care instructions. Of course he'd been on the phone half the time with his life-partner, Kyle, back in San Fran where the two of them run a small gallery. Kyle is a photographer and Dorian, eager to make an extra buck when he'd been new in town, had been one of his models. That is, until he became more.  I met Kyle once, when I visited San Francisco a few years ago. No one else in the family has though. I don't think they even know Dorian is gay; it's certainly never come up in discussion. I know that when my parents stopped there on their West Coast RV trip, Kyle had grudgingly moved his things out of their joint house temporarily. Don't ask me how Dorian's been able to keep it a secret this long, it boggles my mind. As far as my family knows, Kyle is merely Dorian's business partner.

"How's Kyle?" I ask innocently, earning me a weary look.

"Business is fine, so is Kyle."

"He must miss you."

"Don't start, Viv," Dorian answers, the warning evident in his voice.

"Come on, Dor, surely at forty-two it's getting old to hide who you are, isn't it?" I'm not sure why I'm prodding, but something makes me want to push him. Don't know if it's the knock on my head, or our father's health, or what. I don't want my brother to live with regrets. Ever.

"Are we talking about hiding? You really want to go there, Sis? Because I'm guessing I could learn a thing or two from you on that subject." With one eyebrow raised he throws the challenge my way.

*Ouch.* Right between the eyes.

He's right. I have no right to call him out when I have enough shit tucked away in nooks and crannies myself. Fuck, if my family knew all, the shit storm would be so massive, they wouldn't even flinch at the fact Dor is gay.

I pout in silence. Having been bested by my brother is nothing new, he's always been much sharper than me.

When he drives past my exit, I put my hand on his arm. "Hey, where are you taking me?"

"To the 'rents. Mom's been worried about you and wants to see you for herself. Besides, you have to drop me off, I'm driving your car."

Oh, right. The last five minutes of our drive I close my eyes, mentally preparing.


"Did I do that?"

With a shaky voice and big eyes, my father points his finger at my face when he spots me.

"No, Dad, you didn't," I say.

At the same time Mom exclaims, "Fergus! What in the world?" Before turning to me and clapping her hand over her mouth. "Oh dear. I wish ..."

"Mom." I cut her off, knowing she will go on about how there are jobs much more suitable for a young woman, yada-yada-yada. "I'm fine. Honestly, it was a bunch of young kids, who happened to pick The Skipper to wage their turf war. Nothing to be concerned about."

"Really, Vivian? What on earth are you doing? You're almost forty, and you're jumping in to break up bar fights? Look at you."

I roll my eyes at the reference to my age, something Mom likes to remind me of, from time to time. Usually she points out to me how at my age she had five children already. I've always been a tomboy, at least I turned into one in my teens. Never been one to shy away from the occasional fight, either. At least not when I was younger. The pendulum swung the other way after meeting Frank. He much preferred me to look feminine and act more appropriate for a *girl*. His words, not mine. In love and eager to please, I changed, only to change right back in defiance, a few years later. It wasn't until a few years ago, under the guidance of Pam, my therapist, that I seemed to find a happy medium that suited me. Of course last night's display fell a bit short of the norm, but I couldn't stand back.

"She's fine, Ma," Owen's voice comes from the kitchen. Must be his lunch break or something. He walks right up to me, wiping the hair off my forehead so he can take a good look at my shiner. "Nice one," he hisses between his teeth, looking rather pained.

"Yeah? You should see the other guy."

Lame joke, I know, but it gets the boys chuckling, and that cuts through the thick tension in the house.

"Coffee?" Owen asks as he tugs my hair, before turning to the kitchen. I follow him in. "Here." He pushes a mug of steaming black liquid into my hands and scrutinizes my face. "Black and blue anywhere else on your body?"

Taking a sip, I shake my head. "Nah. He just got a lucky lick in, stupid kid. He'll likely feel sore this morning too. I might've broken his arm," I boast, a smug smile on my face.

"No shit," Owen chuckles. "Gunnar told me you were swinging that steel pipe of yours like a fucking bat."

I casually shrug my shoulders. "It did the job."

Suddenly he turns serious. "He also told me the guy was wielding a broken beer bottle, Viv. Did you have to put yourself out there?"

I push down my instinct to jump on the defensive, and take a deep breath before I answer. "Know Arnie? The old guy who comes in a few nights a week for a beer and a chat?" I wait for his affirming nod before continuing. "The kid wedged him up against the bar, too drunk out of his mind and too stupid to know Arnie would never hurt a fly. He was just in the kid's way. Couldn't let him cut Arnie, Owen."

Dropping his chin on his chest, he sighs. "Fair enough. But, Viv, something happens to you ..." He doesn't need to finish the thought. I get it. Putting my mug down, I step up to him, wrap my arms around his waist, and plant my forehead in his chest.

"I know." We stand like that for a minute when I step back, letting go of him. "How's Dad been?" I want to know.

"Much the same. Seems to be able to find his way around the house, well enough, with the walker. Also recognizes Mom, most of the time, but seems confused when it comes to Dorian or me. Aaron hasn't been by yet. He'll come tonight and Lydia's bringing dinner, no need to worry about that. In fact, I think we've got the weekend covered. Maybe when you come over Monday night, you can bring something for dinner?"

Not looking forward to the prospect of a long night in my old bedroom, but I'll manage.

After spending another ten minutes reassuring my mom and avoiding my father's eyes, which seem to follow me everywhere, I get up to go.

"I'll walk you guys to the door," Dorian offers, when Owen announces he has to get back to work too. "You're taking it easy today, right?"

I stop and turn, patting his cheek lightly. "I will. No need to worry, I can take care of myself."

"Whatever. Let me fuss a bit." He tries to hold back a smile and failing when Owen starts to chuckle behind me.

"I'll make sure she gets home," he says, closing ranks with our brother. Traitor.

I make sure both of them see the exaggerated eye role, which has me swaying on my feet. *Whoa.* Bit too much, that made me dizzy. I'd planned on going in to work, but perhaps I should hold off 'til tomorrow. Would make the boys happy.

*I love my brothers—pains in my ass.*

# CHAPTER SIX

*Viv*

"'Lo?"

From the lack of morning light, I can only deduce it is still the middle of the night. Despite my two hour nap in the afternoon when I got home, I was ready for bed again at nine. Gunnar had been pissed I'd even considered coming in when I called him to let him know I was staying home. Syd came over with some grub at five, and we ate our fish and chips at my kitchen counter, before she walked back to the pub. I'd tried for a movie after, but when I dozed off for the second time, during *Magic Mike XXL* no less, I knew I'd be better off in bed. At this rate, I'll never get to ogle those pretty boys. Of course, that sent my mind on a recap of my last and only sexual encounter of the past few years. With Ike. I'd fallen asleep satisfied, until the ringing woke me.

"Vivian, it's Frank."

I takes me a while to process and when the penny drops in my sleep-fogged mind, I scramble up in my bed, back to the headboard. "Frank?" *Fuck. Why does my voice sound so weak?*

"That's what I said. Are you drunk?"

"What? No! I just woke ... What do you want?" I stop myself from explaining. It's none of his goddamn business what I'm doing. Can't get my head around why he'd be calling me, out of the blue, after years of nothing. And in the middle of the fucking night. My eyes wander to the alarm clock on my nightstand, and I'm surprised to find it is only eleven.

"Just checking in with you. I want to know how you're doing." Those are the words he uses, but the tone of his voice is clearly irritated. I know, I've heard it used for years when he would talk to me.

"Do you even know what time it is?" I ask incredulously, hearing a rustling on the other end.

"Oh, right. Sorry, still on West Coast time. Were you in bed?" He doesn't sound sorry at all, and I'm starting to get pissed.

"Look, I don't know why you're calling, and I don't give a flying fuck. I have nothing at all to say to you, so don't bother calling again." I hang up the phone, turn off the ringer, and resolve to get my number changed tomorrow. I wonder if I should call Gunnar, who'd made me promise to let him know if I was ever contacted. Deciding against it, I figure I can tell him in person tomorrow.

I crawl back under the covers and pull them high up over my ears, but just as I close my eyes, something Frank said registers. *Still on West Coast time.* Does that imply what I think it does? Scrambling, I flip back the covers and rush around my apartment, making sure all the doors and blinds are closed before I climb back into bed. Where I lie wide awake for hours, before finally dropping into a restless sleep when the first birds are starting to chirp outside.

## *Ike*

I manage to stay away from The Skipper all weekend.

After a restless few hours of sleep, riddled with those fucking nightmares, I found myself on the floor next to my bed on Saturday morning. It'd been a while, but apparently the events of the night before had triggered something. I dragged myself into the shower and washed the sticky layer of sweat off. A bike ride along the coast north to Bar Harbor cleared my head.

Bar Harbor holds some good childhood memories for me. Summers spent in a cottage on the coast, my parents watching my brother and me clambering over slick rocks to see who could catch the most crabs. Evenings spent around a fire pit with Frenchman Bay in the background. Good times. Bittersweet memories.

By the time I stopped for a bite of lunch, in the quaint center of town, my ass needed a break. Nowhere is the lobster as fresh as in Maine and the moment my teeth sank into that lobster bun, I groaned. Fucking phenomenal.

That brought my thoughts right back to Viv. *Jesus.* The woman is like a virus. I can't seem to get her out of my system. After lunch, I wandered around the town center, surprised at how little it had changed. Looking in the window of a small art shop, something caught my eye, and without thinking, I pushed the door open and went in. A small statuette had caught my eye: an intricately crafted mermaid, entirely made of sea glass, sitting on a rock. A siren. I ended up taking the fast way back to Portland, the fragile package tucked away safely in my saddlebag.

The rest of the weekend I spent tinkering around the house. Hanging blinds, a few pictures, and making a list of shit I discovered needing. No more nightmares. Maybe it was the little glass siren sitting on the nightstand.

When I push open the door to the pub, I tell myself I'm only there for a well-deserved drink after two busy days at work. Still, my eyes immediately zoom in on the bar, where instead of a blonde, I see a smiling redhead.

"Hey," she greets me, as I sidle up to the bar.

"How are ya, Syd?"

"Good. Was wondering how long it would take you." There's a teasing glint in her eyes when she tilts her head in question. Not quite sure what to say, I simply shrug. "She's in the kitchen, in case you were wondering. Doesn't want people gawking at her face," Syd continues, assuming I know who she's talking about. Of course I fucking know.

"She doing okay?" I ask, as much as admitting Syd's take on things is on point.

"Nothing stops Viv. Not even a knock-out punch."

I nod when she raises an empty beer glass my way and watch as she draws a brew from the keg with considerable skill.

"She's cooking tonight, you know," Syd mentions, when she slides the glass in front of me. "Seafood chowder and biscuits."

If I hadn't been thinking of food, I would be now. My stomach responds for me by growling loudly, making Syd laugh. "Shall I put in an order?"

"Please."

Syd walks out the back, and I turn around to survey the pub for any familiar faces. My eyes are caught by a young couple sitting in one of the booths, in the middle of what looks to be a heated argument. The girl seems to be near tears, as the angry looking guy stands up and leans over the table to get in her face. His voice is getting louder and drawing more attention, and the girl backs away but is trapped in the booth. She looks scared. I slide off my stool, ready to intervene when I hear a familiar voice behind me. "Fuck!" Before I even have a chance to react, Viv barrels past me, dropping a tray on an empty table. My dinner, I guess, watching the content of the bowl splash over the sides. I take off after her, but she's already up in the kid's face when I get there.

"Feel like a big guy? Huh? Real nice, bud, yelling at your girl … scaring her." Viv has firmly wedged herself between the angry dude and the cowering girl. "I think you should take a hike. Cool off."

"None of your business, bitch," he bites off. Dumb kid.

I can't help the grin on my face when Viv steps closer to him, poking her finger in his chest. "Guess what, Einstein? You just made it my business. My place, my rules. Get out, right now!"

"Or what?" The kid apparently has a death wish.

Her hand drops down and Viv leans in closely. "Or you'll be singing soprano in the next boy band."

His eyes go big and for a second he looks like he's going to fight her. But with her hand holding his balls in a death grip, and his eyes flicking over her shoulder to spot me with my arms crossed, he throws up his hands.

"Fine," he grits out between clenched teeth, and steps back from Viv gingerly, as she releases his jewels. With one last, very dirty look at the softly crying girl, he takes off.

"Thanks," Viv says softly, turning to face me. I'm surprised she even knew I was here. My eyes track her face, taking in the dramatic discoloration, even though the swelling has gone down quite a bit.

"Wanted to make sure I could step in before punches were thrown. This time."

"I know. I could sense you."

With that rather interesting remark, she turns toward the girl and slides into the booth beside her, mumbling softly. Dismissed, I saunter back to my stool at the bar, where a fresh bowl of chowder is steaming. Courtesy of a stern-looking Gunnar, who is watching me closely.

"Thanks," I mumble when I sit down, picking up the spoon.

"You were looking out for her," he says, as I have my first little taste of heaven. Damn, that woman can cook. "Yup," is my monosyllabic answer, not sure where this is going.

He surprises me with his next words. "Finally, someone who doesn't feel the need to jump in and take over."

I look up with my eyebrows raised. "How do you figure?"

Gunnar shrugs and looks over my head to where Viv is still huddled with the young girl. "You stood at her back, while letting her take care of things. Offered your support without interfering. It's rare. Especially for her, growing up with all the chest-pounding males in the house. Not to mention that idiot …" His voice drifts off. He shakes his head, picks up a dishrag, and starts wiping down the bar.

He never quite finishes that sentence. Doesn't need to, I figure his reference to an *idiot* may have something to do with the *shit* he mentioned Viv was dealing with.

I eat my chowder in silence, using my biscuit to mop the remnants from the bowl. It's that good. When I throw a glance over my shoulder, I see that Viv is just coming this way.

"She okay?" I ask, tilting my head in the girl's direction when she gets close enough.

"No, but she will be," she says as she disappears through the door, only to come back through a minute later, holding a purse. I watch her dig through the contents and come up with what looks like a card. Waving it triumphantly, she walks over to the girl, now waiting by the front door, and hands her the piece of paper, before giving her a hug, and opening the door for her.

This time when she passes me to go behind the bar, her eyes stay on the floor in front of her. I reach out and loosely grasp her wrist, stopping her in her tracks.

"Hey," I try gently, and she looks up at me. Those crystal blue eyes stormy like a churning ocean.

"What?"

"Are you okay?" I ask, letting go of her wrist, and instead reaching up to brush the blue lock of hair off her forehead. The move startles her a bit and seems to soothe the storm in her eyes.

"I'm good now." Her smoky voice stirs my blood. "I gave her my friend's card. She's a counselor," she says by way of explanation. "She runs a shelter for battered women. She'll be able to help her."

Her gentle smile about floors me. She's said more to me, just now, than at any other time, and I don't just mean in words. Whether I'm meant to or not, I hear her story underneath. Not in detail, but the gist of it is becoming much clearer.

I should probably leave right now. I've had my beer and my dinner, I should just head home. I'm really not looking to get involved with, nor am I equipped to deal with, a woman who comes with obvious complications. Yet despite the thoughts in my head, my mouth has a different plan. "I'd like to take you out."

Something flickers in her eyes before she shakes her head and looks down at her hands. "Don't think that's a good idea."

"Actually—" I sit up straighter, suddenly determined to get her to agree. "You already said yes." I hold back a chuckle that wants out when I see her frown in confusion.

"I did? When was that?"

"You agreed to talk to me, so that's what we'll do: talk over dinner." I try for a disarming grin, afraid I'm botching it up and making myself look slightly deranged.

She presses her lips together, but amusement sparkles in those eyes. "Didn't know you were talking about a *date*, nor can I remember saying yes to anything." She left that door wide open, and I'll be damned if I don't go barging in.

Leaning closer I pin her with my eyes. "I fondly remember a time you were saying yes to *everything.*"

When the meaning of my words register, her eyes darken, and she sharply takes in a breath. "No fair," she whispers.

"I know," I whisper back, never losing eye contact.

A war wages on her face before she finally concedes on a sigh.

"Oh, fine."

Despite the grudging response, the words are music to my ears. It's only later, when I finally do leave the pub to go home, that I remember my earlier resolve to steer clear of complications.

Well, so much for that.

# CHAPTER SEVEN

*Viv*

"Oh my God, Syd, what am I doing?"

My best friend rolls back on the bed and laughs at me. "I've seriously never heard you whine this much, Viv," she snickers. "You sound like you're being dragged, kicking and screaming, in front of an altar tonight. It's just a date, for God's sake." She leans up on an elbow and regards me pensively, a slight smile still on her face. "Really, honey, just go and enjoy yourself."

"You don't understand," I plead, looking around me at the outfits discarded all over my bedroom. I don't have any *date* clothes. At least none that I want to be wearing. I've gotten used to my daily garb of jeans and either some comfy top or a "Skipper" T-shirt. The only dressy stuff I have dates back to a time I'd rather forget and should've thrown out a long time ago. "I don't date. Haven't since ... well, you know, since Frank. Hell, I don't even fuck and run, at least I didn't until ... well, you know that, too." Syd knows everything. Almost everything. Back when I met her, I had to open up to her in order to get her to open up to me. It worked and we hold each other's secrets close. I've told her more about my days with Frank than even Gunnar knows, and she's assured me it's not her place to tell him. I trust her, which is why I'm not afraid to behave like an infant. "And I have nothing to wear!" I slap my hands over my face and sink down on the bed beside my

63

friend laughing her ass off. "Thanks," I mumble, making her laugh even harder.

"You're a nut. You're gorgeous, and I'm pretty sure he'll be thrilled for you just to show up. He's not gonna care one bit about what you're gonna be wearing, and you know it." She sits up and slips her arm around my shoulders, tugging me into her. "Now why don't you tell me what's really bugging you?"

I want to. I really want to tell her how I didn't sleep a wink two nights ago at my parents' house. How it took everything for me to help Mom get my father ready for bed. How although he seems to be getting better, remembering more, he still reverts to calling me, "Vivvy," every so often and it makes me cringe. I wish I could just let it all out, but I'm afraid even a single word will make me come apart at the seams. As it is, I'm hanging on by a thread to keep an even front. My father's use of that old nickname, a couple of weeks ago, has pulled on a scab and pus that had been collecting underneath is seeping from my skin, a flow already barely containable.

"I'm not ready," I sob on her shoulder.

"Nonsense," Syd declares firmly. "It's been years since that asshole, and you clawed your way out of that situation. Don't tell me you're not ready, when I know damn well, you've got googly eyes for the guy."

I snicker through my tears at her word choice. "Googly eyes, Syd?" I laugh harder when she dramatically rolls her eyes.

"Whatever, you know what I mean. Now wipe the damn tears and throw something on. Anything will do at this point." She gets up, starts grabbing random clothes, and throws them at me. Picking through the pile, I find a pair of nice dark jeans and a bohemian-looking, flowing tunic in a turquoise paisley.

Once dressed, I pull out an old shoebox that holds my jewelry and pull out some big hoop earrings and a silver bracelet with big solid links. I slip on my favorite tube ring and a couple of knuckle rings and turn to Syd for approval.

"Perfect," she coos, digging through her purse. "All you need is a touch of ..."

Shaking my head sharply, interrupting her, "No. No make-up. You know I don't wear that shit. He'll take me as is or not take me at all."

"All right, all right. Just thought I'd give it a shot. Better get your ass in gear, if you don't wanna keep him waiting. Why is it again you won't let him pick you up here or at the bar?"

When Ike told me, before he left last night, that he would pick me up tonight, I insisted on meeting him in the parking lot of the small bistro downtown he was taking me to. He didn't like it much but conceded.

"It's because I have overnight duty again at my parents. I'll have to go there straight from dinner, since they're expecting me at nine."

"Sneaky. Let me guess, you didn't tell Ike this, did you?" She eyes me, shaking her head slightly.

"Let it go," I tell her, grabbing my purse and my overnight bag, and head to the door, Syd following behind me, grumbling.

I pull into the parking lot of the restaurant and see Ike already there, leaning on his bike. His eyes follow me as I park the car in a vacant spot. He's already opening the door before I have a chance to stuff my cell phone in my purse.

"Hey." His gruff voice is a low rumble as he looks me up and down. "Nice," he says, in a tone that clearly indicates his appreciation, and I feel a blush heating my cheeks. I'm glad I opted for casual, given he's in dark jeans and a henley. It's mild out and there is no need for coats. Even the gusty winds, which have been blowing almost the entire week now, seem to have lost their chill.

"Hi." I cautiously smile back, gingerly grabbing the hand he reaches out to me. He doesn't let go when we walk over to the restaurant, squeezing a little in reassurance when I try to pull my hand back.

"Hawkes," he says to the hostess, who greets us at the small counter at the entrance. I'm surprised he's thought to make a reservation somewhere between last night and now.

"Right this way," she says, grabbing a few menus and leading the way to a small table by the window, on the far side of the restaurant. "Your server will be right with you." She smiles and returns to her station.

Ike pulls out my chair, like a real gentleman, and for some reason it makes me giggle. Nerves I guess. I have no idea what to do with my hands once Ike sits down across from me. I am mangling my napkin until our server shows up, introduces herself, and takes our drink orders. The moment she leaves, Ike covers my hands with his big one. When my eyes look up, I find amusement dancing in his.

"Nervous?" he voices. Slightly mortified, I try to yank my hands back, only to have him hold on tight. "My kick-ass, take-no-prisoners, princess warrior? Say it ain't so."

The ridiculous comment has me giggle inadvertently and immediately lifts some of the tension. I feel like a fucking teenager on her first date, when his rugged face cracks a smile, a combination of butterflies and mild nausea. Following his lead, I open one of the menus to consider my choices.

## *Ike*

*Damn.* She's skittish as a newborn calf.

I quietly observe her from behind my menu, even though I've already made my selection. The tightness I noticed around her mouth, the moment I opened her car door, is still there. I know I have to tread carefully to make sure she doesn't bolt; finesse not particularly my strong-suit. All I can do is my best to see if she'll open up.

"Have you made your decision?" Our server steps up to the table drawing my attention, but not before Viv catches me looking at her. I nod at her to go ahead. I'm grateful to find out she is not one of those salad-only women when she orders the prime rib, which happens to be my choice as well. The girl takes our menus and promises to be back with our orders shortly, leaving us to stare at each other across the table.

"I don't ..."

"I think ..." Both of us chuckle when we start talking at the same time. "You first," I suggest, but Viv shakes her head.

"No. You go."

*Okay.* Still nervous obviously.

"I was going to say that I think we started off backwards." I watch closely for her reaction, which is the slightest lift to an eyebrow, before charging on. "We seem to have bypassed all the usual, tentative explorations and went for the payoff, right off the bat. Don't get me wrong," I quickly add, when I see her face turn guarded. "It was a phenomenal payoff, but I'm afraid it's not enough."

"Not sure what you mean. It was a one-night stand, a quick fuck. I wasn't and am not looking for anything more. And I thought it was the same for you."

I figure she's purposely using bold language to put me off, but she only manages the opposite. I find it refreshing and honest. "It was. And then it wasn't—isn't. I just want a chance to get to know you. Something about you had me return to the pub, and then seeing you in action ... Let's just say you're getting under my skin." There. I've laid my cards on the table as directly as I know how. She'll either engage or give me my walking papers. Once again an assortment of emotions plays out on her face. She really is quite transparent. The fiddling with her napkin starts up again, but this time I don't stop her, so much for finesse. I guess her dismissal of our night together as a simple *fuck*, nothing more than getting our rocks off, stings.

"I don't know what to do with that," she finally says honestly. "I'm not really in the market for anything else."

"I appreciate that. Even though your body language doesn't seem to be in sync with that statement," I observe, noticing her bristles go up again immediately. "Be that as it may, for now, I'm only interested in getting to know you. Talk. That's all. Let it play out however it plays out."

I can tell she's nowhere near convinced, but the arrival of our server with a basket of bread seems well timed. A reprieve of sorts, as Viv takes her time slathering butter on a chunk of the fresh bread. The sight of her small white teeth ripping off a bite shouldn't be erotic, but I'll be damned if it doesn't turn me on. I shift inconspicuously in my seat and try to focus away from her long, slim neck moving as she swallows. I'm so fucked.

"So what exactly do you do?"

Her question surprises me. My reaction must be visible, because a deep chuckle escapes her, making me smile in response.

"You did say we're getting to know each other, right?" The glint in her eyes tells me she's teasing, and I like it.

For the next forty-five minutes or so, we talk. Our work, our pastimes, and we tentatively broach our families. It seems that's where both of us hold back. For me it's my lack of one, but all I want to say at this point is that both my parents died of health-related issues not too long ago. My brother's death is something I can't talk about. As for Viv, she seems happy to discuss her brothers with me, even going so far as to tell me her youngest brother is gay but still firmly in the closet. I'm not sure what she expects from the way she's scrutinizing my reaction, but I've never had an issue with another person's sexual preferences, and I don't hesitate telling her that.

"Men, women, little green men from Mars, it doesn't matter to me. The only thing I draw a line in the sand on is messing with children. That's something that is never acceptable."

The silence at the table is deafening. Viv's face a blank mask as she slowly folds her napkin. Something happened here. I feel it, and I know for sure at her next words. "Thank you so much for a lovely dinner, but I have to get going. My father has not been well and Mom needs my help."

With that she simply gets up, smiles that blank smile at me again, and walks to the exit before I can even get my head around what's happening. What the fuck did I miss?

I get the bill paid in record time, despite the fact I'm sure she'll be long gone by the time I get outside. To my surprise, her car is still sitting in the lot, with Viv behind the wheel staring straight ahead at the windshield where a piece of paper is tucked under her wipers.

Walking over, I snatch up the paper and look at it closely.

## *I STILL HOLD ALL THE CARDS*

Viv doesn't move at all, not even when I pull open her door and crouch down in the opening. "Honey?" I try, reaching over to cover the hands she has clasped in her lap. When she turns her head, she seems startled to find me there. "What's going on?" I show her the note and see her shiver in response. "Do you want me to call the cops?"

"No. Please don't. It's just … it's nothing. Really. Just a prank, I'm sure."

I can tell she knows I'm aware she's lying through her teeth, because her eyes plead with me not to push it. Feeling how on edge she is, I give in, but only because I've already made up my mind to mention it to Gunnar. I bailed on the ball game tonight, but know he'll be at The Skipper later.

"Okay. Why don't I follow you to your parents' house, though. Just in case." I stand up to get my bike when her voice stops me.

"I can't." Her voice wavers a little before her eyes lift to meet mine. "My car won't start."

After I get her to pop the hood, the problem is immediately obvious. Her entire battery is missing. What the hell? This is no joke. When I close the hood, I see Viv has stepped out of the car and is looking at me expectantly.

"Where is the spare key to your car, babe?"

"Why?" she wants to know, uncertainty on her face.

"Because someone took your battery and the only way to pop the trunk is with the inside lever. Was your car door locked when you came out?" I ask, leaning past her to grab her purse from the passenger seat. She's coming with me.

"I popped the locks with the remote, walking up. I don't have a spare set anymore. Never got it replaced."

"What happened to the first set?"

Just like that, I see her eyes fill with tears. Stepping in, I fold her in my arms. "Could this in any way be related to the reason you have a good friend who runs a shelter? Or why Gunnar is so damn protective of you? Talk to me, honey." I stroke her back, waiting her out.

"My ex," is all she says, her voice muffled by my shirt, but it's a start.

"How long ago?" I prod gently.

"About four years. I was thirty-five when I finally left him." Her voice is so quiet, I have to strain to listen but at least she is talking.

"Good for you."

She pushes her face even harder into my chest before she speaks again. "Hardly, considering I was just twenty-three when I met him."

Twelve years. I'm reeling with that bit of information. Hard to fit that with the strong, hard-nosed woman I've had a chance to observe a few times, not only standing up for herself, but others as well. "You figure it's him?" I still ask, even though my gut tells me it is.

"Pretty sure," she responds before she steps out of my arms. "I was gonna tell Gunnar, because I promised him I would if anything like this ever happened, but when morning came I thought maybe I'd overreacted."

I shake my head confused. "What do you mean, when morning came?"

"Frank has never contacted me since moving to the other side of the country, right after I left him. Until Saturday early morning, or technically Friday night I guess, when he called me out of the blue. I shut him down quickly, but it bothered

71

me that he pointed out he was 'still on West Coast time.' The night we had the bar brawl? I thought it was him standing outside the pub, but I'd dismissed that too. Now I'm thinking maybe it was him. Maybe he moved back."

I feel a surge of anger and frustration but suck it down when I see how forlorn she looks. Instead I hold out my hand. "Give me the keys and I'll lock up. You can hop on the back of my bike, and we'll sort your car tomorrow morning."

Within minutes we're on the road, Viv tucked in close behind me, her arms holding on tight. Reminiscent of the first night we met, but a hell of a lot less carefree. She directs me to her parents' place, and I pull into the driveway, just as Viv's phone starts to ring in her purse. Hopping off, she digs it up, checking the caller before tucking it back in her purse.

"Was that him?" I ask, perhaps a bit sharply.

"Mom," she says, pointing over her shoulder at the house. "Guess she's wondering where I am. I better go in and talk to her."

"Wait," I call out, reaching for her and pulling her close. She gives me a little resistance but not too convincing. "Let me have a little taste." Before she can answer, my mouth is on hers. Just as her body softens against me, and I can kiss her more deeply; a loud shattering of glass breaking has both of us swing toward the house. The big bay front window is gone, with only a few large shards hanging precariously from the top of the frame. Some piece of furniture is lying on the porch outside, looks like a folding table or something. From inside, a loud voice is calling.

"Vivvy! Vivvy!"

72

# CHAPTER EIGHT

*Viv*

I stand cemented to the spot.

Ike steps around me and runs toward the house, his long legs taking the steps to the porch in one. The moment he disappears in the house, I become dislodged and run after him. The sound of my father's voice, still repeating my name at the top of his lungs, leading the way. On the porch, I have to side step to avoid the glass and the TV table we've used to slide in front of my father's chair for dinner. Charging through the door, I run into Ike's broad back, who is blocking the doorway to the living room.

"Stay back, babe," he says in a soft voice, and I notice his hands up in a defensive manner. Like hell I'll stay back. I slip under one of his raised arms to take in the scene before me. My father is on his knees by the broken window with blood on his hands. When his wild eyes come to rest on me, he calms instantly.

"Vivvy," he breathes, and I can't help the soft shudder that runs through me. When my eyes roam the room, I find Mom on the other side of the dining room table, with a gun in her hand, aimed at Ike. *Fuck.*

"Mom? What happened?" I slowly walk toward her, stepping in front of the gun, making sure she focuses on me and not on Ike, who swears under his breath behind me.

Confusion mars her face, and she looks from me, over my head at Ike. "Oh, honey," she sobs, dropping the gun on the

73

dining room table, and I wince at the impact against the
wood. "I ... Dad ... he's been ... the window." By the time her
tears start flowing in earnest, I've reached her and slip my
arm around her, holding her tight while she cries. Behind me I
can hear rustling and the low timbre of Ike's voice. He's
looking after my father. I barely know the man, but I gladly
leave that task to him. Don't know what that says about me as
a daughter, but my mom deserves my attention. Gently, I
guide her into a dining chair, fetch her a glass of water before
kneeling in front of her chair, running my hands over her face
and body to make sure she's not hurt.

"I'm fine," she hiccups. "Your father started asking for you
a while ago. Was persistent, even though I'd told him several
times already that you would come after dinner. I got tired of
explaining, so I went into the kitchen, tried calling you, and
when you didn't answer I took a minute to wash some dishes
in the kitchen. That's when I heard the window shatter."

I grab her hands, which are shaking so hard she can't
even bring the water to her lips. After taking a sip, she can
continue. "He was yelling your name, and I didn't know what
happened, so I grabbed the phone and the gun from the top of
the fridge." The guilt for ignoring her call, just now, in favor of
kissing Ike is sharp and bitter. Mom continues without
noticing my wince. "When I came in, he was sitting on the
floor by the window, with blood all over. Then this man walks
in, and ... I thought ..."

"Shhh. It's okay, Mom. That's Ike, he was my date tonight,
he was just bringing me home. I think Dad broke the window,
his TV tray is outside on the porch." I try to keep my voice
calm, but my insides are shaking as hard as Mom's hands.
"You thought Ike—?"

She nods. "I hadn't had a chance to take it all in, and then
he comes walking in, and I thought we were being robbed. Or

invaded, like you hear about from time to time on the news." Her eyes travel over my shoulder to where I can still hear Ike's calming voice, before coming back to me. "I'm so sorry," she says, and the crying starts all over again.

"Babe?"

I turn to look at Ike, who has my father up in his chair and is holding on tightly to his wrists. Large shards of glass are clenched in each of my father's hands and blood is dripping on either side of his chair.

"Need a hand, Viv," he says, his eyes communicating calm. Right.

Standing up, I pull Mom out of her chair. "Mom, can you get the first aid kit from the bathroom and grab some towels, please? Dad has a cut." It's probably the understatement of the year, given the amount of blood collecting on the carpet, but I can't panic. Not now. I try to block as much of her view as I can and guide her into the hallway. Once she slips into the bathroom, I run to take some bottled water from the fridge, a few kitchen towels, and grab the phone off the table, before racing to Ike's side.

"Good girl," he mumbles, and I throw him a fierce look.

"Don't say that," I bite off. I don't wait to see his reaction but instead look at my father. "Dad, is it okay if I take the glass out of your hands? I'd like to put it somewhere safe," I try.

His unfocused gaze lands on me and slowly recognition dawns. "Viv?"

"Yeah, Dad. I'm here. Listen, you seem to have cut yourself, can you let Ike and me have a look?"

He never looks away from my face but slowly opens his hands, letting the shards fall to the ground. *Holy Christ.* His hands are pretty cut up. Just then Mom comes in, her arms piled with towels and the much too small first aid kit teetering on top. She almost drops the lot when she sees his injuries.

"Crimeny! Fergus, good Lord." Handing the contents of her arms to Ike, who's let go of my father's wrists, she sits down on the coffee table. For once, I'm glad for all the shit my brothers put her through. She's seen worse. Still, she wasn't seventy-three at the time.

While she distracts my father with questions, Ike starts rinsing the blood off his hands and arms so we can see the damage. In the meantime, I grab the phone and call Owen, who simply says he's on his way. He lives only five minutes away from our parents, and by the time we have wrapped the wounds in the measly little sterile wraps and then towels, he comes barreling in the front door, with Aaron closely on his heels.

"It's like a fucking bloodbath in here!" This from Aaron, who immediately gets scolded by Mom for his language. Aaron is the perpetual bad boy, and I suspect Mom secretly likes it. Especially when he plays coy with her, like now, leaning down and pulling her in a quick hug. "You okay, love?" When she smiles at him, he turns to look at the injured party. "Dammit, Pops. Did a number on those shovels of yours, huh?"

Owen just looks at Ike. "Who's he?" he barks, getting my back up right away, and I scramble to my feet. "Owen! That's Ike, he's with me. Try to be civil."

"Yeah, Owen, behave." Aaron, gives our older brother a punch in the arm, trying to make light of an already tense situation.

"By the way," I ask him, "how did you get here? Owen call you?"

"Nah. I was at his place. Red Sox game on Owen's sixty-inch tiny dick compensation." That earns him a slap to the

back of his head. I swear, my brothers, in their forties, are no different than they were as teenagers.

"Shut up, moron."

"Boys!" The deep baritone of my father's voice stops everyone. He was always good at restoring order with just that one word. "Think you can stop that for a minute? I think I may need some stitches." I'm sure everyone in the room is as stunned as I am to hear him talk lucidly and to the point. Mom appears to be the first to recover from the shock and jumps up to grab her purse.

"Well, come on, kids. You heard your father. Viv, Owen, see what you can do to clean up here first. Find something to board up that window. Aaron, grab the keys for Dad's car from the kitchen counter? You're driving."

This is my parents at their best. Taking control during chaos, and believe me, there was plenty of chaos in this house growing up. Aaron does as he's told, and helps Mom get our father to the car, while Owen continues to throw dirty looks at Ike. He is still on his knees, calmly trying to mop up the blood with a towel, as if he's done nothing else for years. In fact, he hasn't said much at all, just calmly does what needed doing without a word. I feel guilty for dragging him into this mess, and also ashamed, especially ashamed. This was a bad idea. This whole date thing: I should never have let him talk me into it. Hearing my father go on like that, getting a gun pointed at him for trying to help, while I'm still standing outside paralyzed. It's too much. Too close.

"I think you can go now." God, I sound like a bitch. I watch him slowly raise his head and look at me.

"When we're done here," he says slowly and deliberately.

I'm not sure what to do with that, and I don't want to make what is already a messed-up scene, an even bigger one. Owen, however, has no issue starting something.

"She said for you to leave."

Ike turns his head slowly to Owen, and I can feel the tension ratchet up. "Not what I heard and frankly, given the anger coming from you, I don't know if I'd leave her alone with you."

"That's my fucking sister you're talking about. I'd never hurt her. In fact, I'd kill anyone who would."

I'm standing by, watching this train wreck happen. I see it coming and there isn't a thing I can do about it. "Guys," I try, but neither is listening at this point. Ike has gotten up off the floor and stands with his arms crossed over his chest, feigning calm.

"Yeah? So how come that douche of an ex of hers is still making her life miserable?"

And there it is: the crushing impact.

## Ike

I knew it. The minute I brought up her ex and saw the look of shock on her brother's face, I knew he hadn't had a clue. She'd never told her family. Fucked that up good, because it didn't take a second for Viv to turn to me and let me have it.

"Get out."

"Babe ..." I tried to no avail.

"Don't you fucking 'Babe' me. You had no right to say that." She was almost in tears and I felt like the biggest ass.

"You're right. I'm sorry. But, Viv ..."

"Please just go," she said, her voice no more than a whisper.

I reached out to wipe the tear rolling down her cheek, but she closed her eyes and turned away. Right. With a last look at her brother, who appeared to have completely lost the plot, I made my way out the door, over the glass still littered around the porch, and to my bike.

That was last night. This morning I found the keys to her car in my jeans. The car that is still sitting in the restaurant parking lot. I make a quick call to the shop, arranging to drop the keys off so they can pick it up before it gets towed.

Sitting in my office, I'm waiting for David to come in to discuss some last minute problems they apparently have on the project in Boston. I've already gone over the list of available mechanics who could go have a look. I'm wondering if I shouldn't head out myself, having just been there, it might be easier for me to figure out what the problem is.

I've already pulled up the drawings and am pinpointing potential trouble spots when David calls a, "good morning," outside my door.

"David!" I call after him, and his face pops through the door. "They've hit a snag in Boston," I announce, watching his eyebrows rise.

"What, again? You were just there. What kind of mechanics do those guys employ?" He sits down in the visitor's chair, running his hand through his hair. "Hell, I can even understand those drawings you did, and I'm no engineer. What went wrong?"

"Rotation speed on the screws, they found one of them is lagging when they did their dry run." The screws are the big propeller blades moving the ship, and if they don't move in tandem, the ship would have a hard time staying on course.

"Any ideas?" David wants to know.

"Couple of them, but I'm thinking rather than sending out one of our guys, it'll be faster for me to head down."

David easily agrees, wanting as much as I do to keep this customer happy.

Three to five days, I'm guessing. Just long enough to pinpoint the problem, fix it, and do another dry run while I'm still there.

*It really is easier to go myself.* Who the fuck am I kidding? I'm jumping on the opportunity to get out of town. What does that say about me? The thought of heading off, leaving Viv to deal with all these problems, ones that I've added to by crossing the line, is a coward's move. But she did send me packing, although everything inside me screamed to stay. The urge to stay and protect her from the backlash of my big mouth, and whatever else has her so tightly coiled around her family, disappeared when she actually begged me.

Maybe it's better like this, the woman obviously has some major issues to deal with, and I'm not sure I can help with that. Now that I've let the cat out of the bag on the ex, I just hope she's smart enough to tell her brothers, so they can look out for her.

Steering my bike through traffic, I realize I don't even have her number to check up on her. I almost turn around and head back to Portland. I can always call The Skipper. Yeah, I'll do that tonight when I get back to the hotel.

When I get to the yard, the foreman runs through the problems they have in greater detail, and it doesn't take me long to figure out what went wrong. The bad news is, it means taking half of the damn engine apart again to fix it. I sit down with my laptop at the drawing table and start mapping out a schedule for the coming days. That alone takes me most of the afternoon. By the time I'm done, the sun is slowly sinking into the ocean, coloring the sky a vibrant red. Going to be a nice day tomorrow. I take a minute to enjoy the view and

I immediately think of Viv. Managed to keep thoughts of her at bay all afternoon, but now she's back.

A rumbling stomach reminds me other than the sub sandwich someone picked up for me this afternoon, I haven't eaten, and it's got to be close to nine. I need some grub.

I chew down the fast food I picked up with vague distaste and grab my phone. If I'm not careful, the food at The Skipper is going to spoil me for anyone else.

"Skipper," Gunnar's deep voice comes over the line.

"It's Ike. Viv there?"

The silence on the other side should've been a warning.

"Gunnar?" I prompt.

"Trying hard not to slam this fucking phone to pieces on my desk, pretending it's your head, you bastard."

Should've known. He did tell me Owen was a friend. I should've called him last night when I got home, like I'd intended to.

"I fucked up. Never occurred to me no one knew. The situation was ... tense."

"Been fucking dealing with a pissed off Owen all day. He's furious because he found out she came to me right after and let me help her on her feet. All this time, he didn't have a clue what her ex put her through. Viv's got her game face on, smiling like she's getting paid for it, but I know she's a fucking mess. And you ... you fucking disappear? What the fuck, man?"

I spend the next few minutes recounting the events of last night, trying to explain, but Gunnar won't have any of it.

"Should've stayed. Should've ignored her and fucking stayed, man. She needs a man who's got the balls to stand beside her, while allowing her to battle her demons. She's carried those with her long enough."

81

It stings on a couple of different levels. Gunnar challenging my balls for one, but also the confirmation this woman is carrying this load alone. As someone dragging his own share of crap along, that last one burns. He's right, I inadvertently opened the can of worms, and then left her to deal with it. Guilt, a familiar sensation, coils in my gut.

"I'm in Boston. Last minute problems with a rebuild," I say by way of explaining why I'm not there, rushing over to the pub. A grunt is my only answer, prompting me to continue. "I need a few days to get this sorted. I figure I'll be back Sunday, or Monday, at the latest."

It's silent for a minute on the other side, before his gravelly voice comes back over the line. "Gonna be a tough nut to crack. If you decide she's worth it to step in *and* manage to locate your balls, it's not gonna be a cakewalk. Shit with Viv goes deeper than I even know."

Dammit. Other than that one night of great sex and no commitments, we've barely even touched. I'm surprised I even care this much.

"I hear you. Not sure if I'm the right guy, though." That draws a harsh chuckle from him.

"Hell, I sure have my doubts." With that he hangs up, and I realize I didn't think to ask how her father is doing. Evidence I'm not the right guy for this? I have serious doubts myself, but somehow over the course of my phone call with Gunnar, I've come to the conclusion I want to be that man.

# CHAPTER NINE

*Viv*

"Jesus, Vivian—he hurt you?"

The moment Ike walks out the door, Owen turns to me, anger evident on his face. I don't want to fight with him, not now. Not until I have a chance to push down the emotional toll the night has taken on me. A not insignificant part of that was sending Ike packing. He hadn't even known the half of it, and yet he'd thrown down with my brother over me, standing up for me. And idiot that I am, I turn it against him.

Barely forcing down the tears that I can feel welling in my eyes, I get busy mopping up the mess around my father's chair with a discarded towel. When Owen's firm hand lands on my shoulder, I whip my head around. "Don't," I hiss at my brother. "Not now."

As expected, Owen can't let it rest for long. After we clean the mess, and manage to haphazardly board up the hole in the window, he confronts me on my way to the laundry room with my arms full of dirty towels. "This is killing me, Viv. Talk to me."

It's his pained expression that prompts me to speak. "He changed. Well, that's not entirely true, since he managed to show the same him to the outside world for all those years, but he changed with me. And I changed right along," I mumble the last.

"How long?" Owen's strangled voice breaks open the last of my resolve and I finally let the tears flow.

"Maybe about two years in before I realized what was happening. Oh, don't get me wrong …" I hurry to clarify when Owen throws his hands up in confusion. I know what he is wondering: why the hell hadn't I walked away then? Good question. One that still hasn't really been answered, despite my years of therapy with Pam. "… at that time, he hadn't hit me yet. That came later. I just noticed that where before I would make him happy, then I only seemed to be able to anger him, no matter what I did. I thought it was me."

"Damn, Sis," Owen groans, pulling me roughly into his arms, burying his face in my hair. We stand like that, in a pile of discarded towels, for minutes before he speaks again. "Why? Why not come to me, to any of us?"

"I couldn't," I mumble in his shirt. "You guys always tried to fight my battles, get me out of trouble as a teen, but I'd brought this on myself. Had to get out of there myself."

"Is that why we barely saw you? Why you took off to places unknown, for months at a time, driving Mom crazy with worry?"

"I was in Bangor for a while in a safe house. Then when I found out he'd moved to California, I came back to Portland and finally called Gunnar, but it still took me a while before I could face any of you guys."

There is no stopping the flood, and despite not getting into too many details, I tell Owen everything. He listens quietly, I'll say that for him, although the range of emotions playing out on his face require little clarification.

"Mom will be devastated," he finally says. He has no idea how hard I have to bite my tongue not to spill every last one of my secrets. Devastation doesn't even come close to what that would do: annihilate her—surely; destroy the family— definitely. So I just nod, wiping away the tears.

"No reason for her to know. Let it go, it's water under the bridge," I tell him firmly before grabbing my purse. "Can you give me a ride to the hospital?"

"I will, if you promise to get a restraining order filed first thing tomorrow."

By the time I roll into bed, after hearing my father will spend at least the night in hospital for observation, it's close to four in the morning, and I am completely worn out. Owen insisted on driving me home after the hospital staff evicted us for the night. The roller-coaster of emotions has taken its toll, and other than a perfunctory washcloth over my face and brushing of teeth, I manage little else than to strip and collapse.

It feels like only minutes have passed before the shrill peal of my alarm goes off. Eight fucking o'clock. Four hours of sleep, and I'm dragging myself out of bed and into the shower. Syd's on schedule to come up with the menu special for today, but I promised I'd be there early to help with prep. It's all I allow my mind to linger on, because everything else is just too raw.

The first person I bump into is Gunnar, however. He's in the kitchen creating a vegetable massacre.

"What on earth?"

He turns around, a large chef's knife in hand. Gunnar never helps with prep, for good reason; his chopping and slicing skills are barbaric. He also creates more work than he does, as is evident from the litter of discarded peels, cores, and ends both on the counter and the floor.

"I'm helping," he says almost proudly.

"I see that."

He apparently doesn't hear the sarcasm in my statement. "Syd's not feeling well this morning," he says by way of explanation. I'm immediately concerned for my friend, who rarely takes a sick day.

"Why? What's wrong?"

I don't expect the big smile that breaks Gunnar's usually stern face almost in two. *Oh hell.*

"Are you saying what I think you're—?" I swallow the rest of what I was going to say when the smile impossibly gets larger. Last night forgotten, I squeal and rush into his arms, deftly avoiding the large knife he still clutches. "Put the knife down, you bonehead!" He immediately complies and wraps me up in one of his signature bear hugs, reserved for only a few. "A baby ..." I whisper into his shirt, feeling happy for my friends, who deserve all the good life has to offer.

"I know." His voice rumbles under my ear and once again I wish I could've felt more than brotherly love for this man. But then I wouldn't have Syd, wouldn't have seen first-hand what devoted love looks like. Right on the tail of my elation, a wave of sadness settles heavily in my chest, a feeling of emptiness.

Gunnar sets me back and tilts my face up with a finger under my chin. "Happy tears, I hope," he smiles, but a hint of concern sounds in his voice.

"I'm so, so happy for you." I work hard at being convincing.

"I know you are, honey, but there's something else. You look like shit this morning. Your date last night didn't work out?"

I can't help it, I snort at what might be considered the understatement of the century. Before I know what's happening, Gunnar has me by the wrist and is dragging me to his office down the hall.

"Sit," he barks when I try to protest. "I can't be around knives when you tell me what that asshole did."

I assume he's referring to Ike, who really doesn't deserve this. "Ike did nothing. The night was a clusterfuck of epic proportions, but I don't want to get into it now. We have good news to celebrate." The smile on my face is plastered on thick, but as with all the men in my life, Gunnar doesn't take no for an answer.

"Talk, dammit. I'm not gonna let you leave this office until you do."

The dirty look I throw him makes absolutely no impression on him. I didn't really expect it to.

"Fine, you bully. But you've gotta promise not to overreact, because Ike really hasn't done anything wrong." I proceed to tell him about the nice date, the note on the windshield, at which point he almost launches from his chair, and the scene at my parents' house. As an afterthought, since there's a good chance Owen will be ticked once he discovers Gunnar already knew something about my history with Frank, it seems like a good idea to fill him in on that.

"He did what?" Was the expected reaction.

"In all fairness," I try to soothe, "Ike had somehow guessed I had some bad history, and it wasn't hard for him to put the pieces together when he saw the note. There's no way he could've known my family was unaware of my troubles. It was me who overreacted when I got mad at him."

"Yeah, well he should never have left." Gunnar, still grumbling, looks at me from under his frown.

"I sent him," I reinforce.

"Still." The stubborn ass won't let it go. He's at least, if not more protective of me, than my brothers. "How's your dad?" He turns the conversation into questionably safer waters.

"They'd sedated him last night by the time I got to the hospital. He was combative when they'd tried to stitch the cuts on his hands. They kept him overnight and are getting a psych evaluation today. Based on that, they'll talk to us about how to move forward."

"Gotta be tough. Always respected your dad. Such a proud, strong man. Must be tough to be slipping away like that."

Gunnar's sentiments are real, but his words slice through my threadbare shield. I can barely contain the derisive snort that wants to escape, but my face must've shown something, because Gunnar squints his eyes as he studies me.

"Yes, well, we'd better get back in the kitchen and get going on that special. What did our little momma have planned for today?" I babble, as I get up from the chair and move toward the door. Men are easy to distract, and the mention of Syd pregnant with his child, immediately draws Gunnar's full attention. An instant smile on his face, he follows me down the hall. To my relief, the only further talking we do while working, is about the new baby and how Gunnar's two older children reacted to the news. It was a close call, though. Too close. All this shit happening around me is seriously eroding my ability to erase certain things from my mind. First thing, once the lunch rush lets up, is to call Pam at Florence House. She's the only person I can talk to, and I need to decompress before I explode, which would be bad. Very, very bad.

"Holy shit."

That's the most unprofessional response from my therapist to date, when I update her on the most recent events.

Pam has been a friend ever since I knocked on her door that first time. I remember being startled by the statuesque black woman with short-cropped hair, peppered with gray, which seemed to only add to her stern beauty. She'd taken one look at me and let me in at face value. I spent two months at Florence House, licking my wounds and letting Pam help shore me up to where I was able to talk to Gunnar, the one man who was close enough, and yet sufficiently removed, to face. Pam knows me at my worst. The only person who knows all about Frank and although I kept the rest close to my chest, she's made it clear she's well aware there is more history I'm hiding. I guess that should make me feel self-conscious, but oddly it doesn't. She doesn't. She simply is an amazing, nonjudgmental, warm-hearted listener, who didn't so much as blink when I spilled my story and has since become a good friend.

That's why her reaction tickles my funny bone, it's so out of character. I throw my head back and laugh through the tears that have been threatening. She chuckles as she gets up to refill our teacups; something so warmly familiar, like the feel of the kitchen around me.

Since my own stay at Florence House, I've been working off and on here in a volunteer capacity, as much as my work schedule allows. Another secret I had guarded close, until Syd came along last year. I recognized the pain she was carrying around and put her in touch with Pam, who was crucial in her journey back. Syd now volunteers as well, as do most of the Florence House former residents. At least those who still live in the Portland area.

Setting my refilled mug in front of me on the kitchen table, Pam looks me deep in the eyes. "Here is my take. I know you've been resistant all these years to sharing your experience as an abuse survivor, despite my strong suggestions you share with your family. I understand your reasoning for it. I just don't and never did agree." She waves her hand in my direction. "This? What's happening right now? Is what I've feared. It's blindsided you, and you are scrambling to regain your so-called control, when you know just as well as I do, that your idea of controlling the situation is really the situation controlling you." The somber look on the face of the woman across from me fills me with trepidation, and I catch myself wringing my hands clasped on the table. "I don't think there is a way back—only forward. No way to get the lid back on the can, my dear, you must forge ahead." She leans in to cover my hands with hers. "And you are strong enough."

The dreaded tears seem to have won the battle as I consider what Pam is saying. She's right, I knew it before I came here but needed to hear it, I guess. I am strong. At least as far as my relationship with Frank goes. I'm not so sure about the rest. Time has not erased the memories, and now it would appear, it isn't even my memories that are the problem.

Pam doesn't let the silence hang for too long before she tackles a subject of her choosing. "So tell me about this Ike," she prompts, a big grin on her face.

"I think it's best we keep your husband, and father, here until we can find him placement in a full-time care facility. This new tendency to violence is not something your mother is equipped to handle." The geriatrician, who has taken over my father's care, addresses the last to us. With Dorian still out west and Nolan kept up to date by phone, it's just Aaron, Owen, and me in attendance. "And I'm sure with everyone's help, we could find a full-time licensed nurse for home-care, but a full-time facility, in this case, would be the safer option," he continues.

Poor Mom is crying softly, her world changing so much and so rapidly, I'm sure she isn't ready for this. She looks over at each of us and carefully considers her words. "I've never lived alone. Married Fergus right out of my parents' house and there haven't even been many nights I've slept alone. But I've never felt so frightened and vulnerable as I did last night. Not even when Fergus had his stroke. It was terrifying to see the man who's always been the stronghold of our family, always so emotionally contained, be completely out of control."

"Mom ..." Owen grabs her hand. "I think it's the right thing to do. For him *and* for you. Let's face it, since his stroke, you haven't been able to leave the house. Haven't had a chance to meet up with your friends for your games of euchre, haven't even had your hands free long enough to go for your daily walk. You have a life yet to live, Mom. After almost fifty years of looking after us, after Dad, I think you deserve it."

Mom's eyes meet mine and I smile through my tears and nod, my emotions too confusing to express with words. Aaron simply smiles at her and shrugs his shoulders. "You know what to do, Mom. We don't need to tell you."

With that, she straightens her slumped shoulders, lifts her chin, and faces the doctor. "If that is the best way to care for him, then that's what we'll do."

One of the strongest women I know, my mom, which makes my mixed feelings of pride, love, and anger, even more difficult to understand.

"Very well," the man interrupts my musings. "We have some paperwork for you to go over and sign, so we can expedite his placement."

It's already four-thirty when I finally walk out of the hospital and hail a cab. I've been missing in action from The Skipper for the past three hours and need to get back. I'll deal with the car tomorrow. The vague feeling of emptiness, when thoughts of last night surface, has nothing to do with the man with eyes the color of the gray sky after a storm. At least that's what I tell myself.

"Hey, momma," I say softly, as I walk into the kitchen of The Skipper to find Syd alone, stirring something on the stove. She swings around with a big smile on her face and accepts my hug.

"He told you? That man—we'd agreed to keep it to ourselves until we passed the first trimester safely. Given my age, there are a few more risks to this pregnancy than with my first one, so I'm being monitored closely. I shouldn't be surprised Gunnar couldn't keep it from you."

She looks absolutely radiant. So far removed from the beaten down, barely existing shadow of a woman I met that first time. Seeing as she'd lost her first child, a boy, in a horrible accident years ago, I can understand why she'd want to be extra careful.

Emotion sits heavy on my chest and clogs my throat when I finally manage to speak. "You have no idea how happy I am for you. You guys ... you *so* deserve this, and that little one is lucky having you as parents. Not to mention a big sister and brother to dote on him—or her," I quickly add referring to Gunnar's two children from a previous marriage: Dexter and Emmy. I can't help the tiny pang of longing for a family of my own, but I forcefully push it down, knowing that's not something that is likely to happen.

Still, a persistent sliver of hope flares when my mind conjures up a little boy with a killer smile and beautiful light gray eyes.

# CHAPTER TEN

*Ike*

The blare of a car horn nearly blows my eardrums as I struggle to keep my bike from flying out from under me.

I should've stayed the night in the hotel and left tomorrow morning, but I got on my bike the minute I was able to leave the project to the local crew, anyway. Which is why, at ten o'clock at night, I'm fighting the strong winds of another storm creeping up the Eastern Seaboard. The Maine Turnpike is surprisingly busy for a Sunday night. An unexpected wind gust almost blows me into the path of a van. Not sure what my hurry is tonight, but I'm eager to get home.

Adjusting my speed to the weather, I manage to make the rest of the trip without risking life and limb. It's almost midnight by the time I hit Portland. Can't wait to fucking get home, so I can take a much needed whiz. Instead of steering home, I find myself driving down to the wharf, where the wind is even stronger. Rather than park in the parking lot, I ease the bike down the alley, parking it by the dumpster in the back of The Skipper. I've barely lifted my leg over the seat and the back door opens. Although I can't see the face of the person backlit by the light from the hallway beyond, I'm quite familiar with the shape of that body.

"I owe you," the smoky, rich voice says, the moment I take off my helmet.

"How is that?" I ask, not moving from my spot.

Without answering, Viv walks over to the dumpster, two large garbage bags in her hands that she carelessly tosses inside before turning to me. Now that I can see her face, which is showing no signs of anger, I slowly make my way over to her.

"Got a call Thursday. A guy named Mike. Said he worked for Cumberland Avenue Garage. Said my car was in his shop."

"Uh-huh," is my wordless response.

"You had my car fixed," she says, tilting her head as she squints her eyes.

"I did," I tell her, inching closer so our toes are almost touching.

"Brand new battery *and* new locks. With a spare set of keys." She closes the space and puts her hands on my chest, and my mouth twitches into a half smile. This could've gone either way, and by the looks of it, I'm catching a lucky break.

"You don't say." I slip my arms around her waist and rest my hands on her lower back. With her head back to look at me, I can see fatigue on her face, but it doesn't dim the sparkle in her eyes.

"Thank you," she says simply, before her brows pull together in a frown. "But you know I'm gonna have to pay you back, right? Mike wouldn't take my card—said it was taken care of. You realize I can't accept that. My car—my responsibility."

Tugging her in a little closer, I slide my hands lower, feeling the upper curve of her fine ass in my hands. "Figure it's mine, actually. You see, I've got a vested interest in keeping you mobile and in one piece."

"Is that so?" She raises an incredulous eyebrow, but amusement dances in her eyes.

"Yeah. I've got plans." The moment she opens her mouth to respond, I slip my mouth over hers and slide my tongue inside. She tastes like a cool drink on a hot day and despite a slight initial stiffening, she soon has her fingers clawing at my shirt. The tangle of our tongues, Viv gives as good as she gets, quickly cranks the heat and my hands squeeze down on the globes of her ass. I reluctantly let go of her mouth, fighting the urge to take her up against the damn dumpster. My cock is straining against the fly of my jeans, and my bladder is about to blow. One of her hands slides into my hair, tugging at it to pull me back down. Instead of going in for another taste, I rest my forehead against hers. "Slow down, baby. That was a much better welcome home than expected. Doesn't mean we don't have to talk. But first, I had a long ride home and I'm gonna need to use the facilities before I have problems."

She doesn't say anything, just nods, but by the look on her face, I'm thinking she might be a bit worried about our talk. I follow her inside where she points me to the men's room, while I try to wrestle my hard-on in the right direction. By the time I walk into the bar, Viv is already slinging drinks for final call. The Skipper closes at one a.m. Long days, if you start at lunch time.

Taking a stool, at what is becoming my favorite side of the bar, I observe Viv interacting with what I assume are some of the regulars. At least, I've seen them here the few other times I've been in. Even the older guy, who almost had a broken bottle shoved in his face, was back in the same spot.

Viv walks up and slides a pint in front of me. "From Arnie." She nods in the direction of the guy I just recognized. "Says he never thanked you." I pick up the glass and raise it to him before taking a sip. It's good—not as good as that taste of Viv I just had, but refreshing all the same.

"Hungry?" The object of my thoughts is leaning across the bar. "I can whip you up something, you know."

I'm about to say no, when my stomach disagrees. "Yes. But let me do it. I know where the kitchen is. You finish doing what you're doing." The look of surprise on her face is pretty cute.

"Okay, fine. There's some leftover meatloaf and mashed potatoes in the small fridge. Seemed a waste to throw out along with the rest of the leftovers," she says shrugging her shoulders, having obviously intended to take it home.

I slip behind the bar, tugging her to me for a quick hard kiss, sending a chorus of whoops and hollers through the remaining patrons and putting a blush on her cheeks. With a satisfied smirk, I make my way down the hall to where I saw the kitchen earlier.

Bladder empty and belly full, I spend the next hour or so watching Viv do her spiel behind the bar. At some point, Arnie sidles over to me, and I have a chance to buy him back a drink while shooting the shit. Somehow it comes up in conversation Arnie is a Vietnam vet, and I identify myself as a vet as well, albeit more recently than Vietnam. The last fifteen minutes fly by while we talk shop. The minute Viv starts shooing some stragglers out and gives Arnie a pointed look, he pushes off the bar with a smile.

"That's my cue," he says, tilting his head in Viv's direction. "You know I've had a chance to observe that one. Friendly and cheerful as all get out, but she's carrying a load. You want dibs on that, you'd better come heavily armed."

Not sure how to respond, I simply nod and shake his hand when he offers his. Viv lets him out and closes up behind him.

I watch as Viv shuts and locks the back door to the pub and turns tentatively toward me.

My leg is already over the seat and my helmet is in my hands when I call out to her. "You coming?"

## Viv

Just like that, the nerves are back.

I never expected him to show up tonight, but I can't say I wasn't secretly wishing he would, at some point. The thought he drove his bike straight here from Boston, in a pretty decent storm, created a niggle of hope in the pit of my stomach. Of course, the first thing I blurt out is confrontational. That seems to be my style and I wince at the impression I might've thrown off. Seeming to take it all in stride, he made short work of my misgivings around the car, cutting off my protests with a kiss that about burned my top layer of skin off. I'd been about to suggest a talk, but he beat me to it. Coming from him it sounded almost ominous, yet his behavior was anything but.

I've seen Pam once more since Thursday, and she relentlessly pushed me to give this *thing* with Ike a try. Said that since he's friends with Tim, and appears to have been invited to join Gunnar's ball team, he obviously has their stamp of approval. Not that I am looking for that, but it is nice to know. Safe.

With that in mind, I climb on the bike behind him and wrap my arms around his waist.

"Your place or mine?" he asks over the whistle of the wind.

"Mine. It's the apartment building at the other side of the parking lot." It takes me less than a second to consider the options, but with it being so late already and not wanting to end up at his place without transportation, just in case, the decision isn't hard. I try not to think about the fact that other than Gunnar and my brothers, no man has ever been in my apartment. I promised Pam I'd try.

Much too soon I find myself standing opposite Ike in the elevator. Neither of us say anything, which only ratchets up the tension. The moment the elevator doors start sliding open, I rush out. I'm at my door, fitting the damn key in the lock, when the heat of his body presses against my back.

"Relax. We're just talking." The rough sound of his voice sends shivers down my spine. So much promise there, yet so much to fear. Little does he know, I'd be a shitload less nervous if he were here just to fuck. We seemed to do fine on that front the night we met. It's the rest of it: the talking, the sharing, the trusting. Those are what has my stomach churning.

Flicking on the lights I take in my place the way a newcomer would see it. An old couch, picked up from Goodwill and covered with old quilts and random burgundy pillows. The sunflower yellow paint on my walls that always makes me feel like I'm walking into sunshine. An old trunk that serves as a coffee table and second-hand barstools that I recovered in faux cowhide myself, just about rounds out my decor. Other than the wall-sized shelving unit that houses a small TV and my treasured book collection, there isn't much more. The kitchen is relatively tidy, which is a good thing, since its open concept is visible from the doorway, but I can't say the same for my bedroom. The only room, other than the bathroom, that has a door and can be hidden from view.

"Nice," Ike mumbles behind me. An innocuous remark that nevertheless warms me. This is my haven—my

98

sanctuary. To have him approve of it gives me unexpected pleasure.

"Thank you," I turn, walking into the kitchen. "Want a drink?" I ask over my shoulder, trying to play off a casual attitude.

"Wouldn't mind a beer, if you have it."

Armed with two bottles, I round the small island to find him seated in the corner of my couch. He's tossed the pillows on the other end and has his arm up along the backrest. I hand him his beer, and sink down on the opposite end. Beer in one hand and the other clutching a pillow in my lap, I take a leap into the deep end.

"Why did you come tonight?"

A smile slowly tugs at the corners of his mouth before taking a slug of his beer and swallowing. "The project in Boston, the one I was working on? They ran into some trouble earlier in the week, and with the launch coming up, I needed to get out there to get it sorted." He looks down at the bottle in his hand before his eyes meet mine again. "I'm lying," he says, surprising me. "I could've sent someone else, but I chose to go myself. After what happened Wednesday, I wanted to get as far as possible." What he says stings, and I'm sure he can see the wince I can't hold back. Reaching out with his fingertips he runs them slightly over my shoulder before continuing. "But even halfway down to Boston, I was regretting my decision. You see, I keep trying to distance myself, but it never lasts. I keep wanting to return to you. You're like my siren. Even tonight, after almost killing myself on the road, and with an empty stomach and a full bladder, I was all set to go straight home. But I didn't. I had to see you."

I swallow hard. Part of me wants to fight the way his words are like a balm to my battered soul, but I can't. They overwhelm me. They also make me feel so much worse about the way I treated him that night.

"I'm so sorry," I whisper, blinking fast to stave off the guilt that is threatening to manifest itself in tears.

"So am I," his voice rumbles, settling in my bones. Leaning over, he plucks the forgotten bottle from my fingers and sets it on the table. Then he grabs my hand and pulls me over to his side of the couch where he tucks me under his arm. "I had no right to throw that at your brother. And I should've stayed."

"I overreacted," I admit. "I realized later there was no way you could've known I'd never told my family. Any normal person would have." His arm tightens around my shoulders and he presses a kiss in my hair.

"Doesn't matter. It wasn't my place, and I certainly didn't mean to cause any more trouble for you. Seems you have enough on your plate as it is." That draws a chuckle from me.

"Ya think?" I try to make light of the situation, but something Pam said resonates. *Be real.* I'll try—as much as I dare to.

"Tell me, how is your dad doing?" Ike wants to know, and I catch him up. I tell him about the recommendation by the geriatrician and about the spot that just came available at Seaside Assisted Living, where he is to be moved tomorrow morning.

"Good. I'm glad to hear that. It's an incredible strain on loved ones when someone is suffering with dementia or Alzheimer's, not to mention the effects of his recent stroke."

I'm taken aback a little by his insight and the question slips out before I think. "Did you know someone?" The smile he gives me is rather wistful.

"My Gran. She was in her eighties when she started showing signs and at the time was living with my parents.

She'd refused to move into a home when it became clear, running her own household was getting to be too much. Unfortunately my parents were already in their sixties and should have been enjoying their retirement. It became an almost untenable situation. In the end, after Gran finally passed at almost ninety, my mom found out that the persistent pain she'd been neglecting for too long, because she was too busy, was actually cancer." The pain of remembering shows on his face, and I find myself burrowing deeper into his shoulder.

"She was gone not four months after Gran died. Dad couldn't hack it. His mother and wife gone in the time span of a couple of months was too much. He'd barely survived my brother's ..." A quick glance down at me before he continues, "Dad didn't make the year. He was only seventy-five and had given up."

"I'm so sorry." I rub my face on his shoulder and place my hand on his chest. I can feel the deep thump of his heart underneath my palm. His brother, too? I try not to react, but I can tell by his look, he doesn't want to talk about that. "When did you lose them?" I ask him softly, avoiding specifics.

"Two-thousand, and then three years ago."

His brother first, and then the entire rest of his family. My heart aches and pressing my eyes closed, I can feel the burn of tears behind my lids.

"So. How are things with your brother?" he asks, clearly ready to shift focus.

"Nothing I can't handle. I told him the gist of what happened. He was angry, but mostly I think he was disappointed I hadn't come to him. We've been distracted with my father since, and we've had a few run-ins. I warned him I don't want Mom to know. There's no use, not now, but he's trying to force the issue."

101

"Have you talked to Gunnar? To the police?"

I bristle at his questions and start pulling away from him, but his arm keeps me firmly anchored.

"Don't get mad. I know you probably have a handle on things, but I've been worried. Ever since talking to Gunnar ..." This time I shove at him hard enough and his arm slips from my shoulder.

"You talked to Gunnar? When? Why?" I'm probably overreacting again but I can't help myself. The thought of these guys talking about me, behind my back, gets me all kinds of riled up. All I manage is to make Ike snicker with my barrage of questions.

"Easy there, tiger. First of all, I called for you but he answered the phone. Secondly, it was Thursday evening, and I called because I wanted to apologize to you."

Okay, now I'm a little embarrassed. "Oh." I don't look up but keep my eyes firmly focused on my clenched hands. *Damn.*

He leans down and tilts his head so he can look up at me. "Yeah." He smiles. "Oh. And just so you know—for the sake of clarity—apparently your brother called Gunnar that morning to ream him out for not telling on you. I basically told him I fucked up, when he, in turn, tore a strip off my hide and the air is now clear. At least between Gunnar and me. He knows where I stand, and I know where he's at. And, babe?" I reluctantly lift my head to face him. "I don't think anyone can make the mistake of thinking you're not capable of looking after yourself, that's not in question. The point is that those of us, whose knuckles still occasionally scrape the floor, like to take care of what they consider theirs."

"Whatever," I mumble, but do it through a barely concealed smile, which morphs into a glaringly obvious yawn.

"Tired?" Ike asks as he pulls me to his chest. "Let's go to bed."

At the mention of bed, I push back to look at him with my eyebrows raised.

"Get your mind out of the gutter, woman," he jokes. "You need sleep, I need a snuggle, so I'm staying here."

For the first time in what seems forever, I throw my head back and laugh. Hard. "You're a nut," I say, standing up and pulling him up with me. "Good thing I'm partial to them."

Without another word, we make our way into my bedroom where, to my dismay, the better half of my closet is strewn over furniture and floor. The only thing to do is, with one wipe of my arm, at least clear the bed. I swing around, daring Ike to say something.

"Interesting decor," he dares, but quickly pulls his shirt over his head and I'm instantly distracted by the faint dusting of hair on a fine, fine chest. Didn't have the time to check the wares, so to speak, last time he got naked. His soft chuckle brings me to my senses. With a fake dirty look, I disappear into the bathroom to brush my teeth. After me, Ike takes a turn with the new toothbrush I left out on the counter for him. By the time he comes back to the bedroom, I'm already in my sleep shirt, snuggled under the covers, facing the edge of the bed. I can feel the other side dipping behind me when he gets in.

"Night," I say softly when I feel his arm come around and yank me to the middle of the bed, plumb against his delicious chest.

"You get to sleep, but I still need my snuggle," he says with his nose pressed in the crook of my neck, breathing in deep.

"Are you sniffing me?"

"Hush, you need to rest."

With a smile on my face I slowly give into the draw of sleep. His deep voice in my hair is the last I hear before I drift off.

"You give good snuggle."

# CHAPTER ELEVEN

*Ike*

"Hey. Fancy meeting you here."

*I'm in line to grab lunch on my break when Ben shoves my shoulder, almost making me drop my damn tray. It's been at least a week since I've last seen him. My brother and I have both been assigned orders to the USS Cole earlier in the year, only two months apart in fact. But working on opposite schedules, Ben's on nights, we don't bump into each other a lot.*

"Lunch break for me. What about you? Shouldn't you be sleeping?"

"Nah. I had a couple of hours, can't seem to get back to sleep. Besides, there's a bug running through the operations room and half the guys are sick. We're kind of short-staffed, so I thought I'd grab something and head in." *Bold as can be, Ben grabs a tray and pushes in line beside me, instigating a chorus of swearing behind me. As usual, Ben is oblivious to insult, living his life on the half-full side. He lets everything slide off his broad back. His yin to my yang, Mom always says. I'm the pessimist. The deep thinker, broody, and much darker than my light-haired and light-hearted brother.*

"Meatloaf and mashed potatoes for breakfast?" *I note as I watch him load up his plate. He shrugs his shoulders and throws me one of his big smiles. I just shake my head, and take my tray over to a couple of empty seats on the far side of the galley.*

"Fuck. Forgot my drink," *I curse, just sitting down.*

105

*"Shit. Me too. Hang on, I'll get them." Always the helpful kid, Ben plops his tray in front of the empty seat beside me and heads over to the counter, where a new flood of cursing greets him as I see him jump line again. I knew he'd do that, which is why I didn't get the drinks myself. He charms his way through every obstacle.*

*An ear-shattering explosion lifts me right out of my seat, and slams me into the wall. Noise, I can't even process, surrounds me before it turns eerily quiet. A persistent groaning of metal has me raise my head, and I'm surprised to see daylight flood in through a massive hole in the hull where the counter used to be. The water is starting to stream in. My eyes immediately start searching for Ben when chaos ensues. I'm frantically pushing mangled steel and debris off me and crawl over bodies, some screaming, some all too quiet, to search for my brother.*

*Jesus!*

With a gasp I sit up in bed, looking around in confusion.

Slowly I remember last night, Viv's apartment, and most importantly Viv, who when I look over, is still lying beside me, quietly observing me from under heavy eyelids.

"You okay?" Her smoky voice sounds even hoarser with sleep.

I drop my head in my hands. I haven't had one of these since the night of the brawl, but I'm guessing last night's confessions brought it on. Shouldn't be surprised: I'd never quite been able to rid myself of them, despite some counseling.

"Yeah," I answer, laying back down and curving my arm around her, tugging her close. She doesn't resist.

"That seemed pretty intense," she says with a little too much concern.

106

"Just a dream. We all get those from time to time, right?" I play it off. Not something I want to drag up in the early hours of the morning. Not something I discuss at all. Ever.

"I don't dream," she says resolutely, her lips tight and a blank look on her face.

"Everyone does."

"Not me. Not since I turned fifteen."

With that, she slips out of my hold and goes to the bathroom, where I hear the toilet flush and the tap turn on. Huh. That was a pretty clear *do-not-enter* sign, if there ever was one. No dreams for over twenty years? Seems pretty significant, but since I'm not sharing, I can't fault her for doing the same. Avoiding.

I lie in bed, waiting for her to return, when I hear the water shut off. A minute or two passes and still she hasn't come out, so I go to investigate. Need a piss myself. The bathroom is empty but the door to the hallway is open, and I can hear some noises come from the other end. If I had any hopes for some more quality cuddle time, they were definitely killed off when I smell coffee brewing. This night has apparently officially been declared over. Pulling on last night's clothes, that I discarded on the floor beside the bed, I make my way to the kitchen. A quick glance at the clock on the stove tells me it's only five-thirty. Way too little sleep and too damn early to get up. Viv's sitting on one of the cow-stools with her legs tucked underneath, her head bent over a paperback. Totally engrossed.

"What are you reading?"

The sound of my voice obviously startles her, because I barely manage to keep her and the damn stool from toppling over. She feels warm and soft under my hands, and I can't resist sliding my arms all the way around to her front, where the weight of her breasts casually rests on my hands. "You're not breathing," I whisper behind her, prompting her to take a deep breath in.

"Just a book," she mumbles, slipping off the stool and thus from my arms, making her way to the other side of the counter.

"Romance?" I ask, flipping the abandoned paperback over to look at the cover before looking up at her.

She shrugs her shoulder, a slight blush on her cheeks. "Pam told me to try. She lent me that one."

"Who's Pam?"

A quick flick of her eyes tells me she'd rather not answer. She does anyway. "Pam is my therapist. She helped me a lot a few years back. We became friends."

I suddenly recall the scene in the bar a while ago, when Viv jumped in for a girl whose boyfriend was yelling at her. "She's the one who runs the shelter?" It earns me a tiny smile.

"Surprised you remember that. Yes she is, she runs Florence House. I spent some time there a few years ago, after ... you know." I nod, even though I don't really know. I know she's talking about when she left her douche bag ex, but I don't know the whole story. Yet. I'm sure there's a reason why she opted for a shelter, and not the safety and security of her own family, who live right here in Portland. Yet, until I spilled the beans last week, they had no idea she'd even had problems.

"Still see her when I need a little ... tweaking." She laughs nervously when I round the counter and stalk up to her. "A lot has happened, these past few weeks," she says by way of explanation. Not that I need any. I was there for some of it. "She's the one who told me to give this ... thing with you a chance."

"Did she? I'll have to thank her at some point." I wipe a few wild strands of hair off her forehead, before leaning in to take her lips in a soft kiss. "Morning," I mumble against her mouth.

"Morning," she returns, never letting her lips lose touch with mine. "Hmmm," she hums when she ends the contact. "I was gonna make some breakfast—you interested?"

I rub my nose along hers before answering. "Bring it on. If you're cooking it, I'm game." I take a seat on the stool, prop my elbows on the counter, and watch her pull supplies from the fridge and the cupboards.

"Hope you can handle a bit of heat," she quips, waving a few jalapeño peppers at me.

"I'm here, aren't I?" I wink at her, simply glad I'm not out on my ass. Yet.

## Viv

When the persistent groaning, from the other side of the bed, woke me this morning, I'd been momentarily alarmed. Not for long though, because the moment the mattress shifted and I cracked my eyes, I immediately recognized Ike's shape sitting up straight in bed. He seemed distressed and disoriented, yet when I'd spoken up, he'd passed it off as just a dream.

*Just a dream, my foot.*

Concern for him almost had me tripping up—saying more than I was ready to admit to. Even to myself. Denial is a beautiful thing, as long as I can keep a handle on knee-jerk responses, like the one this morning. In an attempt to avoid any further questioning of my enigmatic slip-up, I'd rushed into the bathroom. Deciding I felt more in control vertically than I had horizontally, going back to bed was not an option.

I'm lucky he didn't pursue, although he did catch me off guard when I tried losing myself in the small-town romance novel Pam had shoved in my hands. I've always been a fan of thrillers and suspense. Have looked down on romance most of my life, but I have to admit, this book sucked me in right from the first page. Not the bodice ripper I expected, and the heroine is far from a whimpering, helpless damsel in distress. I've used every spare minute, since I first cracked the spine, to read. Best way to divert focus from the hot mess my life is in. With my head already fully engaged with the storyline, I almost jumped out of my skin when I heard his voice. And another little piece of myself dropped out of my mouth before I had a chance to check it for content. Damn him. And damn Pam, for pushing me to be *real*, whatever that means. It's hard when you've spent years creating a personality that suits everyone yet hides everything. Only a few see the cracks in the armor. Syd was actually the first and I willingly let her see them, but only so she would see my kindred soul. Gunnar, although he'd already proven a better friend than I could ever have imagined growing up, was tentatively allowed in a little further too. But Ike, with eyes that were way too keen, seeing altogether too much, seemed to barge through almost every defense. Getting to see more of me in a much shorter time than anyone else ever had.

Food is always an excellent distraction, and already aware that his stomach is a soft spot, I don't hesitate a second before I wave it around, drawing his attention right away.

Huevos rancheros, otherwise known as *the big guns* when it comes to any breakfast I cook. I stir the wooden spoon through the beans I'm refrying, tossing in a dollop of sour cream to help break down and smooth out the beans.

The smell of chili powder tickles my nose as I season the chopped onions and jalapeño peppers softening in the other pan. A can of tomatoes goes in my big blender, followed by some cilantro and the onion blend and with a few quick pulses, I have the base for my sauce. I almost forget about the man, whose eyes seem to be following everything I do, while sipping the coffee I slid in front of him. Almost, but not quite.

A quick fry of the corn tortillas in the pan before I lay those out on a plate. Topped with a layer of the heated through tomato sauce, slices of avocado and a few spoonfuls of the beans, they're ready for the eggs. Sunny side up, with the yolk still a bit runny. When I slide the plates on the counter in front of Ike, he has a big smile on his face. "Damn, babe. That smells phenomenal."

"Hang on," I say when he gets ready to shove his rolled up tortilla into his mouth, and shove some paper towels his way. "This tends to get messy."

Sure enough, first bite results in tomato sauce and egg yolk dripping down his hands but he just happily chews and swallows. "Best damn breakfast I've ever had," he mumbles, already going in for the next bite.

Smiling at myself, I have my own first taste. Not so bad: breakfast the morning after.

Ike offers to clean up so I can grab a shower first, but I remind him he's the one who has to be in to work early. Mondays are easy days for me. During the winter months we usually close on Mondays, but during the summer we capitalize on the warmer weather, like anyone else making a living in a coastal town tries to do. But Mondays we don't open until three in the afternoon. Deliveries are scheduled in the morning and lucky for me, that's Dino's job. He takes in and checks all the produce and meat that's delivered and I don't show up until one or two. We used to have both food and liquor delivery on the same day but we've since split it up. Works better this way, and I get the bonus of a morning off.

I'm humming with my hands in the warm suds, while listening to the water run in the shower. My earlier spot of anxiety long gone, I actually feel quite content. When the doorbell rings, I almost ignore it, but when I hear my brother yelling my name in the hallway, I quickly wipe my hands on a towel and rush to open up.

"What the hell, Dorian? Way to wake up the neighborhood. When did you get back?"

Dorian walks to the middle of the room before turning around, his hands on his hips. "Last night and fucking hell, Viv! I cannot believe you never said a word. Not even to *me*."

That feeling of contentment is gone as fast as it came. He knows. I'm suddenly overwhelmed with a rush of anger at Owen. He promised to let me do the talking. He didn't like it, but he promised.

"Dorian ... Owen shouldn't have ..." I start, but that's as far as I get. I don't know what to say. Dorian is empathetic and also very persistent. A lethal combo when you have something you'd prefer to keep to yourself.

A sharp shake of his head indicates keeping quiet is a good idea, for now.

"You mean Owen knows? You told him and not me?"

I'm confused. If Owen didn't tell him, then who? "I don't understand. Who told you then?"

"Kyle told me. He got a call from one of his models yesterday morning, saying she needed to talk to him. When she showed up with her arm in a sling and a scar on her cheekbone, he was shocked. She said her boyfriend put her in the hospital a month ago, and she's pressing charges. Guess what her boyfriend's name is?" He pauses to make sure he has my attention, which he does, but I'm afraid I already know the answer.

"Frank Miller."

I flinch at the mention of the expected name and bile creeps up my throat, but I can't get any words out.

"Turns out she met Frank at one of *our* parties, when you guys were visiting San Fran the year before you broke up. He'd stayed in touch and hooked up with her when he apparently moved to Los Angeles—something else I did not know," he snaps with a pointed look at me. "She told him she wanted to get a message to you to be careful. Frank found out that the cops intended to question any previous girlfriends, to see if they could establish a behavioral pattern to support their case, and that's when he disappeared." His head drops and he takes a few deep breaths.

"I'm sorry ..." My voice cracks under the weight of my guilt. Dorian lifts his head and looks at me with tears in his eyes.

"What did he do to you?" The bluntness of his question takes me aback.

"It doesn't matter," I whisper, "it's over."

"Like hell it doesn't matter!" Dorian bellows, and with his long arm, angrily swipes the content of my shelves on the floor before turning and punching a hole in the wall.

## Ike

My first instinct on hearing an angry man's voice when I shut off the water, is to barge in and throw myself in front of

Viv. It sounds a lot like she's under attack. Then what sounded a lot like anger, is laced with pain. This is one of her brothers, and if my guess is right, it's the youngest one. The one Viv told me she'd been closest with growing up. That's why he's upset, he's hurting for her as well as for himself. Instead of interfering, I decide to monitor from where I am: standing in the doorway of Viv's bathroom, drying myself quickly with a towel.

I'm just pulling up my jeans when a loud yell, followed by a crash and the sound of something hitting the wall has me on the move double time. The first thing I see when I turn the corner is Viv cowering on the floor by the door, her arms covering her head, and I see red. Did he hurt her? From the corner of my eye I see her brother moving, and without thinking, I haul out and connect with his face. Only then do I notice the hole in the wall on the other side of him.

"I swear I didn't touch her," he mumbles through the hands he has covering his face. I ignore him, instead kneeling down in front of a whimpering Viv. I carefully reach out and stroke her hair, only to have her try to curl up even tighter.

"Viv, baby, look at me. It's just me. No one is going to hurt you." She doesn't move other than the inadvertent shaking of her body. When I sense Dorian step up behind me, I turn. "Find her cell. Her purse is in the bedroom. Find a number for Pam."

"Who's Pam?"

"Just fucking find the phone. She's a friend and her therapist."

I try to touch her again, but each time I do she flinches. *Jesus Christ.* She even flinches at my soft words. This worries me.

When Dorian hands me her phone over my shoulder, I quickly find Pam's number. While I dial, I turn to Dorian who looks about ready to burst into tears. I did a good number on his face, his cheekbone is starting to swell. "You'd better put some ice on that."

"Hey, girl, miss me already? I've got you down for tomorrow."

"Is this Pam?"

"Who the fuck are you? And what are you doing with my girl's phone?" The switch from friendly to fierce is scary, it's so fast. I hurry to explain.

"This is Ike. I know Viv talked about me because she told me. Listen, can you come here? There's been an incident and something happened to her."

"On my way. Is she hurt? What happened?" I can hear her walking and talking. She didn't hesitate to get moving.

"She's tucked in a ball, flinching at every word I say. I tried touching her but she pulls in even tighter. Her brother, the younger one, came over to confront her about ... well, about keeping her history with that dirt bag to herself. Things got a little heated, and it looks like he took it out on a wall. Don't know whether it was the yelling or the aggression, but she's tuned out. I ... I don't know what to do." I don't. I feel absolutely helpless.

"She's having a panic attack. It's not uncommon with her kind of history. Keep talking in an even voice like you are doing now. Use her name a lot when you talk, to get her to focus on you and not the memories that are filling her head right now, and put the phone on speaker. I'm about ten minutes out, but let me try to talk to her."

"Okay."

I press speaker and move the phone a little closer to Viv. "You're on."

"Viv, honey. You're okay. You *will* be okay. You and me, we've done this before, right, girl? This is not our first parade.

Are you breathing the way I taught you? In sharp through the nose—out slow through the mouth."

I can see Pam's calming voice having an effect on Viv. Her breathing slows and the tight grip she had on her head loosens a bit.

"Are your eyes open, honey? Can you open your eyes? Ike is right there. Can you see him? He's safe, Viv. Ike is safe."

Viv lowers her arms just enough for her to see. Her eyes flick all over the room and her breathing becomes erratic again.

"I'm here, babe," I step in, trying to draw her attention. "Viv, look at me."

Slowly her eyes come around and focus on me.

"That's a good g … job. Stay with me here, sweetheart. Pam's gonna be here soon." Luckily I caught the *good girl* that almost slipped from my mouth. Something she didn't react too well to last time I said it.

"Ike." Her voice breaks on my name and before I know what's happening, she launches herself at me.

"I've got you," I say, as I wrap her up tight in my arms.

"You've got her?" Pam's voice comes over the phone.

"I've got her."

# CHAPTER TWELVE

*Ike*

A knock on the door has Viv clutching to my shirt.

I haven't moved, and I don't think Dorian has either. He's behind me somewhere, hopefully with ice on his face. I didn't look to check, my focus has been entirely on Viv.

"It's okay," I tell her softly. "It's just Pam. I'm just gonna get up and let her in." But the instant I move, she digs her little nails in my chest.

"No-o," she whimpers. "Don't let me go."

"Okay. I won't let you go. Just hang on to me and we'll let her in together."

Her head, which is buried in my chest, shakes a vigorous no. *Fuck.*

"How about I take you to the bedroom and Dorian can let Pam in?" This time I don't wait for an answer, but just struggle myself to my feet, Viv clinging to me like a monkey. I'm not a weakling, but she's not exactly tiny. It's a bit of a challenge, until I feel a pair of hands hook under my arms and lift. Between my leg muscles and Dorian's upper body strength, I get to my feet and walk straight to the bedroom, Viv in my arms.

I leave the door ajar and hear the front door opened, followed by muffled voices. By the time an unfamiliar woman's head pokes into the room, I'm sitting on the bed with my back against the headboard and Viv still hanging on for dear life. Or so it seems.

117

"Hey," the woman says, taking in the scene before her. "I'm Pam. Ike?" she questions me.

Viv stirs a little at the sound of her voice.

"That's me."

Pam gives me a faint little smile before focusing her full attention on Viv. "Hey, girlfriend. You okay if I sit on the side of the bed?" When Viv doesn't move or respond, Pam sits down on the other side of the bed anyway. Kicking off her shoes, she pulls herself into the same position I am on the bed, her back against the headrest. This is pretty weird. I mean, I'm a guy and a stint in bed with two women at the same time has entered my mind on occasion, but these were not quite the circumstances I'd envisioned.

Pam reaches out and tentatively touches Viv's arm, who doesn't move. "Honey, you wanna try and look at me?" she says softly. "Viv? Your breathing sounds okay, maybe you can just turn to face me?"

Slowly Viv's head lifts from my chest and turns toward Pam's voice.

"Hey, girl, tough morning?"

Her hands let go of my shirt and she slips from my arms into Pam's waiting ones, resting her head against her shoulder. But she's no longer shaking or hiding her head.

"I'll leave you guys." I move off the bed.

"Wait."

Viv's lifted her head and looks at me, clear-eyed. "I ... so sorry." She looks embarrassed and unsure, her face blotchy, red, and wet from tears, and still she's gorgeous.

"Don't. Nothing to be sorry for," I mumble and lean in to give her a soft kiss.

"Well, this is a new experience," Pam quips as I end the kiss and find myself looking, at very close proximity, into a pair of deep brown and very amused eyes. "Can't say I've been here before, but hell, I'll give anything a try once."

A chuckle comes from Viv as I back away from the bed, and soon these two are giggling like crazy, arms wrapped around each other. At my expense, no less. Still I pull the door shut behind me with a grin on my face.

"She okay? Shouldn't we call a doctor?"

Right. The brother. I'd all but forgotten about him. I wince when I see his face. Damn, I got him good. His left cheekbone is swollen and I can barely see his left eye. "She'll be fine. Did you use ice?"

"Yeah." He waves his hand at a bag of frozen peas left on the counter.

"Put it back on, I did a number on you."

With the bag pressed against his face, Dorian pulls out a kitchen stool, while I try to find the makings for another pot of coffee.

"I didn't mean ... fuck, I had no idea ..."

I feel bad for the guy. I get it. I get his reaction, his anger, but the truth is, he wasn't thinking about her when he came tearing in here. That was all about him.

"You know she didn't tell your other brother. I did." When Dorian lifts his head, I shrug my shoulders. "I was with her when we found a note on her windshield."

Of course this part is news to him, so I take him through the events of that night, up to and including the part where I spilled the beans to Owen in anger, getting myself kicked out in the process. It seems to make Dorian feel a little better, but I'm not sure whether it is because Viv never told their other brother herself, or because I fucked up too. I'm reserving judgment on that one, but I'd prefer to go with the latter, because who the fuck cares who told who. It's hardly what's important.

"You know, there's a reason she's kept this to herself all this time, right? And from the way you brothers have reacted so far, it's pretty obvious why."

"She changed. With him—Frank—she seemed happy at first, but at some point that tight connection she and I'd always had disappeared. I thought it was because she'd told Frank I was gay, but the first time he seemed to realize that was when they visited San Fran. Actually, she already started pulling away earlier. Before Frank even came on the scene." He seems to get lost in memories as he takes a sip from the coffee I'd poured him. "Viv is the only one in the family I told my sexual preference to, way the hell back when. At first, I thought the change was because of that. Viv had always been outgoing and so damn happy. Loved everything and everyone, could laugh big, and cry big too. Had her heart and her emotions out there for the world to see. Then suddenly, she'd become moody and quiet. I remember Mom telling me it was probably just her "time of the month." His hands make quotation marks in the air.

"How old was she?"

"Dunno. Maybe fourteen or fifteen?"

I avoid looking at Dorian, because the sense of unease I felt a few times when Viv would talk about her family, just became a vague suspicion that has my stomach in knots.

## Viv

It's quiet in the room when Ike walks out and pulls the door closed behind him. Pam doesn't say anything, she'll wait until I'm ready—she's patient that way. And irritating. But also safe and the one person who knows me better than anyone. So just for a moment longer, I'll enjoy the haven my bed and Pam's arms provide. Although I have to admit, Ike gave me the same feeling of security.

"You're waiting for me, aren't you." I throw it out like a challenge, daring her to speak. As usual, she waits me out and is much better and more experienced at this game than I am.

"You said this would happen. You warned me. That one day—somehow—the boys would find out and it would not be pretty."

"Uh-huh," is her only contribution. I push back a little, so I can look her in the face.

"I'm a mess," I throw out there, wincing a little at the truth of that simple statement. Almost worse to acknowledge it myself, out loud. "There's no way to contain this anymore, is there? I mean, I'll have to tell my mom."

A slight tilt of her mouth is all the indication I get from Pam, the rest of her face remains almost impassive. Then finally she speaks. "First things first: what happened this morning? Talk to me."

Her eyes pierce me and reluctantly I comply, telling her how Dorian found out about Frank. How it's likely that before long, the cops will be knocking on my door with questions. How it makes me feel trapped, and when Dorian started yelling and swung his arm around, I just remember being terrified.

"I don't even know what happened after that. I just know I was so scared of being hurt, I did what I could to protect myself. Don't remember much except your voice." I pause before adding, "and Ike's." Disgusted with myself, I hide my face in my hands. "Oh God, I'm such a goddamn victim. I hate this—being out of control. Thought I was done with this a long time ago, and now *he* saw how weak I am. A fucking front row seat. I can't do this, Pam." I sound pathetic, even to my own ears, but I can't stop the feelings, the words, from coming.

"Prefer to think of you as a survivor, but that's just my opinion," Pam says, rather sardonically.

"Whatever," I mumble, feeling Pam's warm hand come to rest on my back.

"Panic attack, girl. It happens to the best of us. Especially when we try to bury things that can, and often will, come to the surface. Often at the worst possible times. You want control? Only way to claim it is to deal with shit, head on. This is not news to you. You've been faking life these last years, it's time to grab it by the balls. Let the chips fall where they may."

I know she's right. I know it, but I don't like it. I thought I could control things by controlling my part in them, but it's an illusion, isn't it? This morning only proves it.

"This is why you wanted me to try a relationship, isn't it? To crack me?" I accuse her, but she just smiles her enigmatic smile.

"Dramatic much? Crack you? I thought perhaps if you opened up a little to someone, it would help you excise that festering sore you've been keeping carefully wrapped. You know—*you know*," she emphasizes, "that it has to come out. Dammit, Viv, you've worked with me at Florence House long enough. You're well aware it has to get worse before it gets better." Pam is stern with me.

One of the things I love about her is that she doesn't sugarcoat things or pat me on the head. She doesn't allow me to hide, and yet I've been working hard at doing just that.

"Ike worked out better than I thought, though. He's getting my stamp of approval." She fans herself, rolling her eyes. "Fine specimen," she mutters under her voice.

I can't hold on to the burst of laughter that bubbles up; before long, the two of us are howling like hyenas. The tears follow immediately after. Mine. But these are real tears, evoked by emotions that are just a bit overwhelming. Pam, probably expecting this release, simply pulls me back to her shoulder.

"Everything okay?"

I zoom in on Ike, who immediately gets up from the couch the moment he sees me. On Pam's suggestion, I took a cleansing shower after my crying bout. She'd left earlier, making me promise to come see her after I've had a chance to talk to my brother. Something I know I need to do.

"Sure," I smile at him. Funny, part of me is surprised he's still here, and yet I wouldn't have expected anything else from him. "I'm good." Then my eyes find Dorian's, dark with pain, at least one of them. The other I can't really see.

"Jesus. What happened to you?" I exclaim, rushing over to inspect his face.

"Your boyfriend," is his sheepish answer. "Clocked me when he found me scaring the life out of you. Christ, Sissy. I'm so sorry, I ..."

I put my hand over his mouth, cutting off his apology. "Stop. How could you have known?" I use my hand on his chin to tilt his head, this way and that, before turning around to face Ike. "You did this?" When he shrugs his shoulders, looking a little sheepish himself, I almost burst out laughing. Instead I walk up to him, tracing my fingers along his jaw. "That's a hell of a hook," I tell him, at risk of getting lost in his mesmerizing gray eyes, so I drag mine away. Only to have them caught on the clock in the kitchen. Almost ten-thirty, holy shit!

"You're late for work." I point out, but Ike doesn't seem alarmed.

"Called in already. It's all good," he calmly informs me, before looking at Dorian and then me again. "But I think I'm gonna head in shortly. Leave you guys to talk." He walks up and pulls me into a hug, his face buried in my neck, where he mumbles, "I can be back here in no time. Programmed my number in your phone, so you know how to get hold of me."

I hang on to him, not wanting to let go, but I know I have to. Got to do this on my own. Pushing back, I look up at him and mouth, "*Thank you.*" His immediate response is to bend his head and slant his mouth over mine in a scorching kiss that has me forget my own name. When he pulls back, my hands are tangled in his hair, and I almost involuntarily tug at the long strands. Another, much lighter kiss and with his lips still against mine, he makes me a promise that has my knees weak.

"Those kisses of yours make great appetizers, honey, but I can't wait for the main course."

The clearing of a throat alerts us to the fact we have an audience. My brother, no less. With a knowing smirk, Ike lets me go and walks toward the door, lifting two fingers in salute to Dorian, and winking at me.

The moment the door closes, Dorian pipes up. "Holy shitballs, Sis. Where did he come from?"

## Ike

It's hard, leaving the apartment, driving home for a change of clothes, and then heading into work. Trying to make like everything is normal, as per usual, when it's really not. I know she needs time to sort through things with her brother—her family. It sucks, but on the drive home I've come to realize my presence might just muddy the waters. I'm not sure. This morning was such a roller-coaster of emotions, I'm not sure I can properly process it all.

On a whim, I turn my bike around, just as I'm about to pull into the parking lot of Maine Maritime Designs, back in the opposite direction. Florence House is on Preble Street. I've driven past it before and remember wondering if the beautiful old Victorian house was a residence or a business. I never realized it was a shelter, until Viv mentioned the name.

"What are you doing here? Is everything all right with Viv?" Pam's face displays concern, but she doesn't invite me in.

"She's doing better. I left her at home with her brother." I grind to a halt here, not sure what I'm doing here.

"I can't let you in. There's a group in session and this is supposed to be a safe house."

Right. I never thought of that. Would make sense they'd have a *no-men-allowed* rule here.

"Okay, well I ..." I'm about to leave when Pam interrupts me.

"Hang on, let me grab my phone. There's a coffee shop on the corner where we can go for a talk. You did want to talk, right?" She tilts her head to one side and I'm suddenly aware of how tall this woman is. Granted, I'm at the bottom of the steps, but at my height it is rare I have to look up at someone. "Yo, Ike. Did you wanna talk?"

"Yeah, if we can?"

Without answering she disappears inside the house, closing the door behind her. I'm about to consider myself stood up, when the door opens again and she walks out, a purse slung over her shoulder.

"That your bike?" She nods to the curb where I parked.

"Yes, it is."

"Nice," she responds, immediately followed by a quietly mumbled, "lucky girl."

Trying to hold back a smile, I pretend not to have heard her last comment. We walk in silence to the small, quaint store, with two little tables with chairs butted up against the window outside. "Sit," Pam indicates one of the tables, neither of which is occupied. "It's a nice day, we may as well enjoy it. Let me guess: black dark roast?"

"If that means a plain coffee, then yes," I tell her. The response I get is a roll of the eyes before she slips inside.

Interesting woman, Pam. Dark ebony skin pulled tight over an almost perfectly proportioned face, mostly gray hair she seems much too young for, closely cropped to her scalp, and the body of an Amazon. Long limbs, ample curves, but with an underlying power that can't be mistaken. This is a strong woman, and if I didn't have a mind full of Viv, she would be a temptation. Even if she is probably a bit older.

"What are you smirking at?" Pam walks out with two mugs and a brown bag, setting it all on the table.

"I seem to be skipping work," I open with, having decided to ignore her question. "I can't remember the last time I did that." I take a sip of the rich black liquid, waiting to see if she'd give me an opening. Not likely. She just holds her coffee in her hands, looking at me patiently over the rim of her mug. Well damn. "This is about Viv," I offer.

"You don't say? Think I gathered as much, my friend. You should know though, that I will not discuss anything that was discussed with Viv in confidence."

126

I wave her off. "Wouldn't ask that of you anyway. No, it's more about my role, if any." Pam lifts an eyebrow, not saying a word, just lets me struggle by myself. "She told me you encouraged her to go out with me."

"I did say that. I assumed you were a decent enough guy by merit of the friends you keep. You haven't disappointed yet. You handled her pretty well this morning."

"See? That's what I mean: I don't fucking know what I'm doing, and she seems to have some real issues around her family. And I don't mean just keeping her abusive relationship a secret."

The eyebrow shoots up again. "Did she tell you that?"

"Not really, but I've noticed things. The way she talks about her mom, but calls her dad her 'father' consistently. I've only heard her say, 'Dad,' when she was talking directly to him."

"Very observant. And astute." Pam sets her coffee mug down and starts digging in the paper bag on the table, fishing out a muffin. "Here," she says, offering it to me. "I got two."

We spend the next few minutes eating. Well, Pam is eating and I'm mostly picking at mine.

"What is it exactly you want to know?" she asks, wiping the crumbs off her lap.

"I'm not sure if this is the right time to try and start something," I admit.

"For who? For you or for her?"

That's a fucking good question, and I take my time considering how to answer. "Both, I guess. I may not be the most stable person for the job."

It's obviously not the answer Pam was hoping for because her eyes narrow to slits, and she presses her lips together. "The *job*?" she finally says. "My friend, if you think dating Viv is a *job;* you can march your lily-white ass right back over to that hot as hell hunk of steel, and ride off into the sunset. She deserves better than the likes of you." With a heave, she pushes her chair back from the table and rises up to her full height. Oh yeah, she's pissed and is doing a good job at making me feel about an inch tall.

"Hold on. You heard that wrong." I lift both my hands in defense.

"Really? Cause I could swear I heard those words come out of your mouth." Her hands are now planted on her ample hips for emphasis. Fuck, I'm bungling this.

"Let me be clearer then: I'm talking about the job of looking after her. Looking out for her." Frustrated, I run my hands through my hair. "Feels like things have gone to shit for her since I showed up in her life. I can't help but think …" Before I have a chance to finish, Pam leans one hand on the table, while the other hauls off and whacks me to the side of my head. *What the fuck?*

"You stupid, boy. You think you're that important in her universe that you can have that big an impact on it? You're a fool. You're what? Forty? Forty-five? Damn, a man like you should know better than to think his way out of a good thing. Let me ask you this, is she getting to you?" She slaps her hand to her chest over her heart. "She getting in here?"

"Looks that way," I grudgingly admit, feeling all kinds of the fool she accuses me of being.

"As I thought. Although I'd love to dig deeper as to why you'd think you can't take care of her—look after her—like you said, I have a shelter to run, and you have a woman to support." With a brisk tug, she pulls her purse over her shoulder and takes a few steps before stopping and turning back. "Think about this: Is she worth the trouble?"

Fuck, what kind of question is that? "Fuck yes, she is," I snap back, irritated as all hell. The result is a little, self-satisfied smile on her face.

"Exactly. Glad you see it my way." With that she turns on her heels and marches at a brisk pace back to Florence House.

Somehow, I feel like I've just been put over the knee and had my lily-white ass spanked.

# CHAPTER THIRTEEN

*Viv*

As expected, my talk with Dorian on Monday was rife with tears and recriminations, both his and mine. He was unable to get over the fact I hadn't told him and still refused to give him details. What's the use? It would only rile him up more. The hardest for me was when he asked how it is possible that someone like me would put up with it for so long. Yeah, that's the million dollar question, isn't it? Truth is, I was already feeling unsure of my place in life and was searching for an anchor. When I met Frank, I looked up to him: friendly, attentive, stable, and all mine. It's not like he started on me right away, that happened gradually, and it was difficult to let go of the person I thought I knew. By the time I knew I was in trouble, when things got really bad, my relationship with my brothers was almost non-existent. We hardly ever talked. It felt like I was eroded, the person I had been was simply no longer there. It took some serious wake-up calls, in the form of hospital visits, and finally a concerned hospital social worker, to force me to have an honest look at my life.

It's fucking embarrassing, that's what it is, dragging along the garbage of a twelve year relationship where you allowed yourself to be humiliated, belittled, beaten on, and chewed up and spit out. I did that, I allowed it, and I have to own that. Bringing it up with family just seemed like such a minefield, I chose to keep it from them. After all, what would be the point

131

to making them feel bad when it's all over? And didn't that just come back and slap me in the face.

Owen is off stewing somewhere, mostly avoiding me like the plague. Dorian is furious and devastated in equal parts, and I still have to tell the others. And Mom. Jesus, Mom—not like she needs this shit on top of what she's been dealing with lately.

Dorian did drag me to the police station, demanding I tell someone what happened, instead of sitting around waiting for them to come to me. That was an interesting experience. Let's just say it took a while for someone to take an interest. I did walk away with a promise someone would be in touch with respect to the charge pending in California. I finally got that temporary restraining order, which seems a bit futile, if you ask me, considering Frank never was one to follow rules he didn't like, but whatever. The officer explained that it would give the police an added handle on him.

Haven't heard or seen him, though. Not in the last two days. Nor have I seen my brothers, other than a call last night that I was expected at my parents' house tonight to have a family meeting. This is supposed to be to deal with Mom's finances and the house, something that does need to be dealt with in the short term, since the facility where my father now lives costs a pretty penny. Yet a nagging feeling that I'll be walking into something else altogether is persistent.

Which is why I'm hiding in the kitchen. It's Wednesday, so the baseball boys will be in here later. Normally my cue to go, since I don't work late on Wednesdays. Then there's the matter of Ike, who's tried to contact me several times these past few days. Not that I've responded, my total and embarrassing breakdown on Monday still too fresh in my mind.

"There you are!"

Owen walks into the kitchen, disturbing my thoughts. I shooed Dino out of here at eight, half an hour ago, telling him I'd handle any stragglers dropping in for a late meal. Owen stops just inside the door with his hands on his hips and a scowl on his face. "You were supposed to be at the house half an hour ago," he says accusingly.

"I forgot," I offer lamely, causing him to huff incredulously.

"Hiding is not your style," he accuses, hitting a sore spot, because it is. It's been my style longer than anyone knows and it's eating me alive. "Good thing Nolan cancelled last minute, he couldn't get up here in time so we've rescheduled to Sunday. Tried calling, but you weren't answering."

That would be because I'd turned off the sound after Ike called for the third time earlier tonight. I don't tell Owen that though. "You did? I didn't hear my phone."

"Vivian. You can't avoid us forever. Dorian told me what happened. We think you should pull the Band-Aid off and tell Nolan and Aaron at the same time you tell Mom."

I shake my head as panic has bile rising up to my throat. Owen walks over and puts his hands on my shoulders. I'm frozen on the spot, fighting down the nausea at the thought of facing my family. Seeing the disappointment and pain on their faces.

"You'll have Dorian and me at your back, Sis. I know you've tried to shove this down, but isn't what happened on Monday proof enough that you can't will this away?" He pulls me in, and for a minute, I let myself feel safe in his arms before I push back.

"Does Lydia know?" I ask, watching as his eyes flit away before returning.

"I told her. I'm sorry, Viv, I ... I was upset, she noticed."

I hold up my hand to stop him. "I'm not angry. Actually, I'm a bit relieved. She gonna be there on Sunday?" Lydia is good with Mom, and I'd feel better if she were there to deal with her.

"I can ask her. If you want her to be, we'll make sure she'll be there. Her mom won't mind watching the boys for a couple of hours."

"It's Mom, you know? I'm worried about her."

"Lydia will keep an eye on her."

This time I move in for the hug. It doesn't feel so bad now, having some things out in the open, and my brother seems to have gotten over most of his anger. Pretty sure I have his wife to thank for that.

"Viv, can we get—Hey, man, how are you?" Gunnar walks up to Owen, who turns on hearing his voice, giving him a few manly slaps on the back. I guess they've kissed and made up since Owen found out Gunnar knew about Frank. Good. Would hate to have any part in damaging a lifelong friendship.

Gunnar is obviously back with his team for their regular after-game refreshments, so I can guess what he was going to ask. Leaving the guys to catch up, I start pulling out the wings and prepping the hot sauce we toss them in after they're fried.

"I need our standard order of wings, honey," Gunnar appears to have remembered why he came in the first place.

"In the fryer, Boss," I shoot back over my shoulder.

"You're an ace, Viv," he says with a wink, before shoving Owen out of the kitchen in front of me.

Well, it would seem things have been smoothed over with my brother, and I've earned myself a stay of execution. Until Sunday.

Suddenly I have a craving for a glimpse of Ike. He's probably in there drinking with his teammates, and I quickly finish off the two giant baskets of wings, so I can personally deliver them.

My eyes immediately scan for the familiar gray ones at the round table in the corner, where the guys like to hang out. Disappointment sours my gut, when I don't see him in the rowdy bunch.

It's my own damn fault.

## *Ike*

"Those wings look sexy on you."

Viv jumps a foot when I whisper the inane comment in her hair.

She didn't see me coming out of the washroom when she stopped in the doorway, appearing to scan the bar. Like a love-sick idiot, I hoped she was looking for me, which is why I snuck up behind her.

"Holy hell, Ike, you about gave me a heart attack." She whirls on me, and I quickly put my hands out to steady the baskets of food before they go flying. I don't miss the faint blush on her cheeks or the happy light shining in her eyes as she does her best to look disapproving.

The woman has just about driven me insane with her avoidance. If I hadn't experienced first hand how she reacts to anger, I'd probably have forced my way in, but I don't want a repeat of Monday on my conscience. Patience is key. I've seen it work with Pam, but it seems to come to her a lot easier than it does me.

Seeing her head into the bar in front of me, when I hadn't been sure she was going to be here, gave me a great sense of relief. I couldn't resist catching her off guard. "Are these for the boys?" I ask, taking the baskets from her hands before I make my way over to the table. I set them down and turn back to the bar, where Viv is standing with her hands on her hips, watching my every move. When I reach her, I turn her around by the shoulders and march her down the hallway. Loud whistles and catcalls following us all the way.

"You're killing my rep," she says when we get to the kitchen, but she does it with a faint smile on her face.

"Good. It's payback for leaving me hanging for days." I've backed her into the counter and with my hands around her waist, I lift her to sit on the edge. "That was not nice, Viv," I scold her in a low voice, wedging my hips between her knees, effectively anchoring her in place.

She doesn't seem to be in a hurry to get away from me though, her hands are sliding over my shoulders and around my neck. "I needed some time."

"Time for what?"

"Time to lick my wounds—consider my options, either way," she says with a shrug.

"What exactly were those options you were considering?"

"I heard you went to see Pam."

"Yeah. I did."

"Why?" I can hear insecurity in her voice.

Putting my hands on her ass, I pull her closer to the edge, so she can feel how much I want to be here. "Because I was ready to walk away ..." A hard shove to my shoulders almost has me lose my grip on her, but I just grab on tighter and press myself into her. "Let me finish. I was ready to walk away, if she thought it would be better for you at this time."

136

The pout she sports is pretty cute, but her words aren't. "So what you're saying is that if she'd told you to walk, you would've? You went for permission? Not sure that makes me feel any better."

"You're being purposely obtuse, babe. Also, you know Pam better than I do, you figure she gave me my answer for me? She actually hit me." I still can't get over the fact I let her cuff me like that.

Viv snorts, "For real?"

"Not lying. Right there on the street in front of a coffee shop full of gawkers, in the middle of day, she stood up, leaned over and whacked me upside the head." The deep belly laugh coming from Viv sounds really, damn good.

"She loves me," she says on a smile, when our laughing slows down.

"She sure does," I confirm, rubbing the side of my head for emphasis, which causes Viv to burst out laughing again. "And for the record," I continue, "it would've killed to walk away, even temporarily, because regardless, I was gonna come back."

That was apparently the right thing to say, because Viv throws her arms around my neck, wraps her legs around my hips, and proceeds to blow my socks off with a toe-curling kiss.

"Ahem," a voice sounds from behind me. Reluctantly pulling my lips from Viv's, I turn to find a smirking Syd in the doorway. "Sorry to interrupt, but the boys were wondering where the blue cheese dip is for their wings."

Immediately a highly flushed Viv starts worming herself from my hold. "Oh shit. Sorry, I'll get it."

But Syd is ahead of her. "No, no. Stay as you were, I'll just be a sec."

I chuckle as Syd walks by us, her smirk morphed into a wide-ass smile, cracking her face in half. With a groan, Viv drops her head to my shoulder, where she mumbles, "Someone, please shoot me now."

"I heard that," Syd pipes up from the other end of the counter. "No need to be so melodramatic, not like I'll go around announcing you two were making out hot and heavy in the kitchen." Armed with two bowls of dip, she slips behind my back, which I smartly keep turned to her given the current state of my crotch. "Atta boy, Ike," Syd stage whispers. "Atta boy."

This time it's my turn to groan. Forty-two years old and I've been called boy by two women this week. Granted, one is a formidable, slightly terrifying Amazon, who's got me by a number of years, but the other is a waif of a girl, younger than me by a few years, if I were to grant a guess.

"You better get back to your teammates, or they'll send out a search party," Viv comments wryly, her face still pressed against my shoulder.

"Hmmm," I mumble, enjoying her heat, scent, and body surrounding me. "Gimme a minute."

By the time I return to the rowdy bunch at the table, there are only two little wings left and my beer is lukewarm. I take the ribbing the guys give me silently smiling. Content in the knowledge I was able to finagle a promise from Viv to let me escort her home tonight.

Half an hour later, I spot her trying to get my attention from across the bar.

"Time for me to go, guys. I'll probably see you next week." To a cheer of *later*, *good game* and a couple of *lucky dogs*, I make my way over to where Viv is talking with Matt, who is manning the bar.

"Ready?" she asks me when I walk up. I don't miss the elbow she throws in Matt's ribs before turning and walking out ahead of me.

I catch up with her by the back door. "What was that all about?" I want to know when I step outside behind her and close the door.

"Just another misguided Y-chromosome set on *brothering* me to death," she complains. "What is it with every male within shouting distance either thinking they have to protect me, or hurt me."

"Hey." I grab her hand and pull her to a stop halfway down the alley to the parking lot. "What's that all about?" She looks to the side, her eyes fixed in the distance, on some point in the restless waters of the Atlantic. I have to lift her chin and turn her face to me before she'll look me in the eyes.

"It's nothing, really. He's just looking out for me."

"What did he say?" I press on, starting to understand her penchant for pushing things down. I get the shoulder shrug again. "Tell me."

"He just reminded me I should be careful. That I haven't been particularly successful thus far in my selection of men."

"Need me to talk to him?" That son of a bitch knows nothing about me, and I shouldn't even care, but Viv obviously does. "Be happy to," I add, trying to ignore my own insecurities. Because frankly, the mention of *men,* as in multiple, sets my teeth on edge, not to mention the question whether I deserve her. I'm still not sure I do. But I do know I'll do my damnedest.

"Please don't you start," she says, pulling away from me.

"Hey. Look at me." I wait for her to lift her eyes before I continue. "When people care about you, they have a tendency to go out of their way to look out for you. Listen, not necessarily because you need it, but more likely because they need it. Your brothers, Gunnar, and Matt, they're guys. They know you've been hurt and there's nothing they can do about it now. For a guy, that doesn't sit well. So they turn a bit overprotective—try to manage your life for you."

"So why aren't you?" she asks, crystal blue eyes boring into mine.

"Who says I'm not protective? Fuck, there's nothing I'd rather do than slay your dragons for you. But I hold back because I'm afraid if I come on too strong, I'll run you off."

I watch her face soften a little before grabbing my hand. "Not running now."

No, she's not. She's looking at me with heat darkening her bright blue eyes. *Damn.*

We barely make it through her front door when the dam breaks.

A frantic clash of mouths, hands hurriedly pulling and tugging on clothing, and in a matter of seconds, I have Viv pressed up against the wall. My shirt is off and my jeans and boxers are wrapped around my ankles, while Viv is only left in her bra and underwear. I tug down the cups of her bra and latch onto the closest breast, my hand covering the other, when I suddenly release her.

"Please don't stop," she whispers, her fingers tangled in my hair.

"Slow down. We need to slow this down, baby." I press my forehead against hers, both of us breathing deeply. "I want to do this right, instead of right now."

Her eyes are fierce as she yanks on the strands between her fingers. "First right now, then we can spend all night doing it right," she hisses through her teeth.

"Fuck me. I like your idea better," I growl against her mouth, simultaneously slipping one hand down and inside her panties to find her swollen and slick. "Jesus, babe, you're so ready."

"Ahhh, I told you," she groans, as I slide a finger inside her and then a second one. Viv grinds herself on my hand and suddenly I can't wait. I have to be inside her. Sliding my hands under her ass, I lift her up and she automatically wraps her legs around me. With a few short stumbling steps, I manage to carry her over to the kitchen island, where I plant her butt on the edge.

"Hold on. This'll be fast," I say, slicking my cock along her crease. I ease the tip in when it occurs to me I'm not wearing protection. "Jesus, condom," I blurt as I pull back, but she grabs my ass and holds me in place.

"I'm protected," she breathes against my mouth. "And clean."

*Thank God.*

"Ditto on the clean," I'm able to tell her, having had a full physical, and my one-night stand with Viv was the first encounter since. "Look at me." I hold myself still with the head of my cock poised at her entrance. "I want you to see me, as much as I want to see you."

Slowly and steadily I slide inside her body, feeling every one of the little shivers that run through her. Her mouth falls open as I fill her up, bottoming out when my balls slap against her ass. I squeeze my eyes closed to regain some control over my body, which is raring to go. She feels so fucking good. I slowly open them again as pull out, and a small whimper falls from Viv's mouth, her eyes big and clear on mine.

"Ready?" My voice sounds rough and brittle.

"Oh yeah," is her answer, as she drops her legs from around my hips. Bracing herself on the counter, she pulls her heels up on the edge, spreading herself wide open. So fucking beautiful. I don't know whether to feast on her or fuck her.

"You're a fucking siren," I groan, as I try to make up my mind. "My ultimate temptation."

All it takes is a slight movement of her hips and my control is a thing of the past. I slam myself home between her legs, hard and deep, my hips pumping strongly; my knees barely able to hold me up. Viv throws her head back, mouth wide open, and lifts her hips slightly with every surge of my cock. God this woman is phenomenal when she lets loose.

"Fuck me," Viv hisses as she lifts her head and focuses on my eyes. One of her hands comes off the counter, and she starts working her clit in hard, fast little circles. The sight of her, so completely uninhibited and in the moment, is enough to pull my balls tight to my body and the telltale tingle to start at the base of my spine.

"Hurry," I manage between clenched teeth, but unnecessary, because I can feel the tightening of impending release in her pussy.

Throwing her head back, Viv groans out my name as her orgasm hits. The pulsing of her body around my cock a trigger for my own.

"Coming, babe. I'm coming. Ahhh …"

I'm blind. I swear I can't see. My head is swimming and my knees are buckling with the force of my climax. Before I end up in a sorry puddle on her kitchen floor, Viv pulls my body over hers, wrapping her legs around my ass. Gratefully, I lay my head on her chest and wait for my faculties to return.

# CHAPTER FOURTEEN

## *Viv*

*Holy shit.*

I can still feel him all over my body. It's been three hours since he left my place this morning, but the impression his body made on mine is far outlasting his presence. I'm almost waddling as I make my way from the pantry back to the counter, my arms piled high with vegetables that need chopping in preparation for today's crowds. Each part of my sweetly aching body represents a memory of probably the most intensely hedonistic and satisfying night I've ever spent. Who am I kidding? I know damn well there've been none before like this. The slightly abraded rubbing between my legs reminds me of Ike's intense silver eyes holding mine in their draw as his mouth sucked tirelessly on the sensitive nub between my legs. With every pull, the scruff on his lips and chin deliciously chafing my tender skin. The proprietary and hungry clasp of his fingers on my hips leaving bruises. An aching in my lungs, deprived of air as his lips and tongue devoured my mouth and stole my breath. And the throbbing empty space where the size of his cock stretched the limits of my body's hold.

What started off as a frantic coupling, when neither of us had the control to wait, moved into the bedroom and onto a slower pace. He took the time to thoroughly familiarize himself with my body, and I had a chance to explore his strong, powerful one at leisure. The wide angle of his

143

shoulders, the light dusting of hair over his solid chest, the strong lines of his long legs, and the feel of his prominently erect shaft in my hand. All the while, his penetrating stare followed every trace of my hands on him, only his breathing betraying their effect.

A soulful sigh escapes my lips as I neatly peel the first potato.

"What the hell's gotten into you?"

Syd is turned to me, one elbow resting on the counter, her eyebrows drawn together. "Had a tough night? You look like you're hurting with the way you're moving around. And with all that sighing you've been doing, I don't know whether to be happy for you that a certain someone showed you a good time, or whether to chase him down for hurting you."

I can't hold back the snicker. Immediately the frown on Syd's face smooths out.

"Well, alleluia! Someone got some serious action," she says, nudging my shoulder with a big grin on her face.

"Yeah. Uh ... didn't need to hear that." Gunnar's voice comes from the doorway, where he is leaning against the post, a pained expression on his face. "She's like my little sister." He pretend shivers with repulsion.

"Quit being such a prude," Syd teases, "or have you forgotten what we were doing this mor—"

Dropping my knife, I reach out and slap a hand over Syd's mouth, cutting her off mid-sentence. "TMI. Please. I feel your pain," I say to Gunnar, who just shakes his head and disappears. "Wait!" I call after him. "Did you need something?"

He sticks his head around the door. "Just wanted to know what time Dino's coming in. I need some more boards for the windows, thought I might try to catch him. Hoping he could drop by Lowe's and pick up some things."

"I don't think he's left home yet. He doesn't usually get in until eleven-thirty."

"Okay, I'll call him." Gunnar's head disappears from the doorway.

I woke up in the early hours of the morning with the wind whipping against the windows of my apartment. The forecast predicted damaging winds for tonight into tomorrow, which is why Gunnar is in early. Since the pub is completely exposed to the elements at the front, he likes to get boards up on the large front windows at the first sign of a storm. It might be a bit overkill for the overnight weather, but you never know with these onshore winds. Besides, right on the tail of this system is a tropical storm building in intensity. That should hit the second half of the weekend, as per the weather predictions. Worse comes to worst, we'll close the pub—it wouldn't be the first time—but Gunnar will do everything he can before that happens, to make sure the building sustains no, or minimal, damage.

"So ... about last night," Syd teases.

"Not gonna give you a detailed report, girlfriend. Not likely." I smile at the look of disappointment on her face, and playfully bump her hip with mine. *Ouch.* Forgot about those bruises. "And even if I did, it would be a glowing one," I can't resist adding.

"I'm glad. I mean, I'm *really* glad. I've been worried about you lately, what with all that is going on. Your father, Frank, your brothers finding out, filing for a restraining order—it's all a bit much. You need something positive in your life."

"Thanks, sweetie." I give her a side hug and lay my cheek briefly on the top of her head. Not particularly hard to do, since Syd is tiny and I'm ... well, I'm not. Hard to imagine that not long ago there was a time I had no girlfriends whatsoever. Whatever ones I had, they had long since disappeared with the control Frank exerted over my life and my relationships. I'm blessed to have found two good ones in Syd and Pam. "Ike was a bit of a surprise, and a little scary, but Pam urged me to give it a go."

"She's great, isn't she?" Syd points out, being no stranger to the quality of Pam's counseling.

"The best."

I chuckle as I start to tell Syd the story of Ike's meeting with her. By the time the potatoes are rinsed and in a pan on the stove, both of us are giggling like idiots at the thought of this big, tall man getting a slap upside the head from a very angry Pam on a street corner.

The rest of the day goes by as most Thursdays do; with a lot of patrons coming in for meals. The Thursday specials have taken on a life of their own, mostly so, since Syd started flexing her culinary muscle. Her creations are all like wholesome home cooking but with an unusual twist. Just like today's, which is carrot mashed potatoes—honey garlic glazed carrots thinly sliced and mixed in with the potatoes— and meatloaf with fresh mango chutney. The woman can cook. She makes what should be a simple meal into a gourmet experience. That's why people keep coming back on Thursdays.

I'm manning the bar when I notice a commotion outside the front door. With the boards up on the windows, it's impossible to see out, but the window in the door provides just enough of a view to see what looks to be a tussle between two men. Hard to keep track of what's going on, since the ruckus outside is drawing attention. A few customers have gotten up to get a good look and are blocking the view. When the door swings open, a huge burst of wind almost blows it off its hinges, and all I can hear is yelling.

"Get Gunnar out here!"

A familiar voice carries over the sounds of the wind. *Ike*.

# *Ike*

This fucking day has dragged on.

I spent it working on a new engine design for a new customer, a large freight company hoping to inject new life into their aging and sluggish fleet. Time is money in today's economy and higher speeds are expected. Unfortunately, their current fleet of cargo ships is at least twenty-five years old, and they're struggling to keep up with current demands. It's one of the things our company is good at, looking at innovative ways to increase productivity. In this case, it is cheaper for them to have new or rebuilt engines installed than it would be to start replacing their cargo vessels. Big job, and for now it had me pinned in my office, behind my drafting table and wishing for fresh air.

I left Viv's this morning without making any definite plans, just a vague reference to seeing her tonight. After last night, I don't think I could stay away if I tried. It's all I thought about all damn day. For someone not comfortable staying in one place, I sure seem in a hurry to get tied down. Not all of it is Viv, though. It started with my house. That had been the biggest commitment I've made to date. The renovations seemed the logical next step—making the place *mine*. Then the changes in my job, keeping me mostly in Portland. Now, here I am getting hooked on one woman. Settling down. Something that just a short while ago would've sent me running in the opposite direction, but that was before I met Viv.

I'm nothing if not adaptable. Which is why, after a meeting with David, that ran well past office hours, I'm now on my way to The Skipper instead of home. Instead of parking my bike in the parking lot, I slip into the alley behind the buildings. The wind is strong coming off the water and the alley acts as a funnel, increasing its intensity. Damn, it's going to be a bitch riding home tonight. Unless of course, I end up staying with Viv again. Not a bad plan.

I'm about to pull in behind the pub, when I see a guy crouching down beside the dumpster. His head whips around the moment he hears my approach, and he takes off running, leaving behind a small box he was holding. I barely have time to set the bike on the kickstand, and yank off my helmet, before he disappears around the front of the building. A closer look at the box has my blood boiling. In large block letters, it has Viv's name spelled out. Without another thought, I take off after him. Coming to the end of the alley, the wharf in front of me is empty. My first instinct is to head right and back up the public pathway running there, but the sounds coming from the opposite side make me reconsider. It could be the wind causing the gate on that side to rattle, but I'm not taking any chances. The moment I turn the corner, I spot the idiot trying to hoist himself over the chain-link fence. In his panic he must've bypassed the public access path and instead was hoping for a quiet getaway around the other side. He'd obviously not counted on the gate. Before he has a chance to act, I'm on him, pulling him down by the back of his shirt.

I'm not sure what I am expecting, possibly that son of a bitch ex of Viv's, but I'm surprised when it's a young kid who turns around and swings at me. That moment of surprise costs me when I am a fraction too late avoiding the oncoming fist. It connects solidly with my jaw, stunning me enough for him to slip from my grasp and bail.

I catch up with him just as he's rounding the other side of the pub, trying to dart through the alley. Once again, I haul him back by the collar, the kid really no match for my larger frame, although he has a mean left hook.

"Let me go, you asshole," he yells. "I didn't do anything wrong!"

"Then why were you running?" I bite off, dragging him with me to the front of the pub. He struggles fiercely, but this time my hold on him is secure. I finally manage to get the door open one-handedly, with a little help from a strong gust. A group of people is blocking my view of the bar, so I call out for Gunnar. To my surprise, the first person to push through the crowd is not Gunnar, but Viv.

"What the hell, Ike?" she demands. With the wind blowing the short blond locks around her face and her hands on her hips, she really does look like a siren. "So much for Gunnar putting the boards up when you're just gonna let the weather in the front door!" Her fire puts a smile on my face, but the youngster still struggling to get loose draws her attention. "Who's that?"

"Good question," Gunnar's voice rumbles from behind her. "You bellowed?" he quips, an eyebrow raised.

"Can you come out here for a minute?" I ask him, trying to urge him with a chin lift. He looks from the kid, to me, and then Viv before turning his eyes back on mine.

"Lead the way," he directs at me, following me out the door and closing it firmly behind us. "The fuck is going on, brother?"

"Found this little bastard when I was parking my bike out back. He dropped a box with Viv's name on it when he heard me and took off. Idiot tried to get over the fence next door when I caught him." I head around the corner, still dragging the kid along, who had stopped struggling when Gunnar took hold of his arm on the other side.

"I didn't do nothin'!" the little punk pipes up. "All I did's drop the box off where the guy said."

Gunnar stops and swings the kid around with his back to the fence beside the dumpsters, bracing his forearm against his scrawny neck. "What guy?"

The kid's eyes flit back and forth, trying to avoid looking at either of us, but a little added force on his neck has them bulging out of his head.

"Who!" Gunnar yells in his face.

"Dunno him. The dude rents a room at the Knight's Inn my mom works at, on the south side of town. Said it was a simple drop off. Said I wouldn't have to talk to anyone." His voice has taken on a whiny quality that grates on my nerves.

Just as I'm about to open my mouth to ask for a description, the back door to the pub opens.

"Gunnar! What's going on?" Gunnar's wife is standing in the doorway, with thunder in her eyes.

"Bird, I'm just ..."

The momentary distraction gives the punk enough of a window to twist loose and haul off. I immediately turn to follow him down to the parking lot, but Gunnar calls me back. "Ike! Leave it. Don't think you're gonna get much more that's useful out of him. Let's deal with this box."

When I meet him by the back door, he's whispering to his wife, the box clutched in his hand. "Go on," he says to her. "Keep her out of my office." With a roll of her eyes, Syd walks ahead down the hallway to the bar, conceivably to keep Viv occupied, while Gunnar opens a door on the right. "In here."

He walks up to the desk and sets the box down. It's a decorative box; green, about eight inches square with a hinged lid. When I reach to open it, Gunnar stops me.

"Don't. Just in case. Let me take some pictures first," he says, as he pulls his phone out of his pocket and starts snapping. Then he grabs a letter opener from his desk and flips the lid with that. "Son of a fucking bitch," he grinds out between clenched teeth. "Gonna kill that fucker."

Inside the box is a stack of photographs, the top one depicting a very naked Viv, tied spread-eagled to a bed. Her body is covered in bruises and her eyes are so swollen, you can't even tell what color they are. Written across that, in red marker, the words:

## A REMINDER

With my vision blurred and blood roaring in my ears, I haul out and knock the box and contents clear across the room. I make another swipe with my arm, but am stopped midway when Gunnar grabs hold of my arm. "Stop. Get yourself the fuck together, you're gonna have everyone come running. Don't want her to see this, do you?"

Viv. Jesus, my poor Viv. I raise my hands to show him I'm done. He cautiously lets me go before walking over to where the pictures are now strewn across the floor. From the expression on his face, the rest of them are not much better. I get down on my knees beside him and start picking up some that are closest to me. Pictures of Viv tied down or held down in degrading positions, a lot of them with injuries visible on her body or face. Even some of her in a hospital bed, a blank, dispassionate look in her eyes. Almost dead. It's obvious from the images these were taken over the span of at least a few years. Viv's hair is different in most of them. Long and falling straight down her shoulders, or in curls, and changing color regularly. It becomes painfully clear suddenly why she keeps it short these days. The fucker obviously had a *thing* for long hair. By the time Gunnar plucks the stack I've gathered out of my hands, my chest hurts and my eyes burn. When I look at him, I can see his are moist as well.

He sticks the photographs back in the box and runs his hand over his head. "I had no idea," his voice croaks. "Don't know what I thought, but this is so far beyond anything I could've conjured up, I just …" His voice trails off as he shakes his head. Leaving the box on the floor, he pulls himself up on his chair and opens a drawer, pulling out a bottle of whiskey and two tumblers. With shaking hands, he pours two stiff drinks and shoves one in my direction. I sit down across from him and toss it back. I don't know if it's the burn of the alcohol or the images of Viv that has tears rolling down my face, but it's obvious enough for Gunnar to reach over and grab a box of tissues off the bookshelf.

"Her family can never see these. Hell, I don't want Viv to see them, but I have to call the police and they will want to have details. I fucking hate this." He tosses his own drink back, slams the empty glass on the desk and uses his desk phone to dial out. By the time he hangs up, I'm more or less composed again.

"We're lucky—Michael Bragdon is coming in himself. He's a friend. He'll be considerate, but we still have to let her in on this. And I think you should do it."

I'm surprised, and although I'm not voicing it, it must be obvious.

"Look," Gunnar rests his elbows on the desk and leans in. "I'm like her brother. Seeing her naked like that, I … it'll be bad enough for her without having me see them with her. You

... you're different. You've seen her ... before." He gestures at the box on the floor as he stammers through his words. So unlike the massive and gruff man he presents. He's badly shaken, just like I am.

*Fucking hell.*

"Better get her in here before the cop shows up." I nod at Gunnar, not nearly feeling as confident as I'm trying to sound. He stands up and moves to the door right away, only pausing to give me one last look before he walks out. Leaving me to stare at the box on the floor, but only for a minute before I get up and retrieve it, placing it on the desk.

"What's going on?" I hear Viv's voice, along with the low rumble of Gunnar's. The door is pushed open and both walk in. I don't hesitate, but take two steps to get to her and pull her against me. "Ike? What's going on, you guys?"

Hearing the edge of panic in her tone, I quickly start talking. "Some kid dropped off a box by the back door. I snagged him before he could run away. He was just a stupid kid doing a job for someone else, for money." Instead of fear, I see anger in Viv's face.

"It's that son of a bitch, isn't it?" She looks from me to Gunnar and back before her eyes travel to the box on the desk. Gunnar backs out of the room before she reaches to open the box. Wanting to slow things down, I put my hand over hers on the lid, keeping it shut.

"Viv, baby—it's bad." I feel a moment's hesitation before she pulls away from my restraining hand and flips open the lid. Gunnar put the first picture back on top and Viv picks it up. A shiver runs visibly down her body, before she seems to pull herself together and says, matter-of-factly, "He sure did a number on me, didn't he? I can't remember him taking pictures, though, but it doesn't surprise me. He always liked to admire his handiwork."

Her cool detachment makes me nervous. This is so not what I was expecting.

# CHAPTER FIFTEEN

*Viv*

It feels like all the blood drains from my body when I get my first glimpse of the pictures in that damn box. I try to stay detached, but each image brings back the memories associated with it: the fear, the pain, the humiliation. Outwardly, I make sure I show no reaction. I'm well aware of the effect seeing them must've had on Gunnar, and *oh my God*, Ike. I don't want to see pity, shame, or hurt in either of their faces. Luckily Gunnar has slipped out behind me, but the raw emotion in Ike's face is almost too much to deal with. *Buck up, girl—tough it out.* Nothing showing in these pictures comes close to the kind of sick depravation I'd already been subjected to before these were even taken. No images exist of the violations that had left invisible scars on my very soul. These were just physical manifestations, but the real damage had been done even before Frank had his way with me. Maybe that's why. Maybe I'd lost my worth years prior and had convinced myself I didn't deserve any better. Guilt? Was there part of me that felt responsibility? All I see is weakness and capitulation. Someone who'd already given up.

With a sigh I close the box and turn to Ike, who is watching me with a mix of compassion and what? Regret? God, I can't blame the man. Who'd want ...

"Stop that. Stop thinking what you're thinking," he growls. "'Cause whatever it is, it'd be so far from the truth, it's not funny." With both hands he reaches out for me, and I can't

155

help the little step back. Ike simply reaches further and grabs my shoulders, shaking me lightly. "What I'm thinking is how fucking incredible it is—how amazingly courageous it is—that you managed to come back from that. The way you are? Babe, you've gotta know how much respect I have for your strength."

I know I'm gaping at him, but I can't seem to help it. *Say what?* Does he not realize I willingly stayed in that situation for years? Can he not tell those pictures span at least five years, if not longer? I open and close my mouth like a fish several times before I can get any sound out. "But I stayed."

Last thing I expected was the low chuckle that rumbled up from deep inside his chest.

"No," he says firmly. "You *left.* You got out—got away from that sick lowlife." There's no denying the venom in his tone. "Fuck, Viv. If only you could see what I see when I look at you." With a firm tug he pulls me against his chest, his arms banding tightly around me, and something inside me desperately wants to confide in him. I want him to know that what's in that damn box is only the top layer of this fucked-up onion of my life. Instead, I squeeze my lips together and press my face to his shoulder, soaking up the comfort he offers. *Weak.*

After reassurances there's no reason to call my brothers or Pam, for that matter, Gunnar finally lets me leave.

The police have come and gone, and taken the pictures with them, as well as the information Gunnar had gleaned from the kid. With a bit of luck, Officer Bragdon said, they'd be able to pick up my ex at the motel. Worst case scenario was still not bad, I guess, because in leaving those images with me, he just put a nail in his own coffin. They are to be shared with the Los Angeles ADA in charge of the assault case against him there. He's inadvertently done the opposite of what he'd intended. He was never the sharpest knife in the block. Violent—yes, cruel—undoubtedly, but bright—not really. Still, as I'm well aware, he doesn't have to be intelligent to be vicious.

Which is why I don't object when Ike insists on walking me home, even though I simply want to go home, curl up in bed, and try to get myself back under control. If I don't, the lid might pop off completely, and there will be no coming back from that. But when we reach my door, Ike holds up his hand for the keys. It's clear he's planning to come in.

"Thanks for everyth—" I try to stop him from coming in, but he's anticipating it, taking the wind right out of my sails.

"If you think for even a minute that I'm leaving ..." he says, glaring at me before he snatches the keys from my hand and unlocks the door, pushing me inside.

"I'm fine," I protest when he swings me around to face him.

"I know you're fine. *I'm* not fine, though. I'm nowhere near *fine.* The only thing that's going to make me feel remotely better, is being able to ensure you stay fine." He tilts up my chin with his forefinger and leans his forehead against mine. Our eyes are so close, I can see every detail in his. Every emotion is on full display in his light gray ones. Pain, worry, and perhaps a little bit of something else. Need?

"Please, let me stay." The words are said so quietly, almost breathlessly, and I feel them in my heart. So I respond in the simplest way I can—by softly touching my lips to his.

Without any need for words, we head straight to my bedroom, where we each take our turn in the bathroom. Emotionally drained, I roll toward him when he slips under the covers and fall into a deep sleep the moment he wraps me up in his warmth.

-

*"I know you're awake."* The familiar voice causes goose bumps to break out over my skin.

*I'd heard the turning of the knob on my door and quickly rolled up in a ball on my side, my covers drawn tight over my ear. Not tonight, please not tonight. Fickle wishes, because I should know by now nothing will stop him. The soft tread of his feet on the carpet, as he comes closer, is evidence of that. But instead of continuing, they stop at the foot of the bed. Did he change his mind?*

*"My pretty princess Vivvy, so innocent."*

*I have to resist the repulsion at the use of that name I've come to hate. I still hang on to the futile hope he'll just leave me be tonight, but that hope is quickly replaced by dread as I feel the covers being lifted off my feet and slowly drawn up over my body until my head is the only thing covered. The thick layer of bedding makes it hard to breathe, but I've learned that to struggle only means prolonging the inevitable. As hands stroke up my legs, I force my body not to react. I fight the will to struggle and kick out. No one would believe me if I told them. No one. I'd tried once ...*

With a gasp, I shoot up straight in bed, a little disoriented until I hear Ike's sleepy rumble from beside me. "Sleep, baby. It's just the wind."

Sure enough, a strong wind is howling outside my apartment building. He must've thought that was what woke me up. Slipping out of bed, I walk to the window and peek out. It's dark, but the streetlamps lining the wharf stay on all night. I can see the churning water in the spread of their light. The sea is angry. The water cruel and unforgiving.

Turning back from the mesmerizing sight, I grab some random clothes off the floor, while keeping an eye on the man in my bed. He seems to have fallen asleep again, oblivious to the storm raging outside or the one tearing me up inside. Unaware that with every piece he chips away from the icy shell around my heart, he's releasing an eruption of hot, festering anger and pain hidden underneath.

## Ike

I know the bed is empty, the moment I open my eyes. The sheets are cool to the touch and I lie back, listening for the sounds of movement elsewhere in the apartment, but it's hard to hear anything over the whistling of the storm. It looks like it's still dark outside, but I'm not sure of the time. Grappling around on the floor beside the bed, I finally come up with my jeans and dig my phone out of the pocket. Five-thirty. Way too early to be up and about, but I swing my legs over the side of the bed anyway, an uneasy feeling pushing me.

The apartment is abandoned, much as I suspected. The uneasy feeling is growing into genuine concern. Where is Viv? The butt-crack of dawn and a storm raging outside, I'm worried about what might have driven her out. *Fuck.* Not to mention where the hell she might've gone. The concern now building into urgency, I pull out my phone and start scrolling through numbers until I hit Gunnar's.

"Yeah ..." his sleepy voice answers, just as I'm about to hang up after the fourth ring.

"Jesus, sorry man. I obviously woke you. Is Viv with you?"

"What?" Gunnar sounds suddenly wide awake. "What do you mean, is Viv with us? Didn't you go home with her?"

"I did, but I just woke up to an empty apartment. She's not here."

"It's a fucking mess out there," he says, the rustle of covers being thrown off in the background.

"Well aware. Where do you think—?"

I'm cut off as Syd's voice comes over the phone. "Ike? Have you tried the pub? Maybe she's gone there. I don't know where else, except maybe … Pam?"

"I'll try them both, thanks." Before she has a chance to answer, I end the call, immediately scrolling for The Skipper's number.

The voicemail comes on after three rings and I hang up without leaving a message. Pam is the next number I try.

"This better be good, white boy," she answers. "You're interrupting the best part of my night."

Any hopes she might've gone there are instantly doused. "Viv left her apartment sometime during the night. I thought she might've come to you."

"Why? What happened?"

I don't miss the slightly accusatory tone of her voice and hurry to explain.

"I don't know. Her ex had a box of photos dropped off last night at the pub. Damn, Pam, the pictures were of Viv, lots of them. A fucking virtual history of his abuse on her." I hear her intake of breath and then silence. "Pam?"

"I'm here. I'm thinking."

"She seemed a bit … detached, but managed detailing most of the incidents depicted to the cop that showed up."

"Did you check with Syd?"

"Just got off the phone with them, they haven't seen or heard from her. Listen, she was quiet but seemed to handle things better than expected last night. Fell asleep just moments after we got home." In my mind, I'm going over everything I might've missed.

"She's good at suppressing things. I'm sure you've noticed. There is stuff eating at her that I haven't even really begun to touch. I'm worried this is just the beginning. I'm coming over." The last is said with a finality that required no response.

"Well, I'm not gonna sit here waiting," I tell her. "I'm heading down to The Skipper. Syd suggested looking there. I didn't get an answer when I called, but I'm gonna have a look around anyway. I'll leave the door unlocked."

I don't have a jacket and when I step outside the building, the storm has me shivering against the unexpected cold. The first thought that pops in my head as I tuck my head down against the wind, is that I hope Viv's dressed warm enough.

It is only a two-minute walk to the back entrance of the pub, but in this weather long enough to have me soaked to the skin and chilled to the bone. I try the back door, only to find it locked. Banging on it nets no results, so I'm about to walk around the front when I spot something under the lights at the very end of the wharf. A slim figure, with legs and arms spread wide against the onslaught of large, angry waves, spraying up and over the concrete pier and my feet start running.

## Viv

The sharp sting of the slashing rain wakes me up the instant I clear the protection of my building. Fresh, cleansing rain that washes away the remnants of my dream. The first conscious dream I've had since I turned fifteen. My subconscious protecting me even as I couldn't.

The connection that is growing with Ike has my defenses crumbling one by one, leaving me raw and exposed. I allow the storm to toss the suppressed memories around in my mind. Breathing in deeply, I suck in the fresh air as I make my way across the parking lot and down the alley. Bypassing the pub's back entrance, I walk out onto the pier, incognizant of my water logged clothing. The thin layer I'm wearing is no protection against the elements, but I don't care. I'm drawn to the roiling seas on either side of the wharf. I feel a need to howl at the wind.

To purge myself.

Bracing against the onslaught of the storm, I spread my legs to keep my balance and raise my arms, screaming out all my emotions. The sound is immediately swallowed up by the force of the gale and the crash of the waves over my feet.

"Viv!"

The yell penetrates the almost deafening roar of the wind and water, and I turn to look.

Just as I spot a figure running toward me, a large wave crashes into me, catching me off balance. My eyes never leave the approaching man, even as my legs are swept out from under me, and I'm washed into the cruel water.

## Ike

"Fuck! Viv!"

The fear I felt before is nothing compared to the sheer terror as I watch a large wave swipe Viv clean off the end of the pier. My heart stops beating but my legs continue to eat the distance. My eyes are focused on the spot where she disappeared in the water, and without thinking, I jump into the churning sea right after her. The moment I hit the water, I kick my legs to get to the surface, but a strong wave pulls me down before slamming me into the old pilings supporting the wharf, knocking the wind right out of me. I grapple the surge of the water to find a hand hold on the surface of the wood structure when one of my hands encounters fabric. Instinctively I close my fist in the material, pulling it up to the surface with me. Gasping for air, I manage to reach for a large metal ring on the side of the piling and hang on for dear life. When Viv's head bobs up from the water, coughing and sputtering, the relief I feel is immediate, but short-lived as another wave threatens to knock us loose. With all my strength, I yank on her shirt, pulling her against me.

"Lock your arms around my neck!"

I need both hands on the ring or we'll both be lost. Viv's arms immediately grab on and her legs wrap around my waist. I twist my body and reach for the ring, while trying to protect Viv's body from the surging water.

"Ike ..."

"Hold on, baby," I manage to get out before a wave slams into my back, and we are pushed against the piling. I'm no match for the force of the water and it's impossible to move. When the water clears our heads, I'm grateful to hear Viv sputtering right along with me.

With each subsequent wave, it becomes harder to hang on, and Viv stops moving altogether. Memories start flooding my mind of another time I struggled against the devastating pull of the ocean. Another lifeless body I was desperately clinging onto. Time stops existing as that past experience blends into the present, and I feel my hands slipping. I don't know how long we can hold on before someone finds us.

"There they are. Grab that chain over there!"

My arms are cramping, and it takes all my will not to let the ring slide from my hands when I hear the yelling right above us. I don't even have the energy to yell back.

A pair of legs drops down in my peripheral vision and when I look, I see Gunnar sitting in a make-shift chain sling, right underneath the ledge.

"Viv! Reach out for me," he yells against the wind, his arms stretched toward us.

Slowly one of Viv's arms releases its strong grip on my neck and reaches up. The moment his hand clasps around her wrist, her hold on me is gone. He pulls her up and wraps his legs around her body, leaving his hands free to hoist her up higher under her arms and lift her to waiting hands above.

My relief is so great, I almost let the ring slip from my hands.

"No fucking way, José," Gunnar swears above me. "Grab hold."

I kick my legs in the water for some lift and with one hand let go and reach, feeling the vice-like grip of Gunnar's big hand around my wrist.

In seconds, I'm pulled onto the pier where my eyes immediately look for Viv.

"You okay, buddy?"

The large cook from the pub is leaning over me, after having pulled Gunnar back to solid ground.

"Fine," I croak. "I wanna see Viv."

I get my knees under me and with Dino's help I'm on my feet. Three figures are making their way down the wharf battling the relentless wind, the two on the outside almost carrying the third in the middle. Taking a few shaky steps, on legs that feel like rubber, I take off after them.

# CHAPTER SIXTEEN

*Viv*

"I really think you should get checked out."

Syd is fussing and I can't blame her, I'd probably do the same. But I really don't want to go to the hospital, only to be held for *observation*. It seems no matter how many times I assure Syd, she's afraid I tried to kill myself. I didn't. Pam took one look at me and seemed satisfied with my denial, but Gunnar and Dino stay uneasy.

I was so confused at first when I noticed everyone in the pub's kitchen. Turns out a tree had come down in Dino's backyard and after making sure his family was secure, he wanted to check on The Skipper; make sure the boards were still secure and in place. Gunnar, Syd, and Pam had come looking for me after Ike raised the alarm. And Ike ... I look over at him and see concern still on his face.

"I promise, I'll be fine," I tell Syd, never taking my eyes of Ike. "I just need a hot shower and some coffee. In that order."

Instead of braving the storm outside, I head upstairs to the old apartment that sits empty most of the time these days, after I'd bunked there for a few months after leaving Florence House. Syd had spent a few weeks there as well, at some point, and these days it is used mostly for Gunnar's kids to hang out when he and Syd are working later than expected. Before I head into the bathroom, I grab some of my old clothes I left behind.

I'm about to shut the bathroom door behind me when it's pulled from my hands.

"Not ready to have you out of my sight," Ike's gruff voice has me turning around.

"I promise you I wasn't trying anything," I try to reassure him.

He drops his head and with his hands now tucked in his pockets and his shoulders slumped, he looks so sad. "I know," he says softly. "I just lost twenty years off my life, Viv. Help me understand?" His eyes peek up from under his eyebrows. "What just happened?"

I don't answer immediately, but simply start taking off my sodden clothes until I'm naked in front of him. His eyes have followed my every movement, and I can tell his hands are clenched in fists in his pockets. I turn away from him and turn on the tap, putting the plug in the tub, before facing him. "Will you take a bath with me?"

He's quiet for a minute before giving me a slight nod in response. I reach out and tug his shirt over his head, his arms coming up willingly. When Ike is as naked as I am, I step into the tub, gesturing for him to sit behind me. I can't face him, but want his arms around me when I try and explain. Once he's settled in behind me, his knees bracketing mine, he pulls me into his chest, leaning his chin on my shoulder.

"Like this, babe?" he wants to know. Despite being a little cramped in the standard tub, it is exactly what I want. I feel anchored and secure, and am slowly warming up.

"I had a dream." I give him a second to clue in and he does, his arms tightening around me, letting me know he remembers me telling him I haven't dreamt in years.

"What do you think brought it on?" he asks quietly, immediately getting to the point.

"I've been thinking about that and I don't think it was one thing in particular, but a combination of a lot of things. The last drop being the little trip down memory lane I was sent on with those photos." I swallow hard, not sure where to take this next.

"Take your time," he mumbles, his lips against the skin of my shoulder.

"It brought a lot to the surface, seeing myself battered and used like that. I think at the time, I minimized everything. Found excuses for a lot of the shit he put me through. I don't think I valued myself right, if I did at all. Frank ... Frank was the first one to make me *feel,* even when I turned into his punching bag, at least I could feel, you know?" Ike is quiet behind me, but his body is still wrapped around me tight, so I continue.

"That first night we met? I'd done something like that only once before, and it hadn't been a good idea then. But you ... you made me *feel* something too, before you'd even touched me. It was both exciting and scary, nothing at all like the one other time I stepped out of my comfort zone. From that night on, it's like my life slid from solid ground onto quicksand." This is when I feel him stiffen behind me and hurry to explain. "Not because of you, well, not directly ... but because of me. And I'm starting to think it's a good thing."

"How is that good?" His voice is deep and even soothing. I tilt my head to the side and twist to look at his face. Handsome, strong, with the scruff he'd been sporting slowly growing into a real beard, and his eyes as beautiful as ever. Gray silvery orbs that shimmer with intensity and warmth. Windows to the soul they say, and Ike's are clear and open.

"Because you woke me up, Ike. And it makes me want more than the limited life I've been living. I have *coped* for many years by focusing on others, to avoid looking inside myself. It's not been a particularly pretty place, the inside of me. I worked through a lot of my own guilt around what happened with Pam, and she's been crucial in getting me back on my feet. But I really just slipped my life in another groove. Frank was like that, a groove I was stuck in. Not the first one either, but none of that is living. Not *real* living. I was scared. Up to last night I was scared. And then I woke up in the middle of the night—I hadn't dreamt in years."

"Since you turned fifteen," Ike mutters over my shoulder, surprising me.

"Yes," I simply confirm. "The dream had to do with that, with things ... things I've willed to the furthest recesses of my mind. Stuff that I've never really been able to deal with properly. When I woke up and heard the storm raging outside, it felt symbolic. Hiding inside from exposure to the force, the rage, the cruelty of the storm, much like I was hiding inside myself, avoiding and not living. Not dealing." I turn my body so I'm laying stomach to stomach with Ike, lifting my hands to cup his jaw. "That's why I went out. I had this urge to rage against the storm, face the whipping winds and cruel waters. You had my back. I'm so grateful for that. I swear I wasn't looking to die."

His eyes close and he inhales deeply, as his hands cup the back of my head and his lips kiss me hard. "Scared me shitless," he mumbles, his lips still pressed against mine.

"I'm sorry. I promise I won't do that again. But Ike, having you show up like that, and the others, pulling us out—I believe I can brave the fall-out I'm facing when I start living for real. When I confront things that I won't be able to put off much longer, or I might not have an opportunity at all."

"It started when you turned fifteen," Ike says matter-of-factly. "I actually, physically hurt when I think ..." He violently shakes his head before pressing my head in the crook of his neck and hiding his face in my hair. "Whatever you need, my siren. I've got your back."

# Ike

I had a suspicion before, but now I *know*.

The abuse at the hands of her ex was not the first pair of hands that touched her uninvited. Whatever happened when she was fifteen is becoming a clearer picture in my mind, and I wish I could shove it back in the shadows.

We've been soaking in the water for a bit, wrapped around one another, just taking comfort from each other when there's a soft knock at the door. Viv lifts her head from my shoulder and answers, "Yeah?"

"It's Syd, honey, you doing okay in there?"

"Yes, Ike's with me. We'll be right out."

"Okay. Gunnar and I are gonna head out to get the kids off to school. We'll be back in a bit, but Pam and Dino are in the kitchen with coffee."

"Thank you," both of us reply, and we hear her footsteps retreating.

Viv pushes off me to sit back on her knees in the cooling water. "Are you all right?" she wants to know. I'm not sure if I am, but I nod anyway. My eyes take in the sight before me, her pretty oval face with large, clear blue eyes fringed with long darker lashes, her short blonde hair curling up at the bottom where it's gotten wet. Full plump lips and a slightly up-tilted nose dusted with light freckles. My eyes track the trickle of water running from the dip between her collarbones down between her pink-tipped breasts. When she pushes up from the water, I lean back and move my eyes back to her face. "You're beautiful," escapes my lips without thinking. She blushes softly at my words, a little smile teasing her lips.

Viv rustles up an old pair of sweats with paint stains belonging to Gunnar and a brand new shirt with The Skipper printed on the front for me to wear. Dressed in a similar outfit, Viv leads the way down to the kitchen where someone is cooking, judging from the smells emanating. I didn't think I was hungry until that smell hit me and suddenly my stomach is growling.

Dino turns at the stove when he hears us coming in. Pam is sitting at the large kitchen table, sipping from a mug, looking at us with assessing eyes.

"Smells good," I say, walking up to Dino, putting my hand on his shoulder. The man is massive. I've barely had any interaction with him before, but I figure he's got to be a good egg, working with these people. He briefly stiffens under my touch before studiously flipping bacon in the pan. "Wanna thank you," I say in a low voice. "If it weren't for you guys showing up, I ..." I drop my head, emotion choking me as I consider how close I came to letting go of that damn ring.

"Brother," Dino's baritone rumbles over my head. "You jumped in after our girl. Wasn't gonna let your ass drown— s'all good."

"Still—" I try but he won't let me.

"That girl? She needs a taste of good. Figure you're the one that can give her that. Figure she can give you what you need too. I can see she's opening up to you, giving you that gift. Might think about giving it back; trusting her with that pain you carry around like a heavy cloak."

I'm dumbfounded. The man doesn't know me and yet he seems to have me pegged. Fucking eerie.

"Dino freaking you out?" Pam's voice comes from behind. I turn to see both her and Viv regarding me with amused expressions on their faces.

"He has a tendency to see more than he should, and he likes to stir shit up. Never you mind him," Viv says on a laugh.

"Ha," he scoffs, "he'd be stupid not to."

I pull out a chair and sit down beside Viv, facing a smiling Pam.

"Knight in shining armor, again. Gonna make a career out of this?" she mocks me, but with a warm smile on her face.

"I might for her," I fire back with a smile of my own, tucking my arm around Viv's shoulders.

"You good, girl?" Pam directs at her. "Gotta say, even bedraggled and just fished out of the water, I saw the fight in you. Not what I was expecting to find."

"I'm good. Well, I should say I *will* be good. I'm thinking I'll need a lot of pep talks from you because it's bound to get ugly first."

I see Pam's eyes shoot open. "You're ready to talk?"

"I'm always ready to talk to you," Viv's evading a direct answer, but Pam eyes squint sternly in response.

"You give me smartass, girl? I wanna know if you're ready to dig up whatever you've tucked down so deep, it'll take a fully rigged excavation team to unearth."

"Ready," Viv answers with a little stumble in her voice. "If you guys'll be my excavation team," she says, looking at all of us in turn. I just answer with a squeeze on her shoulder, she already knows I'm in. Pam just sits back, her arms folded over her chest, and a smile so wide it looks like her face will crack right open.

"'Bout fucking time," Dino rumbles without turning around, causing Pam to swing her head around.

173

"What do you know about it?" she challenges him, and this time he does turn around, scanning her from top to toe.

"Enough," he says before dismissing her by cracking a few eggs over a hot pan.

Pam *humphs*, muttering under her breath, "Everyone's a fucking therapist these days."

Viv chuckles and leans back, resting her head on my shoulder.

Hard to believe that less than two hours ago we were fighting for our lives. Even the wind seems to have died down.

-

"Is David in?" I cut to the chase when I walk into the office and am accosted by whatever her name is. Amanda?

"I thought I saw him go into the lunchroom. I can check for you, if you like?" she chirps, batting her eyelashes.

"I know my way around, Amanda. Thanks, I'll find him."

"Oh, it's Samantha." She feels the need to correct me, like it matters.

I stick my head into David's office as I pass by, but it's empty. I find him having lunch in the small kitchen in the back.

"You made it," he says around a mouthful of food.

"Yeah. I'm sorry about that. I know I've been a bit preoccupied lately, and now this."

"Not aware of having complained," David says with his eyebrows raised. "I know you're used to keeping your own hours when you're on the road, I wasn't really expecting you to slip into a nine to five that easily. As long as the work gets done, I don't particularly care. But just to satisfy my own curiosity, who is she?"

"Sorry?"

"The woman who's got you *preoccupied*?" he clarifies, a knowing smirk on his face. Figures he'd be nosy. He's only been on my case to *settle down* since he got hitched a while back.

Pouring myself a coffee and pulling out a chair, I find myself telling him about Viv, a little about her asshole ex and her family. I even give him a rundown of this morning's events, which leaves him leaning back in his chair, hands folded behind his head.

"I can see why you were a little distracted this morning. Holy hell. She okay?"

"Yeah, I think so." At least she was when I left her sitting at the kitchen table with Pam earlier. I hadn't wanted to go, but they virtually pushed me out the door, Pam reassuring me that she would take Viv to her apartment for clothes before heading to Florence House. I still felt uneasy about leaving her, but the storm had died down substantially, and she wanted to at least help Dino get through the lunch crowd. Gunnar had come back earlier from dropping his kids at school and hadn't wasted any time telling Viv to get herself home, but with limited success. The two of them went toe-to-toe and ended up compromising: he'd already called Tim in to help with the Friday night crowd, but Viv wanted to stay until after lunch. Not like I wasn't leaving her in good hands.

"Am I out of my depth?" Not sure myself where that question came from, let alone why I'm talking to my boss about all this.

"Why? Because she comes with baggage? Everybody does. Some heavier than others, but that's not really the question, is it? Do you care about this woman?"

The answer to that is simple. "Absolutely."

"Then what does it matter if you're out of your depth? You fucking jumped right after her into an angry ocean, without blinking. That should tell you enough."

"Right."

I'm already in deep, so deep I can almost see bottom. That's probably what scares me most. The last time I felt this kind of overwhelming responsibility for anyone, he died right in front of my eyes. I'll never forget my father pulling me aside before we shipped out, asking me to look after Benjamin. I never considered the weight that came with that responsibility. Not until he was killed, and I was powerless to do anything but hold onto his lifeless body to prevent it from being washed out by the endless ocean. It felt like hours, hanging onto the mangled steel of the hull while the constant pull of the water tried to suck us out of the hole. I wasn't going to let him go, just like there was no way I would've let go of Viv this morning. I'm falling in love with her, and it scares me to death. I don't know if I'm strong enough to help her battle her demons, when I can't even seem to get rid of my own.

"Look," David says interrupting my heavy thoughts. "Why don't you take a couple of days off? I talked to the shipyard this morning. The storm has done some damage to the rigging on the ship. The launch has been delayed until they're repaired and the weather settles down some. Likely not before next week. Nothing else is pressing. Go home, take Monday as well, and check in Tuesday."

I drop my head in my hands, suddenly feeling old and tired. My body had taken a beating by the raging water and with the adrenaline worn off, I can feel every last bit of it. Still, I'm reluctant, until David slaps his hands on the kitchen table, making the decision for me. "There. That's set then. Don't want to see you in here until Tuesday at the earliest. Get some fucking sleep, you look like death warmed over."

I manage to mumble an ungracious, "Thanks," as I walk out of the lunchroom and straight out through the reception, where whatever the hell her name is, jabbers on about something. I don't hear a word she says and simply walk past her and out the door.

I can't quite remember how I get there, but I pull my bike on the stand behind the pub, tucking my helmet in the saddlebag. The rhythmic sound of metal hitting metal draws my eyes to the end of the wharf. The water is choppy but no longer washing over the surface with the churning crush of waves like it was this morning. An involuntary shiver runs through my body. God, we'd come close.

The insistent clanging pulls me from my morbid thoughts. A flagpole at the end of the dock, an American flag, or what's left of it, tugging in the breeze making its rope slap into the metal pole, the source of the sound. The flag is tattered and ripped, but still waves bravely in the remaining wind. The reminder of almost losing another life under a waving flag is suddenly too stark.

I walk into the back door, down the hall, and into the kitchen, where I pull a stunned Viv around and wrap her in my arms, burying my face in her neck.

"Ike, what—" she says surprised, trying to pull back but I don't loosen my hold.

"Just let me..." I swallow hard against the ragged sound of my voice. "I just need to hold you."

# CHAPTER SEVENTEEN

*Viv*

"You ready to talk?"

I should've known Pam would cut right to the chase the moment I sat my ass down at the kitchen table at Florence House.

I'd waited until the lunch crowd dissipated before hanging up my apron, and after saying goodbye to the gang, I walked home to get my car and went straight over. She'd made me promise, before she left this morning, to come to her after. She'd wanted me to come with her right away, but I guess she quickly realized I needed some time to process before talking. Puttering around in the kitchen with Dino, who never says more than is absolutely necessary anyway, was the perfect way to let my mind go. And it went, on and on, and round and round. With this morning's decision to open the door further, rather than trying to shut it again, it wasn't so much *whether* I was going to talk, but rather *how* I would go about it. I sensed that Pam was far enough in my head to be ready for me, but I was crapping myself thinking about what this might do to my family. It had been ingrained in me from a young age that family sticks up for each other. No matter what. Well, when you need protection from someone who's part of that family, things become a little complicated. Part of me wants to just see what happens, since I'm convinced the wheels are going to come off at some point

179

regardless. The only way to have any control over when, where, who, and what, is to tell the truth myself.

First, though, I have to test myself and see how I do discussing any of it with Pam.

"No," is my honest answer, but I quickly follow it up with, "but I will anyway."

I start hesitantly, trying to explain the dynamics in the family when I was younger. The slow indoctrination of my young and easily manipulated mind to a point where boundaries were blurring, and I no longer trusted my own sense of right and wrong. The gradual escalation to a point where I finally voiced my discomfort and was countered with a threat that seemed so real, I was afraid to doubt it. Not even when I finally did try to tell someone, was I heard or believed.

Pam says little—asks even less—she mostly listens, and at times I see her surreptitiously wipe at her eyes. Mostly when I lose it and have to stop to gather myself. I have to force the words out at first, and wince when they hit the empty air, recreating a reality I have buried and denied for most of my life. But gradually they start flowing, tumbling faster and faster, creating a verbal diarrhea that continues uninterrupted until I am done. I've not gone into too much detail yet, but I managed to lay out enough of the story, so she can easily fill in the blanks. I'm sure she'll drag them from me at some point.

Without saying anything, Pam gets up and opens a cupboard above the stove, and pulls out a bottle of scotch. She then grabs our mugs from the table, pours a healthy shot in each and tops it up with tea. Putting one in front of me, she takes a hefty swig from the other and drops down in her seat, eyeing me from under her brow. "Don't look at me like that. We need it." Another generous drink goes down before she puts the mug down. "I fucking hate that for you," she says, her eyes dark with emotion. "I knew there was something, you'd even told me as much, but it still shocks me. Don't get me wrong," she hastens to add when she sees me flinch, "it's not the first time I've heard a story such as yours. But what surprises me—shocks me—is how it was able to continue undetected for as long as it did, in a house full of people. Not to mention that the person you probably trusted most, seemed to turn a blind eye."

"She just didn't believe me," I offer, but Pam is not impressed.

"Bull crap. That's utter baloney and you know it. At the very least, it should've raised a red flag, because let me tell you, deep in her heart she knew. She must've. No way that goes on and she not see some evidence. Think about it."

She's stern and my instinct is to jump to the defense, but I realize that's what I was conditioned to do. Family over everything: all for one and one for all. I've heard every last one of those clichés, to the point where I still get nauseated when someone uses one in my presence. Pam's right. As an adult I can see things clearer. It started after leaving an abusive relationship and wrestling through the feelings of self-recrimination, guilt, and doubt. I realized in the process of working through it, that what I had taken on as something I'd brought on myself was exactly what an abuser wants you to think. They take no responsibility and lay it all on the victim. I can also see how those changes in me should've been visible. Hell, they *were* visible, I know they were. Not in the least the dramatic change in my personality. I'd gone from a chatty, outgoing, happy adolescent to a moody, dark, and rebellious teen. Where before I got along with my brothers, although at times we could fight like cats and dogs, normal sibling stuff; I withdrew and avoided interaction with them as much as I could. Dorian was most affected by my dark moods,

181

mainly because he kept seeking me out, and I'd be surly and mean trying to chase him off. It wasn't until I finally turned eighteen, graduated high school—barely—and left home, that I was able to patch things up with Dorian.

"I just feel guilty for letting it happen."

The sharp slap of Pam's hands on the table startles me. "You wanna go there again with this? Didn't we just spend years working through the guilt you felt over what you *let* your crazy ex do to you? Please. Don't insult yourself or me. You were a child. You were at your most vulnerable, and you were being taken advantage of!"

When five o'clock is announced with the arrival of a therapy group, I'm shocked at the time. Two and a half hours we've talked and my voice is hoarse. Not to mention the condition of my face after spending most of that time crying.

"I need you back here tomorrow," Pam decrees, clearly not intending to take no for an answer. I wouldn't say no anyway, I am sitting down with my family on Sunday, and I need help preparing for that showdown. Even though I will just be telling them about Frank ... for now.

"It'll have to be before eleven or between three and five." Pam's eyebrow lifts. "I want to stick to my regular routine, Pam. I've gotta work." That seems to appease her.

"You planning on talking to anyone else?" she asks cautiously, making me smile a little. Pam is generally not in the habit of tiptoeing around. "You know you could benefit from some of the groups. The more you share, the easier it becomes," she suggests.

"I'll think about it. I feel a little wobbly on my feet right now. A bit unbalanced. I need to find my feet before I'd feel comfortable in a group." I lift my eyes to look at her, before I continue. "Ike suspects. Not sure how, but he's sensed something right from the start. He ... he seemed a little shaky when he showed up back at The Skipper not two hours after he'd left. Said he took some time off work, and was gonna make dinner for me at his place."

"He seems like a good man. A solid man. The kind you can lean on, from time to time, to take the weight off."

"Yeah. I'm thinking we'll do a bit of talking tonight." I smile at Pam who stands up with me and folds me in a hug.

"See you back here for nine?"


"How did it go?" Ike asks me, as he pulls the door open to let me into his house, his eyes scanning my features.

After agreeing to see Pam tomorrow morning, I'd pulled out the directions he'd written down for me and quite easily found my way to his place. A regular two-story, family home, not too big, on a street surrounded by similar houses. Not really what I'd expected. It seems almost too suburban for the man I'm getting to know.

I chuckle lightly at his rather loaded question. "Like lancing a painful boil," I offer him on a tentative smile.

"I bet," he rumbles, grabbing my purse from my hands and dropping it on the bench along the wall in the small entrance way. Taking hold of my hand, he pulls me into the living room, where he stops to tug me to him and leaves the lightest of kisses on my lips. "Have a seat," he says, directing me to a large sectional couch with a comfy chaise on one end. "I'll grab us a drink. Beer? Wine? Or do you want something warm?"

"Beer would be good," I answer, taking in what looks to be a newly decorated house. I detect a hint of fresh paint through the mouth-watering smells emanating from the kitchen. "What are you cooking? That smells amazing."

"Only thing I can do decently," he admits. "The poor man's version of shepherd's pie. Mom used to feed us that a few times a month and did her best to teach us, but I still can't seem to get it to taste as good as hers used to."

The unexpected opening he gives into his family history surprises me, as I happily kick off my shoes and crawl onto the chaise and tuck my legs under me. "Why a poor man's version?"

"Not because we had no money," he smiles indulgently. "But more so because Ben and I would consume massive amounts of the stuff. Mom didn't want to spend hours in the kitchen making the standard version. This one is done with ground beef, onions and potato. Simple, fast, and even better the next day."

"Sounds interesting, I can't wait." I throw him a glance before I carefully ask the next question, but he seems to have anticipated it. "Was Ben your brother?" I watch as a hint of pain flits over his face before he evens it out.

"Ben was my younger brother, yes. He uhh ... he died overseas."

## Ike

Evidence her afternoon had not been easy is all over her face when I open the door. Her eyes puffy and red spots high on her cheeks, making it clear she's been crying. A lot. I feel like a fish out of water, not knowing whether to acknowledge what I know must've been gut wrenching or just pretend I don't see. But my mouth just goes ahead and asks bluntly, without any benefit of fine tuning. Then again, Viv is not quite a wilting flower having shown her amazing strength on a few occasions, not the least of which was just this morning. She answers just as direct, and the metaphor she uses illustrates precisely what I would imagine it'd be like.

I indulge in a little taste of her mouth, resisting the urge to maul her on the spot. Now's not the time. Sensing a little uneasiness, and without too much conscious thought, I open the door for her to ask about my family. She's careful, tentative, but as I expect from Viv, direct. Still, I can't escape the stab of pain at the mention of my brother's name from her lips.

"He was stationed on the USS Cole," I offer when I get back from the kitchen with a couple of beers. Her eyes looking up at me are bright and luminous, and also brimming with tears. *Fuck.*

"He was ... I mean ... did he die in the bombing? I remember you mentioning the year."

"Yeah. He never saw it coming," I volunteer, before quickly adding, "so they tell me." I'm not ready to tell my part of it. Not yet.

"I'm so sorry," she says, not shying back from revealing her emotions to me. So fucking strong. The look on her face shows the hurt she feels for me. It makes it easier for me to let the mask fall from my own face, and I don't hesitate to let her pull me down beside her and wrap her arms around me. This is intimacy at its best and at its scariest. Something pretty alien to me, but from what I can tell, it's no less strange to Viv. Somehow that makes it less scary.

"Thank you," I mumble in her hair. "I'm sorry, too. So very sorry."

We sit wrapped around each other for a while, when the oven timer goes off. With a kiss to the top of her head, I untangle myself and make my way into the kitchen.

"Damn that looks good," Viv, who followed me in, says over my shoulder as I pull the dish out of the oven. It does.

The simple meal of sautéed onions, ground beef, black pepper and potatoes mashed together, becomes something entirely different once baked in the oven. A crisp, golden-brown crust and the blending of the simple flavors turns into something rich and hearty. Most of the work is in preparing the fresh applesauce which, according to my mother, is the only proper accompaniment. I find myself smiling at the memory when I'd once asked her why we didn't just eat the applesauce that came in a jar. It actually earned me a lick around the ears.

"Takes about as long to peel a few apples, throw in a cinnamon stick and letting it simmer until softened, as it does to get the damn lid off those jars," was her indignant response. She would've been mortified at the *easy* meals I often buy for myself.

"Tastes even better." I smile at Viv, gesturing for her to take a seat at the table while I set out the food.

"Oh my God," she mumbles through a mouthful. "I'm gonna have to steal this recipe. It's perfect for the pub's Thursday specials."

Over dinner, the conversation is easy and light, but once we have the dishes in the dishwasher and a pot of coffee percolating in the kitchen, the silence stretches heavily. I managed to lure Viv onto the wide chaise with me and comfortably tuck her into my side, letting her take the lead on any conversation. It doesn't take long until she opens with a question.

"How did you know?" she asks, not looking me in the eye.

There's no reason for me to feign ignorance, so I'm as honest as I can be. "You flinch when anyone calls you Vivvy. You mentioned not having had dreams since you turned fifteen and that seemed pretty significant. I could tell something had happened, but I wasn't sure at first, until I noticed the way you call your mother, Mom, when you talk about her, but you only call your father, Dad, when you speak to him directly. At any other time you talk about your *father.* I figured you'd had a major falling out when you hit puberty at first, but then little things started pointing in a different direction." While I'm talking, she slowly lifts her head and tilts it back to look at me. I cradle her face in my hand and with my thumb wipe away the silent tear rolling over her cheek. "He molested you. Your own father." I stop and swallow hard, emotion starting to clog my throat, as her head slowly nods against my hand. "A house full of people and no one knew." At that, her face tightens.

"I tried," she bites off through clenched teeth. "I started telling Mom when she chewed me out one day when I refused to go for a family dinner. I ran off to my room and she followed me. Demanded to know why I'd become so difficult, but when I started telling her, she cut me off. Told me not to blame my *behavioral problems* on someone else. I simply said I didn't like him coming into my room every night—that he made me uncomfortable. I was afraid to say anything more when she wagged her finger in my face, telling me I should be ashamed for creating drama where there was none. Said I should be grateful for growing up with such a loving father and doting brothers. Called me an ungrateful brat." She chokes out a sob, but behind the tears in her eyes anger shines through.

"How long?" I carefully ask and am almost surprised when she doesn't ask clarification but seems to clue in effortlessly.

"Two years," she whispers, shame now staining her cheeks with a fiery red. "I was almost seventeen when Nolan came in late from a date and saw him coming out of my room. He looked right past my father at me, I was crying, had the sheet clutched to my chest. He asked what was going on, but his eyes kept staring at me. My father told him I'd had one of my nightmares and had woken him up, but I could tell Nolan didn't really believe him. I didn't say anything, I just shook my head. The opportunity was right there, but I kept my mouth shut."

I shift my hand so I can tilt her head. "Not your fault," I tell her simply.

"But I could've—"

With a sharp shake of my head I cut her off. "Not. Your. Fault. Whatever you've told yourself over the years, you bear no responsibility for anything that happened to you."

Her almost imperceptible nod shows me it's not the first time she's heard this.

"Pam tell you that, too?"

She snorts in response. "In no uncertain terms."

"I bet. What else did she say?"

A slight sparkle lights up her eyes as she turns her body slightly, so her torso is draped over my chest. "She said I should stick close to you."

"Wise woman," I say, sliding my hands down her back to the back of her legs and pulling her up to straddle me.

"I don't want to talk anymore." Viv pushes slightly off my chest and tilts her head to one side, sporting a little mischievous grin.

"You sure?" I want to know, a bit hesitant to get physical considering the topic of conversation we just abandoned.

"I'm sure," she says firmly. "I want to feel good, and you do an excellent job of making me feel good."

"Hmmm, I have some thoughts on how to do that." I slide one of my hands up her back and push her down toward me, reaching up to slide my mouth over hers. Despite the earlier heavy subject matter, she seems eager to slide her tongue in my mouth, and just like that all the blood rushes from my brain to my cock. With our mouths fused, our breaths tangling, and our tastes blending, it doesn't take long before the heat between us spikes. With both our hands exploring, it's a matter of minutes before pieces of clothing start coming off. First my shirt, then hers; her naked breasts rubbing against my bare chest feels so fucking amazing, it makes the hair on my arms stand on end. The slight scrape of her fingernails across my skin, skimming my shoulders and down my back, the perfect balance of pleasure and pain. A moan slips from my mouth as soon as her lips pull back from mine.

"I want to see you," she says, sitting back and trailing the tips of her fingers through the hair on my chest. A little flick of her fingernails over my nipples has me hiss in a breath. I'm fighting the urge to take over, but I don't want to interrupt the control she is taking. Instead, I lay my head back against the seat and simply watch her. Every thought and feeling clearly visible in her face. The light tip of her mouth when she sees my body react to her touch. The dilation of her pupils and faint flaring of her nostrils as she tentatively slides her hands up and runs her fingers through the beard that has grown in the past few weeks. Finally when she follows the trail of hair from my chest down to the waistband of my jeans, the tip of her tongue appears between her full lips. The red blush that starts between her breasts and covers her chest and neck, a testament to her state of arousal.

*Fuck it.* With a twist of my body, I have her flipped onto her back. One tug and her pants and panties are down her legs. I lift one of her feet from the tangle around her ankles and push her legs wide open to my view. Swollen and slick, her pussy is damn near irresistible. So why the hell bother trying? Slipping her legs over my shoulders, I slide off the couch and to my knees. There is no teasing, just my mouth latching onto her core, tongue searching for and finding entrance. Letting the scent and taste of her permeate my senses. Fucking delicious. My nose gently slides from side to side over her clit, which has her bucking her hips for maximum friction. She's already close from the sound of her moans, so I ease back, letting my fingers take the place of my tongue and my lips settle over the hard little nerve bundle. All it takes is a little twist of my wrist to reach that soft spot deep inside her, as I suck her clit into my mouth, and Viv falls apart.

Before the walls of her pussy even stop massaging my fingers, I pull them out as I guide my body up and over hers, and slide inside her still pulsing body.

By the time we are curled up in my bed, it is two hours and a couple of orgasms later and the coffee has long gone cold in the pot.

"What's that little statue?" her sleep-heavy voice mumbles against my chest. My eyes move to the little blue figure of a siren I picked up a few weeks ago, sitting on my nightstand.

"That's my siren."

She lifts her head off my chest to give it a long look before finding my eyes. "She's lovely."

I gently urge her head down to rest on my chest and press a kiss to her forehead before I answer.

"That she is, my love. That she is."

# CHAPTER EIGHTEEN

*Viv*

"Need a pick up?"

Owen doesn't waste any time on hello, but as is his custom, gets right to the point.

It's Sunday morning, and I'm meeting with my brothers and Mom at the house in an hour to discuss my parents' situation. Not something I'm looking forward to. Not because it's likely we'll have to suggest selling the house to finance some of my father's care; I think Mom knows it's inevitable. She's mentioned before she wouldn't mind downsizing. No, I have butterflies going rampant in my stomach because I have to tell her, Aaron, and Nolan about Frank. I'm afraid it won't be pleasant.

Pam gave me a good boost yesterday morning, after carefully helping me talk through the events that led up to the first time my father crossed the line. I was shocked to find it was much earlier than that fated night of my fifteenth birthday. I'd been eight years old, and he made it a habit to bring me some hot milk before he went to bed. Something that had lingered after I'd had a bout of night terrors a year or two before. He could always calm me down enough to be able to fall asleep again. The routine of him bringing me a hot drink a few hours after I'd gone to bed, helped me overcome the fear of going to sleep. I had gotten into the habit of waking up around the time he'd come upstairs. The milk and his soothing words helped me settle into a deep sleep through the night.

That night, when I was only eight, he'd pulled down the blankets and had run his hands over my shoulders and down my arms. Told me what a big girl I was growing up to be as he slipped up my pajama top and ran his fingers over the tiny little bumps of my nipples. I recalled him saying how it was a father's responsibility to look after his little girl and make sure she grew up to be a woman the whole family could be proud of. I never thought anything of it. Never had cause to distrust the man, who for years had made sure I could sleep without fear. It was right there, not at fifteen, but already at eight that the lines between wrong and right started getting blurred. Before I even had a chance to learn the difference between the two.

The shock at that revelation made me even angrier, and Pam called a halt to that topic, claiming I'd had enough for the day. She was right. After giving me some tips on how to handle this morning's conversation, I was emotionally exhausted and glad to lose myself in the demands of yesterday's crowd at The Skipper. Saturdays are always good for business, especially with the patio open, and time just flew by. Ike came by, and I chatted off and on with him during the night. Nothing too revealing. Not until he walked me home and I asked him to stay.

I could tell from the tension in his body, he was struggling to hold on to his anger when I told him about what had become clear to me that morning. I have to hand it to him, he held whatever he was thinking to himself and simply listened. Only spoke up when I mentioned I was nervous about opening up to my family about one thing, but not yet the other. He offered to come with me, to be my back up. At first I turned down his offer, but after a decent night's sleep in his arms, I changed my mind.

"No need," I tell Owen. "Ike is coming with me."

The silence on the phone is deafening. If I'm honest, it's not really a surprise my announcement doesn't go over well. Owen's first introduction to Ike is not one he'll likely forget.

"Why? Does he think he needs to protect you? From *us*? We're your fucking family, we protect you. He sounds like a controlling asshole, Viv. Probably not much different from that other loser you picked."

I let him rant, knowing that if I opened my mouth now, it would be to blurt out that my so-called family was nowhere to be found when I needed their protection.

"Is that your brother?" Ike walks into the kitchen and points at the phone I'm holding away from my ear. Every word Owen is spouting is clearly audible, and from the tight look on Ike's face, he's less than impressed. "Want me to deal with him?" he asks with a set jaw. I just shake my head and give him a small smile in thanks.

The moment I hear a break in the angry monologue, I get back on the phone. "You done?" I ask coldly and am met with silence. "I hope you are, because I need you to hear this: Ike has my back, because I *asked* him to have my back. This is the last time you get to go off on him, because you go there again and I will disown you so fast, you won't know what hit you." I can hear him muttering on the other end but I don't give him a chance to respond. "As for the low opinion you apparently have of me, given the shit you just threw at me, I promise you, you will eat your goddamn words one of these days." With that I hang up and brace my hands on the counter. I feel Ike walk up behind me and slide his arms around my waist, tucking my back tight against his front.

"So fucking proud of you, babe. You were right, you don't need me to deal with him. I wouldn't have been able to do a better job." His voice is low and gruff as he buries his face in my neck.

I slowly turn in his arms and he immediately lifts them to cup my face in his hands. I can feel his breath brush over my face as he softly rubs my nose with his. "You're good for me," I mumble. "Too good. I'm just waiting for you to run out the door screaming. My life is such a mess, I don't know why you put up with it."

"Shut up." The words are crass but his tone holds nothing but kindness. "I'm forty-two years old and have been allergic most of my adult life to anything resembling a relationship. I tried not to let you matter, but you did from the moment I watched you sling beers that first night. Couldn't believe my fucking luck when I put my mouth on you and felt your body respond. Only reason I let you go that first morning was because I was hanging tight to the *no-strings* method I'd been applying to any encounters I'd had to that point. I just didn't realize I was already too far gone." He kisses me softly, stroking his thumbs over my jaw. "I can't throw a switch and turn off the feelings you bring out, my love. It just doesn't work that way."

It's the second time I hear him call me that. First time was last night, just before I drifted off. I had dismissed it then as a slip of the tongue. A platitude, if you will. Hearing it from his mouth again, in this context, suddenly registers. He really fucking cares about me. He doesn't seem to see the mistakes I've made—the coward I've been—or perhaps he just doesn't care. He sees me for who I am. I press a grateful kiss on his lips.

"Thank you for that. For the record, I can't throw the switch either. And I wouldn't want to."

# *Ike*

The drive to her parents' house is quiet, both of us deep in thought. When I notice Viv wringing her hands in her lap, I reach out and cover them with mine.

"Nervous?"

"Terrified," was the quiet answer.

When we pull up to the house, we have to park on the street, since the driveway is full. At least it's good for a quick getaway. Looks like all the brothers are here already, and one I haven't met yet, pulls open the door when we approach. With an eyebrow raised he pointedly looks at my hand, holding tight to Viv's.

"You must be Nolan," I decide to take the wind from his sails. Successfully, judging by the flash of surprise on his face.

"You have an advantage here. You seem to know exactly who I am, but I have no clue who you are."

*Ah.* A challenge, and one I don't even have to touch, because Viv instantly gets in his face.

"Knock it off, Nolan. I'm not some fire hydrant you need to piss on to mark your territory. Pretty sure the others have filled you in on exactly who this is, so back off."

Apparently amused by his sister's vehemence, he lifts his hands in a defensive gesture. "Whoa, little sister, no need to take my head off." Then he turns to me and sticks one of them out. "You must be Ike. I've gotta say, I'm surprised you let my sister fight your fights for you."

I shrug my shoulders and put a smile on my face as I stare him down. "I wasn't aware I was fighting. Besides, I love seeing her in action."

"Okay, knock it off, you two," Viv interrupts. "We've got better things to do than to shoot the shit in the doorway." With that she steps into the house, pulling me behind her, her hand squeezing the blood from mine. The whole scene gives me a first-hand look at how she covers up her fears and insecurities with her tough exterior.

In the dining room, Viv's mother and other brothers are seated already, and a pretty brunette walks in from the kitchen with a tray. Setting it down on the table, she immediately reaches a hand to me.

"Hi, you must be Ike? I'm Lydia, Owen's wife. So glad you could join us."

From the angry scowl her husband throws her, it's easy to see he doesn't feel that way. All the more reason for me to clasp Lydia's hand and smile at her. "Nice to meet you, too. I'm sure we'll be seeing a lot more of each other." Viv's mom looks a little uneasy, so I turn to her next. "Good to see you again, Mrs. Lestar, and I'm glad it's under better circumstances." That earns me a little smile.

"Have a seat," Lydia offers, taking the empty spot beside her husband.

"Gentlemen." I nod at the other three brothers before sitting down, trying to ignore the glares.

Viv pours coffee quietly, I'm sure to keep her hands busy, even though her mind must be going a mile a minute. I'm starting to reconsider whether coming with her was perhaps a mistake, the tension around the table is palpable.

"Okay, now that we're all here," Owen says with an edge that has Lydia's eyes snap to him. "Let's crunch some numbers. I've done a few calculations." He hands out copies of a spreadsheet, and I purposely don't look at the copy I receive. I really don't have any business with this part of the discussion. I want Owen to know it.

The next half hour is spent going over sources of income versus a new monthly budget of expenses that includes their father's care. It becomes clear that those far outweigh the combination of small pensions they've managed to live on so far. No one seems surprised, including Viv's mom. In fact, she has a print out herself, with details of a small seniors' apartment building not too far from Seaside Assisted Living, where her husband lives. With some concrete plans in place, I speak up for the first time when a suggestion is made about doing a few upgrades to the house to ensure top market value.

"I actually have a house about as old as this one and just had some work done by a contractor, who's done a great job. He will come in and do a free assessment and quote. If you like, I can leave you his number. It's a place to start." I purposely address Mrs. Lestar, since in my eyes, she may need the support from her children, but she's still very much in charge.

"That would be helpful. Thank you, Ike." She smiles at me before turning her eyes on Viv. "Now that that's out of the way, why haven't I seen much of you lately? Is this man keeping you too busy?"

There definitely is an edge to her tone, and I put my hand on Viv's thigh underneath the table, stilling her leg which starts to bob up and down.

"Actually ..." Viv starts, flicking her eyes around the table and receiving an encouraging nod from Lydia in return. "I have been dealing with some things, Mom. I'm sure you remember Frank? He's back in town and he's making his presence known."

Aaron is the first to react. "What does that mean? 'Making his presence known.' Is he looking to get back with you? I thought he was somewhere in California."

Viv's mom leans over the table and puts her hand on Viv's nervously wringing ones. "Honey, why don't you tell us?"

"I've had to take a restraining order out on him. He's been ... rather threatening."

"Excuse me? He's threatening you?" This time it's Nolan who speaks up. Of course both Owen and Dorian are in the know, as well as Lydia I presume, so they remain quiet.

"Well, you know things with him ended rather abruptly." Her mother nods her acknowledgement. Viv takes a deep breath in and steals a quick look my way before continuing. "I had to go into hiding right after the last time he put me in the hospital."

Her mom inhales sharply before covering her mouth with her hands, right before chairs are being shoved back and expletives uttered by two of the brothers.

"The fuck?"

"Why didn't you tell us?"

I stop them with a raised hand. "Let her talk. Please?"

I could care less about the angry glares sent my way, because both of them shut up.

"I just couldn't, I'm sorry," she says, mostly to her mom, who seems frozen on the spot. "All I can say is it built up very gradually and I was ... ashamed? Afraid? I'm not even sure."

"You were with him a long time, honey," her mother struggles to find the words. "Was this going on the whole time?" Nolan steps up behind his mother, putting his hands on her shoulders. Viv looks from one to the other before answering softly.

"Most of it."

"How many times?" The angry question comes from Aaron.

"Sorry?"

"How many times did that bastard put you in the hospital, Vivian?"

I don't like the threatening tone of his voice, but I want to let Viv take the lead. Nevertheless, I'm primed to jump in on one wrong move or word.

"Four. I ended up in the hospital four times." Is the timid response.

"Four," he sneers. "Three fucking times he beat you into the hospital, and still you needed a fourth time to conclude you might wanna get away from this guy?"

"Enough!" Dorian jumps in before I have a chance to, shoving his chair back from the table. Aaron looks at him through slitted eyes before moving his gaze over to Owen, who sits silently with his head bowed, and Lydia who meets his eyes with tears brimming her own.

"You knew?" he says softly, his disbelief clear in the tone of his voice.

Owen lifts his head slowly. "We just found out ourselves."

I lean in and tuck Viv to my side with an arm over her shoulders, noticing the way both her mother and Nolan intensely stare at her. Viv's head is down and I know she's hanging on by a thread.

With a sweep of his arm, Aaron mows the table in front of him clear, china shattering against the wall and floor with a loud crash. "Goddammit!"

Instead of looking up, Viv cowers down even further against me and I've had enough. "Fucking get hold of yourself," I bite off, glaring at Aaron. "Look at what you're doing to her."

His eyes slide to the hunched figure of his sister beside me and his face immediately softens. "Oh, Sis."

Viv's shoulders move under my arm as she tries to hold back a muffled sob.

"Why?" The harsh question comes from her mother, who's kept surprisingly quiet and appears the most contained. "Why would you stay with someone like that? Why not talk to your family? We stick together. Your father and I taught you better."

Even Nolan seems shocked at his mother's tone, as the whole table turns their eyes on her. Too late I notice Viv's shoulders tensing and her head coming up slowly.

"My *father*?" The shrill sound of her voice has me leaning in and whispering in her ear.

"Babe, you wanna do this now?" But my words have no effect as she pushes my arm off and pushes herself up and out of her chair.

"My *father*?" she repeats with a derisive snort. "What my father taught me about family is a bit different than you think. He taught me family loyalty all right—about *duty* and *sacrifice.*" Her whole body is vibrating with anger now, and I slowly stand up and move behind her. Shock is clear on the faces of her brothers, but when I look at her mother, she slowly shakes her head with fingers tightly pressed against her lips.

"*His* duty and *my* sacrifice, that is. He reminded me how easy it would be to take me away from this *precious* family if I said anything—every time he fucking violated me!" The hysterical edge has reached its peak when Viv screams the last words at the top of her lungs. That's when I slip my arms around her waist and pull her sagging body against me.

"Enough, baby. Enough ..." I'm not sure that my voice penetrates the woeful sobs she breaks into.

"Liar," her mom hisses between her teeth, startling me with her venom.

"Mom!" Lydia reprimands, shocked. It starts a turbulent round of shocked and disbelieving comments from everyone around the table.

Fucking hell, what a mess. I can barely hold up the woman in my arms, her legs no longer properly supporting her. Until finally, I half carry, half drag her out of the dining room and into the hallway, ignoring the disorderly chaos still ringing in my ears. Holding her up with one arm, I try to open the door, determined to get her out of here, when I feel a hand on my back.

"Let me help," Lydia says, sadness marring her face, as she reaches past me to open the door. I get Viv to the car, that thankfully sits along the curb and isn't blocked in the drive. She's quiet, and although crying and defeated, seems to be alert and aware.

"Take me home." Her voice cracks on the softly spoken but determined words, when I help her into the passenger seat.

"Oh, honey," Lydia's voice comes from behind me, and I step aside to let her lean into the open door. "I'm so sorry that happened to you. Go home, let Ike take care of you, but know that I'm only a phone call away."

"You believe me?"

The genuine surprise on Viv's face hits me squarely in the gut. I have to swallow hard to push down the lump of emotion lodged in my throat. It suddenly brings home how terribly alone she must've felt all these years. Not anymore. Not if I have anything to say about it.

"Why would I doubt you, sweetie?"

"My brothers do. My own mother doesn't believe me. Not now and not back then," she reveals.

Lydia reels back and straightens up from her crouched position, firming her shoulders. "Well, don't expect that to last," she says determinedly. "I will set them straight." With that she turns to me. "You better take care of her." Her tone requires no answer, so I respond with a simple nod, wondering at her vehement support. With her lips tightly pressed together, she marches back into the house, while I round the car and slip into the driver's seat.

As I pull away from the curb, I glance over at Viv, who is staring out the side window. When we're almost halfway to her place I hear a soft chuckle coming from her, surprising me.

"Well ..." she says, dragging out the word. "I'm thinking that went well."

I have to pull the car to the side of the road, because I can't see a fucking thing with tears of laughter blurring my vision. Hilarity or hysteria, the two seem only a breath apart right now. When the worst of our laughing calms down, I turn to face her, glad to see the lingering humor dance in her eyes. I'm not under any illusion that she is feeling quite as lighthearted as she seems. I know my own heart is heavy, but she's just proved again how fucking unbreakable she really is.

"Proud of you," I say simply, stroking the back of my hand lightly over her cheek.

# CHAPTER NINETEEN

## Viv

"What a clusterfuck," Dino says, his eyes warm with concern.

It's the same thing Pam said when I called her to fill her in the moment we got home on Sunday. I'd been scheduled to work, but Ike put his foot down and called Gunnar himself to tell him I needed the day. I was pretty angry, but when he explained that unless I was ready to discuss my revelations this morning with everyone, I'd do best to stay home. He was right. I was raw and in no shape to ward off probing questions without revealing more than I was ready to. "A day," he said. "Just take one day to let things settle." By the time he had drawn me a bath and left me soaking with a bottle of beer and my phone, I was already beyond grateful. The moment my muscles relaxed under the influence of warm water and cold drink, my emotions released in full force. A slight knock on the door, and a softly spoken, "I'm right here if you need me," told me Ike was leaving me my space. I barely managed to thank him before the tears made it difficult. I heard the slight scrape of his body sliding down to sit in the hallway against the door. Oddly enough it didn't make me feel smothered, but comfortably safe instead. The realization helped stem the flow of tears. By the time I dialed Pam's number, all that was left was the odd sniffle.

Needless to say, Pam was first upset with my family—ready to go kick some ass, like a good friend—but very quickly concern for me won out over her anger.

"Told you he's a good man," she said smugly, after I told her how Ike had positioned himself at my back without interfering much. "Although in this case, I wouldn't have held it against him had he knocked some heads together."

I've agonized about my family's response to my unplanned disclosure on top of the already sensitive bomb I'd just dropped. Pam had mentioned I should give my brothers time. She had no words for my mother, but noted I no longer referred to her as *Mom*, effectively distancing myself. In a lengthy phone call yesterday with Lydia, I was shocked to discover that she had repeatedly shoved off, at times quite forcibly, inappropriate advances my father had made over the years. I had no idea. She'd apparently had issues with Owen over that before when he'd tried to brush those incidents off, saying our father was just being friendly. When she'd tried to bring it back up with him on Sunday, thinking it would lend credibility to my claims, he'd totally shut her down and had left, spending the night in a hotel. As of last night, she hadn't seen or heard from him.

Something like this is exactly the kind of thing I'd been so afraid of: the ripple effect it would have on my family.

Other than Lydia, I've heard from no one, not even Dorian has called. Despite the fact that Ike did his best to distract me with a bike ride up the coast yesterday, I feel the loss and betrayal deeply.

This morning he offered to stay home another day if I wanted him to, but I was ready to go to work. Lose myself in the pub's kitchen. With all my closely guarded secrets basically out in the open, I wanted to be the one to tell my *other* family. Ironically, I never once question *their* support and loyalty.

"Clusterfuck is an adequate description," I agree with Dino, who has listened to my recounting of this weekend's events with no more than the slight twitch of his jaw.

"You okay?" he asks, his head tilted to the side.

"Nope," I say honestly, popping my lips on the denial. "Unloading that shit did not bring any relief. At. All."

"Didn't it?"

I roll my eyes at the challenge in his question and the raised eyebrow he points in my direction. "No. All I've done is add burden to my family. Not like things aren't messed up enough, as it is. I don't like putting it on you either, or anyone else for that matter. It's done. Over. Nothing anyone can do about it now."

"Well, isn't that the biggest load of bullshit I've ever heard," he says, brusquely tossing the mushrooms in the pan of soup bubbling on the stove.

"Excuse me?" I mumble in disbelief.

"You heard me," he asserts. "First of all, your family has let you down in the worst possible way. Not once, but twice. They should've carried this burden along with you all these years because they didn't *listen*. And they're not listening now." He steps toward me and grabs me by the shoulders. "Secondly, your family here at the pub, your *friends,* have not been blind to the weight you've continued to carry on your shoulders, even after we found out about the abuse you suffered at the hands of that son of a bitch. We've been waiting for you to share, waiting for you to trust us, the way we trust you."

His words, more than he usually utters in one go, are a balm to my raw and tattered soul. Overcome with gratitude, I do a face-plant in his broad, warm chest. His arms fold tightly around me, and we're still standing like that when Gunnar and Syd walk in the back door.

"What happened?" Syd asks with alarm in her voice.

I pull back from Dino's embrace, when he mumbles, "Come clean."

"I need to talk to you," I announce, turning toward them. Syd's eyes are big with worry, and Gunnar just nods, a deep frown creasing his forehead.

"Use Gunnar's office," Dino rumbles behind me. "For privacy," he adds.

Following his suggestion, I follow them down the hall, the lead in my shoes getting heavier with each step. Once inside, Gunnar closes the door and instead of sitting on the other side of his desk, he sits down beside me, pulling Syd onto his lap. I smile at his urge to provide comfort to his wife, even before I have a chance to share.

Ironically, it turns out to be Syd giving him comfort by the time I have caught them up. Gunnar's hands are grabbing on the armrests of the chair so tightly, I'm afraid he'll snap them off. Syd's sad eyes are on mine as her hand soothingly continues to stroke his chest.

"I'm sorry for dumping this on you, but I didn't want to run the risk of you finding out any other way," I apologize, earning a sharp look from both.

"I didn't see," Gunnar says, shaking his head. "Was at your house all the fucking time, but I never saw."

"No one did. I don't think so, anyway. As for my mother, I don't know if she saw, all I know is that she didn't want to see. Didn't want to hear. I can think of a few reasons why that might be, but I'll never understand."

"That's because it's unforgivable." This from Syd, who is the most understanding and forgiving person I've come to know.

"How?" Gunnar asks the hard question, but I don't feel defensive with him. I know he just wants to understand.

"I think the milk," I venture, having had some time to mull it over. "Every night he brought me milk to help me sleep. I was always a spirited child. I think he put something in the milk to make sure I was a little more ... agreeable. Some of my memories are a bit spotty, especially the first time he ... he ..." I have to force myself to speak the words. Make it real. "He raped me."

Gunnar flinches and Syd buries her face in his neck. Guess it makes it real for them, too. Rape. Such an ugly word. The flashbacks to that first time are blissfully limited in what I recall. Mostly I remember throwing up for days after.

"What can we do?" Syd asks in a timid voice. "What do you need?"

I reach out and grab her hand. "Just this. What you're doing right now. Hearing—listening—caring—*believing.*"

The rest of the day passes relatively uneventfully.

I had to make Gunnar promise not to kick Owen's ass, needing to believe he'd come to me on his own, eventually. When Matt came in he could sense something was up, but he was barking up the wrong tree when he stopped me in the hallway and started laying in on Ike. I lost it for a minute there. Yelled at him to back off and got both Dino and Gunnar to come running from opposite sides of the hallway. Dino lead me away to the kitchen, while Gunnar took Matt in the other direction. Dino forced a glass of scotch down my gullet, and I have to admit, the slow, gentle burn of the alcohol went a long way to calming me down. By the time Matt came shuffling into the kitchen, with regret all over his face, I was up and hugging him without thinking.

"Sorry," he mumbled sheepishly. Over his shoulder, Gunnar was leaning in the doorway. "I worry," Matt finished. Something told me Gunnar had given him some feedback because when I looked back at him, he lightly shrugged his shoulders.

"You know," I affirmed, looking Matt in the eyes. "If not for Ike, I don't know how I would've gotten through these past few weeks. And I will not have anyone bad-mouth him."

"Gotcha," he said, with his signature cocky grin.

I walk into the bar with a tray of our daily soup, when a familiar voice stops me in my tracks.

"We need to talk."

# Ike

"Is there anything I can get you?"

I look up from my drawing table where I've been working on the new engine design for the freight company, due by the end of the week. My days off have set me back a bit. I had to call Viv earlier, to let her know I was working late, and I'd grab a bite when I got there. Last thing I want is that girl, Samantha, interrupting me. But when I turn around, I see she's already halfway in my office, the too bright smile on her face more of an irritant than a turn on.

"No thanks," I answer politely before turning my back. "I'll close up," I add as an afterthought, dismissing her. I start back where I left off and am drawn right back into my design, when I hear movement behind me. Last thing I expect to see when I swing around is Samantha, in nothing more than a pair of lace boy-shorts. I reel back and lift my hands in a defensive pose. "Whoa. What the fuck? Samantha, I—"

I don't have a chance to say more before she launches herself at me. The only thing I can do is grab her by the shoulders and turn my head away, which only causes her to latch on to my neck with her mouth. *Jesus Christ.* This woman is like an octopus. All limbs, clinging onto me. My instinct is to fling her off me with force, but I don't want to hurt her either. The possibility of this situation turning on a dime is real.

"Stop!" I try to gently set her back, but a sound from the doorway has me lift my eyes. Fucking great. Tim is in the doorway, watching me struggle to push the practically naked girl off me. Before I have a chance to say anything, he mumbles *"fucking asshole"* and turns on his heels, disappearing down the hall. Goddammit.

"Samantha, knock it off!" Finally I get her off me and try not to look at her body. "What the hell has gotten into you? Get dressed." I stand up and gingerly move past her to run after Tim. Last thing I want is for him to get the wrong idea. Pretty damn sure it's already too late for that, but I've got to try. By the time I round the reception desk, I just see the elevator doors closing. *Son of a bitch.*

Knowing I have another situation on my hands, I make a beeline for the phone on the reception desk and call David, who just left half an hour ago.

"Miss me already?" he says, chuckling as he answers his phone.

"Not really. I have a problem here at the office, David."

His tone instantly turns serious when he answers, "Talk to me."

"I just told Samantha to get her clothes back on in my office."

"Say the fuck what?"

"She came in my office, asked me if I needed anything, I told her no and the next thing I know she is draped around me, half-fucking-naked." I'm about to tell him about Tim showing up, when I hear the click of heels coming down the hallway.

"Here she comes now."

"Where are you?"

"Reception."

"Put the phone down and talk to her. Let me hear." I quickly put the phone, face up, on the desk and turn so my body is covering it when Samantha comes around the corner.

"Oh," she says, coming to a halt when she sees me. "I thought you'd left." She fiddles with the hem of her shirt nervously as she looks at me from under her eyebrows.

"What the hell was that all about, Samantha? Why would you do that?"

She looks at the floor, avoiding my eyes, her fingers never stop plucking at her clothes. "I thought you liked me."

I'm dumbfounded. "How do you figure that? I can't even remember your fucking name," I point out in exasperation.

Her mouth opens in a perfect *O* and tears start to pool in her eyes. Wonderful, here come the waterworks.

"I thought you were flirting, playing hard to get. I wanted to move things along."

"By taking your clothes off? How old are you?"

"Twenty-two," she answers timidly.

"Christ! I could be your father." I close my eyes to try and compose myself before I totally lose it. "Samantha, here is a friendly suggestion. What happened in there? Don't ever do that again. With anyone. For God's sake, you could've been hurt."

Her sniffling almost makes me miss the muffled voice calling my name. Fuck, forgot about David. Turning I pick up the phone. "Sorry," I tell David, who immediately asks to speak to the girl.

She looks at me funny when I hold the phone out to her. All I hear is her side, which mostly consists of monosyllabic responses. The conversation is brief, and in a few short minutes she hands the phone back to me.

"Sorry," she mumbles, before slipping past me to the elevators.

I put the phone to my ear. "You still there?"

"I am. I fired her. Warned her that I heard your entire conversation, and that we wouldn't press any charges of sexual harassment if she left quietly."

"You serious? Sexual harassment?" I'm thinking that might be a bit much, but David is obviously of a different opinion.

"Serious as a heart attack. Goes both ways, you know. Not to mention the girl needs a serious lesson before she gets herself into trouble one day. That friendly suggestion of yours wasn't gonna leave a lasting impression. This will."

"Right." There's not much more I can say. The man's got a point.

"Best get to my dinner," David says, and just like that I remember Tim's hasty departure.

After saying a quick goodbye, I lock up and get on my bike, having a pretty good idea where he might have gone, if my suspicions about him are correct.

Pulling in behind the pub, I park my bike and walk around to the front where the patio is pretty busy. Matt and a young girl I don't know are serving. I'm surprised to be greeted by him with a friendly hello. That's a change from before. Inside, Syd is picking up an order at the bar which is manned by Gunnar. No Viv in sight.

"Evening," Gunnar sees me pull up at the end of the bar, where I can keep an eye on the hallway.

"Hey, Viv around?"

"Yep, she's probably in the kitchen with Tim." Gunnar obviously thinks nothing of it, but I know it spells trouble with a capital T. Which is why he looks at me funny when I immediately rush past him and down the hall. I should've called her. Explained the situation to her before he got here. *Fuck.*

I stop at the door when I'm greeted with the sight of Viv, wrapped in a tight embrace with Tim, who sees me but doesn't make a move to let her go, staring me down. The challenge couldn't be clearer. Viv hasn't seen me yet, but she pushes on Tim's chest and steps back.

"You're a good friend, Tim. I don't know what you think you saw, but I'm pretty sure there's a reasonable explanation. Ike is not *that* guy."

His eyes flick up to me before returning to Viv. "She was naked, Viv."

She lifts up her hand. "I really don't need this right now, Tim. I trust Ike. I may even love him."

*Atta girl.* Her words tug my mouth into a smile. Tim, who seems lost for words, spots it and simply nods.

"You sure?" he asks Viv, but his eyes flick to me. "We had a good thing, didn't we?"

She chuckles and moves away from him ... and toward me. The moment she spots me, she swings back and gives Tim a good shove in the chest. "You bastard, you knew he was there, didn't you? Not cool, Tim. Not. Cool."

He throws me one last look before stalking out of the kitchen, his head down. "Lucky bastard," he mumbles under his breath as he passes me. I don't even look at him, I'm too busy staring at this amazing woman I've been fortunate enough to meet and fall for.

"I was gonna tell you," she starts, but I stop her by shaking my head.

"No need. I had that one figured." I smile and take a step closer. She tilts her head to the side as I approach.

"What was this about a naked girl all over you?" The corner of her mouth lifts in a smile, and I can't quite believe my luck. Any other woman would have my balls in a vice, but this one … this one may have drama in her life, but she sure doesn't create it.

"Just that: a girl. One young enough to be my daughter, who got it in her head that I might be interested." I'm close enough to her to pull her flush against my body. "For the record, I'm not. My attention is fully taken by a certain blonde of a slightly more mature nature." She's smiling big now.

"That right?"

"Bet your luscious ass that's right." With both hands I cup her full behind and squeeze, leaning in for a kiss.

"I'm working," she protests weakly.

"Which is why I have to grab a little snack now," I tell her, closing the gap and covering her mouth with mine. The taste of her is enough to make me forget where we are as my body instantly responds. Slow, languid strokes of my tongue along hers, enough to clear all rational thought from my head.

"Don't mind me." Dino's deep voice startles as he unceremoniously marches in on what was turning out to be a full on make-out session. "I just cook here," he says with a smirk, before he adds, mumbling under his breath, "There's a fully functional bed upstairs, you know? Go for a quick break and my damn kitchen is turned into a peep show."

I reluctantly let go of Viv's ass as she softly chuckles in my shirt. Grabbing her hand, I pull her out of the kitchen, and with a last look over my shoulder at Dino I throw out, "Cockblocker." His big booming laugh follows us all the way down the hall to the pub.

Tim is sitting at the end of the bar that's become my hangout. With a quick touch of my lips to hers, I let Viv get back to work, and slide onto a stool beside him.

"Known Viv for close to four years now," he starts, his eyes focused on the beer glass on the bar in front of him. "In all that time, I never saw her show interest in any guy. She gave me one shot, one late night when both of us had been drinking. I took it, and I blew it." His head comes up and he looks me in the eyes. "It would've been easier if I'd just stuck to looking from a distance. At least then I wouldn't know what I was missing out on."

Not going to say I like the thought of Tim knowing her so intimately, but oddly enough I'd rather it be him than anyone else. He's a friend. Both for me and for Viv. Even when he was warning her earlier, he did it out of concern for her. Can't blame him for making that last play, I'm pretty sure I'd have done the same thing.

I clap my hand on his shoulder. "I hear you, my friend," I tell him before ordering a couple more beers from the pretty blonde bartender.

# CHAPTER TWENTY

*Viv*

"Miss, can you fasten your seatbelt?"

The flight attendant leans over to help me when I fumble, still groggy from the deep sleep I fell into the moment my butt hit the big cushy seat in business class.

The cushy seat is compliments of points Ike collected over the past twelve years of working and traveling for Maine Maritime. I assured him it wasn't necessary, but he insisted. What can I say? I've never traveled business class before. Now it seems I slept through the experience. Damn.

When the detective from the Los Angeles PD initially contacted me last Friday, telling me he was planning to fly in for a brief interview, I told him to hold off booking—I'd call him back. I still hadn't heard a word from Dorian, even though I spoke with Kyle a few times. He'd called as soon as he found out. My brother had taken his scheduled flight home the day after our *meeting* and dumped the whole sordid story on Kyle's lap. He apologized for Dorian's thick skull and suggested perhaps if I could fly out for Dor's birthday, in a week, we could have a good talk. I love Kyle, but I was skeptical about the plan. That is, until the detective called, then it occurred to me I might be able to kill two birds with one stone. Three, if you count the brief meeting the LA Assistant District Attorney was hoping for, as well. Something the detective had mentioned when I was talking to him.

After clearing my shifts with Gunnar, I called the detective back and told him I'd be able to fly out on Wednesday and would be leaving for San Francisco the next morning. Ike had not been happy.

"Babe, I have that launch in Boston that weekend. The one that was delayed because of the storm? I can't make it unless you postpone it a week."

"But then I'd miss out on Dorian's birthday. Being able to do both was the reason I decided to fly out in the first place." My face must've shown my disappointment, because Ike folded pretty quickly. Of course he knows how much my family's silence hurts me. That's when he pulled up his frequent flyer miles and upgraded my flight.

It actually worked out perfect. Ike ended up driving me to Boston this morning in my car, and he's going to stay there for the launch on Saturday. Sunday I get back and he'll pick me up before we head home to Portland. Couldn't have worked out better.

As the plane descends for landing, I let my mind wander to the past week, which has been both one of the worst and one of the best weeks of my life. How ironic that the person I have just tentatively been accepting into my heart—my trust—turns out to be the one whose support for me has been singular and complete. Amazing.

The rumble of the landing gear hitting the tarmac stirs me out of my thoughts. Detective Martens said he would pick me up. He told me they hadn't had any luck in tracking down Frank. Something I was already aware of, courtesy of Officer Bragdon, who'd stayed in touch with Gunnar. Normally I would've bristled at that, but given the weeks I've had, I'm rather grateful Gunnar is keeping tabs. As it is, no one knows where he's at. He checked out from the motel in Portland before the cops got there, apparently.

When the plane comes to a halt at the gate, I reluctantly leave my comfy seat and grab my carry-on from the overhead compartment. I didn't check anything: it's summer and what little I need for these couple of days fit easily into the small suitcase. As one of the first to leave the plane, it's easy to spot the older gentleman holding up the sign with my name. He watches my approach with obvious interest.

"Ms. Lestar?" He smiles broadly when I reach him.

"That's me," I answer as he folds the sign up, tucks it under his arm and takes my suitcase from me.

"Detective Martens, LAPD." He flips open a badge before adding, "Follow me. I'm parked outside."

LAX is confusing and very crowded; I would surely have gotten lost without my escort. By the time we get to his vehicle, my legs are hurting. He pops the locks and drops my case into the cavernous trunk of the Crown Victoria, before inviting me to get in.

"I just have to make a quick call," I smile at him, walking away a few steps to dial Ike's number.

"Hey, love. How was business class?" he answers, making my heart jump a little. He's called me that a couple more times over the past few days, and I'm liking it. Interesting, since I'm not a particularly mushy person. Normally. Ike has me in a puddle pretty regularly, though.

"Too comfortable," I chuckle. "Fell asleep about five minutes into the flight and the attendant had to wake me up because we were landing." The deep rumble of Ike's laugh feels warm and comfortable.

"Better than sitting squashed between a screaming baby and a big snoring man with body odor," he jokes.

"Amen to that."

"So you obviously got there okay. You find the detective yet?"

I sneak a glance over my shoulder at Detective Martens, who had gotten in behind the wheel. "Yup. He was waiting with a big sign with my name on it. Made me feel pretty damn special." I smile when I hear his responding growl.

"Tell me he's old, has a beer belly, and buckteeth, please."

"Sorry," I tease him. "No can do."

"Viv ..." he threatens.

"His teeth are perfectly straight. He doesn't have a beer belly. And from my vantage point almost a head taller than him, I can safely say he doesn't have a bald spot either. Although, he's gotta be hitting his retirement soon," I laugh.

"Asking for trouble, babe." Ike makes that sound way too enticing. Especially since I won't see him until Sunday. "Will you call me when you get to the hotel tonight?"

"Will do," I tell him on a smile, marveling at the fact that I don't seem to mind his slightly overprotective demands. Now if it were anyone else ... "Miss you." The words slip from my mouth before I can check them. Wincing slightly I bite my lip, listening to the silence on the other end.

"Me too, babe. Me fucking, too," he finally says.

When I get in the car, I'm still wearing a big dumb grin.

As expected, the happy feeling didn't last. By the time I get to the hotel that night after two grueling hours of questioning by Detective Martens and another hour with the ADA, I'm done. Stick a fork in me done. I declined an offer of dinner from the detective, telling him I would grab something in the hotel. Even though I'd since discovered the man has been married for thirty odd years and has a couple of adult kids, I wouldn't feel comfortable sitting through a meal with him. It's a matter of trust. Or lack thereof.

Kicking off my shoes and tossing my purse onto a chair, I flop down on the bed with the room service menu. Not normally a justifiable expense, but fuck; it's been a long-ass day. As soon as I have my order in, I change into some comfy leggings and a T-shirt and lay back down on the bed, phone in hand.

"Hey," I say when Ike answers. "I'm back. It was exhausting, and I don't really wanna rehash it all again, so tell me about your day instead."

I love the sound of his chuckle. It's deep and a little rough, and it gives me a charge every time I hear it.

"Fair enough," he says. "Just tell me this, have you eaten?"

"Ordered some room service, just now. I'm not leaving this room until it's time to go tomorrow morning."

"Sounds good. What time is your flight?"

"Not until noon. I should be in San Fran at one-thirty."

"Your brother-in-law picking you up?"

"Yeah. Kyle has me booked at a B&B around the corner from their house, just in case." I insisted, worried that Dorian might not want to have me in his house. Kyle thought it was ridiculous and was only willing to book it for the first night. He said if Dorian hadn't seen the light by Friday night, he would kick his ass out and move me in. "So what *have* you been up to?" I ask again.

"Did some shopping."

His voice is serious enough, but still I burst out laughing. "Shopping? You?"

"I did," he chuckles before turning serious once again. "I needed some new bedding."

I can barely contain the snorts. "I can't see you doing Macy's, Ike"

"Crate and Barrel, actually," he deadpans, and that's the end of my restraint.

When I finally catch my breath I hear him say, "You done?" But there is no malice in his voice, just amusement.

"I am. I am done. Thank you, I so needed that laugh."

"I wasn't kidding. I have one sheet set and a bunch of old blankets. I wanted to get some decent stuff for when you come over."

"What?" Any lingering snickers disappear instantly when his words register. "You went shopping for me?"

Now it's his turn to laugh. "Well, it's for my bed, but I'm hoping to have you in there with me at all times. So yeah, I guess so."

## Ike

"Hang on," she whispers, suddenly sounding like she's crying.

Fuck me. What did I do? I thought it might be nice to have some nice sheets and a nice comforter for when she's over.

To be honest, I was bored out of my brain last night. I didn't feel like going out with the guys of the crew, who kindly invited me along. Things are back on track for the launch on Saturday and the mood was pretty celebratory, but I passed. Instead I walked back to the hotel and on an impulse, stopped into a Crate and Barrel store I passed on the way. Can't say exactly what drew me in, although I suspect it had something to do with the mermaid lamp on the nightstand in the window display. *I'm turning into a fucking chick.* I missed Viv. Well, there hadn't really been opportunity to miss her yet, but I was anticipating it. See? Total fucking chick.

The idea for the bedding popped up when I started wondering whether it would be too soon to get her to move in with me. Definitely too soon.

I can hear her talking to someone in the background. Some rattling and then a door closing, before I hear her breathing into the phone.

"Ike?"

"Still here," I tell her. "Who was that?"

"Room service," she explains. "I had to find some cash for a tip."

"I should let you eat."

"Wait." She pauses briefly before continuing. "So did you buy any?"

"Sheets? Yes, and a comforter. A few towels as well," I grudgingly admit, feeling all kinds of ridiculous right now, but Viv isn't laughing at me this time.

"That's nice," she whispers.

"Look, it's not a big deal. I needed some decent stuff anyway."

"Oh, I think it's a pretty big deal and ... I like it."

"Good."

I'm sitting here in my hotel room, clear across the country from where she's sitting in hers, smiling like a fucking dufus.

"Hey, I should probably eat my food before it gets cold," she says, and I can hear a smile in her voice, too.

"Yes, you should. Call me tomorrow when you get to San Fran?"

"I will. Night, Isaac."

"I like that ... Isaac. Night—and Viv?"

"Yeah?"

"I miss you."

*Total. Fucking. Chick.*

# Viv

Another day, another airport.

Kyle doesn't need a sign, I see his tall, lanky figure sticking up, head and shoulders over the other people waiting for arrivals. If that wasn't enough, the moment he spots me, he starts waving his arms and yelling. *Nut*.

This time I managed to maximize my enjoyment of business class. A short flight, there was simply no time to fall asleep, so I took the orange juice offered. I also accepted the coffee in the real cup, with real cream. I spent my time flicking through my totally private little TV screen until I found *Fifty Shades of Grey*. Looking around me first, to make sure no one would see, I pressed play and donned my head phones. I'll admit, I fast forwarded, since the flight was only an hour and twenty minutes, but I made sure I got the *good stuff* in. I didn't care much for the book, but I'd heard some of the scenes were pretty damn hot—this according to Pam, who has a serious crush on Jamie—so I wanted to at least hit those. Of course I ran out of time and didn't get a chance to splash some cold water on my face before landing, so I walked off the plane with a lusty blush on my cheeks.

"Girl, what happened to you?" Kyle asks way too loudly when I reach him and random people are turning to look at me.

"Kyle!" I stage whisper. "Turn it down." Half of what I say gets muffled when he wraps his long arms around me and lifts me clear off the floor.

"So glad you're here, honey. We're gonna straighten that boy out," he says, his volume at a more respectable level now.

222

Kyle is very flamboyant. I guess it's the artist in him, but when I first met him, it had taken some getting used to. It was odd to see my big, built, deep-voiced brother looking at this exotic creature with stars in his eyes. It didn't take long though, the love between them was clear as day. I know they've had some issues, mainly around Dorian living a lie each time he interacts with our family. That's something that doesn't sit well with Kyle, and I have to admit, if I were him I'd be pretty fed up with being kept a secret this long too.

"I hope so," I tell him, not at all sure, but when Kyle gets something in his head it's full steam ahead. I just hope it doesn't backfire. "So what's the plan?" I follow Kyle, who has taken charge of my suitcase, out of the terminal and into the afternoon heat.

"Dor is at the gallery. We're dropping off your bag at the B&B and picking up your key, and then we go shopping."

"Really? Not a fan of shopping, Kyle. I thought you knew that."

"Groceries and birthday party supplies. We're hitting up Costco. Dinner for tonight and snackies and burgers for tomorrow."

We've reached Kyle's little, sporty Beemer and instead of putting my carry-on in the trunk, he tosses it in the backseat before folding his long body behind the wheel.

"I don't mind Costco," I admit, when we're all buckled in. "Maybe I can find him a birthday gift there. I haven't had a chance to get anything."

"Nonsense," he objects, waving his hand in my face. "You're here, that's the best birthday gift ever."

The ride to the B&B, a beautiful sprawling home with immaculate landscaping, is literally right around the corner. No more than a two minute walk. The lady is lovely and shows us to the back of the house, where my *room* is actually a small guest house at the back of the property, beside the massive swimming pool. She gives me the key and shows me the side gate, which is locked, but she tells me the same key will open the gate as well. Handy.

After a bit of *oohing* and *aahing* over the place, Kyle goes on ahead to their place. I promise to be over as soon as I have my stuff unpacked. I want a few minutes alone so I can call Ike, as promised.

"You know you have ridiculous amounts of food, right?" I point out to Kyle, who managed to cram every last item from his overflowing Costco cart into that little BMW. Now that we've unloaded it into his kitchen and have it all spread out over the counter and kitchen table, it is clear that they won't need cheese, crackers, hamburgers or buns for the next year. Twelve people are invited, he says. Well, these quantities are for forty, at least.

"We have a big freezer." He breezes past me with five bags of chocolate covered pretzels "because they were on sale," and dives into the walk-in pantry. "Stop fussing and start packing it away," he calls from the door opening.

I open the fridge and am disheartened at how full it already is. Packing the perishables away is like a fucking Chinese puzzle. As I'm shoving the last salami sausage in the last available space, I briefly consider that unless someone knows what to grab first, the entire contents will come falling out. *Oh well*. I quickly shove the door closed, determined I won't want anything from the fridge. Ever.

I'm actually glad for the distraction Kyle provides, with his constant chattering, as we jointly prepare a stir-fry for dinner. It gives me less time to consider the confrontation that lies ahead. Still, when I hear the front door open and keys dropping on the hallway table, I feel like I'm going to puke.

"Hey, baby," Kyle calls out, rubbing my shoulder as I stand frozen, the chef's knife in the air, prone to cut the bok choy. "In here," he adds, fishing the knife from my hand with two fingers and putting it down on the counter.

I can't take my eyes off the doorway and watch Dorian's face transform the minute he walks in the door and spots me.

"What are you doing here?" Are the first words out of his mouth. Kyle abruptly drops his hand from my shoulder and marches up to stand toe-to-toe with Dorian, who doesn't take his eyes off me.

"I invited her. Deal with it," Kyle says and Dorian faces him.

"Why?"

"Because you're reacting. You're not thinking. Now, you're gonna come keep us company while we finish dinner."

With some reluctance, Dorian ends up following Kyle to the kitchen, pulling out a stool at the counter, and taking the beer Kyle offers him.

The tension is so thick, it's cloying, but I knew this wasn't going to be a cakewalk, so I pick up the knife, and without saying a word, chop up the bok choy.

Dinner is very uncomfortable. Kyle tries to drag both of us into conversation, but neither Dorian or I are much help. Kyle starts piling up the dishes and walks into the kitchen, so I get up and start collecting the rest of them when Dorian stops me with a hand on my arm.

"Why Viv? Why after all these years?" Pain and confusion shimmer in his eyes.

Slowly I sink back down into my seat, his hand sliding down my arm to grasp my hand. I heard Kyle's words to Dorian earlier, and I try to tamp down the part of me that wants to react to his question with anger. But this is not about who's right, this is about salvaging my relationship with my brother. These are my ripples. I tossed a brick into what everyone thought was smooth water. I own that. But I should also own the resulting ripples, just like my father has to own his. That's the crux of it, right there—I've carried the consequences of his abuse for so long; it has impacted every damn aspect of my life to a point where I am … I *was* ruled by it.

"Because what he did has dominated my life. I tried to block it out, but it's not that simple. It scarred me in a way I can't ignore anymore, Dorian."

"But how? I mean, there were so many of us in that house, how …" His voice fades as he drops his head in his hands.

"I tried. Believe me I tried. Think about it, Dor," I prod, wanting to let him figure it out. Wanting him to start putting the pieces together on his own. Those signs that everyone turned a blind eye to at the time.

I watch as his head comes up slowly, disbelief gradually changing to anger in his face. "Your warm milk?" Shaking his head, a tear starts rolling down his face. "Oh my God … that was his thing, every night."

It's painful to watch the truth gradually reveal itself, leaving devastation in its wake. I see it in Dorian's eyes when he looks at me.

"It's not that I didn't believe you, Viv. You have to understand, I just didn't want to believe that of him either." He pleads for understanding with his eyes, and I do. I get it. I remember the same confusion.

"I love him, Viv, but now I hate him too. What do I do with that?" As he forces the words from his mouth, his face crumples.

"I don't know, Dor," I tell him honestly, watching as Kyle comes in from the kitchen and puts comforting arms around my brother. "I've been trying to figure that out my whole life."

Kyle tries to convince me to move out of the B&B tonight and stay with them, but I need some time to myself after an emotionally exhausting evening.

Lots of tears and anger, but we also had some good laughs and even happy moments. Especially when Dorian announced that he needed to "man up" and come out of the closet already. Said that since I had already dropped a bomb, his bit of news should create no more than a dent. Kyle's squeals were ear-shattering and totally understandable. For near twenty years, the man has had to hide to preserve my brother's secret. Even though Dorian has always been part of every aspect of Kyle's life, he never fully let Kyle into his.

When I pull the door closed behind me and start walking down the street, I know I made the right decision to stay in the rented room tonight. The way those two were eyeing each other, it's obvious there will be some celebrating going on.

It strikes me how funny life can be, like a row of domino stones, one event prompting another, and another. Sometimes the stones get stuck, but with a little nudge—a little outside help—their forward flow of energy is restored.

# CHAPTER TWENTY-ONE

*Ike*

"Hey! You can't park there."

A security guard walks up to the car, a scowl on his face.

*Wonderful.* The only fucking available spot in sight and I can't park here. I'm late. Viv's plane was scheduled to get in an hour ago, and I got hung up behind an accident on the bridge over the channel. I've tried calling her cell phone but she's not answering.

"I won't be more than a minute. I'm late picking someone up," I try, already knowing it'll meet with deaf ears. Sure enough, the guard just waves his hand, indicating for me to move.

Dammit. I wanted to be waiting for her at the gate with the flowers I got her. Sappy idiot. Pulling away from the curb I prepare to drive around the terminal once again, when I spot a familiar streak of blue on a head of blonde hair behind a group of travelers coming through the sliding doors. With a quick peek in my side mirror to check on the guard, I quickly double park and jump out of the car.

"Viv! Over here!" I wave in her direction until I see her spot me, a big smile cracking her face. Damn, she's beautiful.

"Hey, you! Didn't I tell you to move?" I turn to the voice and watch the security guard make his way over.

"She's right there," I explain, turning back to point out Viv's approach. She's apparently caught on that something is up, because the smile is gone and she's rushing.

"Not my problem," the asshole says, pulling a pad from his breast pocket, preparing to write me a ticket. A quick glance at the "towing-zone" sign shows that could be a whopping $2,000. *Hell no.* Just as I'm about to unleash my decidedly crappy morning on his ass, Viv's smoky voice pipes up.

"Oh thank you, officer! I was so worried I was going to be too late," she babbles, batting her eyelashes as she shoves her carry-on in my hands. "Now we may just make it in time to the hospital." Turning to me she says, "Let's go, baby, I need to go say goodbye to Daddy."

I struggle to keep a straight face, the minx even manages to produce a few tears. Quickly tossing the suitcase in the back, I'm glad to see the guard, distractedly tuck the pad back in his pocket, never taking his eyes off Viv. A siren indeed. With watery eyes she smiles at him. "We'll be out of your hair now. Thank you again, so much." I'm already in the driver's seat when she climbs in the car, mumbling under her breath, "Drive!" The crunch of paper the moment her behind sits down makes me wince, but I simply put the car in drive and tear out of there.

"What the hell? What did I just sit down on?" Viv tries to push off the seat, trying to get a look.

"Buckle up, babe," I remind her. "Those flowers are for you," I add with a smile.

I just keep driving until we almost hit the I-95. I pull off into a truck rest stop, slam the car in park and turn to Viv, hauling her half out of her seat, so I can finally give her a fucking welcome home kiss.

"Whoa," she breathes when I finally release her mouth, her hands having found their way around my neck. "What was that?"

"That, my love, was how glad I am to have you home."

A bright smile breaks across her face and reaches all the way to her stunning eyes. "Me, too," she says simply, but it says enough.

Reaching around her, I snatch the helplessly crushed bouquet of flowers off the seat and lowering the window, toss them out. "I'll buy you more," I reassure her, seeing her wince. Lowering her back into her seat, I lean in for one last taste of her lips before I shift the car in drive and get us back on the road.

With only minimal prompting on my part, Viv spends the drive recounting the events of her last few days. The occasional glances, I throw her way, catch every emotion she feels clearly displayed on her face. Something I have been able to see from the day I met her. She's an open book to me, no longer holding anything back, and although I've shared some, I realize it's time to even out the playing field. Trust is a precious commodity and not something easily earned or given. Where she's freely given me her trust, I've not done my part in earning it. That's got to change.

"Dorian and Kyle are flying down next weekend. Together," she says meaningfully, before chuckling. "Dor figures now is the best time to drop his own bomb. I'm not sure how that's going fly, but I figure at this point, why the hell not?"

"So he's coming out of the closet? That's good, baby," I tell her warmly, meaning every word. "No word yet from any of the others?" Throwing a quick look beside me, I catch the sadness hit her eyes.

"Nothing," she sighs. "I thought for sure ..." Her voice trails off, and I lift a hand off the wheel to give her hand a squeeze.

"They'll come around. Just like Dorian has. I venture to bet the way they feel is similar to what he described: that it's not so much about believing you but not being able to believe what their father would be capable of. You've always known the perfect family was a farce—they've only just discovered it. It takes time to process." I'm afraid I come across as defending them, but I'm reassured when I see the soft smile on her face as she turns to me.

Lacing her fingers with mine, we finish the rest of the drive in silence, Viv holding my hand tightly in hers. Turning onto the 295 through Portland, I turn to her. "Where do you want to go? My house or would you rather head to your apartment?"

"Actually, I'd really love to unpack, have a shower, give Pam a call, and take a nap. In that order. Just some time to decompress and regenerate. Would you mind if I dropped you at your place and we meet up for dinner at The Skipper later? I've missed my family there." She looks at me, a bit contrite.

"Sounds good to me," I ease her mind. "Gives me a chance to do the same. Catch up with my boss and give him a report on the launch."

Viv claps her hand over her mouth. "Oh good grief, I haven't even asked you about the launch. I'm so sorry. I suck at this relationship stuff."

I throw my head back and laugh. "Babe, seriously? You're the best serious girlfriend I've ever had." That evokes a loud snort from her.

"I'm the *only* serious girlfriend you've ever had," she says with a smile.

"Same difference."

# Viv

After dropping Ike off at his place, and with a full-body tingle from the scorching kiss we shared in his driveway, I make my way home. I still wear the smile at Ike's promise to finish what we started tonight, at my place.

Traffic is light, even for a Sunday afternoon, but with the mid-day sun baking down, I would imagine most people have sought out air conditioning or a spot near the water. It's tempting—it's been so long since I've actually gone to the beach, I can't even remember the last time. But I think I'll stick with air conditioning for now. I really do need to get some rest. I haven't had much sleep all weekend.

Dorian's birthday party on Friday night was an absolute blast. A small group, but the perfect size for Cards Against Humanity, the game Kyle pulled out. It's been ages since I've laughed so hard that my stomach muscles still ached the next day. Ten bottles of wine and hours of hilarity later, I rolled into the guest bed at their house. I think it may have been close to five in the morning. I'm too old for nights like that.

Saturday Kyle dragged me out of bed at ten, after way too few hours of sleep, and the two of them took me to Fisherman's Wharf. Funny to suddenly be looking out at another ocean, clear across the country. A little bit surreal. Of course, Fisherman's Wharf is far more developed than Holyoke Wharf in Portland is. It's one of San Fran's big tourist draws with a large variety of museums, restaurants, an aquarium, a sea lion center, and a whole host of amusement park type attractions. I'd never been there before, and the guys and I spent the afternoon trying to squeeze everything there was to see and do into a few hours. Later, Kyle surprised us with dinner at the Blue Mermaid, a chowder house and bar with the most interesting and eclectic aged nautical decor. The food was amazing and we didn't get home until after eleven. By the time I got to bed, it was once again early morning hours, because the alcohol consumed over dinner had loosened my tongue. In my semi-sloshed state I revealed far more of the abuse I had endured than I ever would've sober. It was painful, it was tearful, but it was also very cathartic. I'm finding the more I talk about it, the easier it is to breathe.

Despite the very rocky start, I'm so fucking grateful Kyle pushed this. I feel, for the first time in twenty-five years, that I might have a chance of finding that sweet spot back—that special connection that Dorian and I used to share.

When I drive down into the parking garage under my building, I'm glad to see my spot open. Slipping my car in, I turn off the engine, and grab my purse. Walking around the car to get my carry-on from the trunk, I hear a noise that stops me in my tracks. *What the hell?* Whirling around, I scan the garage, but I can't see a thing. It sounded like a scraping or dragging of something over the concrete floor. I stand there for a few seconds, listening and looking, but I don't hear anything else. With a little more urgency, I pull my suitcase from the trunk and head for the elevator. A familiar rattling of the garage door opening breaks the silence, and looking over my shoulder I see one of my neighbors pull in. That makes me feel a little better. I was getting a little jumpy there.

I'm in luck, the elevator is already here. I step inside and press my floor number, already looking forward to a long shower and nap as the doors close. At the last minute, a foot wedges between the doors, stopping them from closing all the way. *Jesus.* Jumping back I trip over my carry-on and land on my ass, never taking my eyes off the doors that are slowly being pulled open.

"Are you okay?"

My neighbor from down the hall steps in and helps me to my feet.

"Jeff! Holy shit, yes I'm fine. Just a little … fuck, that's embarrassing," I ramble, rubbing my hands over my ass, which is definitely going to have bruises. "I heard something earlier, and then … Well, you scared me," I finish on a sheepish smile. I mean, not that I've ever been interested, the guy may be built like a Mack truck and have a face that makes Chris Hemsworth look like yesterday's leftovers, but he is dumb as a rock. No, the embarrassment is mostly for making a fool of myself, not that he'd probably notice, concern is written all over his face.

"Want me to go look?" he asks, indicating the garage, which is just visible between the closing elevator doors.

"No. No need. Guess I'm just tired, I'm hearing things."

An uneventful, albeit slightly uncomfortable elevator ride later, Jeff insists on carrying my suitcase and delivering me to my door. I don't have the heart to tell him the thing has wheels.

"Quit laughing. You're an awful friend and a worse therapist!"

Pam doesn't care, her rich, full-bodied laugh rings through the phone. "Then don't tell funny stories," is her retort.

I just finished telling her about my weekend, ending with my little adventure in the garage. Apparently my description of my encounter with my neighbor, Jeff, mainly me staring up from where my ass had landed on the elevator floor, was cause for great hilarity.

"You should at least be concerned for me, shouldn't you?" I complain, but it falls to deaf ears.

"Well, I'm glad you got yourself home in one piece," she says when she calms down. "And I mean that both emotionally and physically."

"Horrible friend," I mutter, as she starts laughing again.

"All joking aside, girl. You did pretty good. Dealing head on with the cops and the DA's office, discussing things that only a month or so ago would have you curling up and sucking your thumb. Not to mention the confrontation with Dorian, where I'm sure you were put through the emotional wringer again. Really—I'm proud of you," she says warmly.

"Yeah. I'm kind of proud of me too." I smile. "What I don't get is why, despite my greatest fear coming true, I still can feel such a sense of lightness?"

"Not sure what you mean? Your greatest fear?"

"It was hammered into me that if I ever said anything, I would lose my family because they would never believe me. How ironic that it happened just like that. They didn't believe me and I did lose them, but it doesn't feel like the devastation I expected. It doesn't feel hopeless. In a weird way, I even feel a little … vindicated, if that's even the right word."

"Listen, first of all you are an adult, you've lived through hell and survived. You are not the same insecure teenager that believed what she was told. You are not in a position anymore where all you know is dependency on your family. You've learned to take care of yourself, you don't *need* anybody. Which brings me to my next point." I can hear the smile in her voice. "You don't need anyone, but you sure as hell have found yourself someone. There is nothing as powerful as the feeling of having someone at your back, no matter what happens. You may not need Ike to be strong, but he makes you stronger anyway."

It's true. I'd like to think that I would've come to a point where I was able to confront and process the trauma in my life. But the truth is, I don't know if I would have if Ike hadn't come along and knocked some life into my heart.

"One last thing," Pam points out. "Thinking in absolutes is something a teenager does. It's either up or down, good or bad, and nothing in between. You know better now, so don't talk about losing your family just yet. That's an absolute and given the outcome of this weekend with Dorian, I'd venture to say that is way too premature a conclusion."

Food for thought, I think as I end the call with Pam. I've perhaps been a bit passive, waiting for my brothers to come to me. From what Dorian's given me to understand, learning what happened to me at the hands of our father, has significantly tilted their world on its axis. Nothing happens in isolation, and as much as I was a victim, they are too, in a sense. I've had a chance to survive. They haven't even started.

With those thoughts going through my mind, I grab some clothes for tonight and head for the bathroom. I never made it to the shower when I first came in. Exhaustion hit me hard and other than tucking my carry-on in the closet and tossing my purse onto the chair, I did nothing but collapse on top of my fully made bed—courtesy of Ike—and fall into a deep sleep.

One of the things I love about my short hair is how fast showers are. I used to have long hair, it's what Frank liked, and I hated it. It would take forever to get ready. As an act of defiance I chopped it off first chance I had, and I've kept it relatively short ever since. It literally takes me two minutes with the blow-dryer to whip it into shape. Since I don't wear more than maybe mascara and some lip gloss for make-up, it takes me no more than ten minutes to get ready.

A good thing, because by the time I got off the phone with Pam, I was already going to run late meeting up with Ike.

Snatching my purse off the chair where I'd dropped it, I hustle out the door, eager to get to The Skipper and Ike.

Since that big storm passed through, the weather has been calm, hardly any wind, but hot and humid. The moment I pull the door shut on my apartment, I can feel the shirt sticking to my back. Each apartment has its own thermostat, but the hallways and lobby of the building are always either too cold in the winter or too hot in the summer. Trying to save a buck, I guess. It's a little better outside, a cool, soft breeze coming from the water hits me the moment I open the door. Walking across the parking lot to get to the alley, I hear footsteps behind me. I turn around, but can't see anything. The moment I stop, the sound stops as well. I'm being paranoid. Shaking my head, I set off walking again, but this time at a faster pace. I tell myself it's because I'm late, but I'm listening with half an ear for any sound behind me.

When I reach the head of the alley, I relax a bit. From here I can see the pub's dumpster at the far end and the back end of Ike's bike sticking out from behind it. Suddenly the hair on my neck stands on end, just as the sound of steps picks up again. This time closer and moving fast.

Like a bat out of hell, I start running with the blood roaring in my ears. I don't hear anything but my own feet hitting the ground. I don't even take the time to look behind me. My eyes stay focused on that familiar bike, as I barrel down the alley.

I reach the dumpster, put my hand on the edge and am about to round it, when I'm suddenly yanked back. A large hand slaps over my mouth before I even have a chance to make a sound; the arm around my waist, pinning my arms, lifts me clear off the ground.

I can smell him. An unpleasant, yet familiar combination of sweat and Old Spice. *Bastard.* I try to bite the hand over my face, but I can't even open my mouth, he has it clamped so tightly. Struggling to get free, my legs kick out ineffectively.

"Did you really think you could escape me?" his dreaded voice mocks in my ear. "You were lucky your neighbor showed up when he did, but your luck has run out. You bitch ..." The last is said with such vehemence, I feel the spittle hit my cheek. "... I know all about your little visit to California. What did you think? That I'd let you walk away from that? That I wouldn't make you pay? Surely you know me better," he growls in my ear, and I know as sure as the sun rising in the morning, that I won't walk away from this. My struggles don't accomplish much as he starts backing me away from the safety of the pub, into the shadows of the alley.

Without warning, the back door on the other end of the dumpster slams open and suddenly I find my face shoved into its dirty wall. Here we're hidden from whoever is on the other side, dumping garbage over the edge. This is perhaps my one shot—my only chance to get away.

With every last bit of strength I use my legs to shove off the solid wall of the dumpster in front of me. In his struggle to keep his balance, his hand slips off my mouth for a second and the arm that was holding mine pinned to my side loosens slightly, but it's all I need.

"IKE!" I scream at the top of my lungs, as I manage to get a foothold on the ground and push myself back against him, swinging my elbow as hard as I can into his ribs.

Already off-balance, he trips back, falling and pulling me down with him.

"Help me!" I yell, but instead of one of the guys, Syd's head shows around the container. "Get help—GO!"

My one second of respite as my attacker catches his breath is up, and I am fighting with all I have to keep him from rolling me to the bottom.

"Let me go, you fucking whore!" With a massive shove, he throws me off him, scrambling to his feet. It's then that I realize he's trying to get away. Unfortunately for him, his leg got hurt when he fell, and he hobbles rather than runs away. Without thinking, I take off after him. With the sound of heavy footfalls coming up behind me, I know I'll have some back up. Which is why, without a moment's hesitation, I launch myself forward, jumping onto his back. I wrap one arm around and shove my fingers into his eye sockets.

"This ends now, you fucking son of a bitch," I screech, barely registering his howls of pain.

# CHAPTER TWENTY-TWO

## *Ike*

"Where's Viv?" Syd slides a fresh beer onto the bar in front of me. "I'm surprised she's not with you."

"She should be here any minute." I check my watch. She'd suggested meeting here at seven for a bite, it's seven-twenty now.

"How was she when you picked her up? Did everything go okay with her brother?" Syd's obviously been worried. Not really my story to tell, but I want to put her mind at ease at least.

"By the sounds of it, things went well, but I'm sure she's dying to tell you herself." I smile at her, hoping that was diplomatic enough.

When the door to the pub opens, I turn to the sound, but instead of Viv, who'd probably not come in that way I immediately realize, Tim walks in. He spots me and walks over to join me.

"Hey," Syd fills the silence that stretches between us since he sat down. "Can you get yourself a beer, Tim? I just have to get the garbage, it's overflowing."

"Sure thing," he responds, getting up and rounding the bar. Syd dives under the bar and comes up with two large bins.

"Want me to take care of that?" I offer her, as Tim busies himself drawing a beer from the tap.

"No need. I've got it," Syd throws over her shoulder as she carries her load out the back. "Just gonna round up the washrooms, as well."

Armed with a pint, Tim sits down beside me again.

"I just want—"

"I had no idea—" We start at the same time.

"You first." I nod at him.

Taking a deep breath in, he starts again. "Was gonna say, I just want to apologize. Viv ..." He shakes his head as his voice trails off. "I thought maybe there was something there. She didn't hesitate to make it clear, after ... well, you know ... it was a mistake. Still, I thought maybe one day." He slowly turns his head to face me. "It was an asshole thing to do, throwing it in your face. I can see the way she looks at you."

I let him finish before I respond. "Wasn't news to me. I'd suspected as much from some things she said, and after I had a chance to see you with her, I knew. I'm sorry I didn't see it before, but I won't lie and say that I would've kept my distance. Not for long anyway," I admit.

There's a tug on the side of his mouth that doesn't quite make it into a smile. "It's like that, is it? Fuck, I never thought I'd see the day."

I shrug my shoulders. "You're not the only one."

I take a sip of my beer, thinking about the truth of that statement. Never thought I'd allow myself to get so invested in someone, but I simply had no choice in the matter. I've fallen like a load of bricks.

"She's something else," Tim mumbles beside me, and instead of jealousy, I feel a pang of sadness for my friend.

"That she is," I agree.

A door slams in the back, followed by the sound of running feet.

"Ike!" Syd yells down the hall. I immediately jump into action at the panic I hear in her voice. The scrape of a stool behind me tells me Tim is right behind me as I take off down the hall toward Syd. "It's Viv," she manages when I get close. "Alley."

Without stopping, I run past her and barrel through the back door, trying to get a bead on Viv.

"Let me go, you fucking whore!" I hear coming from the other side of the dumpster. I don't think, I just start running. When I round it, I finally have eyes on the alley, and on Viv running after a limping man. I have no fucking idea what's going on, but I run full out in their direction when I see Viv jump on the guy's back, screaming.

I'm almost there when the large man tosses Viv off his back like she weighs nothing, and she lands on the ground with a loud smack. Before the guy has a chance to take off, I reach out, pull his hand away from his face and land a right hook, right in the jaw, knocking him on his ass. It's only then I see the blood already pouring down his face. Tim catches up and trusting he'll keep an eye on this asshole, I immediately turn to Viv, who's trying to sit up.

"Cops," she says, panting hard. "You've gotta call the cops. It's Frank."

"Are you okay?" She is my first concern. I see angry red marks on her face when I kneel down beside her. I have to fight the urge to turn around and finish the fucking bastard off.

"Yeah, yeah." She waves her hand impatiently. "Call the cops—call Bragdon."

"They're on their way." Arnie, who'd been in his usual spot at the bar earlier, seems to have followed us out, along with a few other regulars. All are standing around Frank, who has his bloody face covered with both his hands, swearing loudly about *the bitch* who blinded him. Even if he could see, there's no way he would dare make a move on her. Not with all of us surrounding him.

With Arnie's help, I pull Viv to her feet, turning her toward me, and folding her in my arms. "Fuck, babe. There went another twenty years. I'll be old before my time with you."

The little snort of amusement from the vicinity of my armpit, where Viv has tucked her face, lightens some of my worry.

"You took him down good," I can't hold back the pride in my voice.

"Took him down like a fucking linebacker," Arnie adds with a smirk on his face. "That's my girl."

I throw him a grin. "Back off old man. The girl is mine."

## Viv

An odd sense of déjà vu hits me as I look around the kitchen. Wasn't that long ago that most of these people were assembled, and once again it's as a result of the actions of my ex. This is hopefully the last time, though.

The police, in the form of Mike Bragdon, the EMTs, and Gunnar, who had been at home with the kids, all arrived at the same time. Apparently I've done some damage to Frank's eyes; something I want to feel guilty about but don't. Call me cold-blooded, but the man has gotten away with altogether too much since that fateful day I met him. No, I'm not going to feel guilty. This is the last time I'll have scrapes and bruises on my body at his hands. My right eye is swollen shut from the impact with the side of the dumpster and the rest of me bears the evidence of the struggle I waged to get away from him.

He's been carted off to the hospital, with a police cruiser following. According to Mike, they'll be charging him with assault and violating a restraining order. The latter is only considered a misdemeanor, but the assault is a felony. It'll be a tug-of-war as to where he'll be tried, since he already has a felony charge in California for the same offense, but I don't frankly care. Only thing that matters is that all of them combined will ensure he gets put away for a nice long time.

Tim had to hold Ike back when the idiot decided to threaten me with an assault charge. Good thing too, since he'd been strapped down to a stretcher already. He might've had real cause for complaint then.

I'd been quickly looked over and although the EMT examining me said it might not be a bad idea to get some x-rays done, I opted out. I've had enough bones broken, I know what it feels like. Not spending another second in the hospital at the hands of that man. Ike seemed to understand and assured the medic he'd keep an eye on me.

"Shall I get out the good stuff?" Syd's sitting on Gunnar's lap and elbows him in the stomach when he tries to glare at her. "It's a special occasion," she adds.

"That's what you say every time you start pouring a two hundred dollar bottle," he grumbles, only half-serious. "And you can't drink," he adds.

"Like I would. Geeze." Syd rolls her eyes for effect, as she pushes off and goes to fetch another bottle from Gunnar's prized collection of exclusive liquor. Gunnar kicked everyone out and closed the pub when he got here, other than Arnie who stayed behind, wanting to make sure I was all right. He's at the end of the table, a bemused look on his face.

Tim's sitting across from me, looking confused. Guess he doesn't know yet that Syd's expecting. Ike is beside me, his chair pulled as close as he can get it; his arm is slung over the back of my chair possessively. His other hand is holding one of mine, restlessly rubbing his thumb over my skin. Almost as if he wants to assure himself I'm still here.

"You okay?" I ask him softly. His eyes, that were staring off in the distance, turn to me. "You seem a little edgy. I'm fine, you know. It's over."

"I know. I'm good." His mouth forms a smile, but it's far from convincing.

Syd comes back in with a tray of shot glasses and a bottle, preventing me from prodding further. Probably not the best place and time to have a heart-to-heart anyway. Not in the kitchen with a room full of prying ears and eyes.

"Ah, fuck, Bird," Gunnar says when he spots the bottle on the tray. "Not the AsomBroso." He dramatically drops his head back and looks up at the ceiling.

"Why not? The bottle seemed appropriate. Looks a bit phallic, doesn't it? We can raise a glass to that cocksucker— may we never hear from him again."

Arnie and Tim burst out laughing at the swearword from Syd's mouth. Doesn't happen often, but when it does, it has maximum impact. I guess that's why Ike can't help but chuckle, even Gunnar has a smile teasing his lips. Besides, she's right: the bottle looks like a complete package, cock and balls.

When we finally head out, I'm half in the bag, but Ike stuck to one shot only. He's fishing the extra helmet from the saddlebag when I come up behind him and wrap my arms around his middle.

"Want to walk to the end of the wharf with me before we go?" I ask with my cheek pressed against his back. I feel his movements still, but it takes a while for him to answer.

"Sure."

Hanging the extra helmet off one of the handlebars, he grabs my hand. I twist it in his so I can entwine my fingers with his. When he looks down at me with a soft smile, I lean my head against his shoulder, and we walk onto the pier.

The sea is calm and peaceful, and the only wind is a gentle fresh breeze coming off the water. Much different than the last time we were out here, getting slammed about in the cruel water. Maybe that's why I feel the need to be out here, just to confirm it is over. That some of the turbulence of the past weeks has finally settled down.

## Ike

I wasn't kidding when I told Viv another twenty years was taken off my life.

Sitting in the kitchen of The Skipper, I wasn't quite able to join in the almost celebratory mood. My mind was stuck on the fact that I almost lost her twice now. Fine—perhaps a bit melodramatic in hindsight—but I can't quite seem to shake the fear I felt, seeing her wrestle with that big man. I think what probably bothers me most, is that every time she looks at me with near hero worship in her eyes, I'm thrown back to a time I used to see that look in my brother's eyes.

I know he idolized me when we were growing up. Followed me willingly into the Navy. If not for me, he wouldn't have been on that damn ship. He wouldn't have been at that fucking counter, fetching me my drink, when hell broke loose. He would've been in college, like my father wanted for him. Or already working at a safe place. That's where he should've been. My father reminded me often enough while he was still alive. Each time driving the dagger further home. Christ, there'd been times the guilt was almost too much.

That look of utter confidence, of complete trust, it doesn't seem right. It's a reminder I haven't earned it yet. I haven't trusted Viv with that dark period of my life.

As I'm walking down the wharf with her hand in mine and her head on my shoulder, I think perhaps it's time.

"Want to sit down for a bit?" I ask when we reach the end. There are no benches, but I sit down on the edge and pull Viv down with me. Our legs dangle over the side with the water far below us.

It's quiet this time of night. No squawking of the gulls or sounds of traffic in the distance like during the day. You might hear the occasional engine of a fishing boat returning late, but other than that, it's just the sound of the water moving against the pilings below us.

I wrap my arm around Viv and tuck her close to me.

"When my brother was twenty-four, he was assigned to the USS Cole. That was two months after me."

Viv raises her head from my shoulder and watches my face as I stare out into the ocean.

"Ben always was a happy-go-lucky kid. Would tag along behind me, which I didn't always appreciate growing up. I was more serious. But when he joined the Navy, I was proud of him. Later when he joined the crew on the USS Cole, I couldn't have been happier. That day, instead of heading to his bunk to get some sleep at the end of his shift, he looked for me in the galley, and found me. We didn't get a chance to see each other often, sometimes weeks at a time, so it was a treat when we were able to connect." I pause for a moment, trying to come up with the words, when Viv puts a hand on my chest.

"You don't have to tell me," she says quietly.

I lean in and kiss her softly before turning back to the water. "I do. I need to tell you how when a bomb blew a forty-by-sixty-foot hole in the hull of the vessel, my brother was getting me a drink. I'd been too fucking lazy to get it myself. While he was charming his way to the front of the line, a couple of suicide-bombing terrorists pulled up to the side of the ship and blew themselves up. My brother's was one of the seventeen other lives they took with them."

She lays her head back down on my shoulder and wraps both her arms around me, not saying a thing, and I'm grateful for that.

"It took me a while, but I found him. The water was trying to pull him out to sea, but I held on to him. I wasn't going to let go." I feel the soft shaking of her shoulders under my arm. She's crying and I feel bad for being the cause of that.

"I can't remember much else. All I know is that my parents were never the same."

I don't even realize I have tears running down my face until Viv crawls in my lap, facing me, with her legs wrapped around my back and her hands wiping at the wetness on my cheeks. I notice the water behind her, and promptly wrap my arms tightly around her, worried she might fall back.

With her hands firmly against my cheeks, she tilts my head to look at her. "You won't let me fall … I trust you."

Overcome with emotion, I press my face in the crook of her neck. She fucking trusts me. The kicker is, for the first time I really believe it.

Don't know if it's been hours, or merely minutes, that we sit at the edge of the water, wrapped around each other, holding the other up. By the time Viv climbs off my lap and pulls me to my feet, I feel empty; yet at the same time, as full as I've ever felt.

# CHAPTER TWENTY-THREE

*Viv*

"What's on the menu today?" Ike's sleep-roughened voice mumbles in my neck.

Every morning I wake up either sprawled on top of his body, or on my side, with him wrapped around me from behind. There seems to be no personal space in either of our beds. We've been alternating between places, but I have to admit, I like his place better. Better mattress, gorgeous big bathroom, and a deck off the kitchen that catches the morning sun—perfect to enjoy that first cup of coffee on. Beats my little three-by-three balcony any day.

Funny how for two people who insisted they didn't want any attachment, we seem to have grown attached at the hip, or thereabouts. I mean, I had no clue sex could be so addictive and so ... satisfying. Ike at twenty-five would probably have killed me, going by the stamina he seems to have at forty-two. Even more intense the past couple of days, since we were out on the pier. We've talked quite a bit too: Ike about his brother, his father's blame, and his own guilt. I opened up a little bit more about my life with Frank after the events of Sunday night. Not easy talks by all means, but cleansing in a way and more intimate than any sexual interaction we've had. There's something about sharing yourself with someone who shares back. The feeling of being completely exposed, physically and emotionally, the most terrifying and yet exhilarating feeling at the same time.

I snuggle a little deeper into Ike and his arms tighten around me.

"Dino is in charge. I'm not sure whether he's gonna throw something else on the menu. May just be our regular fare, depending on his mood."

I groan loudly when my body lets me know in no uncertain terms that it's time to get up. I don't want to. I want to stay snuggled in my warm, safe cocoon.

"Where're you going?"

Ike sounds like he was drifting off again, when I untangle myself from his limbs and grudgingly swing my legs over the side of the bed. Leaning back, I give him a quick kiss, but he's not letting me get away with that. Dragging me on top of him as he rolls onto his back, he devours my mouth with his lips and tongue.

"Mmmm. Much better," he says through a grin.

"Won't be for long if you don't let me go. I'm about to pee all over you," I point out my increasing state of urgency.

Reluctantly he lets me go and I can feel his heavy-lidded eyes follow me to the bathroom. I flip down the seat, thinking I really should work on getting him a bit more *domestically trained*, but I honestly can't be bothered. Seriously? In the grand scope of things, what does a pile of dirty clothes next to a hamper, toothpaste squeezed from the middle, or a seat left up, really matter? Growing up with all boys, I've learned to be grateful for a man actually lifting the seat.

Thinking about the boys, I talked to Dorian yesterday, who is flying into Boston with Kyle on Friday night. Ike suggested maybe I stay with him, and let those two take my apartment. I still haven't talked to any of the others. My resolution to make the first approach stalled after receiving a rather icy message on my phone from my mother, wanting to know when I was going in to see my father, he's been asking about me. I'd been stunned at first and angry after. It's like what I told them wasn't heard at all. In talking to Pam about it, she tried to explain that perhaps my mother had become adept at ignoring what she doesn't want to see or has no control over, as a means of coping, over the years. That maybe given the current circumstances—my father's health, the subsequent move from and sale of the house—my mother may simply be unable to process anything more. Denial is the name of the game.

I pull off a wad of toilet paper, when the bathroom door opens and Ike casually walks in.

"Ike!" I almost scream, having been caught in *mid-wipe*.

"What?" he says, pulling open the shower door and turning on the tap, before turning to me, bending down and kissing the top of my head.

Dumbfounded, I'm totally tongue-tied and slightly mortified as he stops to inspect his teeth in the mirror, before squirting a goodly amount of toothpaste, from the middle, onto his toothbrush. With the toothbrush in his mouth, he proceeds to shove down his boxers and step into the shower. Toothbrush and all.

"Babe ..." Ike's head peeks around the shower door, catching me with my mouth still open, his own mouth foaming with toothpaste, "Don't flush. I'll do it after," before he disappears again.

That jump-starts me. Unfolding from the crouched position I'd taken on, I pull up my undies, and defiantly push the lever. The muffled swearing as I see him jump around to avoid the scorching hot spray through the frosted glass, brings a smile to my face. *Serves you right.*

I slip back into the bedroom, put on some leggings and a T-shirt from my overnight bag and head downstairs to the kitchen.

That's where Ike finds me after his shower, bent over the newspaper I'd grabbed off the front step and sipping on the fresh coffee I made.

"Gonna make you pay for that, you minx," he whispers, his lips skimming the back of my neck, sending tingles down my spine. Pretending to ignore him, I watch his back as he makes his way over to coffeepot, secretly enjoying the view of his wide back and tight ass moving under his dress shirt and jeans. With the sleeves rolled up, I can see the ripple of muscles in his strong forearms, giving me another little shiver.

"You deserved it; walking in on me like that," I finally say, straightening up. The slight tilt of his mouth and the raised eyebrow when he turns around should irritate me. Instead, it makes me feel all warm and mushy.

"Babe," he says in a serious tone. "I've seen you naked. Know every square inch of your body. Quite intimately, I might add."

"It's not the same," I lamely counter.

"Okay then, how's this?" he says as he slowly stalks back to me. "I have nothing to hide from you. Not anymore." He reaches me and slowly swings me around on the stool, inserting himself between my legs and wrapping his arms around my back. "There's nothing you need to hide from me. I've never met anyone I wanted to share everything with, until you. So when I walk into the bathroom when you're in there—don't see it as me intruding—see it as me wanting to be close to you, regardless of where you are, or what you're doing."

"Well," I huff, unimpressed by the smirk on his face as he leans in for a touch of his lips to my nose before going back to fixing his coffee.

Definitely warm and mushy.

-

"It might be after dinner before I get to the pub tonight," Ike says on his way out the door. "I'm presenting the new design to our customer this afternoon, and David warned me he might invite us out after."

I watch him walk down the steps and get on his bike before he turns with a grin. "Later, babe."

"Good luck," I manage before he roars off, with a last lift of his hand in departure. Since I followed him home in my car last night, I don't have to rush so he can drop me off. I close the door and head to the kitchen to finish clearing away the breakfast dishes, and sipping the last cup of coffee, before I fetch my overnight bag from the bedroom. I still have about an hour before I have to start prepping at The Skipper, but I want to get home so I can shower and get ready.

By the time I pull into the parking garage, I have the air conditioner in my car going at full blast. Damn it's going be another hot one today. The stale and stagnant air in the garage has my shirt stuck to my body before I even get to the elevators, and I brace myself for the heat of the building. Ike's house is nice and airy. With windows that can be opened to create a cross-breeze at night to blow out the stale air from the day. Nice.

I'm still considering the benefits of Ike's place over my apartment when movement at my front door has me lift my head.

"Nolan?"

My brother slowly pushes himself up from where he'd been sitting with his back against my door. I don't think he's ever been here before. Nervous anticipation and tempered hopefulness wreak havoc on my stomach as I cautiously approach him.

"Can we talk inside?" he asks uncharacteristically timid, his eyes barely meeting mine.

"Sure," I mumble, digging in my bag for the keys.

Once inside, I walk ahead and toss my bag into the bedroom, before turning to find Nolan watching me, his back against the closed door. "Want some coffee?" I ask, a little too eager. Coffee is a good icebreaker, although I wonder if it's the smartest choice, given that I'm already almost jumping out of my skin with nerves.

"Sure. If you have time."

"Of course," I lie, heading toward the coffeemaker in an attempt to hide my tell-all face from him.

"You're probably wondering—"

"So what brings you—" My eyes shoot up when I notice we're talking at the same time. He's standing at the counter looking a little sheepish. "Go ahead," I say. "I have a feeling you were about to answer my question anyway." I try to keep my hands busy by pulling mugs down from the cupboard and getting half-and-half from the fridge.

"I'm sorry," he starts and immediately has my attention, making me turn around. He is leaning with his back against the counter, his hands holding onto the edge behind him. Looking altogether mighty uncomfortable.

"Want to sit down?" I offer, but he shakes his head.

"I'd best stand, but you might want to sit down for this." His strong-lined face looks very serious when he says this, which is why I walk over to my couch and curl up in a corner, a throw pillow tucked to my stomach. Protection, for what it's worth. I watch Nolan run a hand through his hair, leaving it sticking up in every direction and more than anything, that makes me uneasy. Nolan is the meticulous one in the family. Perfect grooming, perfect job, perfect house, and before his wife left him, he had what looked to be a perfect family as well. Now he looks—rattled.

"For years, I'd successfully pushed down that small voice, telling me something was off. I should've said something then, but ..." His voice trails off as he obviously struggles to find words, and a burning sensation starts in the pit of my stomach slowly crawling up my throat. "I saw him come out of your room one night," he says softly, his eyes on me dark with guilt.

"I saw you too," I whisper, barely moving my lips that feel numb.

"He ... he had just ... Ahhh!" In frustration he screams, slamming his fist on the counter. "I can't even say it. Can't fucking say the words. The thought I was looking at him ... at you ... right after he ... raped you? It makes me so sick. But you know what makes me even sicker? That it wasn't the first time. Part of me always suspected, part of me *knew* he lied to me when he walked out of your room. I just ..." He closes his eyes, shaking his head from side to side. "I'm so, so sorry. It doesn't make up for anything. *God*—as if it could. I should've jumped in for you at Mom's house. Should've fucking told everyone what I'd already suspected was the truth. I guess I'd convinced myself, over the years, I'd been wrong. Had seen things that weren't there. Fuck, the guilt has been eating me alive."

I say nothing. I'm not even sure I can verbalize what I'm feeling. Clutching that pillow as if it were a lifeline, I mutely watch as tears track down Nolan's face. Rather detached, I note that I've never seen him cry before. Not any of my brothers, really.

"I don't know what to say," I blurt out stupidly, immediately regretting having said anything at all. Because, it's as if those few words shake me out of indifference and straight into emotional overload. That burning sensation in my stomach turns into an inferno, and has me jump off the couch and running for the bathroom. I make it just in time.

On my knees, leaning over the bowl, the tears catch up, and I discover that sobbing and retching at the same time is not a good combination. Gasping for air, I don't even notice Nolan has come into the bathroom, until I find a cold cloth pressed on the back of my neck and a large hand lifting the hair from my forehead.

"Oh, Viv. I'm so sorry I—"

"I stink," I announce, not sure if I could handle another apology right now. Not that he wouldn't have noticed by himself, because ... well, I stink.

"I don't care," is the curt response, before he turns me around and uses the cloth to wipe my face. I don't know why that action should surprise me, he raised, or at the very least helped raise, a child of his own. I'm sure he's wiped a face or two in his day. He surprises me even further when he pulls me into his arms. Nolan. The brother who never was one for public displays of any kind.

"Just let me, okay?" he mumbles when I stiffen a little.

I let myself forget about being gross and smelly, and allow him to hug me. By the time he sets me back gently, the normal stern expression is back on his face.

"I'm making you toast. Get in the shower," he orders. "You stink."

## Ike

Been a long-ass day.

It started when I came into the office this morning. I could hear swearing coming from behind the reception desk. Hillary, the unflappable grandmother of two David hired on in short order to replace Samantha, was cursing at the printer and banging it with a stapler. This morning of all mornings, the printer had decided to eat paper instead of spit it out. Normally a pretty easy fix, but whatever Hillary had done by the time I walked in had permanently sealed its fate. Since there were eight proposal packages to prepare, I had to turn around and try to find us a new printer on very short notice. David was in Boston this morning for a brief meeting before he would join me for the presentation this afternoon, so it was up to me. Two hours out of my day I wouldn't be getting back any time soon, and I still had finishing touches to make to my design.

The rest of the day had been more of the same: last minute glitches to be ironed out, details to be considered, and loose ends to be tied up. By the time David walked into my office, I was already worn thin, wishing I'd never left Viv's warm body this morning.

"Ready?" he asks, a bit too chipper.

"As ready as I'll be," I grouch, not good at working with an empty stomach. The only response to my sour mood is a raised eyebrow from David.

"Remind me to tell you about my day later," I offer as explanation.

The proposal in hand, along with the PowerPoint presentation I'd managed to throw together last minute, I follow him into the boardroom where our new clients are waiting. Thank God it went off without a hitch. The proposal accepted, with handshakes and backslaps, and before I knew it, we were roped into the dreaded celebratory dinner.

I don't socialize well. Sitting around a table just shooting the shit with people you have little in common with is not my strong suit. In fact, I feel comfortable saying a visit to my dentist for a root canal would be preferable. When I finally manage to excuse myself during a lull in the very boring conversation about the stock market, something I know blissfully little about, it's already past eleven.

Walking into The Skipper, I'm not even sure if Viv's still going to be here. She was supposed to open this morning, which normally means an early night. Still, I spot her right away, not behind the bar, but sitting perched on a stool in an animated conversation with Arnie. Matt, who is leaning over the bar listening in, is the first one to spot me.

"Beer?"

"Please." I barely manage to get the word out and my body jolts back with the impact of a very excited Viv, jumping into my arms. "Whoa, babe."

"And?" she asks, a big smile on her face as she wraps her arms and legs around me. My hands tuck under her ass to keep her there. Not a hardship. She feels good clinging to me, and I can't stop my own smile from spreading.

"They approved," I answer, knowing she was asking about the design.

"Yay! That calls for a celebration." She hops down, turns to the bar and slaps her hand down. "Round of shots!"

I step in behind her and slide my arms around her stomach, trapping her against the bar. "Babe, I'm thinking you started your celebration without me."

"Oops," she says, as she twists her head around to look at me, a wide, goofy grin on her face. Of course I have to kiss her, something she seems quite willing to participate in. She tastes like beer and Viv, and I get lost instantly. The hooting and hollering around us is just about the only thing stopping me from laying her down on the bar and tasting all of her, and I reluctantly break our kiss. The little whimper from her lips tells me she's as far gone as I am.

"Gonna drink my beer and you need some coffee. Don't want you to fall asleep on me when I finally have my way with you, when we go do some celebrating of our own."

Her beautiful, clear eyes darken as her pupils dilate with hunger. *That's right, baby.*

Next thing I know, Viv has roped Arnie, myself, and Matt into a mean game of euchre. Of course with frequent interruptions when Matt has to pour drinks. I don't notice time slipping away until Matt locks the door behind the last person, except for Arnie that is.

"I'm out guys. I need my beauty sleep." The old geezer winks and gives Viv a hug, Matt a wave, and grabs me by the shoulder. "Walk me to the door, son."

I do as asked and follow him. "She's had a tough day. Ask her about it," he says turning to me at the door. He immediately puts up his hand to silence me before I can even ask what happened. "Ask *her*. Make her tell you. She looks happy enough, but it's only on the outside." He unlocks the door and steps outside, but before I have a chance to say anything, he repeats, "*Ask.*"

So I say nothing, simply nod at Arnie, and close and lock the door behind him.

With all three of us, it takes only ten minutes to clean up. Viv's in the kitchen loading up the dishwasher for an overnight load, and Matt is walking out the back door with the garbage. When he comes back in I intercept him.

"We can lock up," I suggest, trying to keep a poker face.

"Sure thing," Matt says, a small smile betraying he knows exactly where my mind is at. He's a guy, after all.

When I lock the back door and turn around to join Viv in the kitchen, she is standing in the doorway, her hands on her hips, and a grin on her face.

"What are we doing?" She tries to act innocent, but can't quite mask the coy tone of her voice.

"What we didn't finish earlier," I tell her as I stalk toward her, the shiver running through her visible at a distance. Reaching her, I bend down and pick her up over my shoulder before making my way toward the bar. Viv doesn't offer any resistance, no yelling or complaints, just laughs her deep smoky chuckle that sets my blood on fire.

# CHAPTER TWENTY-FOUR

## Ike

With all the lights off, it's just the indirect glare from the lamp posts on the wharf that illuminate the bar.

"Get naked," I tell her when I set her carefully back on her feet. She's about to protest when I pull my shirt over my head and toss it aside, waiting for her move. It takes her a few seconds, but once her decision is made, it takes her only a few more to get herself totally, buck-ass naked. If I thought my hard-on was uncomfortable in my jeans before, the remainder of my blood surging to my cock at the sight of her in front of me, makes it outright painful. I carefully unbutton the offensive jeans, but only to create a bit more room. What I have in mind first, only requires my mouth.

Her breath hitches as I grab her by the hips and lift her up onto the bar. Gently I push her back and swing her legs up so she is lying stretched out across the bar. Like an offering. She looks at me intently as I caress every inch of her glorious pale body with my eyes. My hand follows, tracing the dips and valleys of her skin, where the diffuse light from outside touches her.

"Isaac ..." she moans softly. My name from her lips is like a trigger. Bending slightly over her body, my mouth finds hers. Licking my way between her lips, I eat at her mouth hungrily, as my hand never stops moving across her skin.

"You're so fucking slick," I growl into her mouth when my fingers find her warm, wet folds.

263

"Honey ... please." Viv pulls her mouth away and arches her back off the gleaming wood of the bar.

"Stay," I instruct her, sliding my fingers from her and raising them to my mouth for an appetizer. Her eyelids heavy, I see her breath hitch as she watches me.

I grab the closest chair, shove a few stools out of the way and sit down, my mouth now at level with the bar. Viv's mouth falls open when I swing her legs around and place her feet on my shoulders on either side of my head. *Fucking perfect.*

"Ike ..." she breathes, and I watch as she pushes herself up on her elbows.

"You take my breath away."

Her face softens and her mouth tilts up at the ends, but I don't give her a chance to say anything. I keep my eyes on hers as I pull her closer and open my mouth over her gorgeous pink, lush pussy. I'm insatiable. Her scent and her taste stir my appetite for her. I tease and play her with my lips and teeth, pulling back each time her hips lift up, begging for completion. I'm as close to coming as she is. I slide two fingers inside her, and with my other hand, I pull my cock free. When she sees me stroking myself, her inside walls spasm around my fingers, and her teeth bite her plump bottom lip.

"Come for me, baby," I growl, tugging hard at my cock as the fingers of my other hand furiously pump inside her. My tongue flicks out over her clit lightly, but just enough to send her over the edge on a moan. With her pussy still pulsing around my fingers and her taste lingering on my tongue, I let myself come in my hand.

Gently dropping her legs, I stand up and bend over her flushed body, pressing my lips to her belly.

"Beautiful siren," I mumble against her soft skin.

# Viv

*Holy shitballs,* goes through my mind as I catch my breath.

"So how was your day?" he says. The question so totally catching me off guard, I flop down over Ike's chest and bust out laughing.

I'm still trying to breathe after my second explosive climax of the night. With Ike still lodged solidly inside me, his deep chuckle vibrates in my ear.

After our little, erm—encounter in the pub, and after I finished disinfecting the entire bar—something I felt could not be left until morning, we ended up at my place. Closer and therefore more convenient for round two. Something Ike had set his mind on, and I have to admit, I wasn't all that adverse to. This time starting slow and sweet, but ending with me riding him furiously. As a result, I'm now a little raw and a lot tired.

A quick peek shows it's two-thirty in the morning, and I groan. I'm getting too old for these late nights. Luckily Syd is in early tomorrow to do her own prep for the Thursday special, so I can sleep in a little longer.

"Babe ... your day?"

I push myself up so I can take in his fabulous face. The heavy brows, startling eyes, and the full lips, now partially hidden by the rapidly growing beard, like a delicious little surprise. The same lips that are right now slightly tilted in amusement.

"Right," I say, even though the last thing I particularly want to do is to rehash my morning. *Fast, like ripping off a Band-Aid*, I tell myself. "Nolan came by to apologize," I start in my breeziest voice. "He told me he'd suspected something was going on, but didn't want to believe it. He was sorry he didn't have my back." I can feel Ike's body going rigid under mine, but decide to ignore it. "He offered to talk to my mother and the others, but I told him no."

"No?" Ike's voice is clipped.

"No," I confirm. "I've decided it's up to them to figure out I'm telling the truth, it would be worse if they only believed me because they believe Nolan. Does that even make any sense?"

"It does," he says immediately, much gentler this time.

The soft stroke of his large hand over my back soothes the tears that have started dripping down my face. Dammit.

"I still want to pound my fist into his face," he admits, making me snort.

"Stand in line. I'm so angry with him. Sad too, and sick, but mostly just angry, and I don't really know what to do with that."

There. I've said it out loud. I'd talked a little with Arnie tonight when he remarked I looked sad. Not that I went into detail, I'd just mentioned that something had happened that made me confused about what I actually felt. Wasn't sure whether I was sad or something else. Arnie had listened patiently to my confusion, and suggested it wasn't so strange to have mixed emotions. He had brought up the idea that even love and hate, two of the strongest emotions we can experience, are often only a hair's breadth apart and can sometimes exist at the same time. It got me thinking.

"Time," Ike says sagely. "I figure it's one of those things you can't really force a decision on, one way or another. So you let time settle it for you. Trust your own heart in this, my love."

"I know ..." I let my voice trail off. I do know—it's just that trust is so very hard to give. Even to my own heart.

Exhausted, physically and emotionally, I drift off. My body heavy and lethargic on his.

My alarm clock says it's after eleven when I wake up to an empty bed. I have to look again to make sure. *Fuck.* Whipping my blankets back, I dart into the bathroom to take care of business. Dammit, I had hoped to have some time to do much needed grocery shopping this morning, but now I'd be hard-pressed to make it to the pub in time for noon. I pee, brush my teeth, and am about to hop in the shower when my phone rings from the bedroom. Naked, I hurry to my nightstand and snatch it up without looking at the screen.

"Hello?" I answer breathlessly

"Did you sleep well?" Ike wants to know.

"You turned off my alarm."

"I did," he admits casually. "You obviously needed sleep since you didn't even move when I got up this morning. So I turned off your alarm and gave Syd a heads up. She says she'll be fine until three, when she has to go pick up the kids from school."

I have a healthy head of steam building up. It's not sitting right with me that he makes decisions for me without asking.

"You turned off my alarm," I repeat.

"I thought we'd gone over that already," his sardonic answer, only serving to fire me up more.

"You called my work, rearranged my schedule, and you turned off my alarm! Why is it every fucking man in my life wants to manage me? What is it about me that makes you all believe I can't think for myself?"

My little tirade is met with silence. A very pregnant silence. I'm starting to feel the head of steam dissipating, leaving behind a dull throb, and consider I may have overreacted a bit. Finally I hear Ike.

"I gather you didn't read my note," he says, followed by, "I'm not going to make excuses for trying to take care of you, which is what I was intending, but don't make me out to be like the assholes who purposely controlled and hurt you. I don't deserve that."

Before I have a chance to respond, I hear a click as he hangs up.

When I flop back onto the bed, thoroughly disgusted with myself, I hear the crinkling of paper. There, right on Ike's pillow, is a note I completely missed in my haste. Well, double damn.

> *Morning, beautiful.*
> *I hope you don't mind I turned off your alarm. I wish I could've stayed in bed with you.*
> *Believe me when I say there's no place I'd rather be.*
> *I thought about what you said last night, about feeling angry, sad, and sick all at the same time, and I realize there is little I can do to help you work through that but listen. And maybe buy you a few extra hours of much needed sleep.*
> *No need to panic at the time, Syd says she's going to stay until three.*
> *Love, Ike*

My stomach lurches at the realization I completely fucked up. Worse, I really have no valid excuse.

I went totally off the deep end, when all he tried to do was be considerate and sweet. So very, very sweet that a lump of regret gets stuck in my throat. It hasn't escaped me how he signed off. It's not the first time he seems to slip that word in, and somehow I don't think he does so lightly. What do I do now?

*Stupid question.* I still have the phone in my hand and quickly dial his number. I'm about to hang up after the fourth ring, when I hear his voice.

"Viv," he says softly. Any trace of anger is gone from his voice. I'm *such* an idiot.

"I'm sorry. I was ... I feel ... Aw shit, I have no excuse. None. Nada." My voice cracks and I'm furiously blinking to stave off tears.

"Viv, I get it. I got pissed, thought about it, and was just about to call you back."

"You were?"

"Look, I never considered how it might come across as controlling, and I should have. With you, I should've had more care."

I wince when I hear him say that. "Please, it makes me feel like you can't be yourself around me, and I would hate that. Just be you. You're amazing and I'm an ass." The low rumble of his laughter sounds good and instantly makes me feel better.

"Hardly." I hear the smile in his voice. "Although the one you own is one of my favorite parts on your body."

"Isaac?"

"Love it when you say my name." His voice hums in appreciation. "I wish I didn't have a boss waiting in the boardroom for me. I wish I could whip back there and show you how much."

"Go. Go to your meeting," I say with a smile. "I'll see you tonight?"

"Fuck yeah, you'll see me tonight: it's Thursday night special," he jokes.

"I'll keep some warm. Later, Ike."

"Later," he says, pausing for a moment. "Love you, honey."

I'm still sitting here five minutes after he hangs up, my mouth open, and a flock of butterflies turning loops in my stomach.

# Ike

"You coming?"

David sticks his head inside my office, where I've been alternately smiling and kicking my own ass for blurting that out. It's not something that rolls easily off my tongue. Not ever. But it felt right, so I let it roll. Right into a deadly silent phone.

"Ike?"

Right. David.

"On my way," I say, much more together than I feel.

I get through the meeting, barely managing to keep on topic, David throwing me questioning glances. I'm about to step into my office when he calls out behind me.

"Ike, hold up a sec?"

I pause in the doorway, allowing him to catch up.

"Are you okay? You were notably *absent* in there," he points out, luckily not too unfriendly. I step aside and wave him into my office, closing the door behind him. He sits down across from my desk and watches me curiously as I slip behind it.

"I think I fucked up," I blurt out, needing an unbiased opinion.

"How so?"

"Viv. We had a ... misunderstanding," I search for the right word. "Over the phone. I hung up angry. She called back and I told her I love her." I wait for his reaction, but only see a look of confusion on his face.

"Sorry? That's it? I'm still waiting to hear how you fucked up," he says shaking his head.

"It's too soon. She's been through hell. Fuck, she's still going through hell, and I just dumped that on her. Probably the last thing she needs." I drop my head in my hands, pulling on my hair.

David's laugh isn't subtle. It's insistent, obnoxious, and irritating the crap out of me. When I lift my head to glare at him, willing him to shut up, he doesn't seem impressed. Finally it reduces to a more tolerable chuckle, and he leans forward, planting his elbows on my desk.

"First of all, you're an idiot," he says.

Goddammit, I knew it.

"Secondly, women generally enjoy declarations of love. Especially coming from the man they've been spending a shitload of time with. She may not have been ready to hear it, but you can bet your bike she likes it."

"She didn't say a damn thing. Mind you, I didn't give her much of a chance before I hung up, but it came as a bit of a shock to me too," I admit grudgingly. *I'm turning into such a fucking chick.*

"I bet," he chuckles. "You haven't fallen, you've plummeted. Probably a shock to your system, and I bet she'll be over the shock much sooner than you."

I hate to admit it, but he's possibly right. I am shocked and slightly disturbed at what came out of my mouth. And still—I meant it. I don't want to take it back. I know she's still dealing with a lot, and the last thing I want is to put extra pressure on her. But I also just told her the other day that I wasn't going to hide anything from her.

271

"Is it too soon?" The question slips out before I can catch it. I sit back, folding my arms over my chest and brace for David's mockery. He doesn't leave me waiting very long.

"And that brings me to my final point." David leans back in his chair, mimicking my movements exactly. "You. Are. An. Idiot." He clearly emphasizes every word, setting my teeth on edge.

I'm about to object when my phone, which I'd left on my desk during the meeting earlier, alerts me to a text. I reach out for it, but David beats me to it, breaking out in a big smile when he looks at the screen and stands up.

"Case in point," he says, as he hands me my phone and walks out of the office.

On the screen is a message from Viv: a smile emoticon and a little heart.

Don't ask me why I pull into the Ford dealership on my way home. I've been managing fine with just my bike since the old truck died. Granted, I haven't gone through the winter on two wheels yet, given that I was traveling most of the time. If I couldn't take the bike, the company would cover a rental car wherever I was sent.

It's an impulse. One that I don't really care to examine too closely but am sure has something to do with the fact that for the first time in many years, I'm looking ahead further than my next project. Fuck, I got the house done, might as well have something to put in the garage too. Still plenty of room for the bike, even with a second car in there. The moment I walk into the showroom, a slick middle-aged salesman tags me, walking up with his hand out in greeting.

An hour later, I've parked my bike in the garage and wait for the complimentary shuttle to fetch me and take me back to the dealership, where I've just bought last year's model

Expedition off the lot. Pretty good deal too, decked out with all the added options, but since it had been a floor model, I managed to negotiate a decent price. The fact that I don't need any financing and plan to pay on the spot, doesn't hurt either. My whole life I've had little cause to spend the money I earned, and I earn a decent living. First major expense had been the renovation to the house, and although it put a substantial dent in my bank account, it still leaves a solid enough cushion.

From the dealership I head straight to The Skipper, where I slip it into a parking spot as far away from other cars as I can find. Call me anal, but it would really fucking suck if some dumb idiot, half drunk from a night at the bar, would put a dent in it.

Ten minutes later, I have Viv by the hand and am dragging her through the alley.

"Ike! I'm working, I can't just take off like this," she complains halfheartedly. The other half is trying to hold her giggles in check. I found her in the kitchen and with my arms around her, I lift two hands—ten fingers—to Dino. Smart guy that he is, he clues in immediately and waves me out of there.

"I told you, I've gotta show you something. It'll only take a minute."

We cross the parking lot, and I stop beside the flawless, dark green SUV, with the kick-ass shiny rims, Viv looks at me oddly.

"What am I looking at?" she asks in a mock-whisper, only to continue in her normal voice. "I mean I *know* it's a car. By the looks of it pretty new, but why are we looking at it?"

"It's a Ford Expedition and I bought it." I'm fucking excited, like a kid on Christmas morning, and I sound like an idiot. Last time I felt anything close to this was when I bought my bike. That was the start of a new life for me. *Shit.* I guess this is too. When I turn to face Viv, she's not looking at the truck, she's looking at me. And she's wearing a funny little grin.

"You bought a car—"

"An Expedition," I correct her. *She* drives a car; *I* ride a bike or drive a man-sized vehicle.

"Okay," she says slowly, obviously indulging me. "You bought an Expedition. Just now?" I nod in response.

"Drove straight here from the lot."

Viv's face softens and her eyes turn liquid. "Because you wanted to show me?"

"I did," I admit a tad defensively, waiting for her to point out my uncharacteristically weird behavior. She would be right. Can't say that anything I've done today would fall under my *normal* behavior. The welcome slide of her arms around my waist drags me out of my self-examination, and mine immediately wrap around her back, pulling her close. Her head tilts back and her smile lights up the dark parking lot.

"You bought a ca—an *Expedition*," she says with a snort before she turns serious, her eyes like two big question marks in her face. "And you said you loved me."

"Love," I point out softly.

"Sorry?"

"Present tense. As in, I love you, Vivian Lestar."

Her eyes go liquid again, but it's the little smile stealing over her face that settles in my chest. David knows his shit.

"I—" Viv barely gets a word out before she's interrupted.

"Viv! Phone!" Dino's voice rolls over the parking lot, just as he appears at the top of the alley. When he spots us, he adds at a slightly lower volume, "Emergency."

# CHAPTER TWENTY-FIVE

*Viv*

The moment we walk into the hospital waiting room, the tension hits me like a concrete wall, and I have trouble getting the first word out. Luckily, Ike insisted on coming with me, and with his arm around my waist, tucking me close, he faces off with my family.

"How is he?" Getting straight to the point, his eyes focus on Nolan, the one person not glaring daggers at us.

"Semi-conscious, confused, and combative, so they've had to sedate him to examine him. It's likely he'll be staying here, he broke his hip," Nolan replies. "Once the orthopedic surgeon has had a chance to look at him, they'll decide what needs to be done."

I finally manage to speak, focusing only on him. "What happened?"

"Like you care." The deriding comment comes from my mother, her face twisted in pain and anger. I barely recognize her.

"Mom," Nolan softly admonishes her before turning to me. "They couldn't find him in his room when they came to give him his medication for the night. Took them fifteen minutes to find him at the bottom of the stairs, tangled up in his walker, in the stairwell. He was confused and said he was looking for someone when he got lost."

Both Owen and Aaron are uncharacteristically quiet. They sit on either side of Mom, like quiet sentries. I don't

275

know what's going through their minds; where my mother is openly hostile, the two of them now seem to avoid looking at me at all.

I don't want to be here. I don't really know why I came to begin with. When Nolan called the pub, after he couldn't reach me on my cell, he'd been on his way to the hospital and didn't know much. Only that my father had a bad fall and was taken by ambulance. I guess it was conditioning, or maybe obligation, that had me grab my bag and follow Ike to his new truck. Maybe I harbored hope that somehow this would be an opportunity to bridge the divide in my family. But the animosity that hit me the moment I walked into the waiting room with Ike, brought me back down to earth. Brutally so.

I'm not sure how I feel about my father. I try not to think about him, but that's kind of hard under the circumstances. It's just so confusing to love and hate at the same time. I tried picking one and sticking with it, but it didn't last long. The thin line separating them was easily blurred. So sitting here beside Ike, who gently guided me to a chair and sat down beside me, feels like a lie. Yet leaving is not even an option.

"Okay, baby?" Ike's soft voice sounds close to my ear. I have my eyes closed, it seems the only protection I have from the resentment hanging thick in the room, but I can feel Ike. He's wrapped himself around me like some protective cloak.

"Yeah," I whisper back, lifting my eyes to him. There it is, clear as day in his warm gray eyes: the love he has for me. Despite the current circumstances, I feel very blessed.

I was about to tell him I felt the same way, when Dino showed. Even now, I want to tell him, let him know what he's come to mean in such a relative short period of time. But I don't want to tell him here, not with my angry family as witnesses. It would take away from the beauty of such a statement.

276

I try to show him with my eyes, and in the kiss I press to his lips in thanks. I take the gentle smile he gives me as understanding.

Our little *moment* is interrupted when two men in scrubs walk in.

"Lestar family?" one of them asks.

"All of us. Yes," Nolan answers before anyone else.

"X-rays show that Mr. Lestar has what we call a femoral neck fracture," the same doctor continues. "A break in the narrow part just below the ball of the hip joint. We will need to do a partial hip-replacement."

"When?" Owen asks and the second man turns to him.

"They're prepping the OR for him now, and we're on our way up. If you'll come with me, you can briefly see him. But only two at a time."

My mother and Owen follow the doctors out, and Aaron trails along. Nolan turns to me. "Are you coming?"

I don't want to. I don't want to mostly because I'm afraid it would invoke my mother's anger, and I really don't want her more upset than she already is. Not like she's a spring chicken herself. So I shake my head.

"I better not," I tell him with a reassuring smile. "It might not go over well."

"Fuck that," Nolan immediately throws back. "This is about what you want."

Ike goes rigid beside me at Nolan's intensity, but I put a gentling hand on his leg.

"Just go, Nolan. You go in with Aaron. I'll see him after."

"This is so fucked up," he mumbles as he turns and walks out the door.

"He's got that right," Ike contributes, before standing up and pulling me up with him. "Come, let's see if we can find something to eat or drink."

I allow him to lead me down the hall in search of
nourishment.

Breakfast for dinner, is what Ike opted for. I'd forgotten
he never had a chance to eat the food I'd set aside for him.
Since there was nothing decent to eat this time of night in the
hospital, except for some crap from a vending machine, Ike
suggested a twenty-four hour diner just around the corner. I
managed to eat a few pancakes at his insistence. He was right,
it might well be a long night.

"I'm sure this is not what you signed on for," I say
pensively as we make our way back to the hospital hand in
hand.

"What's that?"

"This continuous cycle of drama that seems to follow me
around."

I'm abruptly stopped with a jerk, and Ike steps right into
my space, his hands holding me by my upper arms.

"Enough," he says firmly, his lips a straight line. "I've said
it before, I'll say it again and again until you *hear* me. This?"
he waves his hand in demonstration. "Is not your fault. None
of it is. Not one little bit. You have done *nothing* wrong. Just
because your family prefers to think you're the problem
instead of your father, is not in your control. It never was."
His hands slide up my arms, along my shoulders, and finally
come to rest on either side of my face, as he holds me in place
and rests his forehead against mine. "The storm around you is
not what defines you, Vivian. What defines you is your ability
to get up each time a new wave knocks you down. That's not
drama, babe—that's life. I'll take the storm, over any kind of
smooth sailing, simply because it comes with you. And one
last thing," he adds. "Don't think for one second that I don't
realize exactly what I have in you. That I don't know how

lucky I am. A beautiful, *strong* woman, who knows how to stand on her own, yet trusts me enough to let me have her back."

Okay. That's fucking beautiful. I swallow down the lump of emotion his words evoke.

"Isaac," I breathe, blinking furiously to keep the tears from spilling. "I was just thinking how blessed I feel and you just illustrated perfectly why. Don't catch me, though—I think I like falling in love with you."

## Ike

"Dorian—Jesus, has anyone thought to call Dor?"

Viv stops just inside the waiting room where her family is once again assembled.

"Taking a red-eye. His flight comes in first thing tomorrow morning." Nolan once again steps up as the family spokesperson, something that is starting to piss me off. I hate seeing Viv treated like this. She fucking doesn't deserve the barely contained blame radiating from her mother. Owen and Aaron are slightly better at it, and from what I can see, Owen in particular, keeps checking Viv from the corner of his eye. I can't help wonder if this is more a case of divided loyalty, than a question of believing for them.

"Do you know what time they're coming in?" Viv asks, once again ignoring everyone but Nolan in the room. "I was going to pick them up."

"You were going to pick *them* up? Why do I get the feeling I'm missing something?" This from Owen, who suddenly found his voice apparently. I don't like the way he squints when he looks at his sister. It reeks of mistrust. Of course, now every eye is on Viv and she squirms in her seat. No one knows her brother was already planning to be here this weekend, together with his partner, Kyle. That was going to be surprise, all by itself, and something Dorian had to do himself.

"Didn't you say your brother has some business in Boston? That he might be coming in with his boss?" I direct this at Viv, hoping she'll pick it up and run with it. Last thing I want is for her to be the one to drop another fucking bomb on her family. Viv slowly closes her eyes as she exhales audibly before turning her face to Owen.

"Ike's right. He wasn't a hundred percent sure yet, but he mentioned the possibility last time I talked to him."

*Fuck*. And she was doing so well.

"When did you talk to him?" Suspicion is laid on thick when this time Viv's mother speaks up. Viv instantly realizes her mistake, given no one knows she went to San Fran.

"Last weekend." She gives away as little as possible, which is probably a good idea.

"I'm surprised he took your call." Her mother looks away as she says it, and I have to bite my tongue not to say anything. Turns out I don't have to, Nolan does.

"Enough. Unless you are ready to have the entire load of family laundry hung out in public right now, I suggest you knock it off."

His mother flinches at his words, obviously not used to being spoken to like that. But more surprising are the other two brothers, who don't say anything. In fact, they both avoid looking anyone in the eyes, even their mother, who throws out a silent appeal for support with her eyes. Nothing. Stuck in the middle.

"I wanna go home," Viv whispers, her mouth pressed against my shoulder.

"I know, baby. As soon as we hear something, we're out of here," I say just loud enough for her to hear.

Luckily we don't have to wait long. About two hours after they took her father to the OR, the surgeon and his sidekick are back.

"Went well," he says to Viv's mom, sitting down in the chair across from her. "The surgery, in this case, is probably the easiest part. What is going to be much harder is the recovery. Given that your husband is still recovering from a stroke, has dementia, and is often confused already, makes it even more difficult, since a successful recovery requires a lot from the patient. I will put a note in the file for our social work department to set up a meeting with you. For now he's in recovery, we're letting him wake up slowly to minimize his confusion. You'll be able to see him soon. A nurse will come get you." He stands and looks around the room. "Only one at a time and only direct family. I'll be in to check on him tomorrow."

A chorus of "thank yous" follows him out of the room.

"Well, thank God he got through that," Owen says, rubbing his mother's back. "I'm just gonna skip out and call Lydia, she's probably waiting up to hear."

As soon as he leaves the room, I jump into action. "Glad he came through surgery okay, Mrs. Lestar," I address her directly. "We'd better head home; we need to figure out what time your son's flight comes in and catch some sleep before picking him up at the airport." I stand up and pull Viv up with me. "We'll come straight here after to see how he's doing."

No response from their mother, but a barely visible chin lift from Nolan and a flick of the eyes from Aaron. It's something. Not much, but something. I wrap my arm around

Viv's shoulder, and she slips both arms around my waist, hanging on like I'm her anchor. She hasn't said anything either. Whatever gain she's made over the past few weeks, these few hours in *hostile territory* have been toxic for her. Nolan opens the door and steps outside with us.

"Viv, I wish you would let me—"

I can feel her head shaking against me already, when she stops him.

"No. She's my mother, no one should have to remind her what that means," she poignantly says. Right on the mark, and I notice that Nolan gets it too. Wordlessly he reaches out and pulls her into his arms. Viv goes willingly but doesn't seem to reciprocate, her arms now limply at her side.

"All right. Let's get you to bed."

Nolan grudgingly releases her, and I slip my arm around her, while hers wrap tightly around my middle again. I turn us toward the exit when the big looming figure of Owen blocks our way. His face a mask of regret and guilt. He must've heard every word.

"Viv," he starts, but she turns her face into my shoulder immediately. I know she's had enough.

"I'm taking her home," I tell him resolutely before walking past him to the elevators.

"I have to call Dorian," she says when we walk into my house. I didn't bother asking, I just drove straight there.

"Babe, you're dead on your feet. Why don't you crawl into bed. I'll call and find out what time their flight comes in. You get some rest."

Surprisingly she doesn't object. Of course it's been a long day again and these late nights are becoming more the norm than the exception. It sure the fuck is wearing me out.

I drag my ass into the spare bedroom that doubles as my office and flip open my laptop to see if I can find the flight they're coming in on. Too many fucking choices. Going to have to call Viv's brother.

I use Viv's phone, since it has the number, and Dorian obviously thinks it's her when he answers.

"You okay, Sis? We're just about to board."

"It's Ike."

"Ike, everything okay? Is she all right?"

"Just tired. We just got in, it's been a tough night for her." I run a hand over my face. Been a tough night all round.

"Damn. Yeah, I can imagine. Listen—we've gotta get on the plane, but tell her I'll be there soon. We checked flights directly to Portland, but with the stopovers we'd still get there later than flying into Boston and driving in. We land a little after six tomorrow morning and will rent a car at the airport. Kyle says he needs his independence. Should be in Portland around nine, at the latest."

"Dorian?" I jump in before he hangs up. "Do me a favor and come straight to Viv's apartment. We'll wait for you there."

"Will do. Take care of her," he says before signing off.

Viv is curled up on her side on the bed, fully dressed, with her knees drawn up so tight to her body, she looks like a child. I'm tempted to leave her like that, but decide against it. She doesn't look comfortable.

The moment I touch her ankle to take off her sneakers, she startles and kicks up with her leg, catching me hard on the chin. Her eyes wild, she scrambles up against the headboard, pulling her legs up tight against her chest.

"Baby, it's just me." I reach out to touch her arm, but she flinches away, her breathing erratic. "Hey," I try again, this time her eyes focus on me.

283

"Dream," she croaks out as recognition settles on her features.

"Yeah, I got that. Let's get your clothes off and get you some proper sleep."

This time she doesn't resist as I pull her shoes off. Her arms come up willingly when I pull her shirt up. When she's left in nothing but panties, I pull back the covers and tuck her in. I strip in record time and slip under the covers with her, half expecting her to have dozed off already. Instead, her eyes are on me when I go to pull her in my arms.

"What happened to your chin?" she asks, reaching out to touch my face with gentle fingers.

"Your self-protective instincts," I grin at her. "You kicked me."

"No shit?" She leans in to examine my jaw a little closer. "That's gonna leave a mark," she says, and I catch the hint of pride in her voice.

In one move, I have her laying on my chest, one arm going up her back, my hand on her neck, and the other hand is splayed over her ass.

"Your brother's gonna be at your apartment around nine." Viv starts to object, but I cut her off with a shake of my head. "His man says he needs his independence, so they're renting a car. That means you and I can sleep until eight."

"But your work, don't you start at eight?" Her brows are raised in question.

"Babe, your very gay brother is about to drop a giant bomb on an already explosive situation. Do you really think I'll let you deal with that alone? I'll take the day."

Leaning down, she gives me her soft lips and a little smile. "Thank you," she whispers before tucking her head against my shoulder.

It doesn't take long for her breathing to deepen when sleep moves in. I listen to her breathe but can't find sleep myself. My thoughts are very much keeping me awake. Thoughts that are mostly centered on Viv; how she puts up a great front on the outside, making it look like she's dealing, but tonight's episode makes it clear how deep the damage runs.

A faint band of light filters through the bedroom blinds by the time I finally find sleep.

# CHAPTER TWENTY-SIX

*Viv*

"I love it! This is so *you.*"

Kyle flitters around my apartment, touching every throw pillow, and admiring my colorful walls with the few prints I have up.

Ike and I barely made it here in time, because not five minutes later a bleary-eyed Dorian and a far too chipper Kyle were buzzing to be let up.

We'd been running late, because I woke up this morning with Ike's prominent erection wedged between us. Surprised to find his eyes still closed and breathing deep with sleep, I couldn't resist taking the time to admire his body. All of it. It felt illicit and deliciously wrong to lightly run my fingers over his skin, and follow them with my mouth, tasting every inch I explored. As I worked my way down his torso, I could hear his breathing change. By the time my tongue licked down the light trail of hair and reached the crown of his cock, his breath hitched and a low groan rumbled up from his chest. He didn't move, not when I ran my tongue the hard length of him, and not when I reached my fingers to stroke the delicate skin behind his balls. It was when I slicked my lips around the head and slowly eased his cock deep into my mouth that his hands shot up and fisted my tresses on a deep moan. Already so turned on, I felt the wet heat spread between my legs. I let my tongue massage him as I moved my head up and down his shaft, until his hips almost involuntarily surged up off the mattress.

"Fuck, baby. So fucking good," he started growling in a voice I could feel in my bones. "A dream; waking up with my cock deep inside you. Fucking perfect."

I didn't bother holding back the appreciative hum that bubbled up and vibrated against his skin. His sharp hiss was enough to tell me he felt it. I couldn't resist glancing up. His heavy-lidded eyes were dark with heat and his mouth fell slightly open. A dark flush stained his cheeks, and his breathing had become ragged, as his cock became even thicker in my mouth. Empowered by the effect I was having on his body—on him—I took him as deep as I could and swallowed down on his tip, tugging on his balls as I did.

"Christ! Gonna come, baby."

The warning wasn't necessary, I'd already felt the tightening of his sac in my hand. So when he bucked in my mouth, and the hot streams of his release hit the back of my throat, I was ready to swallow every drop.

He didn't need much time to recover. Before I knew it, I was hauled up and over him, and he was pulling me down on his mouth. By the time we came out of the shower, where he'd ended up lifting me against the wall and making me see stars again, it was eight-thirty. Thus ensued a frantic scramble for clothes and a mad dash to my place.

Sans coffee or breakfast, I'm not at my best, to put it mildly. Still, having both my brother and his man here fills me with enough happy feelings to be able to handle Kyle's loud and abundant cheeriness.

"So how is he?" Dorian asks carefully.

"Had a quiet and uneventful night. They're apparently still keeping him on mild sedation." Seeing as I had placed a quick call to the hospital on our way here, I'm able to answer.

"Good. Did you sleep?" He wants to know, worry in his eyes. God, I love my brother. Here he rushes to fly a gazillion miles through the night to land knee-deep in some seriously messed up family dynamics, to which he is certain to add, and still he worries about me.

"I'm good, Dor," I tell him as I snuggle up against him for a hug. "How are you doing?"

He huffs at that. "Million dollar question, Sissy. Don't know whether I'm coming or going." When I lean back to look up at him, he has his eyes fixed on Kyle, who is very animatedly talking to a mildly amused, but very tired-looking Ike. "He insisted on coming. Even when I said the timing's not right, he still insisted. Had a pretty big fight about it, actually. He said he had already spent years waiting patiently for me to allow him to stand, not only at my back, but by my side as well. Said he was done waiting."

I lift a hand to turn his dark face to me. "I'm sorry, Dor, but he's right. Timing will never be perfect. You deserve to live your life unrestricted, and so does he," I add, nodding in Kyle's direction. "Besides, family is supposed to love and support you unconditionally. They're supposed to be happy if you're happy."

Dorian drops his forehead to mine. "How can you say that? You, of all people?" he whispers. "After how we all treated you, how can you?"

"Hush. You and I, we already worked this out. No need to do it again. As for family; Nolan came to see me." At the surprised look on his face when he pulls his head back, I fill him in on the latest, before shifting the focus back on him. "You're his world." I flick my eyes back at Kyle, who is now watching us closely. "And he deserves to be yours." With a last squeeze, I let him go.

Ike already has his arms open when I reach him and I tuck my head in his neck. "I really need coffee," I whine, making him chuckle. When I turn around, I watch my brother grab Kyle around the neck and lean his forehead against his, just like he'd just done with me, talking intently.

"Never really paid much attention before, so I don't know how accurate my observations are when it comes to men, but those two *really* seem to love each other," Ike rumbles behind me.

"Hmmm," I hum, settling in his arms as I watch Dorian put his hands on Kyle's face and pull him in for a kiss.

"Another first," Ike mutters in my hair. "Now I really need coffee. And something to fucking eat." I tilt my head back and smile at him.

"Nice, right?"

His eyes turn warm when he looks from them to me. "Yeah." His mouth slides over mine, gently sucking on my bottom lip before letting it go. "Hungry."

"All right, all right. We need food," I call out to the guys, who are still pretty much lip-locked. "And coffee. STAT."

We end up back at the same twenty-four hour diner, around the corner from the hospital, about twelve hours after we ate there before. A different waitress this time, though.

All of us order simple bacon and eggs, and more importantly—coffee. I actually moan out loud when I finally get my first hit of caffeine. Kyle snickers when beside me, Ike does the same.

"I'll know just what to get you guys when you make it official," he smiles, ignoring the admonishing elbow Dorian plants in his ribs and my shocked gasp. "Nespresso. Those machines are da bomb. Ask your brother, he got me one for my birthday." Said brother is currently rolling his eyes heavenward.

I sneak a peek at Ike, who is calmly sipping his coffee, apparently totally unfazed by Kyle's outrageous suggestion. He actually looks at me and winks.

Thankfully, we don't have to wait long for breakfast. In pretty short order, we stand on the sidewalk, well fed and caffeinated, ready to head over to the hospital. Ike casually throws his arm around my neck and starts walking. I obviously have no choice but to move as well, although I'd rather be doing anything else than going back in there. Dorian and Kyle are behind us, at least I hope they are. My poor brother was unable to finish his eggs, nerves apparently getting the better of him over the course of breakfast. My mind is still kind of stuck on the whole offhand remark by Kyle about *making it official*. I've known Ike for all of maybe two months now, if that. Granted, it has been intense, and we've somehow managed to spend every night together these past few weeks, but surely it's way too soon to be thinking of anything of a more permanent nature. Isn't it? That calm and confident look on his face, though. Not to mention the wink. What was that all about? Of course he did tell me he loves me and I believe that. He's given me absolutely no reason not to. He made it so easy for me to say it back, and I meant every word. But now in the light of day, walking into whatever we're walking into, it all seems very ... fast.

"Babe, I can hear the wheels grinding over here," he murmurs over my head. "Do you need a minute?" He stops right outside the entrance to the hospital and waves Dorian and Kyle inside, without waiting for my answer. "You guys go ahead, we'll be right in. Just follow the signs for the ICU."

"Ike," I start, but I don't get any further, because now Ike is pulling me toward a bench to the side of the door.

"Talk to me," he says, turning his body toward me and cupping my face in his hands, those intense silver eyes completely focused on mine.

"Isaac ..."

"Spit it out, baby. Whatever it is that has you tensing up under my hand, just let it out. Talk." The last he says in a rather commanding tone, and it immediately makes me bristle.

"Christ, but you can be bossy." If I thought that would have any impact whatsoever, I'm sadly mistaken. No, instead of getting defensive and argumentative, which I'd secretly hoped for I realize, he smiles at me instead.

"I know. But only for good reason. Now tell me." This he says gently, and before I know it, all my thoughts come tumbling out my mouth. Kyle's remark, his reaction to it, my own concerns about moving so fast: everything. Credit to Ike, he calmly listens to my rant and makes sure I'm done before he opens his mouth.

"Let me ask you something," he begins. "Why does this freak you out so much? The thought of a future with me?"

"I don't know," I tell him honestly. "It's not that I don't want it, because I do. I just don't want to hope and have things blow up in my face. For years I've learned to be content just floating around without a rudder. Watching others find their anchor and I'd just be happy occasionally drifting by. It seems safer that way. Storms come and I can simply ride the waves, get bounced around without getting ripped from my moorings."

Ike's hand brushes at my forehead, where the same blue chunk of hair has fallen into my eyes. His expression is thoughtful, pensive. When his eyes land on mine, they're warm.

"I like your metaphor," he says unexpectedly. "It helps me understand what's going through your head. Thing is though, floating through life is not living it. Something I've learned recently, because I was much the same. No real direction, nothing to ground me. I got tired of constantly being in motion, going from one place to the next. That's why I decided to finally turn the house, that I'd bought a few years ago, into a home."

I was listening, my eyes focused on his fingers stroking the top of my hand, but a light squeeze gets my attention. The look on his face is soft when I lift my eyes.

"As soon as that decision was made, you came along," he continues. "Unexpected, for sure, but in a very good way."

I smile at that, because I feel the same way. "Yeah," I acknowledge softly and he smiles back.

"Yeah," he repeats before continuing. "So, maybe it's too soon to talk about dropping an anchor, but Viv, what's so scary about hanging onto each other and floating round the harbor a bit? Enjoy the view? No rush, no reason to be in a hurry."

He's right. Of course he's right.

Feeling infinitely better, I lean in to kiss him softly on the lips. "Thank you for talking me off the ledge."

"Anytime, my love."

## *Ike*

The moment we walk into the waiting room, the tension is already thick. Viv immediately goes to sit down beside Dorian, who looks absolutely miserable sitting on the other side of the room from Kyle, who just looks angry. I'm content for now, leaning against the wall beside the door. Viv's mother is missing and so is Nolan, but the other two brothers are there.

"Where's Mom?" Viv asks.

"She's in with Lydia, to see Dad," Owen answers after a moment's hesitation. "Nolan had to head back to Boston, but he'll be back tonight." His eyes linger on Viv a little longer before turning them back to the floor. Aaron just glares at everyone.

"Oh, okay," she says tentatively. "Any new developments?"

Kyle huffs audibly, loud enough to draw everyone's attention. "Nothing new from where I'm sitting. Nothing new at all," he says with a scathing glare in Dorian's direction.

"Oh," Viv says again, worriedly looking between her brother and Kyle.

"Think she meant with her father, Kyle," I point out and watch his face fall.

"Right," he says softly. "Of course."

"He's a bit combative this morning, Mom and Lydia are trying to calm him down. I tried, but didn't get very far," Owen volunteers, surprisingly. His eyes keep flitting back and forth to Viv in the silence that follows. The feeling I got yesterday that he was starting to soften toward her is enforced.

"I'm gay."

The declaration is loud, too loud for the small waiting room, and Dorian, who just blurted that out of the blue, looks panicked. Viv grabs his hand and leans her head on his shoulder in support. Nobody else in the room moves, but Kyle suddenly looks as if the heavens opened up for him. I scan the face of Owen and Aaron for a response, but all I see are blank faces as they look at their younger brother.

"Kyle is not just my boss, he's my husband. I met him a year after I moved to San Francisco, and we've been together ever since," Dorian pushes on, his shoulders squaring as he does. Kyle is practically beaming from the other side of the room, and Viv throws me a little smile, which I gladly return. The two brothers still stare unmoving.

Still Dorian plows on. "Whenever one of you would visit, Kyle would move in with a friend or stay at a hotel until you were gone. Well, all of you except Viv—she's the only one who's always known."

Now there's movement from Aaron, who jumps up, swearing loudly, "Son of a fucking bitch!"

I push off the wall, ready to intervene, if necessary, when he steps in front of his younger brother with his arms crossed over his chest.

"You fucking got married and didn't invite us?"

Dorian's mouth falls open, as does Viv's, and I have to chuckle when I see the two of them looking up at the looming figure Aaron makes, gaping like fish. Then my chuckle turns into full-fledged laughter when Owen reaches over to ruffle Dorian's hair.

"This is not news, brother. Although I have to agree with Aaron, you owe us a wedding party." Kyle's smile splits his face in two, when Owen turns to him. "Welcome to our fucked-up family, Kyle."

When I look back to my girl, she's pulled away from Dorian, who apparently found his tongue, since he is talking animatedly with Aaron. Viv looks around the room before her eyes land on me, and what I see in them is not good. I tilt my head, inviting her to come to me and after a moment, she gets up and walks straight into my arms.

"Get me out of here," she hisses under her breath. Without questioning her, I pull her against my side and step outside the room. With a last glance over my shoulder, I see Owen watching our departure, his face inscrutable.

Rounding the corner on our way to the lobby, we almost bump into Mrs. Lestar and Lydia.

"Hey, sweetie." Viv's sister-in-law gives her a quick hug, before smiling at me. "Hi, Ike."

"Lydia," I return, but Viv says nothing. She's looking at her mother, whose face is a mask of anger.

"All he wants is his precious *Vivvy*," she almost spits out. "He won't even look at me, won't let me touch him to calm him down. Just *you*—his *good girl*."

"Mom," Lydia pleads, trying to pull her back by the shoulders, while throwing Viv an apologetic smile. Viv stands beside me frozen, just staring at her mother, until Lydia firmly guides her past us and down the hall.

I turn Viv in my arms and tilt her head up. "Wanna go? Let's go," I tell her, but she shakes her head.

"I'm done with this," she says through gritted teeth. "I want to have a word with my father, and then I'm done with this, and with them."

"Sure?" I check.

"Abso-fucking-lutely. My brother reveals his sexual orientation and the double life he's lead since he was a teenager, and my family simply accepts it. No recriminations—no argument—no blame." Her bark of laughter sounds hollow. "I deserve that, but he has taken that away from me too. I at least deserve to tell him what he's done." She turns down the hall and starts walking. I easily catch up and put my hand on her neck, just as a point of connection. Perhaps more for me than for her, because this will be gut wrenching.

The nurse at the desk cautions us. "He's very restless this morning. We've had to place him in a separate room. Family only, though," she says, looking between us.

"I'm his daughter and this is my husband."

I try not to look surprised. I just squeeze Viv's shoulder.

"Very well, end of the hall, last door on the right." With a finger pointed in the general direction, she turns back to her monitors, effectively dismissing us.

Determinedly, Viv pushes the door open and steps into the room, only faltering slightly at the sight of her father, who looks fragile and gray. She seems to take strength from my hand on her back.

"Vivvy ..." he whispers the moment his eyes spot her.

"I need to tell you something," she says, her voice wobbling a bit but her spine strong under my palm. "You almost ruined me. Almost," she repeats as her father's eyes grow big. "I adored you, growing up. You were always larger than life to me. Superman, a hero, someone who always made me feel safe and protected. Until you turned into someone I needed protection from. And there was no one, Dad. No one. I lived in a house filled with people and no one saw. No one listened. No one cared enough. And every night you came into my room—every time you violated my body and my mind—you isolated me further. I lost my family because of you. You took everything." A sob rips from her chest and I slip my arms around her stomach, holding her up when she looks like she'll collapse.

"Always my good girl," he mutters, a smile on his face, his eyes distant with vile memories. It takes all I have not to beat the life out of the brittle man in the hospital bed.

"Yes," she spits out with renewed fire. "And after I stopped being your *good girl*, I was a shell: confused, betrayed, and empty inside. Nothing but a mark for another predator in search of a *good girl* to find me. Belittle me. Beat me. Rape me. I blame you. It's all on you ..." She whispers the last, silent tears streaming down her face when I turn her in my arms. My own eyes are blurred when her hands go around my neck and she climbs up my body, wrapping her legs around my hips.

With my hands under her ass for support, I turn to walk out the room but stop in my tracks. Owen stands in the doorway, his face as white as the hospital sheets.

"Take me home," Viv pleads, oblivious to her brother in the room. Her brother, who looks like his entire world just collapsed.

"My God, Viv." His soft voice cracks on his sister's name and she jerks in my arms.

"Home, Ike. Home." The sound coming from her is thin and weak, but insistent.

"I'm taking her home."

Without waiting for an answer, I carry Viv through the hospital and out to the truck, ignoring the curious glances. She pulls herself up into a ball when I deposit her in the passenger seat, lowly keening. The moment I get behind the wheel, I send a text to Pam with my address, before dialing her.

"Meet me at my house," I say simply as soon as she answers. "I just sent you a text with my address."

"What hap—" she starts asking but I cut her off.

"Viv needs you."

# CHAPTER TWENTY-SEVEN

## *Viv*

"Babe, you've got to eat. You heard Pam, if you don't eat even a little, she insists you be admitted. Please."

I hear Ike's voice, just like I've heard Pam's voice whenever she's been here, but I can't bring myself to react.

I've watched the sun go down and come up again. I've heard life go on outside and in the house. I've even made it to the bathroom when the need arose, and yet here, in my safe cocoon of blankets I can pretend the world outside doesn't exist. Nothing matters.

Suddenly the covers are yanked down my body and Ike's pulling me up by my arms.

"What the—" I start, but Ike shoves his face in mine.

"This is not you," he barks, startling me. "This is not you and not how you handle things. We're having a shower and then we deal. No more hiding under the covers, it's been four fucking days you've lain there with that blank look on your face and it's enough."

He's angry. So, so angry and a niggle of fear starts working its way up my spine when he picks me up and walks me into the bathroom.

"Stay," he says in a tone that warrants no objection, before he turns around and turns on the taps, putting a plug in the bottom of the tub. Turning back to me he grabs the hem of my shirt, the same shirt I've been wearing all this time, and looks me in the eyes. "Lift."

Without thinking I do as he says and lift my arms up. In a single move he has my shirt up and over my head. He undresses me in record time, turns me toward the tub, and orders me to get in. The moment my butt hits the porcelain bottom, I pull up my legs and wrap my arms around them, turning my face to the wall. I hear rustling and then feel him get in the tub behind me. When his legs slip around me, I hold myself stiff as a board. Still, he's persistent and his hands come around to loosen mine, which are tightly clasped together around my legs.

"Baby—let go." This time his voice is soft, coaxing, but still I hold on tight and shake my head.

"I can't." My voice sounds scratchy and alien, even to my own ears. "I'm scared."

"Last time you were scared and we had a bath together, you let go. You felt safe enough to let go." He absently strokes my arms, before his voice drops. "I don't know what else to do, love."

It's the hitch in his voice that hits home. I let go of my knees and slowly lean back against his chest. His arms immediately band around me, pulling me tight. Suddenly it's not enough, I need more contact—more Ike. I twist my body, partially turn my front to his chest and bury my face in his neck.

"I'm so dirty," I mumble against his skin.

"I'll clean you." Ike's deep rumble feels wonderful against my skin.

"You can't clean this kind of dirt," I try to explain, and his arms tighten around my body.

"Baby," he argues softly in my hair. "That dirt is not yours, it never was. And if they made you dirty—I will make you clean."

That's when the dam breaks. Bottled up emotion I thought I could safely tuck away, like I did once before, pours out of me. Again, like before, it's Ike who won't allow me to hide. My fist comes up and strikes him on the chest. And again and again.

"Why?" I cry. "Why won't you let me be?"

One of his big hands folds around my fist and presses it against the chest I've been pounding.

"I can't," his voice breaks with emotion. "I can't let you go back to just existing, and not living. You have to *live*, honey. All that beauty, it's gotta shine."

While I sob myself empty in his neck, Ike grabs the soap and starts washing every last inch of my skin with a tenderness that fills me from the inside out.


"There she is."

I turn around from the kitchen island, where I've been trying to force down a piece of toast Ike made me, to find Pam in the doorway, smiling from ear to ear.

"Damn, girl. For a bit there, I thought we'd lost you for good." Her eyes track to Ike, who is leaning against the counter, his arms crossed over his chest. "You'll do, my friend. You'll do." She then claps her hands. "Right. Coffee. Bring it on. We've got work to do."

That's Pam. No frills or flowers, just painfully direct and to the point. With the cup of coffee Ike served her in hand, she calls me with a wave of her hand before walking into Ike's living room. The pleading look I throw back at him is met with a little shake of his head and a soft smile. *Drat.* Grabbing my own cup, I pop the last piece of toast in my mouth, which earns a pleased nod from Ike, and follow Pam into the living room where I curl up on the chaise.

Ike comes in moments later and leans over the back of the couch to kiss me lightly. "Gonna leave you girls to it, for a bit. Heading out to pick up some groceries, the fridge is empty. Need anything?" he asks, and I simply shake my head. Nothing I can think of now, anyway.

Before he has a chance to back away, my hand shoots out and grabs his arm. "Wait. What day is it?"

"Tuesday."

"Aren't you supposed to be at work? Oh God—The Skipper, I have to—..." But I don't get the chance to finish my sentence or get up from the chaise, because Ike's hands push firmly on my shoulders.

"We have the week off."

"But—"

"It's done. Taken care of." I'm about to protest when he leans down, slips his hands under my arms and lifts me half out of the couch to hug me to his chest. "Beautiful—let me." His words are heavy with meaning and his eyes hold a message that registers. He needs this.

So instead of protesting, I lift my mouth, pressing a small kiss to his. "Thank you."

After we watch him leave, Pam turns to me with a smirk on her face. "He loves you."

I nod. "I know. I love him back."

Pam's eyes shoot up into her hairline. "You seem ready to accept that?"

Again I nod. "He's giving me every reason to."

"Good," she says with a last sip of her coffee, before she puts her cup resolutely on the table. "Let's start with you telling me what happened at the hospital on Friday. Ike already gave me the outline, but I want you to tell me what happened to *you*."

That starts a long session of soul-cleansing talk, tears, and analysis that leaves me feeling ultimately better. Being forced to put to words my confusing emotions helps place them in context and therefore easier to understand. Pam coaxes and cajoles until she squeezes the last drop out of me, and I finally throw up my arms. "Enough! I'm done. I need a nap," I beg.

Pam tilts her head to the side and squints her eyes at me before answering. "Okay. Enough for now, but you have to promise me—*promise* me—not to close off again. Because, girl, it would've broken my heart, but I was *this* close to having you hospitalized. Don't you fucking scare us like that again."

Guilt hits me square in the chest. Those words, uttered with such emotion behind them, illustrate without any doubt, the worry I've put them through. Both Pam and Ike, and who knows who else. I've been so hung up on shutting myself off, I never properly considered what it does to those who care for me. Who love me.

Ike is right. I'll never fully live if I'm too scared to struggle through the bad to get to the good. And that would cause a ripple effect on those around me. People I care about. People I love.

Feeling exhausted, but a million pounds lighter, I look Pam straight in the eyes. "I promise," I tell her before repeating more strongly. "I *promise*."

# *Ike*

When I came home earlier, Pam was waiting on the couch, by herself. "Where's Viv?"

"Having a nap. Don't worry," she added quickly. "It was a good session. A great session actually, but it wore her out. Wore me out, too. So now that you're back, I'm heading out." She stood up and her eyes zoomed in on the duffel bag I had in my hand. "What's that? I thought you were going for groceries," she said, her eyebrows raised in question.

"Swung by Viv's apartment to pick up her stuff. At least the beginnings of it," I explained. "Figured she's not ready to face anyone in her family just yet."

"You would be right. Best give her some time. So Dorian is still here?" She wanted to know.

"His partner apparently flew back home Sunday night. Dorian's staying indefinitely."

"Because of Viv?"

"Partially, he says. Says he's done avoiding confrontation and wants to stay close for now. Their father's deterioration is part of it, too. This whole fucking mess is taking its toll on everyone in that family. Everyone is on pins and needles around each other. I made it clear to Dorian, I don't want that for Viv. She doesn't need it." I dropped Viv's bag at the bottom of the stairs and the bag of groceries I had in my other hand on the kitchen island.

"And how are you coping?" Pam's surprisingly gentle question startled me.

"Me? I don't know," I admitted to her. "Managing. I know, probably better than most, how important family is. Their acceptance, their trust. How painful it is to lose that. I'll do whatever I can to make sure that doesn't happen for Viv. She fucking deserves better." Turning back, I started putting away the groceries, but my movements stilled when I felt Pam's hand on my shoulder.

"So do you, Isaac. So do you."

I didn't start moving again until I heard the soft click of my front door behind her.

That was a few hours ago. In the meantime I've spoken to Syd, Gunnar, and Owen on the phone. The last was a surprise. He said he got my number off Dorian and wanted to know how Viv was doing, but didn't want to disturb her. I told him the truth, which clearly didn't make him feel any better. Don't fucking care. I also don't care that telling him there's no way in hell I'd let him come talk to her—not now—pissed him off. "I'm her brother," he said and I snorted. Told him he sure hadn't treated her like a brother, like family should. Told him Viv has good people around her, who love her and never once questioned her honesty, her integrity. Never betrayed her trust, like her family had. That shut him up. I did end up promising him I'd let him know if or when she was ready to see anyone. That's when I turned off my phone and started dinner.

"What's for dinner?" Viv's sleepy voice drifts in from the doorway.

Rinsing my hands under the tap, I snatch a towel to dry them as I turn around to a very sleep-tousled and sweet-looking Viv. The moment I put the towel down, she takes the few steps that separate us and molds herself against my front, my arms slipping naturally around her body.

Kissing her hair, I mumble, "Oven-roasted chicken breast, potatoes, and Caesar salad."

"Mmmm, sounds good. I'm actually a little hungry."

I lift her chin with my finger and smile down at her. "Glad, baby. Really glad."

"What's my bag doing here?" She turns and points to the duffel bag I'd left at the bottom of the stairs.

"Picked up some of your things. Enough to last a few days, I hope."

She looks at me questioningly. "I'm staying?"

"Relatively speaking. I'm taking you away for a couple of days. We're taking the bike, so we have to pack light. But I figure a bathing suit, some shorts and shirts would be enough. Whatever else we need we can buy."

It's easy to see the internal struggle she wages, but finally she turns to me with a smile. "Where are you taking me?"

I silently heave a sigh of relief. I'd worried she wouldn't want to go, but I thought a few days away from Portland might be good. Give her a chance to do some healing. Fuck, if I'm honest, I need this for myself. It'd been easy enough to get time off work. My last design had gone over well and everything else could wait, David said. Not like I was in a habit of taking vacations, so I had quite a bit of time due. Gunnar had been even easier. "As long as it takes, I don't fucking care. You just make sure you take care of her."

"Up to Bar Harbor. Got a cottage sorted right on the water. It's basic but clean. We leave tomorrow morning at the crack of dawn."

"Sounds perfect," she says with a sniff, as she tucks her head back in my neck.

*Viv*

"I don't want to leave tomorrow."

I turn on my side to face him, putting a hand on his stomach.

We've been in Bar Harbor three days, and tomorrow we have to vacate our cottage for the next vacationers. I don't want to.

I didn't expect my showdown with my father to have quite the impact it did. Not that it would've stopped me if I had. It'd been cathartic in a way. Like a crude excising of a dormant cancer, it left a raw, gaping hole that would take time to heal. Those first few days after I almost disappeared into that hole, had Ike not forcibly pulled me out. I owe him. I owe him big. He told me the day we arrived here that he'd been in touch with Dorian a few times. Apparently he will be sticking around for a while. Although I'm grateful for that, I'm not ready to face him, let alone anyone else in my family. It's not necessarily that I'm upset with Dorian, but I envy him. Ugly emotion, jealousy, and one I didn't think I harbored a lot, if any, of. I was wrong. In my talks with Ike, and also the sessions with Pam we continued over the phone, it's become clear to me that part of me has always felt insecure being the only girl in a family of guys. Their unquestioned loyalty to each other became evident when Dor's sexual orientation was so easily accepted, without question or resentment for keeping that part of his life from them for decades. I was not granted the same loyalty, the same trust. My brothers turned on me as one when I shared my painful secret. Then there's my mother, to whom the boys can do no wrong, yet who did not hesitate to push me out of the nest, choosing not to believe me. Again. That fucking hurt. Standing on the outside of the family unit looking in. I realized it had been like that most of my life. I had a connection with Dorian that kept me tethered, but when that disappeared at fifteen—admittedly by my own doing—there was nothing left.

Funny how highly charged emotional situations can unearth complexities and dynamics that weren't so visible before. At least, not to me.

Only a short time here and so much of it was spent lying on the beach, talking about everything and anything. It feels like we spent weeks instead of days. Still, I'm not ready to leave, even though I know we have to. Reality awaits and oddly, even with my life a bit of a mess, I feel better having everything out in the open. Of course it helps I have a man who, despite all my layers, has seen me for who I am from the very beginning. I'm blessed, I realize that now. He makes it easy to be open and real, because he no longer hesitates to show his own vulnerabilities and insecurities. A man I've only known the summer, but who's stuck with me through some pretty fucked-up shit. That should count as dog years, right? Sure feels like that, in a very good way. Which is why I don't particularly want to leave our bubble.

"Baby," his voice rumbles low in his chest; I love that sound so much. "Don't know what you were just thinking but every last thought was visible on your face." He smiles under his beard, which has become even fuller over the last week. "We have to be out of here tomorrow, but I checked with the owners this morning and booked a week for us here in September."

"You did?" I sit up, pushing my hair out of my face and smiling brightly. "I love that! We probably won't be able to lie on the beach anymore, but we can take long walks on the beach, and maybe go whale watching. I haven't done that since I was twelve." I'm already looking forward to it. "Oh! And we have to go back to Galyn, I loved their crab cakes."

Ike smiles and runs the back of his hand over my cheek. "Glad it makes you happy, love."

I lean forward and press my mouth to his, but when I try to pull back, his hand cups the back of my head and holds me in place. He tilts his head and licks his tongue along the seam of my lips. The moment I slightly open my mouth, his tongue slides in, touching mine boldly. Using his bigger body as leverage, he rolls me on my back and settles his body on top of me. The slight abrasion of sand between our bodies sensitizes my skin and I moan softly in his mouth. Abruptly he lifts himself off me, holding on to just my hand. With the other he snatches up our towels and starts walking toward the cottage, dragging me behind him.

It's not that we haven't been intimate these past days, because we have, but it's been gentle and sweet. The fire I see in those silver eyes looking back at me, promises heat I don't mind getting scorched by.

The moment we step through the door, Ike tosses the sand-covered towels on the couch, but I don't get a chance to protest. Kicking the door shut, he backs my body against the wall by the door, using his to hold me in place and slamming his mouth on mine hungrily. Ike one-handedly has his swim shorts down and off, rubbing his gloriously naked body against mine. I'm not that fortunate. I manage to get hung up in the one strap of my damp one-piece I manage to pull down. My other hand is too busy roaming over his strong back and tight ass to be any help. I struggle, whimpering with frustration into his mouth. I want my skin against his. I need it. I barely have a chance to protest the loss of his lips when Ike releases my mouth, grabs the straps on my bathing suit, and peels it right off my body. With his mouth back on mine, his hands mold and knead my body, driving me wild. One hand slips between my legs, lightly stroking the wetness gathered there, before I'm pulled away from the wall, twisted and pushed down over the back of the couch, my ass sticking up in the air. His hand comes around my chin and lifts my head back as he surges his cock inside me in one thrust. No words, no sounds, other than the crash of the surf on the beach outside, and the deep guttural grunts that fall from his lips and the moans from my own. The hard, furious pumping of his hips, the slap of his balls against my skin, his hot breath on my neck. *This,* flits through my mind as my body convulses around his cock, and my knees are no longer able to keep me standing. He plants himself deep inside me, his hips flush against my ass and roars out his release, dropping his head in the crook of my neck.

"Fucking hell," he pants out of breath.

"No shit, Sherlock," I respond, equally breathless. Both of us burst out laughing before Ike pulls out, swings me up into his arms and walks me into the bedroom, where we start from the beginning.

We miss seeing the sunset on our last night at the cottage.

# CHAPTER TWENTY-EIGHT

*Viv*

"Viv!"

The moment I come walking into the back hallway of The Skipper, Dexter, Gunnar's eleven-year-old son from a previous marriage, comes tearing down the stairs and throws himself at me.

"Hey, kiddo." I ruffle his hair and hug him back.

"Saw you coming down the alley on the back of that bike. That bike is sweet!" The little Gunnar clone lifts his face at me with a wide grin almost splitting it in two. "Who's the dude?" he asks, without taking time for a breath.

I snicker and feel Ike's warm chuckle in my back. Stepping aside I make introductions. "Dex, this is Ike, and Ike, meet Gunnar's son, Dexter." I bite back a smile as I watch Dex pull himself up to his full height, which is still a couple of feet shy of Ike's, and stick out his hand.

"Nice to meet you," he mutters politely, with something akin to awe shining in his eleven-year-old eyes. "My dad's got a bike, but it's nowhere near as cool as yours."

"Thanks, man," Ike answers back, Dexter's shoulders squaring a bit more at being called "man." "Had her for almost twelve years now, but she's indestructible."

"Wow," the youngest of the Lucas clan breathes. "That's older than me."

With a chuckle, Ike does his own version of the hair ruffle. "You treat them right, machines like that can last a lifetime. Maybe two."

From the kitchen Syd's head comes poking out. "Eeep, you're back!" she squeals, stepping around Dex to give me a hug.

Back in town and glad I asked Ike to drive us here for lunch before heading over to his place, since Dorian is still at mine. I need this place, these people, to bolster me up for when reality sets in.

I was sad to watch the cottage disappear in the distance. Our stay there had breathed new life into me. Hope. I turned away from the view and pressed my cheek against Ike's back as he turned onto the road heading back toward my life. *Our* life.

I gladly hug Syd back, who next turns to Ike for a warm hug. "Thanks for keeping us in the loop," she tells him. My eyes shoot up to meet his somewhat guilty ones.

"I thought you said no phone, other than Pam?"

He'd insisted when we got to Bar Harbor, that other than my daily phone call with Pam, we were to keep our phones powered off. Seems he didn't follow his own rules.

He shrugs his shoulders. "Babe, she needed to know you were okay." I want to be upset, but the flare of anger is already dying down. It disappears altogether when he puts his hand on my neck and pulls me into him. "You needed the space, your friends needed the reassurance."

"I don't like being managed," I protest weakly, more for show than anything else.

"You trust me?" he asks, as Syd gently but firmly sends Dex back up the stairs and disappears discretely into the kitchen.

"Yes." The answer is that simple. I do trust him, trust that he's looking out for me. Doesn't mean I always have to like the way he goes about it.

"Good, then I better tell you that I spoke with Owen, too."

I stiffen up at that. I'm still so angry with Owen. Only believing what his eyes couldn't deny any longer in that hospital room. Not before—not my word.

Ike must feel it because his arms around me get tighter. "Spoke to him before. On Tuesday, while you were having a nap. You have a right to be mad at him. Be disappointed in him, but Viv, that doesn't make him any less worried. I wanted to give you time to get your moxie back before you were forced to deal with any of your brothers directly."

"My moxie?" I lean back and raise my eyebrows up at him.

The side of his mouth tilts up. "Getting that fire back, baby," he says on a growl. "Felt the heat of it all over me last night."

I feel his words down to my toes and my body remembers exactly. Lifting up on my toes I press my lips against his.

"Before that goes any damn further in my hallway, best come say hello and grab some food." Gunnar comes walking down the hallway and turns into the kitchen with a pointed look in our direction.

"Fuck," Ike swears against my lips. Fuck indeed.


"This is fucking amazing," Ike mumbles around a mouthful of Dino's pulled pork.

Just our luck to have waltzed into the pub at lunch hour. Our breakfast long since processed and digested, Ike's stomach loudly makes its current empty state known the

313

minute the scent of food hits our nostrils. Which is about a second after walking into the kitchen.

"You good?" Dino steps into my path and gives me a thorough once-over before bumping his fist under my chin lightly. "Yeah. You're good," he says, answering his own question and not paying Ike any mind. I'm pretty sure Ike is starting to get used to his occasional asocial behavior. Dino doesn't talk much, and when he does it's concise, to the point, and usually of value to him or whomever he's talking to. His words *mean* something. Therefore, it's hard to be insulted when he snubs you—and certainly not after he carelessly tosses a plate with the most mouth-watering pulled pork sandwich down on the kitchen table in front of Ike. "You look hungry. Eat," is all he says before he turns back to the massive Dutch oven sitting on top of the stove. Ike doesn't hesitate and digs in.

"Who's up front?" I ask, looking from Syd to Gunnar, who cautiously look at each other. Gunnar answers, "Matt and a new girl, she's full-time. One of Pam's women. Hired her Monday."

*Really.* As manager, it's always been on me to hire full-time staff. Occasionally, Gunnar or Syd would take on a part-timer for the busy season, but full-time, year-round staff is my job. Syd must've noticed my reaction, because she reaches across the table and grabs my hand. "Viv, she's had a rough few years, been staying at Florence House since March. You know how hard it is to find a place to start. We thought you'd be all over it."

I'm an idiot, a self-absorbed, insecure idiot. A flush of embarrassment heats my face. "Of course. Absolutely," I say quickly. I know what it's like to be given that first chance at climbing out of the hole. I've been paying it forward since I got my shot; pulling Syd into the pub when she was destitute, volunteering as much as I can at the shelter. Syd and Gunnar had simply done what they knew I would've, had I been around. "Look, I'm sorry my hours have been messed up lately. So much has dropped in your laps."

"Couple of things," Gunnar starts, but is stopped by the kitchen phone ringing. Before Dino can get to it, the ringing stops. Matt must've picked it up and turning back to me, Gunnar continues. "Syd being pregnant, I don't want her on her feet long hours." From the glare she throws her husband, I can tell Syd is not necessarily in agreement with that decision. Gunnar ignores her. "You having a man, the stuff you've been dealing with—all of that plays into it, too. Business has been good. We all benefit from another pair of hands and Ruby is working out well. Syd needs more time to focus on the baby and her foundation work, and you need to have a life."

Syd had come into some money a few years ago, which she used to start up a foundation to aid families with devastatingly ill children. She organizes regular fundraisers to raise monies and has been written up a few times in various newspapers around Maine. Tragically, the applications far outnumber the families the foundation is able to ensure appropriate medical care to. So although Syd has chosen not to be involved with vetting the applications, a board was set in place for that, she does take on the responsibility of fundraising. A full-time job in itself, which this summer, she hasn't been able to do much work on. For the most part because she was covering my shifts at the pub.

That's why I choose not to get my hackles up at Gunnar's comment that I need a life, because even if I'm not ready to admit to that, his reasoning on Syd's behalf is valid. More than valid. But before I have a chance to say anything, an out of breath, short, rounded woman of obvious Latin descent rushes into the kitchen. This must be Ruby.

"It's urgent," she says to Gunnar, who pushes out of his chair immediately. "I'm sorry, he said he was looking for Viv?" Her dark brown eyes scan the kitchen table and land on me where they stay.

## Ike

I watch Viv get up from the  table and tentatively grab the kitchen phone off the hook. "Hello? Yes, this is Vivian Lestar."

I don't even realize getting up until I find myself standing right behind her. Her shoulders are pulled up and her head is hanging down as she listens to whoever is talking on the other end.

"What the hell?" She whips around, suddenly face to face with me. "Dorian needs me to come get him from jail," she informs me, disbelief in her eyes when she hands the phone over to me.

"Dorian?"

"Shit. Shit. Shit. Ike, man, I'm glad you're there, I tried calling your cell, but it kept going to voicemail. Can you come instead?" That's probably because I still have it powered off in my pocket.

"What happened?" I ask, ignoring his question.

"Jesus, look, I'll tell you when you get here. I'm in a holding cell where they just handed me the phone after dialing for me. I'm not exactly alone."

"Where are you?"

"The main one, on Middle Street."

"Give me fifteen minutes," I tell him before hanging up. When I turn around I see a kitchen full of people, but no Viv. "Where'd she go?" I want to know, but the answer comes with the slam of the back door. *Son of a bitch.*

I ignore the questions thrown at me and take after her on a run. By the time I get through the door and past the dumpster, I can see her hoofing it down the cobblestones in the alley. Fuck, she's moving.

"Viv, hold up!" I yell after her, but all she does is throw a quick glance over her shoulder. It's not until I call out, "You don't even know where he's at," that she slows down, allowing me to catch up with her. "Jesus, babe," I groan, Dino's pulled pork sandwich sloshing around in my stomach. "My bike is back there." I point to where it is parked behind the pub.

"Can't fit him on there with us. Let's go, my car is in the garage." Before she can take off again, I snag her hand, making sure she keeps a more reasonable pace.

"Thought you were taking off without me," I note, working hard at suppressing my irritation.

"Nope," she says popping her lips. "Was just getting the car. I'm pissed at my brother—I needed fresh air."

She looks pissed, walking at a decent clip beside me, her shoulders still pulled up tight. But it's not until we are in her car, which I insist on driving given her agitated state, plus the fact that I know where we're going, that I break the silence.

"We don't know what happened yet, babe. Maybe it's a bit premature to be pissed at him," I suggest carefully.

"*If* that was why I'm pissed, I'd agree with you. But that would not be the reason. I'm fuming, because he counts on me being there for him, they all do, without thinking."

It takes me a minute, but then I clue in. He knew she'd come running, no questions asked. Trusted on it. Yet that's not something that's been afforded her. She's right. I wasn't pissed before as much as curious, but now I'm pissed too.

Viv is not happy to be relegated by the desk sergeant to sit in the waiting area and is virtually bouncing in her chair. Sitting down beside her, I take her hand in mine, holding it firmly when she tries to pull it free. "Settle," I tell her softly, to which she glares at me.

"I can't settle. You heard her," she says, tilting her head in the direction of the officer. "He was picked up for drunk and disorderly after getting kicked out of a bar for fighting last night. What the hell is wrong with him?"

I have to clench my jaw, so I don't make the mistake of pointing out to her that she had thrown herself into the middle of a bar brawl not that long ago.

Despite my efforts, she must be picking up on my thoughts because she says, "Not the same, Ike. That is so not the same."

At that moment, the door beside the front desk opens and another officer comes through with a rough-looking Dorian right behind. Shirt bloodied, a cut on his cheek, and that whole side of his face swollen, he looks like he got as good as he gave.

"Shit, man, you brought her?" is the first thing out of his mouth, and I feel rather than see, Viv steam up beside me.

"More like she brought me. You should know your sister better than that."

It wasn't intended to have a double meaning, but from the wince on Dorian's face, it was received as such. I don't feel sorry. If he chooses to read something more than was intended into my words, that's his problem.

"He's all yours," the officer says, handing Dorian a slip of paper.

"Viv," he says when he stops in front of her, but he gets a hand stuck in his face.

"Not a fucking word, Dorian. Not even one. Not now." With that she turns on her heels and leads the way out of the police station, the two of us following behind. Dorian meekly and me not just a little amused.

Viv gets in the front, without a word, leaving Dorian to fold his big body in the backseat. We're about halfway home when she suddenly blurts out as she twists in her seat, "Are you out of your skull? Getting drunk and fighting? What the hell, Dorian?"

"Fuck, Viv. I was missing Kyle, dealing with our ... family shit, and I just went over to The King's Head for a drink. Escaping for a couple of hours. How was I to know it's Aaron's favorite hang out? Didn't waste time getting in my face either."

"Aaron? You were fighting with Aaron?" Viv's voice rises to a level distinctly uncomfortable for the confines of a car, but I can't blame her. I lift my eyes to the rearview mirror, where I can see Dorian grimace before answering.

"We had a difference of opinion that got a little out of hand," he confesses. "I lost my cool, shoved him when he got up in my space, and he tripped over a stool. I felt bad right away, reached out my hand to pull him up, and he repaid me with a fist in my face."

Viv twists herself back to face the front, pulling on her hair, and mumbling under her breath. "I can't believe this, I can't fucking believe this."

Knowing I am risking possible physical harm with her wired so tight, I count on the fact that I'm driving to work in my favor as I reach over with one hand to still hers. The moment I touch her, she drops her hands and turns her eyes on me. "Do I even want to know what they were arguing about?" Her voice carries the sound of defeat. I don't like hearing that.

"First bump, beautiful. We knew there'd be some. Hang in there." Next I address Dorian. "You gonna need medical care?" I meet his eyes in the rearview mirror. He shakes his head.

"EMT looked me over at the police station. He superglued the cut. I'm good."

Just as I pull into the underground garage of Viv's building, she turns back to her brother. "Does Aaron look anything like you?"

"I may have returned fire a time or two."

"Jesus."

The moment I turn off the engine, Viv is out of the car and marching to the elevator. Dorian and I follow a little slower. Glad to see she's holding the elevator for us, even though she doesn't look at Dorian once.

The phone is ringing when we walk in and Viv rushes to get it. She barely gets her hello out before her face goes completely blank and her back shoots straight. Both of us move to her side, but Dorian gets there before me, snatching the phone from her hand and putting it to his ear. I put my hands on Viv's shoulders and turn her to me. "Who is it?" I ask, just as she does a face plant in my chest, but the answer doesn't come from her.

"Mom!" Dorian yells in the phone. "Yes, I know you thought you were talking to Viv, and now I know why she's upset. I can't believe you, Mom. I'm the one who got into it with Aaron. Viv has shit to do with that. I'm telling you right now, you keep this crap up, just like you've been doing all week, and you won't just alienate Viv, but Nolan, Owen, and me too. Yes, Mom, them too. We talked—Nolan saw him, Mom. Coming out of her room, he's always suspected. No, that's not what happened, Mom, and you fucking well know it.

Owen overheard Dad in the hospital. You wanna try and convince us all that his hands are clean? That your daughter is making this shit up? Think hard, Ma, think real hard." With that, Dorian slams the phone down. "Son of a fucking bitch!"

During his tirade, Viv's hands have been digging into my back, and I've mumbled nonsense in her ear. I'm glad Dorian took a stand, and did it loudly. "Babe," I lean back and tilt my head to the side to catch Viv's eyes. When she lifts her face I see unspilled tears shimmering in her eyes, but she surprises me by snorting loudly.

"How's that for a dysfunctional family?"

# CHAPTER TWENTY-NINE

*Viv*

"Want me to stop at Standard? Pick up some pain au chocolat?"

"Dor, you can stop buying my good graces with pastries already, I'm gonna end up twice my size."

Dorian is on his way over for dinner. It's been two weeks since we got back from Bar Harbor and our tumultuous homecoming. Ike will be home tonight after a three-day trip and Dor offered to man the BBQ. My brother already redeemed himself by a mile, but seems insistent on making up with me. I've seen him a couple of times. He's come in to The Skipper, every time with a bag of something fresh-baked and delicious. Then he sits at the end of the bar, chatting up Arnie while waiting for me to speak to him. I relented the second time he appeared. Tonight will be the first time he comes to Ike's place, where I've been staying all this time. Something Ike brought up again last night, when he called me from his hotel room. He wants me staying with him to be a more permanent arrangement.

Two weeks ago, after my semi-hysterical burst of laughter, I left Ike and my brother in the living room, escaping before the tears would come. The moment I walked into the bedroom, where my brother had made himself at home, I decided I'd done enough crying. Enough. That's why, when I walked back into the living room fifteen minutes later, my bags in hand, both of them looked up in surprise.

"Where are you going?" Dorian asked, pointing at the bags in my hands.

"Ike's," I told him. "If he'll have me a bit longer, that is," I added, suddenly a bit insecure. The big smile behind his beard quickly dissolved any concerns I might have had. "Don't know how long you'll be staying, after … well, after today, but I feel the need for some distance. From everyone," I throw in for clarification.

I'd had enough. I never thought I would hear my mother spout garbage at me like she did. It shocked me. So much for easing into my reality. It fucking smacked me in the face. First with my brothers getting into a fucking fight over me, and then mommy dearest. *Jesus.* Dorian having my back with my mother, leaving no room for doubt as to where his loyalty lay, went a long way to soothe my initial anger. But my God, what a hot mess. It's enough to make me want to head right back to Bar Harbor, but Ike's house will have to do.

So I talked to Dor on his second time to the pub, and a bit more the third. That was last weekend. Tuesday Ike had to go to Norfolk, Virginia, to put together a local crew for work on his new design. He didn't want to go, felt it was too soon, but I convinced him that as long as he was fine having me stay here, I would be fine by myself. The fact that Pam promised to pop in on Wednesday night, went a long way to settling it as well. That was the first time he brought up me moving in permanently, giving up my apartment. I'd hauled over the stuff I'd need daily, but I was missing my *things.* That, and the fact we haven't known each other that long, has held me back from jumping in with both feet. Because, truth be told, I love Ike's house. It doesn't have my view, but it does have a nice backyard with a deck, perfect for having morning coffee. I can still hear the gulls and the fishing boats leave in the morning, and when the wind is right, I can even hear the water.

"So, is that a yes or a no?" Dorian pushes.

"Okay, fine, bring the damn chocolate croissants."

"So easy," I hear him tease as he hangs up the phone.

Just as I put mine down on the counter to finish the potato salad I'm making, it rings again.

"Dor—just the croissants, nothing else," I say, assuming it's my brother calling back. It is, but not that brother.

"Viv? Nolan here. Look, I'm driving up from Boston and staying the weekend. Any chance I can see you when I get into town?"

I don't say anything right away. Not quite sure what to say to be honest. I wish Ike was here so I could bounce it off him. Am I ready? Is he expecting a serious talk or is this just a visit? I could do a visit, I'm pretty sure I could manage that. Not so sure I'm ready for a heart-to-heart.

"Viv? If you need more time, I understand. We'll try for next time I come down."

That decides it. Hearing that he's not planning to give up on me, regardless of my answer, prompts me to say, "No. I mean, no, I don't need more time. I'm not at home though, I'm staying at Ike's."

Nolan chuckles. "I know, Dor told me, gave me his address too. Talked to him not ten minutes ago."

Dorian is a pain in my ass. I'm onto his game now, buttering me up with pastries just to smooth the ride for Nolan.

"Okay, but just so you know, I'm not sure I'm ready for a heart-to-heart," I admit.

"No worries, Sis. Hadn't planned on one, I just want to see you. Be there in thirty," he says softly, which makes me melt a little inside.

"Okay."

The dead air in my ear tells me he's hung up, and I snatch some paper towels to dab at my eyes. *For fuck's sake.*

Half an hour later, Dorian arrives, toting not one brown bakery bag, but four.

"Geeze, Dor. I thought you were bringing me *a* chocolate croissant, not the entire contents of the display case."

"Oh hush. Nothing wrong with a little sweet from time to time," he huffs past me and deposits his bags on the kitchen counter. "Whatever doesn't get eaten can be frozen. Or eaten for breakfast, that always works for me."

I'm still standing with the door open when another car pulls into the driveway. Nolan gets out, comes up to me, and saying nothing, pulls me in to hug me tight, before setting me back and also disappearing to the kitchen. Amazing how my brothers can't find a pair of clean socks to save their lives, but put them in a strange house and they easily find the kitchen.

I close the door and join them. Already they're pulling back the plastic wrap on just about everything I have set out on the counter and dipping their fingers in. "Hey, guys!" I warn before doling out a few well-aimed slaps on hands. "Back away from the potato salad and get out of my kitchen."

"Your kitchen, Sissy?" Dorian teases.

I glare at him. "Whatever, Dor." Only serving to make both my brothers start chuckling. Assholes.

In seconds they've located the beer, cranked up the stereo, and are popping one open outside on the deck. Looks like Nolan is staying for dinner as well. Fine. Not like there isn't enough. One of the drawbacks of occasionally cooking at the pub is that you don't have a good gauge on appropriate quantities anymore. Hence, whenever I do cook at home, it's generally enough to feed an army. Just in case, I pull another French stick from the freezer to go with the herb butter I made.

I'm about to wrap it in tinfoil to defrost in the oven, when there's a knock at the door. I hustle to the stereo and turn the volume down. Shit, way to get friendly with the neighbors, Vivian. I'm assuming one of them is here to complain about the loud music, so I pull open the front door, apologizing as I do. "I'm so, so..." my voice sticks in my throat. Because it isn't an annoyed neighbor on the doorstep, but Lydia and Owen looking very uncomfortable.

"Viv, I'm sorry we're barging in, but Dorian said—" Lydia starts, but doesn't need to finish. My youngest brother has been busy, for which I will have to kick his ass.

"No heart-to-heart," I repeat the conditions I expressed to Nolan not that long ago. I'm pretty sure I see relief flit over Owen's face at that. Dorian is the only one of my brothers reasonably comfortable with displays of emotion. The others, not so much.

"Okay," is Lydia's soft answer, before I step back and let them walk in.

## *Ike*

I'm surprised to find my driveway full of cars, and along with a healthy dose of irritation my homecoming will obviously not be able to play out the way I'd imagined, an uneasy feeling creeps up my neck.

Call me pathetic but three nights away from Viv, after having spent the summer falling asleep and waking up in her arms, was not conducive to good sleep or a good mood. Having to listen to her smoky voice over the phone, sounding even sexier than in person, with only my hand as companion, didn't help either.

The plan was to pull the Expedition into the garage, leave my shit for later, walk in, catch Viv as she'd jump in my arms, and march her right into the bedroom, where I'd waste no time getting her naked. No, there would be no hard, fast fuck to get rid of bottled-up frustration.

I've already battled heavy Friday afternoon traffic from the airport home. Now I was relegated to parking in the street. Fuck me.

With my bag hoisted over my shoulder, I walk in the door to hear the makings of a party. Music, voices, and laughing coming from the backyard can be heard through the open sliding doors. I drop my duffel on the floor by the stairs, walk through the house and outside, where I'm stunned to find Viv, Lydia, and three of her brothers. All toting beers, and all laughing.

Dorian is the first to spot me and smiles like the cat who ate the canary. No doubt he had something to do with this unplanned gathering. Unplanned, I'm sure, because Viv would've mentioned something last night otherwise.

Viv is the next to turn her head and squeals when she sees me, jumping up and running to me, still holding on to her beer. I barely get my hands under her ass in time when she jumps in my arms, spraying herself and me in beer. I don't care. Viv is beautiful any day and in any situation, but when she's happy and smiling that smile, which makes the lines at the side of her eyes pop out, she is fucking breathtaking. Not particularly needing an audience, I turn back into the house, Viv clinging to me like a monkey.

"You're home." She smiles at me big, her eyes shining when I plop her butt on the kitchen island.

"I'm home, and in need of some lovin'," I point out. Viv doesn't hesitate for a second before she has her mouth pressed against mine, her tongue seeking entrance, while her fingers tangle in my hair. My beautiful siren and beer—tastes fucking phenomenal. I have a mind to carry her to the bedroom and follow through with my original plan, ignoring the fact her brothers are on my deck, but I have a feeling Viv may take issue with that.

"Babe," I mumble against her lips, trying to pull back, which she is making very difficult. "Beautiful," I try more firmly before she loosens her hold on my head. "We've got guests," I point out with my eyebrow raised.

"Right. It's Dorian's fault. He invited them all without my knowledge. I was ambushed," she babbles, not appearing to be in the least riled by her brother's ministrations. "But don't worry, I laid down the law." She looks smug and I smile, because that looks seriously cute on her.

"You laid down the law," I repeat for clarification, to which she nods.

"Told them no heart-to-heart and they've stuck to it."

Before I have a chance to react, Dorian sticks his head in the door. "Can I light the BBQ now?"

Wait. Dorian's going to mess with my BBQ? "Hold on to that thought," I delay him, quickly lowering Viv back on her feet and opening the drawer for my lighter. It's not there. "Babe, where'd my lighter go?" I look at her and she in turn points to Dorian, who is waving said lighter in the air before disappearing outside. I take off after him, Viv's laughter following me outside. Laugh, but no one lights my BBQ but me.

I feel a hand on my back and a mug of coffee appears from around me, which I gratefully take. Reaching behind me, I pull Viv to my side with my arm resting at her waist.

"How's it going?" she asks, with a smile in her voice.

I glare at her brother, who is currently warming up chocolate croissants on my BBQ. I'd almost given him the green light too, seeing as the chicken he cooked earlier— something that to do well, requires a bit of skill—was delicious and moist. Of course he had constant supervision from me. But once the food was eaten and I'd started a pot of coffee, he announced he was gonna "BBQ the pastries" and I almost had a coronary. Visions of melting or worse, burning, chocolate on my grill had me almost snatch the bag of croissants from his hand. But Viv was quicker, and calmly wrapped the croissants in tinfoil before placing them on a baking tray. "There," she said smugly when handing the tray to Dorian.

"No leakage," I say, referring to the dreaded melting chocolate, making Viv chuckle.

"Glad to hear it. Now are you coming to sit down?"

With just a nod I follow and sit down beside her around the small fire pit off my deck. Everyone has dragged their chairs onto the grass, and Nolan and Owen are arguing about the best way to stack the wood for a good fire. Lydia is sitting back in her chair, sipping her coffee and observing.

"You should bring your kids next time," I suggest, surprising even myself. "I think I have a volleyball net somewhere in the garage."

"We will. They'd love that," Lydia says with a smile, as Viv snuggles into my side.

With the fire built and the admittedly fucking awesome chocolate croissants eaten, Viv and Lydia are talking in hushed tones beside me, while I listen to the brothers share funny childhood stories. Makes me think about some of the shit my brother and I would get into from time to time. Mostly with me instigating and Ben executing. It makes me sad to think that we'll never have times like this, where we can relive our history or even share with our kids at some point. Really fucking sad.

"Hey," Viv says softly, with her hand on my arm and her face tilted up to me. "You okay? Looking a little sad."

"Just listening to your brothers talk—I miss that. Miss Ben."

Her face goes soft. "I get that. I was just saying to Lydia that although it's hard to hear how different their experience growing up was compared to mine, I'm glad they have that."

"Yeah." My mouth agrees, but inside I'm cursing myself. I miss Ben, but I love the good memories I have of him, growing up with him. I didn't consider that Viv doesn't have those kinds of memories, and I'm once again struck at the strength of heart this woman has. Despite the shit they put on her, she still manages to be happy for her brothers.

All but one, who is glaringly absent.

I'd asked Dorian earlier, if he'd been in touch with Aaron, and he said he'd tried a few times, without success.

"I miss Aaron," Viv suddenly says, staring in the fire, as if she'd been reading my thoughts. It immediately silences any conversation and all eyes turn to her. She seems to realize she has everyone's attention and blinks a few times. "I'm sorry, you guys, I know I'm breaking my own rules. I'm just so goddamn sorry for everything," she finishes on a sob and buries her face in my shoulder.

"Jesus, Viv," Owen is the first to speak. "Nothing to be sorry for. Not you."

"Yeah, none of this is on you, Sissy," Dorian adds.

Nolan gets up, walks over and hunches down in front of her. "Vivian." He draws her attention in a firm voice. "The responsibility for this lies with one person and he's in a hospital bed. The only other people who should arguably share some of that responsibility is everyone else in the

331

family ... except you. Not your burden to carry, and not your problem to solve. Been a shock to the system, that's for damn sure. Finding out that what all of us had chosen to believe was a great family to grow up in was actually a farce, was a harsh awakening. And the way each of us responded to that is on each of us. Including Aaron, and including Mom." He leans in and cups her wet face between his hands, tipping his forehead to hers. "There is no way you can take this on, sweetheart. You tried to carry this family singlehandedly on your shoulders for years, when all this time it was us failing you. That ends now."

I reluctantly let Viv's body slide from under my arm as she leans forward into her brother's arms. There is some clearing of throats all round and a sniffle from Lydia.

"I need a fucking beer," I try to break the emotionally loaded atmosphere, as I stand up.

"Thought you'd never fucking ask," is Owen's response and Lydia giggles.

"I'll take one," she says, and Dorian nods when I look at him.

"Just bring two," Nolan grumbles, as he sets his sister back in her chair, ruffling her hair before he retreats back to the other side of the fire.

"Honey?" I look at Viv whose watery smile reaches in and squeezes my heart. "Just bring out the whole damn crate."

It's past midnight and the last of the wood was tossed on the fire a good half hour ago. Aside from the few minutes of high drama, the evening has been really good. So good in fact, I've lost any lingering resentment over the thwarting of my plans for a very different welcome home a while ago.

But it's past midnight, and Viv is yawning loudly beside me, while Dorian is nodding off in his chair. We've all had plenty to drink, and I don't feel good about letting anyone drive home.

"I have a spare bedroom and a couch that sleeps two, in a pinch. You may wanna consider crashing here for the night."

Dorian and Nolan readily agree. Dorian mainly because it means he can stumble inside and simply go back to sleep. Since Nolan was planning to stay at Viv's apartment with Dorian, his is an easy decision as well. Owen objects, at first, until Lydia points out that with the kids at her mother's until tomorrow anyway, it would be safer and more convenient if they stay. Seeing as, even with her soft manner, Lydia obviously is in charge, Owen eventually gives in.

I grab extra sheets and blankets, while Viv scrambles to dig up extra toiletries and sorts out a sleep shirt for Lydia. By the time one o'clock rolls around, everyone is tucked away. I've just had a quick shower to wash off the residual travel and beer stench when I walk into the bedroom to find Viv curled up on her side, already fast asleep. Without wasting time I slip under the covers behind her, curl my body around hers, and with my nose in her hair, feel sleep taking me too.

The insistent ringing of a phone wakes me a few hours later. I reach for my cell, which I left on the nightstand, but the blank screen tells me it's not mine, must be Viv's. By the time I get around to her side of the bed, Viv's phone stops ringing, but another phone starts up, somewhere else in the house.

"What's going on?" Viv's sleepy voice comes from the bed, as I'm already pulling up my jeans.

# CHAPTER THIRTY

*Viv*

The ride to the hospital is chaotic with Nolan and Dorian piled in the back of Ike's Expedition. Lydia and Owen, who had their car at the end of the driveway, are just ahead of us.

Nolan ended up answering his phone, and was zipping up his pants when Ike and I came down the stairs. "Be there soon," is all he said before he hung up. He spotted us and looked over at Dorian, who was by now awake as well. "Get dressed. The hospital called; Dad's bad. Aaron is taking Mom to the hospital. We're meeting them there."

I was frozen, until a warm hand on my neck and Owen's warm voice got me moving. "Get dressed, Viv," he said. I hadn't noticed them coming down behind us. I rushed into the bedroom and started pulling on the first piece of clothing my hands encountered. Ike was already waiting by the bedroom door for me by the time I was dressed. Grabbing my hand, he pulled me down the stairs. Luckily he had the presence of mind to grab my purse, something that hadn't even occurred to me.

Now we're on our way and I am just letting myself get swept along. Because honestly? I have no idea what I'm supposed to be doing. Where I'm supposed to be. But for once I'm going to trust my brothers, who gave me back a whole lot last night, and I will let them lead the way.

A warm hand slips over mine in my lap. *Ike.* The small squeeze around my fingers reminds me, I don't stand alone. If

I want it, he'll give it all to me. In that moment, regardless of what is heading our way, I decide I'm giving him everything too. "I love you, Isaac," is what I say. "I love you and I'm moving in with you."

His hand convulses around mine before he lifts it and brings it to his mouth, peeling my fingers back and pressing his lips in my palm. "I love you back, and I'm glad, baby. It's where you belong." I can feel his words soak into the skin of my hand and carefully fold my fingers over top, keeping them close.

Surprisingly there is nothing but silence from the backseat where, as I'm a bit late in realizing, my brothers just got a front row seat. When I throw a quick look over my shoulder, both of them are silently grinning. Whatever.

It's Owen's idea to first find out exactly what happened from the night nurse, before walking into my father's room and have emotion take over. It's a good idea, and the nurse is very forthcoming.

What I didn't know, because everyone had been avoiding the topic of my father, was that he had developed pneumonia over the past week and as it turns out, antibiotics have done little.

"He's deteriorated quite dramatically over the past few hours, and we felt it prudent to warn the family. I'm afraid it will be a shock." The kind nurse looks at each of us as she warns us. "We tried to make him as comfortable as possible, but the reality is that the build up of fluid in his lungs was very fast and is substantial, so breathing has become very difficult. I encourage you to use the suction clipped to his headboard, to give him a bit of temporary relief."

Ike's hand squeezes my shoulder as he leans in. "Breathe, beautiful," he mumbles. I've been holding my breath and I didn't even notice. The nurse smiles at me sympathetically. If only she knew how very conflicted I feel about being here. Then I look at my brothers and remind myself that being here for them outweighs anything else I might or might not be feeling.

"There won't be any restriction on numbers, since your father has a private room and, well, because of the circumstances. There is also the waiting room next door, which is free for your use. One last thing," she says, a wistful smile on her face. "Your father is surprisingly lucid. He is aware and seems cognizant of everything and everyone around him."

"Thank you," Owen says, and with his arm around his wife's shoulder, leads the way.

I can hear his labored breathing from well outside the room, and it has me hesitate on the doorstep. I listen to the gurgling of the suction wand, as I watch Aaron clear our father's mouth. One by one, the boys walk up to the bed, acknowledge Aaron and kiss my mother on the cheek, before leaning over my father to let him know they're here. Neither my mother or Aaron look at me. I feel completely out of place. Yet I can't take my eyes off the figure in the hospital bed. I know in my bones I'm supposed to be here.

"Viv," Aaron's voice, hoarse and unexpected, drags me from my thoughts. I see him flick his eyes at our mother, who sits stoically on the other side of my father, then back at me. "He's asking for you." The hair on my neck stands on end, as I glance at my father's mouth and watch his lips move. I inadvertently take a step back, bumping into the hard, solid, secure wall of Ike's chest. I can feel the panic rising up from the tips of my toes, taking control over every muscle in my body, making me shake violently. It's only the safe hold Ike's arms have around my middle that holds me back from slipping into that dark place, where panic rules me.

I don't want to come any closer. Don't want to hear what he has to say.

"Babe," Ike's voice sounds concerned.

"Come here," Owen suddenly speaks up as he walks up to me. "I'll take you." I'm pretty sure he's not aware the minefield he's walking into, yet when his arm comes around my shoulders, I'm surprised to find it grounds me. I let my eyes travel through the room, locking in on each of my brothers, before making the decision I can do this for them. Give them a sense of closure as I don't expect to receive any. I didn't realize my feet were already moving, and I find myself by my father's bed, Owen by my side and Ike at my back, my father's eyes clear on me.

"I'm so ... sorry," his voice comes out on a rattle, but the words are clear. Clear enough for everyone in the room to have heard. A slow building keen comes from the other side of the bed where my mother has her hands clasped to her mouth. Oddly detached, as if everything is moving in slow-motion, I watch Lydia and Nolan fuss over her. Ike's arms band tighter around my waist as Aaron's, "*Jesus*" hits my ears. When I look back at my father his eyes have closed, but still his breath rattles.

"Give me that," I tell Aaron, who lost all color in his face and is holding the suction wand uselessly by his side. Moving away from the safety of my brother and my man, I take the wand from Aaron's hand, nudge him aside and carefully clear my father's sagging mouth from the fluids that are slowly drowning him. I don't do it for him. I also don't do it for my family, but I'm doing this for me. With every touch of his skin and every sweep of his mouth, I remind myself that this is my choice.

# *Ike*

Everything in me wants to follow her as she moves away, but I hold back and watch in amazement as she carefully, and with a surprising amount of tenderness, ministers to her father. I know I'm watching a victim turn into a survivor before my eyes.

-

Three hours later, never having regained consciousness after repenting, Vivian's father rattled his last breath. She never gave him her absolution, but gently eased him as he slipped out of this world.

The room had stayed oddly quiet after her mother quieted down, but Viv's eyes never left her father.

When it is done, she turns into my arms and I fold her in. A nurse comes in and quietly starts disconnecting the various tubes and wires. I move Viv out of her way and sit down in a vacant chair against the wall, settling her on my lap.

"He's gone," her soft whisper is barely audible.

"Yes, beautiful. He's gone."

She lifts her head from my shoulder and looks me in the eyes. "I want to cry for him, but I can't."

"Maybe not for him, but you can cry for you and for your brothers."

Her head swings around and she finally takes in the scene around her. Lydia in Owen's arms, their heads bent together. Nolan with his arms around their mother, softly stroking her back, his eyes closed. Aaron still standing close to his father's bed, his hands in his pockets and his jaw clenched. Finally she turns to Dorian, who is leaning against the far wall, silent tears streaming down his face.

"I have to go to him," Viv says softly when she turns her eyes back to me. "And after that, take me home."

I lean in, kiss her lightly, and let her look after her brother, waiting until she's ready for me to take her home.

"Make love to me."

This is not what I expect when I finally slip between the sheets and pull Viv back to me.

We'd left the hospital, which had been strange. Other than Dorian, no one even seemed to notice us leaving. Still, Viv stopped in the doorway and turned to her family. "I'm sorry, I have to go," was all she said and with understanding nods from every one of her brothers, we walked out. Once out on the street, she stopped me. "Take me to the diner?" she asked. So I did. We shared an order of pancakes, most of which I ended up eating. Then she asked me to take her to the wharf, where we silently watched the sun come up at the end of the pier.

But I really didn't expect this. Part of me understands she is taking bits and pieces back, somehow reclaiming herself with these seemingly random requests, but still I have to ask. "Babe, are you sure?"

She rolls over to face me and puts a hand to my cheek. "Yes, I am. This is a choice I make for *me.* Just like breakfast and the pier. Just like making my father as comfortable as I could, and leaving when we did. These are my choices. Make love to me, Isaac."

I don't hesitate this time, my eyes zoom in on her tongue licking along her bottom lip. No hesitation at all, when I slip her shirt off over her head, before showing her with my mouth, hands, and cock how fucking much I love her.

-

Four days later we're standing at the gravesite, a little distance from the rest. The crowd is very small. The brothers had asked for a private ceremony and burial, given the circumstances. Viv had opted to stay away from any funeral arrangements, asking only to be told where and what time.

She'd felt guilty when she found out her brothers had limited the funeral to immediate family only, but I reminded her of what Nolan had said; not to take on what didn't belong to her.

Dorian's husband had closed the gallery and flown in two days ago, and with his effervescent nature, managed to lighten up the heavy general atmosphere when we'd had the family over for another BBQ last night. Without Aaron and their mother, but with Owen and Lydia's children and Nolan's daughter. Since Gunnar and Syd would not be at the funeral the next day, Viv had asked them to come as well, insisting it was beyond time for Owen and Gunnar to patch up their differences, as well. Of course with them came Dexter, who eagerly fist-bumped me when he walked in, and then without reservation walked over to Owen and Lydia's two boys. The youngest introduced himself as Jacob and the older one, about the same age as Dex, said his name was Benjamin, but to call him Ben. I hadn't paid much attention to their names to be honest. They'd come tearing through the house to the backyard, and I'd barely seen them since. "Boys" seemed to be the preferred way for their parents to address them, which is why when I heard the name of the older boy, a warm shiver ran down my spine.

Gunnar's eldest, the very pretty and rather shy Emmy, took ten minutes to warm up. By then she was giggling with Nolan's girl, Chloe, on the couch inside.

I've had little exposure to kids. I was actually surprised how easy it was to have fun with them. It also made me think of having kids of my own someday, and wondered how Viv would feel about that.

The kids are part of the reason why Viv wanted to stay back from the gravesite, she didn't want any dramatic outbursts to mar what was already a traumatic event for those kids. Not even Dorian's pleas swayed her from that decision.

We wait until the priest finishes his final prayers over the casket, watch it being lowered slowly into the ground, and watch as everyone, starting with their mother, picks up a clump of dirt and drops it in the grave. The last one to turn their backs on the grave, are Aaron and his mother. It surprises me when after a few steps toward the car, she stops Aaron and turns back to the cemetery employees, who are about close the grave. I can't hear what she says, but there's no mistaking her intention when she turns and points at us. One last look in our direction before they continue their trek to the car.

"For an apology, that was pretty weak," Viv dryly remarks beside me. A chuckle bubbles up that I don't bother hiding. She smiles at me before taking my hand. "But that doesn't mean I don't appreciate the gesture," she says, before walking determinedly over to her father's grave, where she bends to pick up her own handful of dirt. "I hope your soul can find peace," she says before dropping the dirt on his casket. The soft thud has the sound of finality.

"Shall we brave the house?" she asks, when we get to the truck.

"Absolutely," I smile at her, proud of the way she is handling this.

Of course Pam has been by every day this week, making sure Viv was as okay as she made it seem. After Viv assured her that she'd said goodbye to the only father she cared to remember a very long time ago, Pam seemed satisfied.

A few close friends and neighbors had been invited to attend a small reception at Viv's parents' house. It was also meant to double as sort of a last hurrah for the house, since ironically it had sold the day before Fergus Lestar passed away. Viv's mother was scheduled to move out by the end of next month, giving her time to sort through forty odd years of belongings and condense it to a living/dining room and one bedroom in her new apartment.

Walking up the walkway to the house, the front door swings open and Aaron steps outside.

*Viv*

This past week I'd expected to be confronted with Aaron—was prepared for it—but nothing happened.

And nothing will happen now. The minute I see him come out that door and wait for us on the front step, I know he has something to say, but today I don't want to hear it. Any other day, I'd be willing to listen but not on the day we put our father in the ground.

"Viv," he starts, and I immediately cut him off.

"Aaron, I appreciate you have things you want to say, but here and now is not the time or place." I see his shoulders slump and his jaw clench, as he slowly closes his eyes.

"You're right," he says, before taking a deep breath, stepping around us, and walking away from the house.

"Was I cold?" I ask Ike, not sure if I made the right call and a little worried when he walked away.

"No. You were honest and also right. Let's go in."

The next few hours aren't as bad as I thought they might be. Mostly because Lydia totally intervenes each time my mother even looks at me. I don't know yet if I will ever have a relationship again with my mother, all I know is if I do, it will never be the same.

Kyle makes the afternoon go by a lot smoother too, with his outrageously effeminate charm. He breezes through the house, playing hostess, and making sure everyone's drink stays topped up, serving hors d'oeuvres and flirting with women and men equally. Mostly to the women's delight and for the men uncomfortably so. Still, by the end of the afternoon there isn't a person here, including my mother, who doesn't return the warm smiles he shares freely. I have to remember to thank him, for this and for being the first to reach out to me when the proverbial shit hit the fan.

Aaron never came back to the house.

"Babe. Need you to come," Ike growls in my neck.

I'm on all fours, holding on to the headboard, and Ike is powering his cock into me from behind. I'm so close, but I can't seem to let myself fall over the edge. "I can't." I woke up with Ike's head buried between my legs, already fully engaged in eating me out and making me come the first time. I can't come so soon after.

"Vivian, you can," he pants, as his hand slides around and down, while his middle finger presses down hard on my clit. A magic button because the moment he starts rubbing in tight little circles, my inner walls start pulsing and I fall. Before I know it he's on his knees, his hand cupping my breast, the other arm around my waist, and he has me flush against his chest. It only takes seconds of him thrusting up inside me until he comes on a deep groan. Falling forward, he rolls us so that he ends on his back with me on top of him. I worm around until I'm comfortable, with my legs tangled in his, my hand on his chest, and my cheek to his shoulder.

"How many babies do you want?"

It's early morning, a few days after my father's funeral and he wants to talk babies? I try to push up, but his arms keep me in place.

"Don't think so much, Viv. Just answer, first thing that comes to mind."

"Three," I blurt out.

"Three? Okay," he chuckles. "But you know what that means, right?"

No. I have not the faintest what he's talking about. "Nope."

"We have to start right away."

"Ike!" I slap his chest because he's still laughing.

"I'm serious. I think we should have our kids before I turn fifty and if you count two years in between each kid, for gestation and a little break for you, I figure we'll have to get going now."

"A little break?" I manage to lift my head and rest my chin on his chest, looking up into his beautiful eyes that are currently sparkling with amusement. "Kids, huh? Where did that come from?"

He shrugs his shoulders and his eyes turn serious. "Never had much cause to be around them. It's hard to miss what you don't know. I didn't know I wanted any, but I want children with you."

He's dead serious, which is why I pull myself up and kiss him sweetly on the lips.

"You know that I'm a little old to start, right? I mean it would likely already be considered a high risk pregnancy because of my age. Besides, isn't it a bit soon to start talking about that?"

He growls as he gently rolls me, so I'm on the bottom and he's on top. "Woman, you're contradicting yourself. First you say time is ticking and next you suggest we take our time. Which is it? Or is it that you don't want kids?"

My hands come up to cup his face. "I'll have them with you." I smile, seeing his face light up.

"Excellent," he says after kissing me breathless. "We're getting the rest of your stuff this weekend. Decide whether you want to keep the apartment, so your brothers have a pad when they're in town, or get rid of it. And I'm going to want to make this legal."

Too early to keep up with his warp speed, so I don't even try, and kiss him instead. The moment Ike takes over the kiss, the shrill ring of the phone interrupts our morning play time.

# CHAPTER THIRTY-ONE

*~Three weeks later~*

*Viv*

I walk up the stairs to the courthouse, Ike's hand on the small of my back, and shaking in my sensible pumps. Wear something conservative, ADA Phillips had instructed me. So I did, a pencil skirt, a plain white blouse and these butt-ugly sensible pumps. Kyle had taken me shopping yesterday.

We'd arrived two days ago and I'd been grilled by the ADA, who wanted to make sure my testimony would be solid, even under cross examination. It was brutal and I almost walked out when he'd gone so hard on me, I had to fight back tears.

"Don't fight those tears, they can make the difference between winning or losing. We need you to be as human as possible. Let the jury see you're broken."

That's when I picked up my now cold coffee off the table in the little office and flung it with all my might against the wall. Shocked that bastard good.

"I'm not fucking broken!" I yelled at Phillips. That's when Ike came flying in, followed by a security officer. He'd been waiting outside on a bench when he heard me yell. Told the ADA in no uncertain terms that he was *done*, while looming over the guy with noses almost touching. Ike irate was scary. Phillips apparently thought so too and confirmed that indeed he was done and would see me in court on Wednesday. The day I was scheduled to testify.

He is an asshole, calling us on a Saturday morning, shooting off location, date, and time when I was expected in LA. Frank's assault case, obviously, but little else was shared with me. I'd known it was likely I would have to testify at some point, but with everything going on, my father's death and his funeral, I swear it had been relegated to the far recesses of my mind.

Needless to say the past few weeks have been stressful, but as Kyle so typically pointed out yesterday, it was also almost over. Which is what gives me the strength to pull open the courthouse doors, walk in, and start looking for courtroom nine. Ike, as always, close on my heels.

We've been waiting for almost an hour, when I hear, "There they are!" from the end of the hall. Kyle is dragging Dorian toward the bench where we were told to sit.

"What are you guys doing here?" I want to know.

"Nothing better to do," Dorian grumbles, and Kyle elbows him in the ribs.

"Don't listen to him, sweetie, we're here to support you. And after it's all said and done, we'll go celebrate."

At that moment, the double doors open and the court clerk walks out. "Ms. Vivian Lestar?" His warm brown eyes zoom in on me, since I'm the only female I suppose.

Ike presses a quick kiss to my head and whispers, "You've got this, beautiful."

I manage to throw a nervous little smile in the general direction of my brother and his husband, before trotting on my ridiculous shoes after the big, black and very long-limbed court clerk. I focus on the back of the man in front of me and try not to look into the gallery on the side, or the curious glances from the folks in the jury box. Most of all, I avoid looking at the man sitting behind a desk on the left side of the aisle beside his lawyer. The clerk holds the little gate open, and I notice Phillips, the ADA, get up from his seat the moment we pass. I'm told to sit in a chair to the right of the judge, on the side of the jury. I feel all eyes on me but keep mine down.

"Miss." The deep bass of the clerk is gentle and hushed, and I raise my eyes to meet his warm sympathetic ones. "You gotta look up when I swear you in."

"Okay," I whisper back, which draws a little twitch at the corner of his otherwise straight mouth.

So with his eyes calming me, I place my hand on the Bible and repeat after him, as instructed. I almost want to hide behind him when he turns away and exposes me to the whole courtroom. Instead I focus on the ADA, who is standing in front of me. I don't like the guy, would go so far as to say I actively *dis*like him, but he's the only person I know for sure will try to get Frank put away. Even if he has to make me bleed to do it.

His questions are surprisingly gentle, much more so than in his office, and I realize pretty quickly he's playing to the jury. He repeatedly asks me to "tell the jury" something. After the first time, when he had to gesture to the gallery of twelve people sitting to my left, I soon clued in that at some points during my testimony, he wants me to face them and talk directly to them.

The first time I show emotion is when a few slides of my battered body are entered into evidence. I'm asked to pinpoint each one as to time and place, and a few times when a new slide came up I could hear soft gasps from the jury box. That got to me. Then I'm hit with what he says is his last question.

"Miss Lestar, do you see present here the man responsible for the injuries as shown?"

I've managed to avoid looking directly at Frank so far, but now I have to.

"I do," I say, as my eyes find his angry ones, and suddenly I'm not nervous anymore. I fucking bested the guy once before, I can do it again. I feel my back straighten. I'm in the driver's seat this time.

"Can you point him out to the court?"

"Gladly," I say, pointing my finger at his scowling face. I come *this* close to sticking out my tongue and singing, *neener-neener-neener* as I do it, but manage to control myself.

After that, the defense does their best to shake my testimony. One question in particular, in which I was asked whether I was sure I wasn't a willing participant in some *rough play*, rattled me. I longingly look at the doors I came through, hoping for a quick escape, when I happen to spot a number of familiar faces in the last row.

## *Ike*

I can tell the moment she spots all of us sitting in the back row. Her eyes widen and the smallest smile hits her mouth as she turns back to the defense attorney.

"Never," she says loud and clear. "Mr. Miller was never interested in my opinion, my wishes, or any preferences I might have. Sexual or otherwise. The man wasn't even able to beat an orgasm out of me."

At that, Frank shoots out of his chair, kicking it over. "You lying fucking bitch!" he yells, moving to climb over the table.

The entire back row, which includes all her brothers, Kyle, Gunnar, and me are on our feet. Before we have a chance to move though, the court clerk, who'd been standing in front of the gate, launches himself at Frank and has him to the ground in seconds. I glance over at Viv, and instead of the shock I expected to see on her face, a smug little smile tugs at the corners of her mouth. *I'll be damned.*

It takes the judge five more minutes to bring the courtroom to order. And another five to shoot down the objection the defense tries to enter. In the end, Viv is excused from the witness stand, escorted past us, and out the door by the big clerk, who returns promptly and stands legs spread and hands at his back in front of the door, blocking my way out. Thank fuck it doesn't take both prosecution and defense long to rest their case. Before adjourning, the judge instructs the jury and tells the court that final arguments will be heard after lunch.

I watch with no small amount of satisfaction, as Frank Miller is taken by guards, handcuffed and shackled now, through the small door leading presumably to his holding cell. Good fucking riddance.

The moment the door is clear, I hurry out to find Viv, wringing her hands, on the other side.

"You fucking rock," I tell her as she throws herself in my arms. "You nailed him, beautiful." I reluctantly release her as one after the other wants their turn with my girl. Standing off to the side is Aaron, who apparently flew in this morning with Owen, Nolan, and Gunnar. Viv's eyes are shiny with tears, but she also has a big smile on her face.

"You crazy guys. What are you all doing here?" She turns from one to the other.

Owen finally speaks up. "It was Aaron's idea. Said it was about fucking time we showed our sister we had her back. Wasn't that hard to convince us."

Viv immediately moves to Aaron and is about a foot from him, when he reaches out and pulls her the rest of the way, wrapping her in his arms.

"Fucked up, did it big and I know I can't ever make it right, but I promise I'll fucking well try."

"Means a lot," Viv tells him before turning around and looking at everyone, clearly having lost the battle with her tears. "All of you—it means the world."

After a quick lunch, not too far from the courthouse, we are back, but this time Viv joins us in the back row. Frank is back behind the table, still in cuffs and shackles, and his lawyer is pontificating in front of an obviously uninterested jury.

The prosecution had been smart to keep their prior closing argument to a single line. "Unless you are deaf, blind, or no longer breathing, what you've heard in testimony, what you've seen in evidence, and what you've been able to witness today in this courtroom, there is only one possible verdict. Guilty."

From the nods of the members of the jury, it's safe to say he impressed. Not so his opponent. By the time he insisted the jury enter a not guilty verdict, most of them were staring at the ceiling or picking their nails.

It was not a surprise when not even an hour after the jury was dismissed, we were back in the courtroom to hear the verdict. Guilty. Applause went up as that piece of shit was led out of the courtroom, knowing he would have to return in a week to receive his sentence.

We are not going to be around for that.

On our way down the steps, Viv suddenly bursts out laughing. I pull her close and smile down at her. "What's so funny?"

"I feel like Snow White with her seven dwarfs," she snorts, as she looks at her entourage of seven men of rather large stature, before her eyes come to rest on me. "Well, actually, you probably can't be my dwarf and my prince at the same time. I may have to rethink that."

In the meantime, the guys have passed by us and are waiting and chatting on the sidewalk below. That gives me a chance to pull her body into mine, bend my mouth to hers, and kiss her until I can feel her melt in my arms.

"You know," I mumble, my lips still on hers. "For you I'll be frog, dwarf, prince, it doesn't matter. As long as I can end up as your husband, you won't hear a single complaint out of me."

"Love you, Isaac," she smiles, bright eyed, up at me.

"To the moon and back, babe."

"Guys!" Kyle yells out. "Let's go! My hors d'oeuvres are getting soggy."

It's that evening, with a goodly number of celebratory drinks in the system, that I come up with my brilliant plan.

"Guys," I address the group the moment Viv disappears to the washroom. "How would you like to change your flights around, and add one overnight stop?"

Once I have formulated my idea, Kyle, as expected, is all over it. So are the others, although Gunnar makes a good point. "What about Syd? And Lydia and Pam? I know they'll be upset if they miss it."

"Dammit. Didn't think of that. Okay, what if we FaceTime them? They could see her surprise firsthand."

"Bud," Gunnar calmly draws my attention. "I'm sure that half bottle of Courvoisier you soldiered through, by yourself, is reason your brain cells are working at half power, but have you considered how much of a surprise it'll be when we all end up flying to Vegas tomorrow? I mean, she does have to get on the plane. Your surprise will be null and void, the moment we board."

"What surprise?"

*Fuck. Shit.*

I don't have to turn around to know Viv is standing right behind me. She's at least as buzzed as I am, although her drink of choice had been chocolate martinis that Kyle has been more than happy to ply her with. Still, not nearly drunk enough not to remember the conversation she walked in on. To make it worse, her brothers burst out laughing. Even Gunnar chuckles, although that's a rare occurrence.

"Ike?" She moves around to stand in front of me, hands on her hips, clearly conveying she expects an answer.

Only one thing left to do. "Stay here," I tell her as I get up and turn her around, pushing her down in my vacated spot. "And you," this I direct at the guys. "Not a word." Before they have a chance to respond, I run up the stairs, to the spare bedroom, digging through the small side pocket in my shaving kit, where I'd hidden the ring I bought her last time I was in Norfolk. I tuck it into my pocket and race back down the stairs, ignoring the mild swaying of the steps under my feet. I come to a stop in front of Viv, who is looking with suspicion around the room before her eyes lift to mine.

Never thought I'd do this. Fucking positively never figured I'd do this in front of an audience. I sink down on my knees, hitting the floor a little harder than intended, sending a sharp jab of pain through my knee. "Son of a bitch," I bite off, which gets the gang behind me snickering again. "Shut up," I throw over my shoulder before grabbing Viv's hands. She looks a little like a deer caught in headlights. "Love you, Vivian Lestar. Thought I would die single and wandering the roads. Never expected anything else, until you. Never hoped for anything more, until now. Marry me?" I let go with one hand and start digging in my pocket for the ring, which I triumphantly fish out, when I notice she hasn't said anything. Her eyes are big and welling with tears, but she's not giving me any words. "Viv, honey?"

"I can't believe you asked, I mean, we talked about a future, but I thought we'd keep it simple and uncomplicated. No muss—no fuss." A single tear rolls down her face.

"Baby, I—"

"No." She cuts me off, putting her hand on my lips. "You don't get it. You're fussing, Ike. I never thought you would, but you're fussing."

I'm so lost. I'm worried I bungled this because I don't have a fucking clue what she's talking about. Slightly panicked, I look to Kyle who's sitting beside her, *his* eyes full of tears. With a big smile he gives me a thumbs up. *That's good, right?* Should've done this sober.

"Beautiful, help me out here?" I'm trying to ignore the snickering behind me when Viv slides down on the floor with me and wraps her arms around my neck, tilting her head so she can look me in the eyes.

"I love it that you're fussing. I thought I'd made it clear a while ago, but for the record: yes. Yes, I'd be thrilled to marry you."

"Great," Nolan says deadpan. "Now that we have that out of the way, Planet Hollywood sound okay to you?"

"Right," I say when I see Viv's confused face. "I was trying to surprise you. We're eloping. We're all flying to Vegas tomorrow."

Viv leans in close to my ear, but still manages to say loud enough for the room to hear, "Honey, it's hardly eloping if you're dragging my entire family along."

The chuckles last long after the outburst of laughter has subsided.

I wake up with Viv's hair tickling my nose. Aside from a slight throbbing, my head feels surprisingly good. Of course it helped that we all switched to water and coffee, while we spent a couple of hours shifting and changing flights, booking rooms and most importantly a chapel. Kyle even managed to find Viv a dress that will be delivered at the hotel at midday tomorrow.

Still, in the bright light of day, and with a much clearer head, I have to ask again. "Beautiful," I whisper against her hair. "Are you awake?" My hand snakes around her waist and slips down between her legs where I loosely cup her.

"Mmmmmm."

"I really need you to look at me." With slow strokes, I rub my finger along her crease. Almost immediately she becomes wet as she hums again, spreading her legs slightly. "Turn around, baby." Slowly and with her beautiful eyes sleep swollen, she rolls over on her back, keeping my hand trapped between her legs. "Got a question for you," I tell her, enjoying the slight arch of her back off the mattress, as I slide my finger inside her heat.

"What?" she hisses when my thumb finds her clit, but her eyes never waver from mine.

"Will you marry me? Today? No regrets, no complications, just you and me. Oh, and four plus two brothers." She smiles at that, tilting her hips when I slip in a second finger.

"Yeesss," she moans, and I stifle the sound with my mouth on hers. Slowly pumping my fingers in and out, I let go of her mouth and trail open-mouthed kisses until I reach one of her deep-red, perky nipples and suck it against the roof of my mouth. A slight change of pressure of my thumb against her clit, and she explodes with my name on her lips.

# EPILOGUE

*~Three months later~*

*Viv*

"Honey, can you swing by Standard Baking on your way home and pick up some pastries?"

"Anything specific or a selection?" I can hear the smile in Ike's voice.

"Selection, but make sure there is at least a few pain au chocolat in there."

"Mmmm, you know I love it when you speak French to me."

"The only French I know. Better yet, the only French I need to know," I smile at his teasing sexy banter.

"Gotta go, my love. Have to finish this design if I want to be home in time for dinner."

After we say our goodbyes and hang up, I let my eyes drift to the dining table, which is set for ten.

This is the first time Dorian will be back in Portland since my father's funeral, and Nolan is driving up from Boston. Aaron will be here, as will Owen, Lydia and the kids. The tenth person will be my mother and that scares me a little.

Although I haven't seen her, I've spoken to her on the phone a few times. The first time was a week after the trial and Ike and my impromptu wedding in Vegas. She caught me by surprise and my stomach was immediately in knots when I heard her voice. She simply congratulated me on my wedding and told me she was happy I'd been able to put a bad guy in jail and managed to drag a good one in front of the altar, all in two days. I chuckled at that, as did she. The silence that followed was a tad uncomfortable, until she asked me timidly if she could call again sometime. I told her that was fine and two weeks later she called again, and again two weeks after that.

I asked Pam if that was normal, and she, very sagely, responded that we all make our own normal. I guess she's right.

The moment I heard Dorian was coming, I contacted my other brothers and organized this get-together. As an afterthought, I decided to call my mother as well. She seemed happy and a bit surprised that it was me calling her this time, but readily agreed to dinner at my house. Ike's house. Actually, our house.

We've hung on to the apartment, for now, and will occasionally rent it out short term. The rest of the time it's there for whomever needs it. Although I have to admit, I've thought about offering it to Ruby, she's looking for an affordable place so she can finally move out of Florence House. Not sure what we'll do.

I grab the asparagus from their little footbath in the fridge and start cleaning them over the sink. My eyes drift out the window as I think about the changes in my life this last half year. It's enough to make your head spin. Before, my life had been The Skipper and Florence House, with very little else in between, except perhaps sleep. Existing, is what Ike called it and he was right. I haven't felt it as clearly as I do now, the difference between existing and living. In my kitchen, preparing food for ten dinner guests, after having already worked the lunch shift, and my husband on his way home with fresh-baked goods from Standard.

May not seem like much to some, but to me it is full, rich, and meaningful. More so because I never thought I could have this. Now look at me. I still struggle with things, especially when it comes to my family. Some resentments still pop up, from time to time, but I talk through it with Ike, or I hit Pam up for a visit. Either way, I don't keep it buried anymore. I guess what happened to me will always be a part of me, but the difference now is that I don't let it dictate my life, my choices. My past no longer defines me, but it shapes me. It's made me aware of a strength I never realized I possessed. It's given me an endless appreciation and love for all the amazing people in my life. Not the least of whom is my husband. My rock.

"Anybody home?"

I quickly toss the last asparagus in the bowl and grab a towel to dry my hands as I walk out of the kitchen. Dorian is standing on the mat pulling a beanie off his head, making his hair stand on end.

"It's fucking cold here, Viv," he says as he opens his arms for a hug. I willingly walk into them and smile.

"End of October, little brother. Summer's over," I tell him.

"Not in San Fran it isn't."

"Not in California anymore, Dorothy." I love my brothers. All of them, but Dorian and I have that connection. One that had disappeared for a while, because neither of us worked on it, but now we do, and it's growing back. That makes me so happy.

"I thought Nolan was picking you up from the airport on his way up? Where is he?"

"Decided in your driveway that he should've made a stop at the bakery, pick up some sweets. So he's doing that now."

I smile, thinking that we won't have a shortage of desserts.

"Who else is coming?" Dorian says on his way to the kitchen, where I'm sure he'll be sampling every pot and pan on the stove.

"Owen and Lydia and their gang, Aaron, ... and Mom." It's kind of expected but still funny to see his eyes bulge and his mouth fall open as he swings around.

"No shit," he states, when he finally gets his mouth to move.

"No shit," I echo in the affirmative.

By the time Nolan walks in with a very full Standard grocery bag, Dorian is up to date on the *Mom* thing and is sitting at the island, sucking back a beer he appropriated from the fridge.

"Got another one of those?" Nolan asks, as he dumps his bounty on the counter and dives into the fridge, coming up with his own bottle before giving me a chance to answer. "Never mind. Got it," he says helpfully, and all I can do is roll my eyes. My brothers.

A ruckus from the front hall is a sure sign Lydia and her men have arrived. I step out of the kitchen, just in time to see the boys pull open the drawer underneath the TV and grab the controllers. Ike's introduction to children, in particular Gunnar and Owen's boys, has resulted in the purchase of the latest PlayStation and enough games to supply an arcade. I don't mind. I love seeing him mess around with the boys. "No shoes on the couch," I call out to them.

"Hey, Aunt Viv," Benjamin, the older of the two, twists his head around so he can see me over the back of the couch.

"That's it? That's all I get from you?" I ham it up a little, putting a smile on Ben's face. Then I turn to Jacob. "And what about you? No hugs, no kiss hello?" Ben is already by my side, hugging me awkwardly—it's the age—before jumping back on the couch.

"Auntie Viv, where's Ike?" Jacob is looking up at me, his little arms around my hips.

"Uncle Ike." My brother, who apparently already made his way into my fridge by the sound of it, corrects his youngest.

"But Dad ..."

"Jakey, listen to your father," Lydia's warm voice sounds behind me as her arms slip around my waist. "Hey, you."

I cover her hands on my stomach with my own. "Hey back." I lean my head back on her shoulder. Another blessing I have to remember to be thankful for. I'd always gotten along with Lydia, but since this summer, our relationship has changed. She no longer just is my brother's wife, but has become like a sister.

"By the way," she says as she lets me go. "Owen insisted we stop at Standard."

I can't hold back the chuckle as I follow her into the kitchen.

I'm just sliding the asparagus into the oven, next to the roast, when another "hello" sounds from the front of the house. From the enthusiastic greetings from my nephews, I know it's Aaron and my mom. Before I have a chance to go and greet them, Mom comes walking in the kitchen and it hits me how good she looks. Old, sure, but with a lightness in her eyes that I can't remember ever seeing.

"Oh look," she says looking around all the bodies crowding my kitchen. "All my favorite people are here." Then she lifts a bag up. "Here, I thought I'd stop by Standard to pick up some pain au chocolat. I managed to snag the last ones. They said there'd been a run on them today."

I burst out laughing and step aside to show her the two big bags already on the counter.

# Ike

I'm a little ticked when I walk in my door. Viv is one of those people who never asks for much. In fact, it's rare I get calls like today, which is why I'm pissed I couldn't get what she asked for.

But the sound of laughter coming from the kitchen, and the two boys scrambling off the couch and throwing themselves at me, makes the minor irritation disappear instantly. "How are my two best commandos?" Two faces beam up at me and Ben takes the lead.

"We beat the next level. You should come see, it's so cool."

I'd taken to playing the odd game of *Call of Duty* with these two, and although I never grew up with electronic games or owned a system, I really get a kick out of it. "Maybe later, kiddo. First I have a delivery to make to your Aunt Viv."

I kick off my boots and shrug out of my jacket as the boys wander back to their controllers.

"Babe," I say when I walk into the kitchen holding up the bag, figuring it's best to pull off the Band-Aid. "Standard was all out of your chocolate croissants, but I managed to grab a few Danish pastries." I'm not quite clear why this is funny, but the whole kitchen bursts out in loud laughter. Viv can barely speak, she's laughing so hard.

"Just ... put them over there. By the others," she manages before dissolving in a new round of giggles.

On the counter by the sink are three large bags, exactly like the one I'm still holding in my hand.

-

"You have to admit that was funny." Viv tilts her head back to look at me.

Dinner was wholesome and amazing, as most everything Viv cooks up tends to be. Coffee and dessert was cause for renewed hilarity. It was good to see the family healing.

I lost all of mine, but fuck if I didn't feel I gained one back. I look around the table and feel part of them.

"It was funny," I admit to Viv, who's been sitting on my lap since the chocolate croissants came out. Enough to feed an orphanage.

I look over to find Cora's eyes on me. When I first arrived, it had taken her two minutes to come to me, offer me her hand, and say, "Let's try this again, shall we? Please call me, Cora." That took guts and although there are some things I will likely never understand, I decided for the sake of this family, I could do this. I could try this again. I lightly squeezed her hand in mine. "By all means, Cora."

Now she was looking at me again. Has been off and on during dinner, just quietly observing me. I figure we're all trying to figure out how to be a family again, so I don't really mind her sizing me up. I've got nothing to hide.

Owen and Lydia are the first to leave. The youngest was falling asleep on his mother's lap. Next are Nolan and Dorian, who are both staying in the apartment. That leaves Aaron and Cora, who seem to be in deep conversation with Viv. Nothing stressful, if Viv's face is anything to go by, she looks totally relaxed. I head to the kitchen to do a bit of clean up, but as I walk in, the phone rings. Being closest, I answer, feeling Viv's eyes on me from across the room.

"Hello?"

"Ike. It's a boy. Mercy Hospital, room 612. Syd wants to see Viv."

I never get a chance to say anything, before he hangs up in typical Gunnar fashion, but my smile is big when I turn to my wife. "It's a boy," I tell her and watch as realization sets in, along with the tears. Happy ones.

"Ohmigod," she suddenly jumps up. "We've gotta go."

The next five minutes consists of Viv running around frantically, trying to find the gifts she had bought about a month ago, insisting she can't go to the hospital without them. When she finally comes downstairs, gifts in hand, her mom catches her in an unexpected hug. Viv doesn't even seem to register, her mind is set on babies.

"Congratulate them for me," Cora says, smiling at her daughter's antics. Then she turns to me, and with her hands on my shoulders, pulls me down for a kiss on my cheek. Her eyes are bright with tears. "Thank you for standing by my girl. She deserves that. She deserves a good man in her life."

I don't even have a chance to react before she's out the door, Aaron right on her heels, with only a, "Later" in our direction.

Viv is almost jumping up and down, as I pull on my boots and shrug into my jacket. I lock up behind us, leaving the mess for another day.

We're stopped at a traffic light when I feel Viv's eyes on me. "Another boy," she says, a smile in her voice. "I'm thinking it's up to us to dilute all that testosterone with a girl."

I turn to her, reach out, and with a hand at her neck, I pull her in for a quick, hard kiss. "We'll find out soon enough," I smile into her eyes.

With my hand still holding hers, I pull away as soon as the light turns green.

We have a baby to welcome.

# THE END

# NOTE FROM AUTHOR

I seem to be drawn to write about situations that are difficult. Topics that are painful and complex. I was not an abuse victim, but I find myself challenged by the emotional complexities that those who where, struggle with. I want to understand what it takes to be that survivor.

I do however, have a father who suffers from dementia. I was blessed with parents, who are nothing like Viv's parents in Cruel Water. My father has never touched me inappropriately. My mother has always gone to battle for me without thought.

My Dad is slipping away. His body is still here, but a large part of his mind is lost. My Mom, just as she fought for me growing up, now fights for the man she has been married to for over sixty years.

Dementia is devastating.

I hope that I have been sufficiently respectful and insightful in my writing. The last thing I would want is for this story to have a negative impact. It is meant to show the strength, the resilience and the courage of those who have lived it.

Thank you so much for reading 'CRUEL WATER'.

# ACKNOWLEDGEMENTS:

As always I need to thank some amazing ladies.... My Barks & Bites group of friends who always, always have my back. They pimp, they tag, they promote—all for the love of my books. I don't know how I got so lucky with this incredible group of women.

My beta-readers who never fail me. I message them to let them know another book is ready (often with little or no warning and on a pretty tight timeline) and they do everything in their power to make sure the manuscript I need to get into the hands of my editor, is as clean as can be. They can be brutal, but they are always brilliant and are indispensable.

Catherine, Lena, Deb, Kerry-Ann, Sam, Pam, Debbie, Nancy and Chris—Love you! Don't EVER leave me.....

My fabulous friend and editor, Karen Hrdlicka, whose dry humor is right on line with mine and who seems to understand my characters as well as I do. It is an absolute pleasure to work with you and I'm just thrilled I manage to make you blink away the odd tear. I adore you, woman!

Daniela Prima, a dear friend and a meticulous proofreader, who has made it her mission in life to not only spit shine my writing, but to educate me on the appropriate use of punctuation. You have become invaluable to me. MUAH!

I need to include my wonderful, awesome and

delightfully politically incorrect friend, Dana Hook in my acknowledgements. She was my Alpha reader on this book and always forces me to be better than I believe I can be. If not for her ongoing encouragement and faith in me, I might have thrown in the towel a time or two. You have my heart, babe!

Linda Funk, my twin, my cheerleader. This woman is why I create flawed but indestructible heroines. She is one. She is also that special friend—the one you can have silent conversations with and who will stand by you no matter what. I'm so incredibly blessed to have you in my life.

I'm always grateful to my family who quietly support, and are quietly proud. I'm the loud one of the bunch and I know it. But they give me the time , the space, and the courage to pursue this 'wild hair' of mine into a writing career. I love you and am eternally grateful for you.

Finally my readers, my reviewers and my critics: With every book I write, you push me further, demand more of me and make me a better writer than I ever thought I could be. Thank you from the bottom of my heart, for your kindness, your wisdom and your friendship. I hope we have an opportunity to meet face to face one of these days. Love you all.

# ABOUT THE AUTHOR

Freya Barker inspires with her stories about 'real' people, perhaps less than perfect, each struggling to find their own slice of happy, but just as deserving of romance, thrills and chills, and some hot, sizzling sex in their lives.

Recipient of the RomCon "Reader's Choice" Award for best first book, "Slim To None," Freya has hit the ground running. She loves nothing more than to meet and mingle with her readers, whether it be online or in person at one of the signings she attends.

Freya spins story after story with an endless supply of bruised and dented characters, vying for attention!

## *Freya*

https://www.freyabarker.com
http://bit.ly/FreyaAmazon
https://www.goodreads.com/FreyaBarker
https://www.facebook.com/FreyaBarkerWrites
https://tsu.co/FreyaB
https://twitter.com/freya_barker
or mailto:freyabarker.writes@gmail.com

# ALSO BY FREYA BARKER

CEDAR TREE SERIES:

### SLIM TO NONE
myBook.to/SlimToNone

### HUNDRED TO ONE
myBook.to/HundredToOne

### AGAINST ME
myBook.to/AgainstMe

### CLEAN LINES
myBook.to/CleanLines

### UPPER HAND
myBook.to/UpperHand

### LIKE ARROWS
myBook.to/LikeArrows

PORTLAND, ME, NOVELS:

### FROM DUST
myBook.to/FromDust

# COMING SOON

The seventh and final book in the Cedar Tree Series is
scheduled to be released Spring 2016.
Not to worry, following Cedar Tree, a spin-off series: Rock
Point, will be coming your way!

But first, here is a taste of:

# HEAD START

## (UNEDITED)

## CHAPTER ONE

*Kendra*

"No, Karly, I'm not going on a singles' cruise with you."

I roll my eyes at Naomi who is chuckling as she walks by the
front desk. Naomi is Doc Waters, technically Dr. Morris since she
married Joe, but everyone still knows her as Doc Waters. We
opened this clinic in Cedar Tree over a year ago. Already Naomi is
almost at capacity with patients, and I'm at a point where I'm here
almost full time as well. Just two shifts a week left at Southwest
Memorial in Cortez. Most of my regular physical therapy patients
have already followed me here to Cedar Tree.

Two weeks from now, I'll be moving out of my beloved
apartment in Cortez and into a cute rental here in town. Actually
the house belongs to a friend, who is happier renting it out than

selling it. The rent is actually slightly less than what I pay for my apartment so it wasn't a particularly difficult decision. Not to mention I will have a backyard, a great L-shaped living/dining room and two good sized bed- and bathrooms. The place  even has a swing on the porch and I'm really looking forward to drinking my morning coffee there. And the best of it? I can walk to work every day. I love walking.

The grating high pitched sound of my sister's lament drags me back to the conversation.

"Why not? It's half-price, one of those short notice deals." My sister resorts to the pre-adolescent whine that gets our Mom to cave every single time. Unfortunately, Karly hasn't yet figured out that it does the opposite for me.

"Because those things are like floating sausage fests."

"You're such a stick-in-the-mud. Mom said she'd come too."

Oh my God. Like that is enticement. I have to swallow hard to bring the content of my stomach back down where it belongs. I automatically turn my back to the waiting room when I hear the telltale ding of the door opening. "Not helping your case, Karly. Just sayin'... I'm not into quick, convenient fucks. Especially when most of the guys on those trips are looking to score as much and as many as they can manage in the shortest possible time frame. Not keen on being the dessert buffet for a bunch of young idiots, hopped up on Viagra. Besides, as I told you a month ago, I'll be moving house in two weeks so I can't come. End of story. You and Mom have fun, but count me out."

By the time I get my nympho sister off the phone, my eyes have rolled heavenward a few more times. I should have spared one eye-roll to confirm it actually was my next patient coming in. It wasn't. A familiar face with a toothy grin is leaning on the damn counter, right behind me. Instantly my German ancestry betrays me with the robust blush I feel burning on my cheeks. Fabulous.

"What can I do for you, Neil?" I say none too kindly. One of his heavy eyebrows lifts all the way up, and the grin slips into a smirk.

"That, is a loaded question," he teases, "especially given the tantalizing conversation I just overheard." The heat on my face has now reached my hair line while I curse myself six ways to Sunday. "By the way, I like that color on you," he mumbles, tapping me on the cheek.

"Neil—that was fast, I just called like twenty minutes ago." Naomi smiles as she walks in, and leans in for a peck on his cheek. I release a sigh of relief at her timely interruption.

"I much prefer that kind of greeting," he rumbles in that raspy dark voice of his, giving me a pointed look. A sound inconsistent with his youthful surfer boy looks and bright blue eyes, yet unfortunately has me steady myself on the edge of the counter.

"Maybe I should introduce you to my sister then, she'd be about your age," I snap back and grab the file for my next patient, but not before I see the flash of anger in his baby-blues. Deciding to ignore it, I make my way around the desk only to be held up by Naomi.

"Have you been on your computer yet? I had problems this morning logging on," she asks.

"Haven't had a chance. Why?"

"Well if Neil is here anyway to fix whatever's wrong with mine, he might as well have a look at yours; make sure all the upgrades are up to date and stuff."

I shrug my shoulders. "Be my guest, here is my next patient, I'll be busy for the next hour anyway." With that I motion to Mrs. Winkler who I've been treating for a frozen shoulder. "Come on in. The needles are waiting for you." With a small smile for Naomi and Neil, she follows me into my treatment room.

"How have you been?" I ask her once I've closed the door behind us. "Are you noticing any improvement?" I have treated her with acupuncture twice a week for the past three weeks and I'm hoping to see some loosening in the joint. She was so seized up by the time she came to see me, there was no movement whatsoever in that arm.

"I'm still have trouble with the kitchen cupboards and getting dressed in the morning isn't much fun, but I do believe I have a bit more movement." She says as she sheds her blouse and lays on the bed in just her undershirt.

"That's great. Let's have a look."

379

The next twenty minutes I manipulate her shoulder joint, finding mobility indeed a bit improved and carefully place the needles. With the tens-machine hooked up to the needles and doing it's work, I slip out of the room to quickly grab a coffee. Just as I pass by my office, Neil sticks his head out the door, causing me to almost drop my mug. "Holy shit."

"Sorry," he mumbles a bit sheepishly. "I just wanted to have a quick word if you have a minute."

"I do if you follow me to the kitchen. I need more caffeine."

I can barely hear him behind me. For a large man he is surprisingly light on his feet. I pull my one indulgence, hazelnut flavored creamer, from the fridge and wave it in his face. "You want one?" The look of disgust on his face is comical, and I can't stop the snicker. "Guessing that's a no?"

"I'll have my coffee plain, thanks," he says, opening a cupboard for a mug.

I'm still smiling as I pour our coffees and almost burst out laughing again when I see him watch me pour enough creamer in my mug to turn my coffee a delicious beige. "So what's up?" I ask, closing my eyes automatically as the taste of hazelnut with a hint of coffee hits my tastebuds.

"Two things actually," he corrects himself. "First do you need any help moving? I have my old truck which can haul a shitload of stuff."

I look at his youthful face with the far too serious eyes. Sure, most of the time they shine with a teasing glint, but there was darkness behind it. His eyes seem ancient. "Sure," I accept, because really—when a young guy built like a tank offers to help you move, especially after your family ditched you for an aquatic meat market, you don't pass it up.

"Great. Just let me know when and where, and I'll make sure my schedule's clear." His smile is genuine and I'm struck once again by how utterly tempting it is to give in to his charms. Even though I know he'll bore of me soon enough in favor of something 'fresher' and preferably younger.

"Sounds good," I say quietly.

"Oh, and secondly: I was cleaning your drive when I noticed your cache file pretty full," he says, receiving a blank look from me, since I do not have a clue what he's talking about. I can work a computer, but I don't understand it. "Are you getting a lot of pop ups when you're online? Those little screens with shit you don't wanna see that suddenly cover your monitor?" he clarifies, thankfully, and I now understand exactly what he's talking about. I shiver thinking about the vile, sadistic porn sites that have started popping up on my screen.

"Actually I do. Disgusting. How did they get there?" I half expect Neil to make fun of me, but instead he looks concerned.

"One of the sites you've visited has left something behind on your computer. An imprint that generates these links popping up. I want to have a look to see where it comes from."

"Go right ahead. I've gotta get back to Mrs. Winkler." I wave my hand in his general direction, not even half understanding what he just told me.

It isn't until much later, when I'm lost in thought with my hands working the tension from my patient's shoulder, that I realize Neil is going through my history with a fine tooth comb.

*Holy schnikes.*

*****

*Neil*

Oh, I'm pissed.

No sooner had my hopes flared when Kendra agreed to let me help her move, or they deflated instantly on finding the links to the MatureDatingOnly website. She'd been busy. *Fuck me.* Here I am thinking I might finally be making some headway with her, convincing her that the age difference between us means fuck-all, when reality hits me in the face. I know I'm crossing a line when I check her emails for evidence of some douche nozzle trying to hook up with her, but I figure the end justifies the means. Nothing. Not a damn thing. Which probably means that she didn't sign up with her clinic email, because beautiful, and fucking funny as she is, there's no way she wouldn't have had any interest. *Christ.*

I just finished clearing all the crap from her history as well as cleaning up her drive, when my phone buzzes in my pocket. I pull it out and see Gus' number, swearing softly at the site of my boss's name on the screen. I was about to go talk to her about accessing questionable websites. Frustrated I slide my thumb across the screen.

"Yeah?"

"Neil, you almost done? Meeting in my office in twenty."

"On my way."

Slipping the phone back in my jeans, I quickly finish installing the upgraded firewall and log off. With one look back at the still closed door of her treatment room, I pull her office shut and head for the front desk, where Naomi is just showing her patient out.

"You done?"

"Didn't take much," I tell her. "Yours is up and running, was just a glitch with the automatic updates, and Kendra's is cleaned up. She's still in with Mrs. Winkler so I'll catch up with her later."

"Thanks, Neil." She smiles at me and it hits me again how fucking lucky my colleagues at GFI are. Every last one of them has found their match and are building a future. Fuck, how I want that. I'll admit, I've had fun sewing my wild oats, but I've been long done with that. Left that part of my life behind when I came here from Grand Junction, but every good woman that has crossed my path has been snatched up from under my nose before I had a chance to move. The one I've wanted since meeting her is determined to keep me at a distance. Fuck, I almost lost a good friend to this stupid hang up of hers.

I shake my head to clear the frustrations and bend down to kiss Naomi's cheek. "No problem, Doc. I've gotta run, though, duty calls." With two-fingered wave, I step out the clinic into the warm spring sunshine. Damn, it's gonna be good being able to get out again. Winters can be brutal and make the terrain traitorous but with this warmer weather, I can't wait for a chance to try out my new ATV on the trails.

I'm at Gus and Emma's place, also the GFI main office, in about five minutes. It takes that long to get from one end of town to the other. I used to think I'd need a larger place to keep me busy, but since my first trip to Cedar Tree, it has never been boring. For a small town like this, they sure see a lot of action, which is why Gus, after our fist case here ended, moved the office from Grand Junction to here. Of course the fact that that first case netted him his wife, Emma, helped make that decision. The first years I stayed mostly in Grand Junction to run the office there with Dana, our office manager and resident mother. But she has since retired and Gus decided to close down that office. I started out in the guesthouse behind their house, but have recently moved into the apartment above the local diner, Arlene's. She and her husband Seb have become good friends, as have all the other members of the GFI team. Two more members have been added since the office here opened. Joe Morris, Naomi's husband and the former sheriff of Montezuma County, and Mal Whitetail, Caleb's brother. Of course Caleb and his wife Katie have both been operatives longer than I have.

By the looks of the cars assembled in the driveway, everyone has been called in. When I walk in the door, the unmistakable smell of baking greets me. Emma, Gus' wife, is our resident baker and will use any damn excuse to shove a pie or some pastries in the oven, even an emergency GFI meet.

She leans against the counter, wiping her hands on her apron and wearing a big ass smile. "Hey handsome."

"Hey," I smile back. "I swear, if Gus didn't force us to hit the gym at least twice a week to stay in shape, you'd have all of us sporting guts with your need to feed."

Emma flaps her hand. "Whatever, it's just a few cinnamon rolls. You guys look like you might be in there for a while and I didn't have time to make soup in time for lunch. Gus just got the call forty-five minutes ago. You better get in there."

I wrap an arm around her neck and pull her close, planting a kiss on her fiery mop of auburn curls. "You're the best, Ems."

"Coffee in the boardroom," she yells after me when I turn into the hallway attaching the kitchen to the addition in the back that holds the GFI offices.

"Neil, good. Sit. FBI is gonna be here in fifteen and I want to get you guys up to speed." Gus sits at the head of the massive boardroom table with my partners along the sides. I slip in a vacant chair beside Katie, giving her a wink as I sit down.

"Damian Gomez, as you know, is now leading the field office for La Plata County. He called in asking for our help. He's short on staff, been working almost single-handedly on the disappearance of a number of women from this general area."

"How general?" Joe pipes up. He's the one with all the law-enforcement connections and I can hear the wheels turning. Gus turns to him.

"For now, limited to La Plata County, but with feelers out further. Once he brings in copies of what he has, we can talk about what it is we're looking for in terms of matching cases up with other jurisdictions. For now, let me tell you that there are five women missing. All are between twenty-five and forty. Four were single, one married, and as of this morning, three bodies, two who'd been there for a while and one fresh body, that would be number six, were found. A hiker who was out early this morning stumbled on the bodies when he tripped and slid off the trail and down a twelve-foot ridge. He found them at the bottom, between a pile of sizable boulders. According to Damian, they looked to have been dumped there. The latest victim appears to have been there only a few days at most. Police is looking at getting her identified. All appear to be women." Gus stands up, turns to the window and runs his hand through his hair. "We've had our share of trouble in this region, but if Damian is correct, this could be the first serial killer of this caliber since fucking Ted Bundy and Gary Ridgeway made Colorado unsafe."

"Have mercy," Mal breathes from the other side of the table.

"No shit. We'll need it," his brother Caleb adds.

The door opens and Emma pushes her walker in, a tray of sandwiches and the freshly baked cinnamon buns balancing on top. Behind her, FBI Special Agent Damian Gomez walks in toting a case of bottled water and a stack of files.

"She got you working?" Gus smirks, looking at his wife appreciatively. He and Damian go back a ways and not all of it very good, but in recent months, since Damian's taken over the Durango office, things have settled down a bit.

Damian's grudging smile and raised eyebrow is his only response. Mal takes the tray from Emma and sets it on the table, while Damian adds the case of water.

"Thanks, Damian," Emma smiles up at him, leaning in to give him a kiss on the cheek. Something that obviously surprises him and stirs up Gus, whose low guttural growl can be heard clearly. "Oh geeze, Gus," she turns on her husband, one hand on her walker for balance, the other resting on her hip. "Put your balls away, will ya? We all know they are exceptionally large. Now eat!" With that, she shuffles out of the room.

"Well. Now that that's been established, grab something to eat and let's get this show on the road. I'll just be one minute," Gus says, as he pushes his chair back and stalks out the door behind Emma. Most of us have a knowing grin on our faces, except for Damian, who looks a bit confused.

"Just go with it," Katie tells him with a smirk, as she offers him a bottle of water. By the time Damian is done giving everyone a file folder, Gus comes walking back in, a satisfied look on his face.

"All right," Damian starts. "Six missing women, three bodies recovered this morning. The latest one, Cora Jennings, was a nurse at Mercy General in Durango. The report on her was only filed this morning by her supervisor at Mercy. She apparently had a date two days ago, didn't show up the next day and when her supervisor couldn't get hold of her, she went to check her apartment. The woman's car was gone and no one answered the door. Durango PD is over there now waiting for the landlord to show up with the key so they can get in. We suspect the third body found on Smelter Mountain was that of Cora. It hadn't been out there long. All bodies were partially dressed. Looks like their clothes were neatly cut open along the front. They look to have been violated and the cause of death appears to be strangulation. The coroner will make a report hopefully by the end of today on the latest victim. He'll also be able to confirm her identity, but we're pretty sure it's Cora." He sits back and gives us time to scan over the pages in the file.

"Jesus," Joe says. "Are we sure, aside from the bodies of course, that all six of them fell victim to the same perp? Better yet, are we sure six is all there is?"

"That's where I'm hoping you guys can help out. Other than the three bodies, I don't even know for sure the others, still technically listed as missing, are connected. I need someone run a ViCAP search, see if any similar cases might be linked, and then follow up with whatever police department. Then I need sharp eyes on patterns, similarities, anything in the victims profiles that overlaps. Anything that may give us a starting point on this guy." Damian gets up and checks his watch. "I have to run. Autopsy scheduled in an hour and a half and I want to be there. I'll be in touch." With that he's gone.

"Have a bad feeling about this one." Mal is the first to speak.

"Right," Gus breaks in. "Neil, you run ViCAP."

"I'm on it," I tell him, my laptop already open to the sign in page.

"The rest of you, run through the files you have and start digging for similarities."

Katie is shifting in her seat beside me. "I may have found one," she says, flipping back and forth between the profiles of the six women. All of them appear to work in the medical field in one capacity or another."

I grab the file and shift through the papers. Sure enough, a pharmaceutical rep, two nurses, a medical secretary at a private clinic, an anesthesiologist and an ultra-sound technician.

Gus gets up, walks to the dry erase board up on the far wall and starts writing. "Neil, add that to your search and include all of the Four Corners region. Joe, make a note of all the reporting officers on each of these profiles and find out as much as you can about each of these victims. Mal, I want you to follow Gomez back to Durango. Get any information that comes out of that autopsy and keep us up to date. I want you to be our eyes and ears there. The rest of you, keeping going through these files with a fine tooth comb. Going just by what we have this guy has been at it for over a year. God knows how many are out there. Let's stop that fucker now."

31071888R00217

Made in the USA
San Bernardino, CA
01 March 2016